Praise for
The Used World

"Kimmel's true genius is her ability, like Flannery O'Connor, to tell stories about compromised characters we care for, while simultaneously lacing those stories with humor and meditations on time, death, faith, and the unseen metaphysical world. . . . She deploys her arresting prose, her seeker's searchlight, her formidable intelligence, and her generous heart to tell the intertwined stories of Hazel, Claudia, and Rebekah, who work together at Hazel Hunnicutt's Used World Emporium. . . . *The Used World* is so full of riches, it would be downright unwise not to read it immediately. Haven Kimmel has created a convincing, fierce, funny, compassionate novel of grit and faith that shines much-needed light on our ragged, well-worn world."
—*The News & Observer* (Raleigh)

"In her multilayered novel, which gently dissects the entwined thread of friendship, family, love, and spiritual uncertainty, Kimmel focuses on the souls who can't unravel themselves from the past. . . . Kimmel's novel, bright and hopeful as Christmas morning, lets us know we can grow up without losing wonder at the world's small miracles."
—*The Miami Herald*

"Kimmel's novels are more than anything else novels about love: the mysterious love of God and the extraordinary love of human beings for another, a love that is sometimes strong enough to overcome human greed and stupidity and narrowness. She surpasses herself in this novel and has given us a reading experience that can transform the soul."
—*The Charlotte Observer*

"By turns wise and hilarious, tender and fierce, heartrending and inspiring, *The Used World*—with its underlying theme of belonging despite supposed solitude—charts the many meanings of that place we call home. . . . Irrepressibly charming and heart-piercingly poignant."
—*The Sanford Herald*

"[An] impressive novel from a major talent."

—*Big Book Guide* newsletter,
Tanglewood Books

"Kimmel recognizes us . . . she dusts us off, using language to lift us from mundane to miraculous, from foolish to philosophical. . . . Those looking for a can't-put-it-down story will find it here. Belly laughs and thought-provoking situations also abound. With Haven Kimmel, one size fits all."

—*BookPage*

"*The Used World* by Haven Kimmel [is] entertaining and smart, descriptions that too rarely appear together."

—Gale Walden, *Chicago Sun-Times*
reviewers' favorite books of 2007

"These characters are worth knowing. This is one of those books that people will keep handy on a shelf, ready for them to read again every few years or so."

—*American Way* magazine

"Wry humor and sympathetic characters are Kimmel's trademarks, and both are very much apparent in *The Used World*. But with this novel's multilayered approach, she has achieved a new level of storytelling. . . . What Kimmel gives us, in her eruditely homespun way, is hope: hope that we can fix ourselves, hope that we can get up in the morning, hope that things won't get any worse."

—*The Sunday Oregonian* (Portland)

"*The Used World* is a book that's entertaining to read but it's also smart. It takes on the taboo subjects of abortion and religion in unexpected ways, and along the way refers to objects you might have forgotten."

—*Chicago Sun-Times*

"Kimmel returns to rural Indiana in her expansive third novel. . . . It's an intriguing puzzle box of a novel."

—*Publishers Weekly*

"Kimmel's prose is peppered with characters and circumstances by turns peculiar and profound . . . . [She] covers an encyclopedic range of emotions in this tale of love, loss, and the irrevocable acts that define us."

—*Booklist*

"Juxtaposing past with present, Kimmel offers a sumptuous banquet of a novel. . . . This compassionate portrait, rich in detail, sometimes heartbreaking, often hilarious, captures rural Indiana's bleak, unaltering landscapes. Kimmel serves up more than a few twists, considerable mischief, and, most important, surprisingly touching love stories, tempered with tenderness and ferocity. This magical, marvelous novel shines with wisdom, wit, and wonder."

—*Library Journal* (starred review)

"*The Used World* awakens in the used reader the hallelujah impulse, making new all over again the realization that a novel can be honest, stormy, bitterly funny, and not merely worth the time, but necessary."

—Gregory Maguire, author of
Wicked and *Son of a Witch*

"No one can evoke a universe with a safety pin holding up its hem in the way Haven Kimmel can. In her third novel, *The Used World,* she tells a story of an eccentric collective of women with the majesty of a parable and the poignancy of a country song. As Faulkner did before her, Kimmel writes about doing what needs doing."

—Jacquelyn Mitchard, author of
The Deep End of the Ocean

ALSO BY HAVEN KIMMEL

A Girl Named Zippy

The Solace of Leaving Early

Something Rising (Light and Swift)

She Got Up Off the Couch

The
Used World

A NOVEL

Haven Kimmel

FREE PRESS

New York   London   Toronto   Sydney

*f*P
Free Press
A Division of Simon & Schuster, Inc.
1230 Avenue of the Americas
New York, NY 10020

First Free Press trade paperback edition June 2008

FREE PRESS and colophon are trademarks of Simon & Schuster, Inc.

For information about special discounts for bulk purchases,
please contact Simon & Schuster Special Sales at
1-800-456-6798 or business@simonandschuster.com.

Designed by Kyoko Watanabe

Manufactured in the United States of America

3   5   7   9   10   8   6   4   2

The Library of Congress has cataloged the hardcover edition as follows:

Kimmel, Haven.
The used world : a novel / Haven Kimmel.
p.   cm.
PS3611.I46 U74 2007
813'6—dc22 200600053172

ISBN-13: 978-0-7432-4778-8
ISBN-10:   0-7432-4778-7
ISBN-13: 978-0-7432-4779-5 (pbk)
ISBN-10:   0-7432-4779-5 (pbk)

FOR JOHN

I borrow these words from Martin Buber:

The abyss and the light of the world,
Time's need and the craving for eternity,
Vision, event, and poetry:
Was and is dialogue with you.

Part One

We come upon permanence: the rock that
abides and the word:
the city upraised like a cup in our fingers,
all hands together, the quick and the dead and the quiet.

—PABLO NERUDA, "THE HEIGHTS OF MACCHU PICCHU"

The virgins are all trimming their wicks.

—JOHNNY CASH, "THE MAN COMES AROUND"

Preface

CLAUDIA MODJESKI stood before a full-length mirror in the bedroom she'd inherited from her mother, pointing the gun in her right hand—a Colt .44 Single Action Army with a nickel finish and a walnut grip—at her reflected image. The mirror showed nothing above Claudia's shoulders, because the designation 'full-length' turned out to be as arbitrary as 'one-size.' It may have fit plenty, but it didn't fit her. The .44 was a collector's gun, a cowboy's gun purchased at a weapons show she'd attended with Hazel Hunnicutt last Christmas, without bothering to explain to Hazel (or to herself) why she thought she needed it.

She sat down heavily on the end of her mother's bed. Ludie Modjeski's bed, in Ludie's room. The gun rested in Claudia's slack hand. She had put it away the night before because eliminating the specificity that was Claudia meant erasing all that remained of her mother in this world, what was ambered in Claudia's memory: Christmas, for instance, and the hard candies Ludie used to make each year. There were peppermint ribbons, pink with white stripes. There were spearmint trees and horehound drops covered with sugar crystals. The recipes, the choreography of her mother's steps across the kitchen, an infinity of moments remembered only by her daughter, those too would die.

But tonight she would put the gun back in its case because of the headless cowboy she'd seen in the mirror. Her pajama bottoms had come from the estate of an old man; the top snap had broken, so they were being held closed with a safety pin. The cuffs fell a good two inches above her shins, and when she sat down the washed-thin flannel rode up so vigorously, her revealed legs looked as shocked and naked as refugees from a flash flood. In place of a pajama top, she wore a blue chenille sweater so large that had it been unraveled, there would have been enough yarn to fashion into a yurt. Claudia had looked in her mirror and heard Ludie say, a high, hidden laugh in her voice, *Poor old thing,* and wasn't it the truth, which didn't make living any easier.

The Colt had no safety mechanism, other than the traditional way it was loaded: a bullet in the first chamber, second chamber empty, four more bullets. Always five, never six. She put the gun away, listened to the radiators throughout the house click and sigh and generally give up their heat with reluctance. But give up they did, and so did Claudia, at least for one more night, this December 15.

Rebekah Shook lay uneasy in the house of her father, Vernon, in an old part of town, the place farmers moved after the banks had foreclosed and the factories were still hiring. She slept like a foreign traveler in a room too small for the giants of her past: the songs, the language, the native dress. Awake, she rarely understood where she was or what she was doing or if she passed for normal, and in dreams she traversed a featureless, pastel landscape that undulated beneath her feet. She looked for her mother, Ruth, who (like Ludie) was dead and gone and could not be conjured; she searched for her family, the triangle of herself and her parents. There were tones that never rang clear, distant lights that were never fully lit and never entirely extinguished. She remembered she had taken a lover, but had not seen him in twenty-eight . . . no, thirty-one days. Thirty-one days was either no time at all or quite long indeed, and to try to determine which she woke herself up and began counting, then drifted off again and lost her place. Once she had been thought *dear,* a *treasure,* the little red-haired Holiness girl whose laughter sparkled like light on a lake; now she stood outside the gates of her father's Prophecy, asleep inside his house. Her hair tumbled across her pillow and over the edge of the bed: a flame.

* * *

Only Hazel Hunnicutt slept soundly, cats claiming space all around her. The proprietor of Hazel Hunnicutt's Used World Emporium— the station at the end of the line for objects that sometimes appeared tricked into visiting there—often dreamed of the stars, although she never counted them. Her nighttime ephemera included Mercury in retrograde; Saturn in the trine position (a fork in the hand of an old man whose dinner is, in the end, all of us); the Lion, the Virgin, the Scorpion; and figures of the cardinal, the banal, the venal. Hazel was the oldest of the three women by twenty years; she was their patron, and the pause in their conversation. Only she still had a mother (although Hazel would have argued it is mothers who have us); only she could predict the coming weather, having noticed the spill of a white afghan in booth #43 and the billowing of a man's white shirt as he stepped from the front of her store into the heat of the back. White white white. The color of purity and wedding gowns and rooms in the underworld where girls will not eat, but also just white-ness for its own sake. If Hazel were awake she would argue for logic's razor and say that the absence of color is what it is, or what it isn't. But she slept. Her hand twitched slightly, a gesture that would raise the instruments in an orchestra, and her cat Mao could not help but leap at the hand, but he did not bite.

In the Used World Emporium itself, nothing lived, nothing moved, but the air was thick with expectancy nonetheless. It was a cavernous space, filled with the castoffs of countless lives, as much a grave in its way as any ruin. The black eyes of the rocking horses glittered like the eyes of a carp; the ivory keys of an old piano were once the tusks of an African elephant. The racks of period clothing hung motionless, wineskins to be filled with a new vintage. The bottles, the bellows, the genuine horse-drawn sleigh now bedecked with bells and garlands: these were not stories. They were not ideas. They were just objects, consistent so far from moment to moment, waiting for daybreak like everything else.

It was mid-December in Jonah, Indiana, a place where Fate can be decided by the weather, and a storm was gathering overhead.

Chapter 1

AT NINE O'CLOCK that morning, Claudia sat in the office of Amos Townsend, the minister of the Haddington Church of the Brethren. Haddington, a town of three or four thousand people, sat only eleven miles from the much larger college town of Jonah. The two places shared so little they might have been in different states, or in different states of being. Jonah had public housing, a strip of chain stores three miles long, a campus with eighteen thousand students and a clutch of Ph.D.'s. Haddington still held a harvest carnival, and ponies grazed in the field bordering the east end. It had been a charming place when Claudia was growing up, but one of them had changed. Now the cars and trucks parked along the sides of the main street were decorated with NASCAR bumper stickers and Dixie flags. There were more hunters, and fewer deer. And one by one the beautiful farmhouses (now just houses) had been stripped of every pleasing element, slapped with vinyl siding and plastic windows. Eventually even these shells would come down, and then Haddington would be a rural trailer park, and who knew if a man like Amos Townsend or a woman Claudia's size would be allowed in at all.

Amos tapped his fingers on his desk, smiled at her. She smiled back but didn't speak. The crease in her blue jeans was sharp between her fingers. She left it, and began instead to spin the rose gold signet ring on her pinkie. It had been her father's, but his interlocking cursive initials, BLM, were indecipherable now, florid to begin with and worn away with time.

"Can I say something?" Amos asked, startling Claudia.

"Please do."

"I talk to people like this every day. I spend far more time in pastoral care than in delivering sermons. That—podium time—is the least of my job. So I'm happy to hear anything you have to say. Except maybe about the weather, since I get that everywhere I go."

Claudia nodded. "It's going to snow."

"Sure looks like it."

What did she have to say? She could tell him that she spent every morning sitting at the kitchen table, staring out the window at the English gardening cottage her father had built for her mother, Ludie—stared at it through every season, and also at the clothesline traversing the scene, unused since her mother's death. She could say that the line itself, the black underscoring of horizontality, had become a burden to her for reasons she could not explain. The sight of the yard in spring and summer, when the fruit was on Ludie's pawpaw tree, was no longer manageable. Or she could say that looking at the gardening shed, she had realized that the world is divided—perhaps not equally or neatly—into two sorts: those who would watch the shed fall down and those who would shore it up. In addition, there were those who, after the fall of the shed, would raze the site and install a prefabricated something or other, and those who would grow increasingly attached to the pile of rubble. Claudia was, she was just beginning to understand, the sort who might let it fall, love it as she did, as attached to it as she was. She would let it fall and stay there as she surveyed—each morning and with a bland sort of interest—the ivy creeping up over the lacy wrought-iron fence on either side of the front door, a family of house sparrows nesting under the collapsed roofline.

"I suppose I have a problem," she said, twirling her father's ring.

"Yes?"

"It has to do with the death of my mother."

Amos waited. "Three years ago?"

"That's right." Claudia nodded. "I can't say more than that."

Amos aligned a pen on his blotter. Even in a white T-shirt and gray sweater he appeared to Claudia a timeless man; he might have been a circuit rider or a member of Lincoln's cabinet, with his salt-and-pepper hair, his small round glasses hooked with mechanical grace around his ears. "I met your mother once," he said.

"I—you did?"

"Yes, it was just after I moved here to Haddington. She and Beulah Baker showed up at my door just before noon one day and asked if they could take me to MCL Cafeteria for lunch. They were very welcoming."

"I had no idea." It had happened a few times in the past few years that Claudia would find a note in her mother's secretary, or the sound of Ludie's voice on an unlabeled cassette tape, and it felt like discovering in an attic the lost chapter of a favorite novel, one she thought she knew.

"Salt of the earth. I liked her very much."

"She and Beulah were friends for a long time. Though I didn't see much of Beulah after my mother died, of course." She didn't need to say because Beulah's daughter and son-in-law died, and there were the orphaned daughters; Amos knew all too well. "I started coming to your church because of her, because she had spoken highly of you from the beginning."

"Are you close to her again?"

"No—I—I find her unreachable." What she meant was *I am unreachable.* "She's friendly to me, but so frail she seems to be, I don't know. In another country." That was correct, that was what she meant: the country before, or after. There was Beulah in Ludie's kitchen twenty-five years ago, baking Apple Brown Betty in old soup cans, then wrapping the loaves in foil and tying them with ribbons, fifty loaves at a time, to go in the Christmas boxes left on the steps of the poor. Beulah now, pushing her wheeled walker down the aisle at church, nothing and no one of interest to her but the remains of her family: her grandchildren; Amos and his wife, Langston. Nothing else.

"There is something missing in my life," Claudia said, more urgently than she meant to. "I wake up every day and it's the first thing I notice. I wake up in the middle of the night, actually. Sometimes the hole in the day is big, it seems to cover everything, and sometimes it's like a series of pinpricks."

Amos leaned forward, listening.

"I'm not depressed, though. I'm really quite well."

"Are you"—Amos hesitated—"are you lonely?"

Claudia nearly laughed aloud. Loneliness, she suspected, was a category of experience that existed solely in relation to its opposite. Given that she never felt the latter, she could hardly be afflicted with the former.

"Loneliness is fascinating," Amos said. "I see people all the time who say they are lonely but it's a code word for something else. They can't recover from their childhood damage, or they've decided they hate their wives. I don't know, I had lunch with a man once who kept complaining about his soup. It was too hot, it was too salty. I remember him putting his spoon down next to the bowl with a practiced . . . like a slow, theatrical gesture of *disgust*. The soup was a personal affront to him. I knew on another day it would be something else—he would have been slighted by a clerk somewhere, or the rain would fall just on him, at just the wrong time."

"Wait, go back—code for what?"

"Excuse me?"

"Loneliness is a code word for what?"

Amos shrugged. "That's for you to decide, I guess."

They sat in silence a few more minutes, Claudia now fully aware of all the reasons she had never sought counseling before. She glanced at the clock on the wall behind Amos's desk and realized she needed to get to work. "I need to go," she said, standing up. Amos stood, too, and for Claudia it was one of those rare occasions when she could look another person in the eye.

They shook hands and Amos said, smiling as if they were old friends, "It was a pleasure. Come see me again anytime."

Salt of the earth. All through the day Claudia considered the phrase as it applied to Ludie, and to her father, Bertram. She didn't know the provenance, but assumed the words had something to do with Lot's wife, who could not help but turn and look back at the home she was losing, the friends, the family, the—who knew what all?—button collection, and so was struck down by the same avenging angels who had torched Sodom and Gomorrah. Ludie would not have looked back, of that Claudia was certain. They were plain country people, her parents, upheld all the conservative values that marked the Midwest like a scar. But they had been canny, too—they had played the game by the rules as they understood them. They were insured to the heavens, and when they died they left Claudia a mortgage-free house, and a payout on their individual policies that meant she would never want for anything. For her whole, long life, they seemed to be saying, Claudia would never have to leave the safety of the nest.

Ten days before Christmas and the Used World Emporium was busy, as it had been the whole month of December. Claudia thought about her mother and Beulah Baker showing up on Amos Townsend's doorstep and wished, as she wished every day, that she could witness, or better yet, inhabit, any given moment when Ludie was alive. Claudia didn't need to speak to her, didn't need to stand in her mother's attention; she would take anything, any day or hour, just to see Ludie's hands again, or to watch her tie behind her back (so quickly) the pale blue apron with the red pocket and crooked hem. She thought of these things as she moved a walnut breakfront from booth #37 into the waiting, borrowed truck of a professor and his much-too-young wife, probably a second or third spouse for the distinguished man, and not the last. She carried out boxes of Blue Willow dishes (it multiplied in a frightful way, Blue Willow; 90 percent of what they sold was counterfeit, but in the Used World the sacred rule was *Buyer beware*). Over the course of the day she wrapped and moved framed Maxfield Parrish advertisements; an oak pie safe with doors of tin pierced into patterns of snowflakes; a spinning wheel Hazel had thought would never sell. She watched the clientele come and go, and they were a specific lot: the faculty and staff from across the river filtered in all day, those who knew nothing about antiques except the surface and the cache. The gay couples who were gentrifying the historic district, well-groomed men who walked apart from each other, their gimlet eyes trained to see exactly the right shade of maroon on a velvet love seat, a pattern of lilies on a cup and saucer that matched their heirloom hand towels. And behind them the crusty, retired farm folk who knew the age and value of every butter churn and cast iron garden table, who silently perused the goods and would not pay the ticket price for anything. Claudia watched them all, this self-selected group of shoppers, aware that just half a mile down

James Whitcomb Riley Avenue, the Kmart was doing a bustling business in every other sort of gift, to every other kind of person, and she
was grateful to work where she worked, at least this Christmas season.
She moved furniture, took off and put on her coat a dozen times,
thought about Ludie and Beulah, and she thought about loneliness, a
code for something. Everyone she encountered stared at her at least a
beat too long, then talked about the weather to disguise it. She nodded in agreement, as the sky grew dense and pearl-gray.

By three o'clock Rebekah Shook had said, "What a lovely piece—
someone will be happy to get it," approximately twenty-four times,
and had meant it on each occasion. She was always the saddest to see
anything go. She had wrapped dishes and vases and collectible beer
bottles in newspaper until her hands were stained black and her fingerprints were visible on everything she touched. No matter what she
was doing or whom she was talking to, she was also remembering the
number 31 (or maybe it was 32 now), rising up before her like an ani-
mate thing as she was falling asleep, something with power. The 3 was
muscular, with hands sharpened to points, and the 1 was a cold mar-
ble column. She sat up straighter on the stool behind the counter,
closed her eyes. Her lower back ached; the night before, she'd sat down
on the edge of the bed, intending to brush her hair, but before she
could lift her arms the room had swayed like a hammock. She was on
her back, counting the days since she'd last seen Peter, the hairbrush
next to her pillow. She didn't remember anything else until morning,
when she woke to the sound of her father's heavy gait in the hallway
outside her room and realized she'd been reliving, in a dream, the last
conversation she'd had with her mother.

It isn't life, Beckah.

I don't understand.

Of course not, but your father does. I'm going to ride this horse home.

Which horse, what horse?

*Can't you see it? It has blue eyes. Turn that knob and see if it comes in
any clearer.*

"It's almost completely dark outside," Hazel said, coming around behind the counter with a box of miscellaneous Christmas cards. "Sell these for a quarter apiece. Some don't have envelopes, so if anyone complains tell them that the glue becomes toxic over time anyway."

"Does it?" Rebekah asked, flipping through the stack. There were plump little angel babies, snow-covered landscapes, faded Santas affecting listless twinkles.

"Oh who knows. There are a few in there that date back to the thirties, I'm pretty sure. Who the hell would want to lick something that old?" Hazel jingled as she walked. Today she was wearing, Rebekah noticed, one of her favorite outfits, an orange and yellow batik vest with matching pants. The vest sported big metal buttons designed to look like distressed Mediterranean coins. Under the vest she wore a lime-green turtleneck, on her swollen feet a pair of stretched white leather Keds. Her dangly earrings were miniature Christmas trees with lights that blinked red and green. Hazel had less a sense of style than an affinity for catastrophe, which was one of the things that had drawn Rebekah to her.

"I'm going in my office for a minute, listen to the weather report. I'll call the mall, too. If they're closing early, we're closing early." Hazel jangled down the left-hand aisle, past booths #14 and #15, toward the cramped little office. Rebekah noticed that Hazel favored her left hip, something she hadn't done the day before, and she realized, too, that the Cronies, the three men who always sat at the front of the door drinking free RC Colas, were mysteriously absent. Rebekah stood. She glanced at the two grainy surveillance cameras trained on the back of the store; in one a man flipped through vintage comic books. In the other nothing happened. She looked out the large picture window, through the backward black letters painted in a Gothic banker's script that spelled out HAZEL HUNNICUTT'S USED WORLD EMPORIUM, and saw the heavy sky, the absence of a single bird on the telephone line. She knew, as everyone from the Midwest knows, that if she stepped outside she would be struck by a far-reaching silence. In the springtime of her childhood it hadn't been the green skies or the sudden stillness that would finally cause her mother to throw open doors and windows, grab Rebekah's hand, and pull her down the stairs to the basement: it was the absence of birdsong, of crickets, of spring peepers that meant a twister was on the way. It's not the temperature, it's not the sky. It's the countless unseen singing things that announce by the vacuum they leave that some momentous condition is on its way.

Rebekah rang up a lamb's-wool stole and a breakfront from #37 for the professor's young wife, forgot to charge the tax. She said to the customer, whose expression was cold, "This is lovely, this lamb's wool—it's one of my favorite pieces." The woman smiled vaguely, as if made uncomfortable by the familiarity from the Help. The husband, his beard streaked with the marks of a small comb, rested his hand on his wife's shoulder with a proprietary ease. "I shouldn't be buying her gifts before Christmas, but how can I stop myself?" he said, glancing down at his wife.

"Merry Christmas," Rebekah said to them both, and the man nodded, steered his sullen charge out the door.

She sat back down on the stool, felt dizzy just for a moment. Her vision righted itself, and she decided to begin organizing the day's receipts in case Hazel closed early. She lifted the thick stack off the spindle—it had been a busy day—and could go no further. The receipt on top was nothing special, just a box of miscellaneous linens from #27. Rebekah let her hand rest on top of it, felt her pulse pound against her wrist. What had happened on that night thirty-one or thirty-two days before? She had read the events over and over, she had turned every word between them inside out, she had rebuilt from memory every square inch of Peter's cabin, as if the truth were under a cushion or tucked between two books.

All evening he had been distracted, but polite to her as if she were a fond acquaintance. He'd eaten the dinner she had made (chili, a tossed salad), answered her questions about his day without any precision or energy; he'd declined to watch a movie. She had overfilled the woodstove and the cabin was hot. On any other night Peter would have complained, he would have said, "We're not trying to melt ice caps here, Rebekah," but on that evening, the last one, he couldn't be moved even to irritation. He had taken off his gray wool sweater and wore just a faded red T-shirt and blue jeans. There were things he wanted to look up on the Internet, he told her, and because she understood very little about computers he left the description of what he was seeking opaque: something to do with chord charts, a lyrics bank, copyrights.

"It's a doozy," Hazel said, startling Rebekah out of the too-hot cabin.

"I'm sorry?" Rebekah blinked, patted her face as if trying to stay awake.

Hazel swayed in front of her, widened her narrow green eyes. "How many fingers am I holding up?"

"None. What's a doozy?"

"The snowstorm appears to be doozy-like, Rebekah. Let's pull the gates down on this Popsicle stand."

"Oh, the snowstorm."

"If you'll help me round up the customers and chain them in the basement, I'd much appreciate it. And also tell Miss Claudia I'd like us to be out of here by four. I'm going to call my mother, make sure she's okay."

Hazel headed back to her office and Rebekah stood, intending to do a number of things, but instead just stared out the large front window. That night, the last night, she'd gotten into bed without Peter. She'd been wearing a summery yellow nightgown with a lace ribbon that tied at the bodice, and he'd said good night in a normal if distracted way. She'd fallen asleep without waiting for him to come to bed and in the morning it appeared he never had, he hadn't gotten into bed with her. He'd left a note that said he had some things to attend to early at his parents' house, and that he'd talk to her later. That was it, *I'll talk to you later, xo, P.* It was that simple. He didn't call that night or the next day, and when she called him there was no answer. When she drove past the cabin he wasn't there; when she tried his parents, they were also gone.

Peter had been her first in every category, and she had no idea what to do when he vanished. He should have come with an instruction guide, Rebekah thought, or a warning label, turning and heading out to round up customers.

"You'll lock up?" Hazel asked, jingling her keys.

Rebekah nodded, continuing to stack receipts. The Clancys, in booth #68, seemed to be coming out ahead.

"You'll lock up if I go ahead and go?"

Rebekah glanced at Hazel, who had her heavy bag over her shoulder and her car keys in her hand. She'd made the bag herself, out of a needlepoint design intended as a couch cushion: a unicorn lying down inside a circle of fence, trees in delicate pink bloom, a black background.

"God knows traffic will be backed up all through Jonah, and my femurs ache like they did in seventy-eight."

"I already nodded, Hazel, that was me nodding," Rebekah said. "Claudia nodded, too."

"I could stand here all night, waiting for you to nod. In seventy-eight, maybe I've already told you this, after the snow stopped falling, the people who lived in town went out to check the damage and didn't realize they were walking *on top of the cars.* There were drifts eighteen, twenty feet high in some places."

"I remember," Claudia said, changing the roll of paper on the adding machine.

"How on earth could you remember?"

"Let's see, I was . . . nearly eighteen. That's about the time we start to remember things, I guess," Claudia said, without looking up.

Rebekah laughed, put a paper clip on the Clancys' receipts.

"My cats could starve to death, waiting for an answer from you two," Hazel said, jingling.

"Have mercy," Rebekah said, dropping the paperwork and giving Hazel her full attention. Hazel's purple, puffy coat, fashioned of some shiny microfiber, hung almost to the floor and resembled nothing so much as a giant, slick sleeping bag. The hem had collected a fringe of white cat fur. Beside Rebekah, Claudia was sorting her groups of receipts by vendor. She took the largest stacks from her pile and the largest from Rebekah's to add up and enter in the ledger book. Rebekah hardly knew Claudia after working with her for more than a year. She knew only this gesture from Claudia, the taking on of the heaviest moving, the staying later if necessary, the silent appropriation of the less appealing task.

"I could wait if you want me to. We could go get some White Castles and then go back to my house," Hazel said.

"No, thanks," Rebekah said, thinking of the coming storm, the drive home, how perhaps she'd just drive past Peter's house, only the once. "I should get straight home if life as we know it is about to end."

"How's about you, Claude?" Hazel asked, and continued without waiting for an answer, "Mmmmm, White Castles. Hazel Hunnicutt and a bag of little hamburgers. Many a young buck would have given his eyeteeth for such a treat back in the day."

"There's plenty who'd trade their eyeteeth for you now," Claudia said, running figures through the adding machine.

"If they had teeth. This town is nothing but carcasses, and you are sorely trying my patience and that of my cats by making me wait for your answer, Rebekah. I'm adding an episode of *Star Trek: The Next Generation* to sweeten the pot, right here at the end."

"I can't, Hazel. If I got stranded at your house Daddy would kill me."

"Of course," Hazel said, crossing her arms in front of her chest, her purse hanging from her forearm in a way that made her seem, to Rebekah, *old*. "Vernon." She spoke his name with the familiar acid. But in the next moment she turned toward the door, swinging her bag with a jauntiness that wasn't reminiscent of either 1978 or aching femurs. "All right, children. Remember the words of the Savior: 'There is no bad weather; there are only the wrong clothes.'"

"You're wearing tennis shoes," Claudia said.

"Exactly." Hazel opened the heavy front door, and a gust of wind blew it closed behind her.

Rebekah took a deep breath, sighed. She was never able to mention her father's name to Hazel, nor hers to him. She didn't know, really, would never know what it felt like to be the child of a rancorous divorce, but surely it was something like this: the nervous straddling of two worlds, the feeling that one was an ambassador to two camps, and in both the primary activity was hatred for the other.

1950

Hazel had not dressed warmly enough, and so she draped a lap blanket over her legs. It was red wool with a broad plaid pattern and so scratchy she could feel it through her clothes. Snow had been predicted but there was no chance of it now that the clouds had broken open and the moon was bright against the sky, a circle of bone on a blue china plate.

The car was nearly a year old but still smelled new, which was to say it smelled wholly of itself and not of her or them or of something defeated by its human inhabitants. Hazel leaned against the door, let her head touch the window glass. She was penetrated by the sense of . . . she had no word for it. There was the cold glass, solid, and there was her head against it. Where they met, a line of warmth from her scalp was leached or stolen. Where they met. Where her hand ended and space began, or where her foot was pressed flat inside her shoe, but her foot was one thing and the shoe another. She breathed deeply, tried not to follow the thought to the place where her vision shimmered and she felt herself falling as if down the well in the backyard. Her body in air; the house in sky; the planet in space and then dark, dark forever.

"Ah," her mother said, adjusting the radio dial. "A nice version of this song, don't you think?"

"It is. Better than most of what's on the radio these days." Her father drew on his pipe with a slight whistle, and a cloud of cherry tobacco drifted from the front seat to the back, where Hazel continued to lean against the window. She was colder now and stuck staring at the moon. She tried to pull her eyes away but couldn't.

"True enough." Caroline Hunnicutt reached up and touched the nape of her neck, checking the French twist that never fell, never strayed. Hazel had seen her mother make this gesture a thousand, a hundred thousand times. Two fingers, a delicate touch just on the hairline; the gesture was a word in another language that had a dozen different meanings. "But it's a sign that we are old, Albert, when we dislike everything new." Les Brown and the Ames Brothers sang "Sentimental Journey" and her mother was right, it was a very nice version of the song. Caroline hummed and Hazel hummed. Albert laid his pipe in the hollow of the ashtray, reached across the wide front seat with his free hand, and rubbed his wife's shoulder, once up toward her neck, once back toward her arm. He returned that hand to the wheel, and Hazel's hand tingled as if she'd made the motion herself. Her mother's mink stole was worrisome—the rodent faces and fringe of tails—but so soft it felt like a new kind of liquid. Time was when Hazel used to sneak the stole into her room at naptime, rubbing the little tails between her fingers until she fell asleep. That had been so long ago.

Countin' every mile of railroad track that takes me back, Caroline sang aloud, the moon sailing along now behind them. Hazel's head lifted free of the window, and as soon as she was able to think straight, she felt the car—the rolling, private space—fill up and crowd her. There was the baby hidden under her mother's red, bell-shaped coat, hidden but there and going nowhere until she had decided it was time. There was Uncle Elmer, Caroline's older brother, a yo-yo master and record holder in free throws for the Jonah Cougars, drowned in the Rhine as the Allies pushed across toward Remagen in 1945. Hazel did not really remember him but she kept his photograph on her dresser anyway, his home-made hickory yo-yo in front of the picture like an offering to a god.

There was Italy in the car, where her father had served as a field surgeon. He had brought home with him a leather valise, a reliquary urn, and a collection of photographs that revealed a sky as bright as snow over rolling hills in Umbria, a greenhouse in Tuscany. These items belonged to Albert alone and marked him as a stranger. Here was the edge of Hazel, here the surface of her father. And because of Albert's past, Albert's private history, the valise that was his and his alone, something else was in the car with them, a patient and velvet presence that vanished as soon as Hazel dared glance its way. It was the war years themselves, a house without men, a world without men. She tried, as she had tried so many times before, to touch a certain something that she had once thought was called I Got to Sleep With Mother in the Big Bed. That wasn't it. It wasn't the sweet disorder her mother had allowed to rule each day; it wasn't that Caroline had kept the clinic up and running alone. It was somewhere in the kitchen light, yellowed with memory, and tea brewed late at night. Women sat around the table in their make-do dresses, hair tied back in kerchiefs. There was a whisper of conversation like a slip of sea rushing into a jar and kept like a souvenir, and Hazel didn't know what they had said. But she knew for certain that women free of fathers speak one way and they make a world that tastes of summer every day, and when the men come home after winning the war—or even if they don't come home—the shutters close, the lipstick goes on, and it is winter, again.

"It won't snow now, will it?" Caroline said, lit with the night's cold delicacy.

"Not now." Albert tapped out the ashes of his pipe, and made the turn into the lane that would lead to his family's home.

The quarter-mile drive was pitted already from this winter's weather. Hazel studied, on either side of the car, the rows of giant old honey locusts, bare and beseeching against the sky. She could see the automobile as if hovering above it, the sleek black Ford whose doors opened like the wingspan of that other kind of locust, and whose grill beamed like a face. The car seemed friendly enough from a distance, but up close the nose was like an ice cream cone stuck into the metal framework, the sweet part devoured and just the tip of the cone remaining. The headlights lit up were Albert's eyes behind his glasses, and what he and the car were angry about, no one bothered to explain.

Hawk's Knoll was sixty acres on a floodplain leading back to the Planck River; a four-story barn; a metal silo once used for target practice; and a hulking house completed just two months before the first shots were fired at Fort Sumter. Albert Hunnicutt's Queen Anne boasted a wrap-around front porch with both formal and service entries. The doors and windows sparkled with leaded glass, and the fish-scale trim was painted every other year. The three rooflines were so steep and the slate shingles so treacherous that replacing one required a visit by two Norwegian brothers, who set up elaborate scaffolding, tied themselves to each other, and still spent a fair amount of time cursing in their native tongue. The front portion of the house and all of the upstairs were private, but the maid's wing at the back had been converted to her father's surgery. All day long patients came and went, sometimes stopping for a cup of coffee in the Hunnicutts' kitchen. But at night the house and lanes were deserted.

The family stepped into the foyer of the formal entrance, where they hung up their coats and scarves; an inner door was closed against the parlor, the gas fire, and the flawless late-Victorian tableaux her parents had created. "On up to bed," her father said, glancing at his watch. "It's late." They had stayed too long at the Chamber of Commerce Christmas party, her father unable to tear himself away from the town men. Albert came alive under their gaze, stroking the mantle of the European Theater he wore like the hide of an animal.

"Brush your teeth first." Caroline kissed the top of Hazel's head, cupped her palm around the back of her daughter's thin neck, as if passing a secret on to another generation.

"Good night," Hazel told both her parents, without a thought toward argument. She was not merely—then—obedient and dutiful, but anxious for the solitude of the nursery, regardless of whether the *skin* of the room, as she'd come to think of it, had grown onerous. She climbed the wide, formal front staircase, holding on to the banister against the slick, polished steps. Portraits of her ancestors, thin-lipped and metallic, watched her pass, up, up.

At the top of the stairs she paused in the gloom; the gaslights were now wired with small amber bulbs, three on each side of the hallway. To the right was the closed door of her father's study, and to the left, door after door—bedrooms, bathrooms, the attic, closets, the dumb-waiter. Hazel walked silently down the Oriental runner and stopped in the prescribed place. She centered her feet on the pattern, closed her eyes, and wished—even this close to her tenth birthday she was not above wishing—and lifted her arms until they formed a straight angle; she could tell before she looked that she hadn't done it, couldn't yet or maybe ever. There was still nearly a foot of space between the walls and her fingertips. To touch both sides at once: that was what she had wanted for as long as she could remember, and it was an accident of birth and wealth that had left her stranded in a house too large, a hallway far too wide, for her to ever accomplish it.

The nursery was unchanged, unchanging. In one corner were her toys, preserved and arranged by Nanny to suggest that a little girl (who was not Hazel) had just abandoned her blocks, her paper dolls. The tail of the rocking horse was brushed once a week, though Hazel did nothing to disturb it. The dolls were arranged in their hats and carriages. At the round table the teddy bears and the rabbit were about to take tea out of Beatrix Potter porcelain, silver rims polished bright.

The walls of the nursery were painted gray; the floor a muted red. A teacher at the college had been employed to paint a scene a few feet from the ceiling, and traveling all around the room: a circus train with animals and acrobats and clowns. Trailing the caboose were six elephants of various sizes, joined trunk to tail. Hazel's white iron bed frame was interwoven with real ivy—Nanny tended to that as well. Hazel did not love the bed, did not love the down comforter with feminine eyelet trim. What was hers, what was *of* her, were the small school desk and chair, and the white bookcase where she kept the E. Nesbit books her mother had given her over the years.

She slipped out of her shoes and party dress and hung them in the closet, then claimed the flannel nightgown from where it warmed over the back of the rocking chair near the radiator. Her bed was under a mullioned casement window, and each night Hazel moved her pillows from the headboard to the feet so she could lie awake and look at the sky. Such behavior was baffling to Nanny, who would exclaim each morning, finding the pillows at the wrong end of the bed, that Hazel was a *silly* girl.

Standing on the bed, she opened the window and leaned over the sill. The air was cold enough to cast the ground below her into sharp distinction; each tree branch looked knifelike and black. There were fifteen acres between the house and the road. From what Hazel could see, nothing and everything moved in the mid-December wind. A swirl of leaves tumbled down the lane, a barn cat leapt out of the shadows and back again. Hazel got out of bed and turned off the light, then settled against her pillows with the window still open. The moon was high, so she could see its light but not its face. Her best friend, Finney, had a favorite game called What If? What if a robber broke into your house? What if you were stranded on a mountaintop and had to eat human flesh? What if you were charged by a lion? Lying in the moonlight, Hazel thought the real question should have been *What if* . . . without anything following. Because that was what scared Hazel most.

What if the Rhine were freezing? What if her mother did not live? What if there were no difference between the surface of a German fighter jet and Hazel's mind? It was that question that startled her awake, and even after she opened her eyes she didn't understand what she was seeing, because outside her window, in the light of the dipping moon, a plane was gliding silent between two trees. Hazel held her breath, waited for a flash of light more awful for its lack of sound, the vacuum they prepared for during drills at school. Nothing came. The plane disappeared, passed once again, finally lowered its landing gear, and, wings tilted up, it alighted in her window.

The owl was backlit, enormous. Hazel knew she should not be able to see his eyes, but saw them. The stare of the bird felt colder than the air outside. He did not speak or move, and the way he didn't move was so deliberate Hazel couldn't move either, as if she had become one of the toys at the tea table. Her hands lay useless at her sides, and her shallow breaths didn't lift her coverlet. The owl held her gaze so long Hazel feared she might yet return to dreaming, until, without warning, he was off the window ledge, sailing in one revolution around her room, counter to the circus train and the impotent, fading animals, and back out the window. There had never been the slightest sound.

Hazel broke free of the trance, scrambling out of bed and grabbing her brown leather play shoes, which she slipped on her bare feet. Her thick white robe was hanging on the back of her door; she tied it with an unsteady haste. She had to stop and catch her breath before she stepped out into the hallway. *You weigh nothing,* she told herself, closing her eyes and picturing herself levitating past the door to her parents' bedroom. *You weigh nothing.* The brass doorknob felt resistant in her hand, but turned with the polished ease that came with a full-time handyman.

She stepped out into the hallway and closed the door behind her with a slight tick. Two wall lamps were always kept lit, one on each end, and Hazel stood still a moment, as her vision adjusted to the pale yellow light. The pattern of the Oriental was, she saw now, a thousand eyes. If she moved to the left they opened. If she moved to the right they closed.

The floorboards closest to the walls were least likely to complain. Hazel slid along the mahogany paneling, the fabric of her robe whispering. At the top of the formal staircase she looked down into the thick darkness of the parlor, unsure of what she was about to do. What if you let the owl decide? She straddled the banister, a game she had never imagined would have a useful purpose, and slid noiselessly down to the thick newel post, which stopped her like a pommel on a cowboy's saddle.

Her hand grazed the red settee embroidered with gold peacocks, the floor lamp with the milk-glass shade. She was afraid to go out the front door for all the locks, so she slipped around the heavy columns and into the library, where she could make her way to the service door. Here there was just a simple deadbolt, and on the outside screen a hook and eye. The doors closed behind her with such grace she wondered if she had opened them at all.

She made no noise crossing the porch, even though her leather brogans were awkward and half a size too big, as her mother tended to buy things ahead of the season they were in. Down the steps, the metal rail burned her hand. Jefferson Leander, who built the house, realized after moving in that he was too close to the county road. He had the original road closed and moved fifteen acres forward. The Hunnicutts called the remnant the Old Road, and even after ninety years it was clear, and circled their sixty acres. Hazel ran down to the driveway and turned right, following the Old Road past the apple orchard, past the fire ring, the cemetery where no one had been buried since 1888. She ran past the four-story barn where her pony, Poppy, was sleeping, probably dreaming of delivering a hard bite. Hazel ran away from the house and her parents, away from the teacups and the stained glass doors in the library bookcases, the track on which those doors opened with a sound like a metronome. She ran away from the deep dining room with the red carpet and captain's bell; away from the butler's pantry where her parents' wedding crystal flashed, sharp and bright as stars. She tried to forget the ball of gray fur on the barn's unused fourth floor, fur that Hazel had found a year ago and was keeping there as evidence of some unseen but powerful crime. She ran past the farm truck abandoned since the 1930s, a bullet hole in the windshield and a small tree sprouting through the floorboard—ran past it and it might as well have not been there. She ran on ruts, on rocks, on frozen shards of Kentucky bluegrass, until she reached the apex of the Old Road. From here the downward grade was steep enough to give Poppy pause when they cantered toward the first meadow. Hazel stopped because she wasn't sure where she should go. The meadows were mown clear, the line of forest between her and the river too black to consider. She heard herself breathing, felt a fist in her chest. Afraid, she studied the forest at the bottom of the hill. Virgin timber—a wealth of sycamore and birch and oak, trees so tall they seemed more alive than Hazel herself, more real than the words in any history book or any photograph, even of Uncle Elmer. Drowned. These trees had outlived him.

Nanny had told her that if she held her hands against a birch tree in the light of the full moon, the bark would peel away on its own, would roll down the trunk like old wallpaper in steam. Hazel saw the birch then, its silver flesh a streak of frozen lightning; her eyes traveled from the roots up to the lower branches, the scars where someone the size of a giant had rested his hands and relieved the tree of its armor. She studied the tree's dark heart, where anything could be nesting. Her eyes skated up and up until she saw, at the very top, so close to the stars he could wear them like a crown, a man in black, squatting, his legs tucked under him. She thought it was a man, a midget black as coal, the sort of creature who should have been painted on her circus train but wasn't. He will never get down from there, she thought, and before the thought was whole, the man had stretched his legs and was leaping like a diver into a pool of winter darkness. With arms outstretched, he fell, and then with a single downward closing of his wings, he flew. Hazel didn't move, even as she saw that where he meant to land was where she stood. She didn't move until he was so close she could see his claws lower and engage.

The stones of the Old Road cut through Hazel's nightgown and bloodied her knees as the bird's claws caught her on the forehead and dragged backward into her hair. She made a rabbity sound—half newborn, half terror—and tried to cover her head with her arms. There was a split second in which she felt the downdraft of his wings like the heat of a bonfire, and then she was on her elbows and knees and everything around her was quiet. The owl was gone. Hazel stood and looked around her but there was no sign of him. She reached up and touched her forehead, her scalp. Her hand came away covered with blood, and there was blood on her nightgown and robe.

*　*　*

In the morning she would carry this wound to her mother, who would stitch it up tight. The gown and robe would be bleached, mended. Much of the night would be forgotten, in the way that what is unspoken is often unremembered. What would remain, barely visible under Hazel's hair, would be the two scars, tracks left like art on the wall of a cave. That primitive, and that familiar.

Sitting beside Claudia, Rebekah continued to run the receipts, each stack twice. She ran two adding machine tapes, attaching them both to the stack with the stapler that said PUBLIC HARDWARE on the top. Nothing in this building was new—nothing was specific to it. Here groups of furniture that had lived together for fifty years were separated, sold, sometimes destroyed. The place had a powerful effect on Rebekah, even though she'd worked for Hazel for nearly five years. The fluorescent lights flickered and whined, an everyday menace. And in bad weather, like today, the metal walls of the back half of the building seemed to bow inward, growling against their joinings like a chain saw.

Once finished, Rebekah stood, told Claudia she was going to shut down the lights in the back, check the doors. Before her stretched the whole construction, 117 yards long. Rebekah couldn't see the end from where she stood. The front half was cinder block, rectangular—it had been a tractor tire store thirty-five years earlier—and the back half, which Hazel had added, was a tacked-on pole barn, ugly as sin. The floor was poured concrete, rough finished and unpainted, and the cold radiated up through it and right into Rebekah's shoes. The walls were corrugated metal. The ceiling soared, making it difficult to heat, so Hazel had installed two twelve-foot industrial fans originally designed for the corporate-owned pig operations out in the county.

She started in the far left aisle, wandering as if she were checking the stock. Hazel and Claudia didn't seem troubled by what bothered Rebekah the most: these were objects—yes—but they were also lost lives, whole families. They weren't the dead but they stood for the dead, somehow. Here, in the very first booth, #14, was a four-poster bed made of beautiful aged maple, and right in the center of one of the posts was a shiny, hand-shaped groove, as if a woman had held the post right there as she swung around the footboard and into bed, night after night for decades. Rebekah hurried by booth #15, with its cherry dining room table, its chandelier and vintage landscapes, because #15, rented by the Merrills, also contained a collection of leather suitcases. Inside one she'd found an old rain hat and a note on yellowed paper that reminded: *January 7 11:00 mother to Doctor.* Now she could hardly look at #15, the suitcases especially. Everything stung her, everything Peter had touched, everything that bore the slightest mark of him.

Toward the middle of the building, the displays became more manly: #16 was primarily unmarked, narrow-necked bottles caked with dirt, and #17 was preserved wrought iron—tools and frying pans, with some cracked butter churns on the floor. The two parts of the building were connected by a short hallway (Hazel called it a breezeway), lined with cheap landscapes tacked up on fake-wood paneling. As far as Rebekah could tell, none of these paintings or prints had ever sold—even the frames weren't worth anything. The hallway was narrow, then opened up into the massiveness of the back. How had it happened, Rebekah wondered, that a structure so displeasing, so prefabricated and out of scale, could feel so wonderful? It was wonderful. The slight breeze from the industrial fans, even the deep thrum of their motors—a sound so insistent Rebekah could feel it in her stomach—daily pulled Rebekah in. There, stretched before her, more than fifty yards of individual rooms established by Peg-Board walls six feet tall, each room filled with treasure impossible to predict. One booth, the Childless Nursery, contained nothing but wooden toys and rocking horses, the kind covered with real horsehide, with horses' tails and cold glass eyes cracked and cloudy with age. Sometimes when she looked in this booth she imagined not the children who'd owned the toys, but further back: the horses themselves, whose hides now covered the wood frames and stuffing. She couldn't see them whole, just the chuffing of breath on a winter morning, a flank, the shuddering of a muscle under skin.

There was a booth with a baby crib, a carriage, threadbare quilts, an old print of the Tunnel Angel, the guardian who presses her finger against the lips of the unborn and whispers, *Don't tell what you know.* It was the very end of the building that Rebekah loved best. From the breezeway to the back were two long aisles—Rebekah thought of them as vertical—and against the back wall Hazel had set up a horizontal display. Everything here belonged to Hazel. It began against the west wall with Your Grandmother's Parlor: an oval rag rug, its colors dimmed, surrounded by a plunky Baldwin piano, a Victrola, a radio in a mahogany cabinet, a nubbly red sofa with wooden arms and feet. On a low table was a green metal address book with the alphabet on the front—you pulled a metal tab to the letter you needed and pushed a bar at the bottom and the book sprang open—and a heavy black telephone from the 1940s, a number still visible on the dial: LS624.

Rebekah dusted the Victrola with the sleeve of her white cotton shirt, adjusted the dial of the radio, picked a piece of string off the sofa. At the telephone table she scrolled to the letter *S* but didn't push the bar, rested her hand on the receiver of the phone. It was cold like metal, made of Bakelite, a heavy, nearly indestructible thing. She knew the phone worked, because Hazel had tried it with an adapter. The ringer was broken, but the phone worked. Rebekah had been circling it for three years now, waiting for someone to buy it, hoping they never would, because she believed that someday she'd pick up this phone and call the past. She'd call her own childhood, ask to speak to Rebekah, the bright-haired girl in Pentecostal dresses. She'd issue warnings, some mundane (*Don't turn your back on the Hoopers' yellow dog*), some of grave importance (*Don't ever get in a car with Wiley Crocker*). Was there a way to call her mother, back when her mother was young? Or someone even farther away, a boy who'd just enlisted against his parents' wishes, a young housewife confiding in her sister?

Hazel's things were really more beautiful than anyone else's, but she never made much of it, didn't carry around catalogs or talk much business with the Cronies. She just went to auctions, answered ads in the paper, came to work with treasure she'd paid almost nothing for. Her trick was to choose the stormy Saturdays—rain or sleet will drive a crowd away—and stay at the auction until the end, when the prize pieces had been saved back but there was no one there to bid on them. Hazel was a businesswoman, Rebekah knew, but still this pained her, the way Hazel moved around Hopwood County like a shark. It didn't take going to many auctions to see what the truth was: each one was an occasion of sorrow. Either a parent had died, or a spouse who left no insurance. One way or another a life had been foreclosed on, and whatever was earned at the auction would go toward a debt that would never be paid. And there was Hazel, circling somebody's heirloom china and linens, or a handheld drill with a man's thumbprint permanently engraved, trying to figure out how to get it cheap and sell it high.

After the Parlor was Rebekah's favorite place of all and her domain: the Used World Costume Shop and Fantasy Dressing Room.

Of all the things Rebekah had hidden in her years in the Prophetic Mission Church—the doubt at which she didn't dare glance; the sense that the church was a screen between herself and everything she wanted to experience unmediated—there had been no secret as potent as what she kept in her closet. Forced to wear, every day, long denim skirts with white tennis shoes, white blouses or sweaters, and in full knowledge that the slightest violation of the dress code was a sin against God Himself, Rebekah had assembled—slowly, over the years—her own line of clothing. She had begun with items left in the lost-and-found at church, and then, when she could drive, by combing rummage sales for certain fabrics and rare buttons. Her first dress violated every precept of Pentecostalism's radical edge: the top of the dress was a girl's old blue jean jacket, darted beneath the breasts. Rebekah had removed the collar and the sleeves at the three-quarters length, replacing them with rabbit fur from another, moth-eaten jacket. The skirt was yards and yards of pale peach parachute silk lined with white organza, calf-length, 1950s style. Although she had modeled it on herself, Rebekah didn't want to wear the dress. She wanted to make it, and to know it existed; that was all.

Other dresses followed, and men's suits, baby clothes. Once she had purchased a box of Ball jars, and had taken it home, rolled up the smaller things and tucked them in the jars as if putting up tomatoes for the winter. Afterward she sat on the floor of her bedroom studying the gold lids of the jars, each in its own cubicle of waxed cardboard. In that week she had told her father she was leaving the church. She had endured brutal hours with him following the news, days of brutal hours, and yet there she was, still in her bedroom, still hiding things from him. The next week she saw a Help Wanted advertisement in the paper, run by Hazel, that read, *Looking for a woman who believes there is a wardrobe beyond this wardrobe,* and so she had come to the Used World Costume Shop and Fantasy Dressing Room.

Here a U shape of wooden rails held hundreds of vintage dresses, countless old coats, men's suits, sprung leather shoes, which Rebekah found on weekend trips in the spring and summer to the county's yard and estate sales, sometimes filling her car, sometimes arriving back at the store with nothing but a single item. There was a hat tree that looked more like a wildly exotic bush—hats with feathers, hats with fruit, men's fedoras, Russian caps of Persian lamb. Hazel had found a dressing room mirror on a stand that was bigger than a bathtub, and a Chinese screen for changing. Tucked away under the dresses was a traveling trunk, barely visible, on its side and open, the drawers pulled out in graduating degrees, lingerie spilling out as if a sexy woman had left in a hurry. It was in the Dressing Room that Rebekah felt most acutely the presence of lives stopped, or abandoned, and here, too, was the place she most expected someone to return. Who could leave forever the narrow, creamy satin nightgown with the lace straps, or a bespoke suit tailored to a man nearly as big around as he was tall? Rebekah would never understand how some people came to have such style and then *died anyway,* but she could hold the satin nightgown, let it flow over the palm of her hand like cool water, and sense a breath of animation.

In the Dressing Room was the stereo where all day Hazel's favorite songs played: *Big Band Hits 1936–38, The Anthology of Swing, The Greatest Hits of Glenn Miller, Sinatra and Dorsey.* At least once every day Rebekah stood among the clothes, singing along with "These Foolish Things," "Moonlight and Shadows," "Make Believe Ballroom"— these were her new hymns. She stood back here just before opening and closing, when the cool, cavernous space was all hers, taking stock of everything—from the sad, shapeless housedresses every girl with a mother or grandmother recognizes with guilt and longing, to an evening dress made of cheap chain mail—Hazel's costume collection covered the spectrum of the human drama.

Rebekah swayed to Rudy Vallee's "Vieni, Vieni," her favorite song on the tape. *Vieni vieni vieni vieni vieni / Tu sei bella bella bella bella bella . . .*

She knelt down and turned off the stereo, with reluctance. The vast space rushed in where the music had been, a tomblike echo belied only by the bass notes of the fan. She stood too quickly, looking over her shoulder at the two aisles leading directly to her. From the perspective opposite her, more than half a football field away, she was the vanishing point. The next thing she knew, she was on her knees, her face in a wine-colored silk dressing gown that smelled of age and cigarettes. No harm done; her knees weren't scraped, she hadn't hit her head. And there had been nothing there, no one in the aisle, no one just emerging either from the booth set up to resemble a one-room schoolhouse or from #32, the Abandoned Pews. No one was coming for her, and yet Rebekah wasn't alone where she stood, and she knew it.

By the time Rebekah returned to the front counter, Claudia had checked the totals against the day's receipts and prepared the deposit. The green zippered bag was closed and locked, the top and front of the glass estate jewelry case was wiped clean, the lights in the office were off. Claudia was looking at a *Life* magazine from 1954, waiting, Rebekah assumed, for her return, even though the wind outside was picking up and Claudia had farther to drive.

"You didn't have to stay, Claudia."

"That's okay," Claudia said, standing up and pushing her stool in, and it happened again as it happened every day that Claudia just kept rising. First there was the complicated gesture of getting her legs underneath her, and then the slow straightening up. Sometimes she stretched or pressed a fist against her back as if her body constantly came as a shock to her. Sitting on the stools behind the counter, Claudia was the same height as Rebekah standing. At her full height she was five or six inches taller than Peter, who stood at six feet even. All day Rebekah marveled at the basic facts of Claudia, the way her hands were twice the size of Rebekah's. She watched openly as Claudia walked around the counter to the coat rack, removing her blue parka with the orange lining; watched the way Claudia covered the distance in two long steps. No matter what she wore—jeans, slacks, the plain dress shirts she favored, sweaters—it was impossible to tell at first glance that she was a woman. Rebekah didn't think she looked like a man, either, which was a puzzle. Claudia's black hair, just going gray at the temples, was cut short, but it wasn't exactly a man's haircut, and besides, a lot of women had short hair. Her face was both broad and well defined; she had high, pronounced cheekbones, gray eyes, dusky skin. What Rebekah really felt was that when Claudia stood up, it wasn't Claudia who was revealed as too tall; rather, the rest of them were obviously *too short*. Red and Slim, for instance, the Main Cronies, sat all day on the cracked Naugahyde sofas at the front of the store smoking cigarettes, yammering away about nothing, both of them weak-backed and heading for emphysema, while Claudia lifted heavy furniture with one hand, opened the back door with the other.

Rebekah herself—the china doll of the Prophetic Mission Church, of the church school; the backyard, twilit games—was treasured for being smaller than other girls, more frail. Famous among her friends and cousins for her tipply laugh, a laugh so quick and impossible to repress, Rebekah was the embodiment of *Girl*. Her mother said she had Bird Bones, her uncles called her No Bigger'n a Minute. She had felt pride when other girls became coltish and awkward and she was still so neat and childish. Even after she'd reached a normal height, had grown unexpectedly so curvy that her father wouldn't look at her, she continued to think of herself as that princess child, the one girl small enough to sit on Jesus' knee as He Suffered the Children to Come Unto Him, while the others, the tall angry girls and the pimply boys, sat at His feet.

"Bekah, you coming?" Claudia stood next to the heavy front doors, her hand at the keypad for the alarm system.

Someone should have pointed out to Rebekah that it's the summit of foolishness to feel pride for what you lack. Someone might have mentioned that there comes a day, and not long into life, when you'll need all the strength you can get; when the woman who makes it across the prairie and saves her children turns out to be taller than Jesus by a foot and a half.

"Do you want me to follow you, make sure you get home all right?"

Rebekah smiled, shook her head, accepted her coat from Claudia. "That's okay. Thank you, though—I have an errand to run."

The snow wasn't falling yet. Rebekah steered the old Buick Electra, wide and heavy as a ship, down the streets of the east side of Jonah, out to the bypass that would take her to Peter's rural road. She was thinking it had been a Friday that she'd met Peter, a Friday because that used to be Claudia's day off and she was nowhere in the memory. It was Friday now. An anniversary of sorts, but how many weeks? More than seven months of weeks; she was too tired to count.

Before her twenty-third birthday, when she left the church and took up with Hazel, Rebekah had never worn pants or cut her hair, not even into bangs, although lots of girls got by with that one. Rebecca's hair had hung to the middle of her thighs, dark red at the roots and gradually lightening at the ends, until the last three inches were blond, fine as silk. Her baby hair. Her crowning glory. Vernon wouldn't allow her mother to braid the blond hair, or put a rubber band around it. Once a week she had to use a VO5 Hot Oil Hair Treatment to protect it. Every year that passed was like the ring in a tree: blond as a baby; here you can see it starting to darken. Light, then strawberry, then more like a cherry, then like aged cherrywood—her life, her father's life. By the time she cut it, that baby hair was a raggedy mess, most of it broken off and split in two; she pulled a comb through it hatefully, and her head hurt all the time from the weight of it on her scalp.

Until that day five years ago when Rebekah left the church, she'd never seen a movie or watched television or danced or been in the same room with alcohol. She'd never gone swimming or even taken a long bath, as it was considered immoral for girls to do so. She'd never been on a boat, an airplane, a train. She had been on a bus, in cars, trucks, tractors, and hay wagons. Garlic had been exotic to her, as were any spices beyond those in a traditional Thanksgiving dinner: sage, thyme, nutmeg. Salt. Her father ate onions as if they were apples, but didn't hold with spicing food. She hadn't learned the details of any world war, only the barest facts, and she didn't know where on a map the great cities of Europe could be found. If she'd located the cities, she wouldn't have known their currencies. She had never played a sport, had not run since she was a child, and her tendency to take long, brisk walks was frowned upon. At eighteen, twenty, she knew nothing about sex, only what she had heard whispered or otherwise referred to by her friends who'd married young, had children young.

But for all this naïveté, what was forced and what was natural to her, Rebekah had seen many dead bodies. The Prophetic Mission denied her the knowledge of sex and reproduction, but found death to be, in general, quite wholesome. She'd attended the calling hours and funerals of more people than she could recall. Though there were plenty she remembered: profiles—first just a nose, a temple, the back of the head meeting the silk pillow—who became her aunt Lovey; her grandparents; her mother; Sister Parson, who died old, and Sister Lynton, who was only twenty-nine; and children, too, and babies. Martin Peacock, who owned Peacock's Mortuary, was Prophetic, and his funeral home was as familiar to her as any place in the world. The members of her church stood at the wake of every member who died, the extended families of every member, near strangers. They attended funerals when it was politic to do so, or when the service would be interesting, perhaps because a daughter from home who sang beautifully—a daughter who had since gone on to Olivet or Bob Jones University—would be there, singing.

INDIANA: CORN AND DEATH. She'd like a bumper sticker that said that. Ooh, that would vex her daddy, wouldn't it? she thought, then realized she'd already gone about as far as she could where vexing was concerned, and was about to go the distance. The sky seemed somehow too *close* to the car—what was the problem here? The snow hadn't started and yet the tires on the road sounded muffled, the color of a truck in the distance was dulled. She couldn't tell where she was— somewhere on the County Line Road, but how far to go? Hadn't it been a Wednesday? She would remember if Claudia had been there, she remembered everything else.

She had been wearing green, her best color, according to Hazel. A green cardigan because it was a cool morning in early May. She'd been sitting with Hazel at the counter when Peter came in alone. He nodded at the Cronies, gave a little salute to Hazel. Rebekah glanced at him, back down at her book. She had been reading *Other Voices, Other Rooms,* one of Hazel's favorite novels. The mule had not yet hung himself from the mezzanine, but that scene was coming. Peter was average height, thin, wearing baggy blue jeans, a blue nylon jacket, a red knit cap, and later she would have a simple, bright memory of his face as she saw it for the first time, as he looked at Hazel and before he looked away. His cheeks were flushed from the spring wind, and his lips were red. The hair she could see at the edge of the cap was black, curly. Red cap, black hair, pink cheeks, red lips, his wide blue eyes fringed with black lashes. The blue was a surprise, the eyes themselves so round they were almost feminine, and the eyelashes, too.

He was not Vernon's idea of what a young man should be. Rebekah watched him stroll into #14, pull out a drawer in a china cabinet, slide it back in slowly. He was wearing running shoes, something her father would never have tolerated in a son, if he'd had a son. Peter straightened a frame against the wall, tipped a floor-length mirror, rubbed the satin edge of a quilt; this was not how men behaved in her world. They stood still and kept a silent watch as their women committed such shenanigans; it was the province of the female to study objects and engage the earthly. She watched as he picked up an alligator travel case in #15 and carried it a few feet down the aisle, as if he were running late for a train. Rebekah laughed out loud before she could stop herself; the Cronies looked up a moment, and then went back to talking.

She wondered, in the months that followed and certainly now, what the human eye sees in that first moment. Do we know something, or do we decide it in an instant and only later rewrite the scene to imply that something decided on us? Because now, if she were asked, she'd say that he looked smart and funny, whimsical, sophisticated, gifted. She might even say that she saw something in his hands she loved, a certain eloquence, but in truth she didn't, on that Wednesday, notice his hands at all. His eyes, that blue, told nothing about what he turned out to be. There were jokers in the church, men who could do imitations, who could tell jokes, even a few with a droll wit that was lost on nearly everyone. But no man in her life would have run like a girl with a travel case and *make her see the train,* and do it for the benefit of no one.

Rebekah had laughed, and the laugh hung in the air a moment the way a bell will after it's stopped ringing. Peter turned, offered her a slight bow. Hazel glanced at her, went back to her magazine. The Cronies were silent a moment, then Red had said, "I told him I'd rather tow a Chevy than drive a Ford."

"Yep, that's right."

"I don't care if it's a V-8 or a V-80, don't be asking me should you buy a Ford truck."

"That's the way to say it," Slim agreed.

"And then he sets over to the house night after night, watching grown men wrestle on the TV. His mom carries his food in to him like he's a shut-in. I said I sure didn't raise him to set like that."

"His get-up-and-go got up and went, sounds like."

"Hand me another cola, if you wouldn't mind."

Rebekah turned left onto Peter's road, which had a number but everyone called it One Oak. The snow had just begun to fall and now she wondered if she hadn't made a mistake, maybe, coming out this way before the storm. Before she could really regret it, there was his cabin. His mailbox, the short lane, three steps up, the broad porch, the screen door, his storm door, his windows. He was there—the porch light was on, and there was his little red truck. She'd intended to drive by, just drive by the once, but now all she could do was stop and wait for a sign, not from God, but from Peter. She no longer fit in her life and it was his fault and there was no sense going on until something was resolved. A silver strip of smoke curled up from the chimney, away. Snow began to settle in the upward curving arms of the trees, and Peter, if he was really home, gave nothing to go on. A note, a letter, should she leave something behind? But what should she say? That right there, as close as her own breath, she could see the faint scar on his palm where he'd been bitten by a cat? That the shirt of his she slept with was losing his scent, and when it was gone she would see no light in her life? She could say: *The way you shake hands with strangers, play the guitar, know songs about umbrellas—these things have destroyed me. You gave me red wine, venison, you lifted the hair off the back of my neck, which no one has done since my mother died.* Every person wore the look that spoke of this loss, it had happened to everyone, and they could all say these things: his smell, her voice, her body in sleep. What had happened to Rebekah? What has happened to me? she said aloud, and watched the door Peter didn't open. What would she really say to him, if there were world enough and time, a letter like a book he would have to read but never get to finish?

She would say, Peter, there was a sinking-down comfort in my life, as if I knew I was trapped in the belly of a whale, and so I built my little fires and was content to ride the waves out. All my life I'd looked around at the hangar of ribs, the slick walls, and thought, This is the size of the world. But what if the Leviathan opened his mouth? What if the greatest darkest biggest beast in the deepest sea imaginable, my God, the land that was my God and the Mission and the fear that were the swallowing that had swallowed me; what if that very beast opened wide and there above the sky I had always thought was the sky, the hard black whale palate dotted with whale stars; what if that sky opened to the sky above the sea, and I could see the wild spread of it above me, the real stars for once, for the first time? What if I suddenly saw the teeth, the tongue, the cervical curve of the whale's mouth? What then?

Well, she thought, taking a deep breath, I would run for it.

She gave him thirty seconds more, but she knew he wasn't coming. Peter didn't pull her from the sea. He wasn't the shore, the sky, the stars. He was just standing there, agreeable at the time, and while she hadn't even begun to grieve for him, hadn't begun to reckon up what the cost would be to her in the end, she also knew women never *really* die from love. Hazel had told her so.

Rebekah put the car in gear, and headed home.

Claudia stopped at Parker's Supermarket on her way out of town, joining half of Jonah in the joy of the looming crisis. She took what milk was left, the orphaned loaves of wheat bread. Not knowing whether the storm would even come, and if it did what she would need, made her forget what she'd come for. The store was vast, too bright, and both her knees and her will felt porous. Again and again and again, the car door, the parking lot, the groceries, the stares. In the produce section she stood a few moments unmoving, thinking how *odd* the fact of consciousness in beings who spent their lives like hamsters on a wheel.

She ended up buying more fruit than she could ever eat, and a few things she'd never purchased before in her life: buttermilk bath salts, smoked cheese, a bar of bittersweet chocolate. On a whim, she went back and bought two of everything, thinking she might leave a bag on her sister's porch with no note, as if Millie had been the object of a visitation; Millie, who had no need of help from anyone, and didn't care much for food. Everyone in the store gave Claudia at least a long look; and one elderly woman stopped in her tracks and pointed directly at Claudia's chest, while saying to her stooped husband, "Look-a there!" Claudia walked on, never meeting an eye or giving an indication she'd heard their comments, as if she weren't merely too tall, too broad, but deaf and blind as well. It wasn't that she was resigned to her status, although that was part of it. And she hadn't precisely taken inside herself the years of scorn, although for a while she had. Now she relied on something she'd heard Amos Townsend say in church a few months earlier.

He had welcomed them and they'd sung something, Claudia couldn't remember the song, and then he read from Scripture and she didn't remember what that was either—something from the book of Mark, she suspected—and then Amos began to talk about the character of Jesus. He'd quoted a Quaker theologian named D. Elton Trueblood: "Jesus Christ can be accepted; He can be rejected; He cannot reasonably be ignored." Claudia wrote the words in the little notebook she had taken to bringing with her to church. She could see how Trueblood's claim might be true intellectually, and yet ignoring Jesus was as easy as ignoring anyone else in the realm of the dead, as far as she was concerned. He could have easily said that the Civil War cannot reasonably be ignored, or the mechanics of evolution, or the missile silos in the American West. Of course they can't, she had thought, and yet it's in our nature to ignore everything except our survival, and indeed, our survival probably depended upon a narrowness of focus that began in the morning with the hunt and ended at night with shelter. She was thinking of this when Amos said that he'd thought about Jesus his whole life—he agreed with Trueblood—and as an adult his contemplation felt like a combination of what young girls feel for rock stars and what young boys feel for abusive fathers. Claudia had blinked, taken a breath. He imagined, Amos said, a girl lying on a sofa, studying pictures and biographies of the object of her affection, imagining she knew Him in a way no one else did, and also hoping to get closer, to establish greater intimacy and to get to the bottom, finally, of her passion. Or a boy, walking through the house after dinner and hearing his father come up the steps—the wariness, the quick prayer, *Please don't let him notice me.* Jesus, Amos continued, had always struck him as a man filled with rage. Think of Jesus' impatience with His mother, with the Apostles, His chilly distance from the people on whom He performed miracles, how He was so irritated with everyone who simply *didn't get it*. Think of Him with the fig tree. What a world to be born into! How grotesque and cruel to be made manifest by the Divine just to suffer and be killed for a senseless metaphorical principle. Amos shook his head in disbelief, mentioned Abraham and Isaac, Kierkegaard, how the message sent was understood by the Son, but not by the messenger. He paraphrased a passage from a book about cosmic child abuse. Claudia was lost a moment, then Amos said he thought the great message of Jesus might be there, in His anger, in the abuse He had suffered not at the hands of the Romans, but at the hands of His Father, because that's what we really share with Him. We are called upon to love a God who either didn't see fit to protect us from disaster and death, or was helpless to prevent it. What sort of a God was that? And Jesus, in response, created for Himself a sort of daily compassion (not empathy, of which He seemed to have little, at least to Amos), but a cobbled-together will-to-patience that was born not of His divinity, but of His humility. Amos said he'd imagined Jesus so many times repeating under His breath, "Don't smite them, don't smite them, they're really just a bunch of morons and are in enough trouble already," repeating it as He healed the hemorrhaging woman, the blind man, the soldier, people He did not love but took mercy upon anyway. If Jesus hadn't seen His lot as the same as humanity's, He could not have been human. And if He hadn't felt compassion for the people around Him, He could not have been Divine. "Or maybe I'm just mad at my Father," Amos had said near the end of the sermon, with his rueful smile. He ended by saying it was possible to consider Jesus an entire lifetime and find nothing but projections of our own futility, our own fear of death; He was a wild, blank, imaginal screen on which we had cast our looming cultural shadow.

The Haddington Church of the Brethren was completely silent when Amos stopped speaking. Claudia didn't dare look around, but she wondered what the other parishioners were thinking as they listened. At the time she didn't even know what Brethren meant, except that she never thought about her clothes when she was there, and no one and nothing but Amos Townsend and this church really interested her.

After that Sunday, Claudia thought often of the phrase 'He created for Himself a kind of daily compassion,' and she tried to do the same, even though she lacked power, divinity, wisdom, grace. She walked through the grocery store, or stepped into a gas station, and when the toothless women in sweatshirts, their bodies and hair reeking of cigarette smoke and fast food, stared at her cruelly or even went so far as to make a comment, she no longer thought, *They hate me.* Now she tried to remind herself that if we don't feel the weight of the human condition, we must not be fully human. She thought instead, *They hate themselves. They hate being alive. They hate their Fathers.*

As she walked to the car, the feeling in her chest was atmospheric, a pinching there not unlike excitement. The silence was so thick Claudia became aware of her own breathing, and of the sensation that she was actually *in* the sky. The sky was no longer above her, or the clouds at a safe distance. As she loaded her groceries the snow began to fall, heavy flakes at first, but by the time she started the car and turned on the lights, the wind had picked up and the six miles ahead of her seemed too long. She had the second bag of food, the things she'd thought she might leave for Millie, but knew she'd never get to her sister's house and back home before the storm struck. As she made her way through the north end of Jonah, she decided to leave them at Rebekah's; the old house where Rebekah lived with her father was on the way.

The porch light burned at the Shooks', but Rebekah's car wasn't there, and there was no sign of Vernon. Claudia trudged up the sidewalk, the heavy bag obscuring her vision. Rebekah's neighborhood felt abandoned—there were no dogs barking, no movement. She left the bag in front of the wooden screen door, under the porch light, as she would have at Millie's, with just these words written on the outside of the bag: *For Rebekah, a cold night.*

By the time Claudia reached Old 73, heading east toward home, hers was the only car on the road, or the only one she could see. There was a little visibility to the south, but almost none in the north; she could make out the houses, the convenience store, the used car lot to the right of the road, but nothing on the left. She knew her right turn was coming up, and began to look for the mailbox that signaled the V of the additional lane—just a little turn lane a quarter of a mile long. She was too familiar with the road, had driven it too many times, and tended to sail into the turn lane at top speed, then slow down quickly in order to make the turn. Indiana country roads have that effect on most people, Claudia thought; they breed a false security, because the world seems so flat and manageable, the sight line so clean. She didn't see the mailbox and then she saw just the outline of it, and some part of her body led into the swerve to the right, but something else, a voice, cautioned her to flash her high beams into the lane, just in case. There in the lane was a man, dressed in a black coat and walking shoulder-hunched against the blowing snow. Claudia jerked the wheel of the old Cherokee too hard to the left; too late realized her error. The back fishtailed with a skating, liquid ease, and Claudia took her hands off the wheel. She spun in a full circle, then half of another, and when the tires found some purchase, she gently turned the wheel into the spin and felt the truck shudder in her hands.

She could no longer see anything. Her headlights were pointing west, she thought, but she couldn't be sure. The walking man was gone, had vanished as if into smoke, or a high tide. She had to get off the highway—whoever she couldn't see wouldn't see her, so she drove a few feet, then recognized the iron gate of the old nursing home, empty for the past three years. Bear Creek, her road, was due south—so she turned and drove tentatively over what she hoped was the road. By now there was nothing, no shoulder, no fencerow, nothing to indicate if she was still on pavement or heading toward the culvert. Two miles yet from home, and she'd left earlier that day without either boots or gloves, another bit of typical Hoosier folly.

Sometimes the snow blew horizontally across her headlights, and sometimes it seemed to stop altogether. She'd gone nearly half a mile when she saw something off to her right, at the edge of the headlight beam. She angled the Cherokee toward the shape just slightly, just enough to cast light upon it, and got out of the truck. The wind and snow hit her face like an open hand, rocketing into her coat, and for a moment she thought of how silly this was, a woman like Claudia undone by a winter storm. She'd lived on this road her whole life; how could she possibly fail to get home? The wind sang in her ears, rising and falling, and a stand of trees outside her sight moaned along in time.

"Hello?" Her voice seemed to stop in her mouth. The wind had blown it back at her.

There, then: a set of eyes caught green in the halogen light. Claudia took a step backward, saw another set, a third, the vague impression of fur. Three dogs, she thought, long-muzzled, gray. She imagined more than she saw. Three dogs lying on the frozen ground, snow blown up against their sides, the brutal wind. Before she could decide what to do, all three animals rose and ran away from her, deep into the pounding whiteness, the black ground of the field on which they could run all night.

The snow was blinding by the time Rebekah drove home, leaning close to the steering wheel, as if that would help. When she finally reached her house, she parked the car in the general vicinity of other car-shaped, snow-covered mounds, hoping she wasn't actually on the sidewalk, or in somebody's yard. She'd left the porch light on by accident that morning, and now it was the only guide to her door—the too bright bulb her father insisted on and that she usually found distressing.

It was Friday, so Vernon would be at the Governance Council Meeting until it was over, snowstorm or not. Rebekah didn't worry about him driving or becoming stranded; to do so would have been a betrayal of who he was to her, and who he believed himself to be. He had, Rebekah knew, thrived in storms far worse than this, once traveling seven miles on horseback in a blizzard because he'd intended to propose to her mother and would not wait.

Constance Ruth Harrison, called Ruthie, had been seventeen years old in 1958, had known nothing of the world when Vernon set his cap for her. They'd met when Vernon responded to a call from the pulpit to help get a neighbor's crops in; Ruthie's father, Elder Harrison, had fallen to pneumonia, and his family was in trouble. They weren't

Prophetic, the Harrisons, but belonged to a radical Holiness sect that had broken away from the larger body and set up worship in a barn on Elder Harrison's land. At first they called themselves Children of the Blood of the Lamb, and then Children of the Blood, and finally, just The Blood. That was where the truth lay, they believed, in the old story. For some groups it was in Christ's miracles, for some it was the Resurrection. (The Mission preached that demonic sects like the Catholics worshiped only Mary and a group of Mafia-connected cardinals in Italy who carried submachine guns under their red robes, and who communicated with the Underworld through a code involving sunglasses.) But the Harrisons and their little ragtag army, which had remained isolated as long as Elder Harrison lived, believed that the divine message of Jesus was in His Blood, the blood He shared with the Master Creator Father God, and the blood He spilled on the cross to redeem humanity. In them, the Blood rose up and spoke; it told them of the End Times, it said there would be a worldwide slaughter of the unconverted Jews. As the Children of the Blood married and mingled with the Prophetic Mission, and as the secular world slouched toward them, they realized there would need to be a worldwide slaughter of other groups as well. No *hope* of conversion would be offered to Catholics, Lutherans, Episcopalians, Muslims, Hindoos, the Godless Buddhists. A special trampling under the hooves of the Four Horsemen was reserved for Unitarians, and a spectacle of Holy Execution for the mortal enemies of The Blood, the Mormons. The old peace churches, the Quakers, Amish, Hutterites, Mennonites, and Brethren, would be mown down, but gently, like wheat, as the members of The Blood respected their work ethic. Jesus would smite the proclaimers of the Pentecost with a special vengeance, including the Nazarenes, the Assemblies of God, and the Church of God, because their worldliness was evidence of a silent affiliation with Satan. Any branch of the crooked tree that called itself Pentecostalism, then built its ministry around cavorting with prostitutes and self-glorification, had not merely gone astray. It had become a carrier of the Disease.

Until five years ago Rebekah had thought it all perfectly normal, what went on in that barn with her Granddad Elder, her child mother, the members of the fugitive group. It was Worship as they Worshiped. Of course there would be no Children of the Blood without blood, there would be no life, there would be no eternity. The barn was their Temple, and its altar was stained, as had been all the altars of the seven tribes of Israel. And her father riding his great horse Michael over miles of snow-blanketed fields to claim Ruthie as his own—that had sounded normal, too. Ruth had had no say in the matter, wouldn't have dreamed of making any claim to her life or liberty. She'd told Rebekah at the end, lying in the hospital bed the Mission had rented and set up in her bedroom, that although she couldn't say she'd loved Vernon at seventeen, there had been something in the cruel set of his jaw that had thrilled her and made her want to go away with him. So she'd been willing, in her way, then he took her and married her, and it hadn't been her family or her childhood she'd mourned, it had been her girl-friends in the church, whom Ruthie had taken for granted, considered permanent. They'd never been together as a group again, never walked across a field or gathered around a porch swing, never spent the night in the same bed or talked for hours about nothing, chattering like mag-pies, as the men used to say. All those girls were married off eventu-ally, scattered to the winds, kept behind closed doors.

Rebekah hadn't worn boots to work, and so was forced to make her way down the sidewalk in mincing steps, reaching out for trees. She imagined someone watched her do this. Hazel's voice suddenly entered her head, saying, *Oh look, a little redheaded stepchild has escaped from under the porch.* Rebekah laughed aloud, lost her footing, righted herself. She could just see, in front of the screen door, a bag from Parker's Supermarket. When she reached it, she looked inside before picking it up, but it was just what it appeared to be. Who would have done such a thing? Who would have thought of her, now that she'd lost her cousins and all her extended family, the church she'd grown up in, and the love of her father?

The front door opened into a sitting room that contained a piano no one had played since her mother died, but which Vernon had tuned once a year because that's what one did: tune the piano. The walls were painted pale green and decorated with the acceptable notions: family pictures, a print of Jesus knocking on the door—everyone knew the image of Him knocking on the door and awaiting admittance. Jesus knocks, was what the print was trying to say, He doesn't just walk in and help Himself to your old mess. Above the piano was a counted-cross-stitch sampler Ruthie had made that read JESUS IS THE SONG IN MY HEART. The same could be said of everything in the parlor: the bench on which no one sat, the piano no one played, the two wing chairs gathered around the little table on which Ruth had placed her knickknacks and doilies—all of these things were somehow connected to Jesus. It was a wonder to consider, the experiment to make Jesus everything, the effort it contained.

Rebekah unloaded the groceries on the butcher block table in the kitchen as if compiling the clues to a mystery. Milk, eggs, bread, orange juice—that could be anyone. But this French cheese, a bar of bittersweet chocolate, buttermilk bath salts in what was supposed to look like an antique milk jug? And all this fruit: oranges, grapes, apples, as if it were a different season altogether. For a single fluttery moment she thought Peter must have left it, he must have been worried about her, and then she saw the note: *For Rebekah, a cold night*. Claudia's handwriting.

The oranges looked so good she decided to eat one right away— she would puzzle over Claudia's gesture later—but then saw again the bath salts, so she carried them both into the bathroom, ran hot water. She took off her clothes without looking in the mirror, as her mother had taught her, poured part of the milk container into the tub. The salt didn't smell like buttermilk (thank goodness) but it was that color, and the water became creamy, slightly foamy. Rebekah climbed in, surprised by the silky feeling of the water, and leaned back. The water lapped over her, rose and fell as she breathed, leaving a sheen of sweet-smelling oil on her skin. Rebekah closed her eyes and thought of Peter; he had glanced at Hazel and she saw his face again, everything around and behind him gone dark in her memory. She focused on nothing but the color of his skin and the shape of his mouth and the length of his eyelashes. But she couldn't hold on to the image; she kept seeing Claudia's handwriting, the span of Claudia's hand on the glass countertop of the Used World. Span. It was a biblical word for time, Rebekah thought. The smell of the orange rose up in the heat of the room. Water continued to pour from the tap as she claimed the orange from the countertop, thrust her thumb under the skin around the navel. She pulled off large sections of peel and dropped them in the water, where they floated, riding the crests of the small waves around her body. She hummed a bit of Artie Shaw's "My Heart Stood Still" as she peeled the orange clean, then pulled it apart harder than she meant to, not bothering to divide it into neat sections, and ate the whole thing in quick, big bites.

Chapter 2

Snowplows had parted the streets of Jonah like a solid white sea. Claudia drove carefully after the scare with the man in the turn lane the night before. Each season in Indiana carried its own near miss, she concluded, remembering a moment last summer when she'd taken an exit ramp onto the highway. She had been holding tight to the inside curve, then decided—for no reason she could discern—to move toward the outside. At the very end of the curve, just before the ramp opened up onto four lanes, there was a beagle, trotting along happily, following a scent and wagging his tail. Claudia most certainly would have hit him, had she stayed her course.

Keeping her eyes on the street ahead, on the intrepid Midwestern holiday shoppers out in full force, Claudia reached over and lifted the front cover of the book Hazel had lent her, *A Prayer for Owen Meany,* making sure the photograph was still there. It was. She had checked four times since leaving the house, a gesture that now struck her as compulsive; although it was, she supposed, in the nature of a photograph to slip out of a book, in the same way it is somewhere in the nature of glass to shatter.

The prior evening, after surviving the snowstorm and the drive home, Claudia had taken the book to read in bed. The wind was slapping tree branches against her bedroom window, and in the silence of her old farmhouse she experienced the weather as another facet of her nightly dread. She was too tired to read. She closed the novel and reached up to turn off her reading light, and a photograph fluttered out of the middle of the book.

The picture seemed to have been taken sometime in the sixties—all the colors had been muted by the orange pall that marked that decade's snapshots. Two young women were in the back of a pickup truck. One was sitting on the lowered tailgate, her bare legs crossed at the knee. She was wearing shorts and a halter top, white or pale yellow. Her hair was in a ponytail and her sunglasses were pushed up on her head. There was something familiar about her. The other was standing behind her friend, her legs about a foot apart, in a short-sleeved shirt with buttons. The shirttails had been tied around her midriff, showing off her small waist and tan. Her hair was loose and curly, chin length, streaked with light. Her arms were resting on her friend's shoulders, her hands lightly clasped, and the sitting girl had reached up, her right arm across her chest, to lay her own hand over her friend's.

Claudia was aware, again, of the wind, the ticking of the old radiators, absences. She felt her pulse in her throat, heard it in her ears. She turned the photograph over and read, *Hazel and Finney on the way to the Fair, August 7, 1964.* Hazel. Claudia studied the picture for another few minutes before turning off the light and not sleeping; she studied Hazel's young face, her smile, her hand resting so lightly against that tanned, beautiful girl.

The store had only been open for ten minutes when Claudia arrived, but there were five cars in the lot already. She sighed, stepped out of the Jeep. The sky was blue above her, but there was a threatening haze in the east, and the temperature seemed to be dropping. The delivery door at the side of the building was unlocked, which meant that Rebekah had gotten there early.

There were four or five people milling about in the back half of the store, picking up various items, hoping that an ugly little statue of a dog would be marked OCCUPIED JAPAN (not just that the dog would be here and they would find it, but that the dog's origin would have been missed by both its owners and Hazel). Rebekah was playing Frank Sinatra's Christmas album on the stereo and someone had hung a strand of twinkly lights over the doorway to the breezeway. The music, the heat blown down by the industrial fans, all of it worked together to make Claudia feel as if she'd just returned from a war or an epic journey, in time for the holidays. The Used World was, after all, nothing but the past unfolding into an ideal home: enough bedrooms for everyone, a parlor, a chapel, a well-stocked kitchen. Hazel had more books here than the local library, more tools than the craftiest farmer. Claudia stopped in the breezeway, next to a muddy painting of a shipwreck, and felt something come over her, a blast of heat from her solar plexus, overwhelming her like a mortal embarrassment. She put her hand against the wall, fanned herself. Her coat slipped from her hand, landed on the floor, *A Prayer for Owen Meany* beside it. The collar of her shirt was too tight, and her wool sweater was suffocating her. She pulled it off in one swift gesture, took a deep breath. In less than a minute her entire body was drenched in sweat; she reached into her back pocket, pulled out a folded handkerchief, dried her face.

"Claudia?"

She turned, and coming up behind her was Rebekah. A light around Rebekah's body shimmered. Claudia squeezed her eyes shut, opened them again. The light was gone.

"Are you okay?"

"I'm fine," Claudia said, folding the handkerchief and putting it back in her pocket. "I think I got too hot."

Rebekah stepped closer. She reached out to touch Claudia on the elbow, and just before she did, a crack of blue light passed between her hand and Claudia's arm.

"Oh!" Rebekah flinched, pulling her hand back.

"You shocked me," Claudia said, looking down at her elbow.

"I'm sorry, I—"

"That's okay."

"Want me to do it again?" Rebekah asked.

"Excuse me?"

"Want me to try?"

Claudia studied her, the red hair and pale skin, the pale green of her eyes. Whatever had held Claudia in its grip loosened. "Okay."

Rebekah took ten steps backward, shuffling her feet on the grimy dark blue indoor-outdoor carpeting in the breezeway. She shuffled back toward Claudia, reached out slowly, and again, in the narrow space before Rebekah's finger touched Claudia, there was a pop and a flash.

"Ow!"

"Ouch." Claudia rubbed her arm. Her shirt was drying and she was suddenly cold.

Rebekah shook her fingers. "That was fun," she said, smiling up at Claudia.

"In its way." Claudia leaned over and picked up her coat, her book. She opened the front cover and the photograph was still there. Maybe it had been a hot flash, she thought, glancing again at the young Hazel. Or maybe it had been a barb on the shaft of nostalgia that had struck her, listening to Frank Sinatra sing "Have Yourself a Merry Little Christmas."

"I was looking for you, actually," Rebekah said, still standing close. "Hazel needs you—somebody bought that gigantic ugly painting in number forty-two, and also the love seat with the yucky upholstery job."

"The pink one?"

"The pink one."

"Let me go put these things in the office," Claudia said, turning.

"Oh, and also, Claudia? Thank you for the groceries."

Claudia blushed, rubbed her hand over the top of her head, a gesture she'd made since childhood. "You're welcome."

The new owner of the ugly pink love seat fell into one of east-central Indiana's most recognizable categories: the married woman with small children, the kind who might have been adorable or saucy or wild in high school, but who had long since cut her hair, stopped trying to lose weight, and who had donned her I Give Up Suit. In this case she had also plucked her eyebrows too thin, which struck Claudia as a peculiar trend. Everyone seemed to be doing it, creating a county full of startled women.

"Do you think this will fit in my Suburban?" the woman asked Claudia, who had tipped the love seat on its side and was wheeling it on a dolly toward the delivery door.

"Probably," Claudia said.

"Because I could maybe borrow a truck from someone but I don't know who—we aren't really truck people. Well, my husband isn't a truck person. There's a long list of things my husband isn't but I'm sure you don't want to hear them." The woman was wearing the holiday uniform of her class: a red turtleneck, an oversize cardigan sweater embroidered with a Christmas scene, blue jeans, tennis shoes.

Claudia said nothing.

"I'm Emmy, by the way. I just hate Christmas, I hate it," Emmy said, drawing in and exhaling a shaky breath. "I'm buying this love seat for myself when I ought to be Christmas shopping but I'm not, I'm buying a piece of furniture that my husband is going to despise because it isn't new and we didn't get it at Sears."

They passed the shelves of blue, ruby, and carnival glass. Claudia backed the dolly up, turned it until it was straight, started up the breezeway.

"I need a new one because one of my kids set the old one on fire. That's what he's doing these days, setting things on fire. I found hundreds of burnt matches in his closet a few days ago, taken from my husband's matchbook collection. No one is *saying* he set the couch on fire, it's just assumed and kept quiet. Do you hate Christmas? Don't you?"

The answer, Claudia thought, might be: *I have. I could. I can sure see how it's possible.*

Before she could speak, Emmy continued, "I say to my husband, 'Brian, admit it, admit what you expect of me,' but he won't. He says I make my own choices and I should live with them. Does he think I *want* to spend two weeks decorating the house, leave those decorations up two weeks, then spend two weeks taking them down? Does he think I *want* to bake cookies and little cakes for the neighborhood association and the postman? And do all the shopping, all the wrapping, pick out every single goddamn gift, including for his parents who he won't spend two seconds thinking about? And send out Christmas cards with a picture of the kids in it every year when I can't hardly get them to sit still to take the picture, not to mention the furniture is on fire and one of the boys has decided he can't live without a *python*?"

They turned the corner at NASCAR collectibles and Claudia said, "Could you open that door for me?"

Emmy leaned against the bar on the delivery door and it opened, letting in a blast of white light and cold. "Good God," Emmy said, slipping on her red coat. She opened the back of the Suburban, lowered the tailgate. She'd left it running, and the parking lot was streaked with blue exhaust. Two or three loose napkins were picked up in a gust of wind and blown out toward Claudia. She caught one, green with white letters that read, SANTA, IT WAS AN ACCIDENT!

Claudia lowered the dolly, took the ramp from the side of the building. The back of the Suburban was littered with the castoffs of family life: shoes, clothes, collectible trading cards, CD cases, crumpled grocery bags.

"Just," Emmy said from behind Claudia, "just put it on top of all that shit, if you don't mind. Flatten it all, I don't care."

The love seat was light; in addition to the unfortunate color and upholstery, it was shabbily constructed, and might not last the afternoon with the Arsonist and the Snake Handler. Claudia pushed it up the ramp and into the vehicle, where it laid waste to a comic book and a variety of plastic items. After she'd taken away the ramp and closed the tailgate, she turned to find Emmy leaning against the side of the building, her hands over her face.

"I'm done here," Claudia said, wheeling the dolly back toward the door.

"Okay then," Emmy said, standing up straight and clapping her palms together, as if declaring the case closed. "This is going to be great. Everything is going to be fine. I can do this, absolutely." She opened the driver's side door, climbed in. "Merry Christmas," she said, looking back at Claudia.

"To you, too," Claudia said, pushing the code into the keypad lock on the door. She wheeled the dolly inside and turned around. Emmy was still sitting there in the smoking Suburban. She wasn't crying, she wasn't moving; she had slipped on a pair of sunglasses and was just looking out at the traffic as it sailed by.

"I sold the last of the Santa suits," Rebekah said, placing the receipts on the spindle.

"The one with the cigarette burn in the crotch?" Hazel asked.

"That's the one."

Hazel hummed a bit of "I'm Dreaming of a White Trash Christmas."

"Do you want me to see if there are any more out in the storage shed?"

"Please don't." Hazel closed the phone book, unable to find what she was looking for, and slipped it on a shelf under the counter. "Santa is too much with us as it is."

"Hey, Becky," Slim called from his perch near the RC Cola machine. "Want to come sit on my lap and tell me what you want for Christmas?"

Rebekah blushed. Hazel didn't look up but said, "Slim, remember D-day."

Red wheezed out a laugh, put out his cigarette; Jim Hank wheezed out a laugh, lit a new one. D-day, Rebekah knew, referred not to World War II, but to Slim's wife, Della, who had forgone any employment for the past forty years in the interest of maintaining her bitter anger at her husband.

The Cronies were three men in their early sixties who had taken an early buyout from the Chrysler plant. Their histories, ideologies, and fashion tastes were so similar that for the first six months Rebekah worked at the Emporium, she had no idea which Crony was which. Their sons were wastrels, their overweight daughters were married to ne'er-do-wells (if not outright criminals), and their wives disappointed them on a daily basis. Almost every day the Cronies sat on the three couches in a U shape with the soda machine in the corner. Hazel had bought the furniture at some auction; she swore she hadn't been drinking, but without some mental impairment Rebekah didn't understand how the couches could be justified.

One was tan, stained. This belonged to Red, the most knowledgeable, or at least the most opinionated, of the three. He was horse-faced, wore glasses, and the other two accepted his pronouncements as self-evident because he had, in the very distant past, held a county record in pole vaulting. Red rented space in the back corner of the front of the store (not prime real estate by any means), where he sold an assortment of things he swore to be valuable: carved historical figures, forged at the Franklin Mint; commemorative coins; a set of dish towels bearing the likeness of Spiro Agnew.

The second couch was green and missing a leg, which had been replaced with a set of coasters. This was Slim's domain, which he claimed by spreading his belongings around him: cigarettes, lighter, wallet, and keys. Slim seemed to be persistently busy working on a political system at the center of which was advertising and sentimentality. He was in favor of any person, establishment, or event said to promote Family Values; thus he loved Republicans, chain restaurants, NASCAR, and military skirmishes. He choked up listening to Toby Keith, and saluted when he saw a flag, although Rebekah believed he, like his comrades, had sat out all military duty. Slim shared the corner booth with Red, where he sold what Della told him to. She tended toward old bedspreads and a variety of pastel-colored mixing bowls.

The third sofa was black and had been repaired with silver duct tape, not even electrical tape, which would have matched. Jim Hank, unmarried and the least of his brethren, sat on the edge of one of the sofa's three cushions. He never sat back or settled in. Red claimed that a vicious rival for a woman's hand had hit Jim Hank in the back of the head with a crowbar; Rebekah had no idea if it was true. *Something* had happened to him, maybe just a nick on the edge of a chromosome. From a distance he looked as if he'd been handsome and strong, but up close one side of his face dragged and his eyes were all but empty. He limped, couldn't hold anything small in his left hand. When he lifted a can of soda it shook all the way to his mouth. He and Hazel rarely spoke, but there was a file in Hazel's office filled with receipts for his rent, his prescriptions, his groceries. Jim Hank had a table in Red's booth, where he arranged various articles taken from his home: a butter dish, a pocketknife, a wooden box designed to hold a family's silver. Inside were a lone, tarnished butter knife and an ornate meat fork.

Hazel had gotten, in the same auction lot as the couches, two ashtray stands and a coffee table, plastic made to look like leather. She referred to the setup as a Conversational Grouping, and what she'd made at the front of the store was a combination of den (in the home of some poor and tasteless person) and a gas station as they'd been when Rebekah was small, a grimy place where she would sometimes see men gathered, smoking and waiting for an oil change. Her own father never joined in. Rebekah had once heard Claudia ask, aggrieved by something Slim had said, whether Hazel had known what she was doing when she built the Conversational Grouping. Hazel had waved her hand in the air as if Cronies were a fact of life, furniture or no.

"I knew them when they were young," she had said.

"What were they like then?" Rebekah asked.

Hazel had glanced over at the three, all of whom were bent over, elbows on their knees. "Just the same. But younger."

There was a box of books on the counter, something Hazel had just purchased or brought in from the storage shed; Rebekah began looking through them. One thing that puzzled her was the way the men smoked, and drank sodas until their knees began to bounce, and then at some point every afternoon a signal sounded and they all stood up and left, in the way a flock of birds will suddenly depart a tree.

Hazel pulled her knitting out from under the counter and began counting stitches. "A 'ramage,' I think it's called," she said between rows.

"What's called a ramage?"

"It's also possible I invented that word."

Rebekah looked at the table of contents in a 1954 memoir of a woman's first year of housewifery, *Boiled Water*. "But what does it mean?"

"It refers to the phenomenon of a flock of birds suddenly leaving a tree." Hazel's knitting needles—wide, blue with a mother-of-pearl tint—clicked, slid against each other.

Rebekah looked up at Hazel. "Was I thinking out loud?"

"When?"

"Before ramage. Did I say something about the Cronies out loud?"

"I don't know." Hazel shrugged. "Did you?"

Rebekah had to turn only one page and there it was, the sentence *I couldn't boil water!* She had tried many times to think it through, she had even tried to talk to Peter about Hazel, but he had been skeptical, had suggested that Rebekah, because of her history, was gullible. But as far as she could see, the opposite was true. The first twenty-three years of her life had been spent in thrall to prophecy, or at least those years had been spent with a community that valued nothing more. What was it? Pastor Lowell had once said in a sermon that the only test of a prophet was his accuracy. He said this while discussing a passage from Ezekiel. How could that be, though, Rebekah had wondered, if the prophet and everyone who heard him speak the words of his prophecy were dead and gone? Anyone can say the Temple will fall (because the Temple will fall) and be right eventually. And what does it suggest about the nature of time and space, if the future is given to some long in advance? If one thing is true, namely that the future can be known by the prophets, then the future has been predetermined and there is no such thing as free will and the damned are born damned, the saved likewise. The biblical seers and those members of the Mission who were given the fruits of the Spirit foresaw an arc into history, an apocalypse of change, natural disaster, and vengeance. Its ushering in was accompanied by the signs and symbols everywhere in evidence, so the world itself appeared to be in league with the conspiracy.

But what of Hazel? Rebekah flipped past the chapter in *Boiled Water* that dealt solely with Adventures in Ironing. The world *was* Hazel's evidence, it was its own testimony. Rebekah had tried to say to Peter that she thought of the old men in the desert, the way their sight (such as it was) traveled like a bullet through time, puncturing everything in its wake, but Hazel just sat knitting or doing needlepoint, watching *Buffy the Vampire Slayer,* and the ephemeral world was right there beside her. All she had to do was reach out and pluck a strand and she knew your past, your greatest fear, and what you'd be trying to avoid the next day. These weren't the words Rebekah had used with Peter and he'd been irritated anyway. He told her he thought Hazel was a just an old woman with a keen eye, a collection of astrology texts, and a bag of tricks. He thought this even as he courted Hazel, gave her his most level blue gaze. And it seemed that Peter had been right, because Hazel seemed to like him; she seemed unable to see his real feelings for her.

"I'll tell ya what you're gonna have to do," Red suddenly said, pointing at Slim with his burning cigarette. "You're gonna have to drill through the hardwood, the subfloor, right through that concrete, my friend, one them full-inch drill bits, then pump the poison dreckly in the ground, and do the same outside the house. Course you'll have to wait fer spring." He sat back, satisfied.

"Naw!" Slim said, slapping his forehead. "The wife'll kill me, she's gonna kill me!"

"You brung it on yourself, not putting in a basement or a crawl space. Where'd you get that idea, build a house on a concrete slab? You get your house plans with a set of Ginsu knives?"

Jim Hank wheezed his hardest laugh, fell to coughing.

"Lord but it is gettin' cold outside." Red shook his head. "What happens when your pipes burst in that slab, Slim?"

Rebekah glanced up at him, but Slim just shook a Doral out of his pack, lit it.

"Did you see him last night?" Hazel asked, adjusting the pale blue afghan that was lengthening by the minute in her lap.

"See who last night?" Rebekah pretended to be reading.

"Oh please."

"No." Rebekah turned past an illustration, classic 1950s style, of a woman tangled up in the cord of a vacuum, little stars above her head.

Hazel lifted the afghan, let it fall over her knees. "Will you try again?"

Would she try again? Rebekah thought about it. "I feel like," she began, "like maybe he's waiting on me to make a move? Some grand gesture, maybe?"

"You mean because the grand gesture of calling him repeatedly and leaving plaintive messages wasn't sufficient?"

"I stopped leaving messages a long time ago."

"Ah."

"You know, part of the problem is that I miss him so much I want to tell someone every detail of it, the missing him, and the person I want to tell is Peter."

"Why?" Hazel asked.

"Why what?"

"Why Peter?"

Rebekah sighed, rubbed her temples. She was very tired all of a sudden. "Because we were friends, I thought. He's the only boy besides my cousins I ever knew. Men don't—they don't make much sense to me—"

"No."

"—and I feel like if he's still in my heart, I must still be in his."

Hazel let her hands fall in her lap. "But Rebekah, feelings are not facts."

The pages of the mildewy book blurred before her; Rebekah closed it. "Grief is a fact."

"No, grief is a feeling."

Rebekah swallowed hard, tossed the book back in the box. "Whew, I should get back to work. I thought I might put some New Years-y dresses on the mannequins, hats, things like that. Then I'll help Claudia rearrange number forty-two. She wants to show you something, by the way," she said, slipping out from behind the counter.

"All right, dear," Hazel said. Rebekah heard the ticking of the knitting needles resume as she walked quickly past #14, #15, the suitcases, the dining room table at which no one ever sat.

It was four o'clock before Claudia found Hazel alone in the office, putting stamps on a stack of letters to vendors. Hazel glanced up at her, nodded toward the empty chair beside her desk. "Women are the pack mules of the world," she said, pressing a stamp down with her thumb.

"You aren't a pack mule," Claudia replied, gingerly stretching out her left knee.

"True. But I bought my way out of it. Plus I'm too old."

They sat a few moments without speaking. Claudia listened to the faint, tinny sound of the Andrews Sisters coming from the back of the store.

"They were lovely, the Andrews Sisters." Hazel completed her task and dropped the stack of envelopes in her outgoing-mail tray.

"I found this in your book last night," Claudia said, handing the photograph to Hazel.

"What's this?" Hazel slipped off her glasses and held the picture at arm's length. She squinted. "You found this in *Owen Meany*?"

Claudia nodded.

"Thank you for returning it to me." She slipped the picture inside the book she was reading, *The Mysterious William Shakespeare: The Myth*

& the Reality, and said, with a perfunctory clip, "Let's get this store closed down and go home."

Claudia allowed one beat to pass between them, one chance for Hazel to change her mind and speak. It passed, and Claudia stood up, Hazel following her. "Okay." Claudia touched Hazel's shoulder with just her index finger, attempting to make the gesture communicate something. But Hazel left the office without another word.

1961

"I can't be late getting home." Hazel looked at her watch for the fifth time, thrust her hands back into her coat pockets.

"You *can't* be late." Finney's breath smelled like tea. Sometimes she smelled like sleep or cinnamon, but today it was bergamot and lemon.

"That's what I said. If we don't leave here in twenty-seven minutes, it's all over for Miss Hazel."

"Well, we don't want that." Finney leaned farther over the scrollwork railing of the mezzanine, let her body tip just slightly past the fulcrum of her own weight.

"Hey, how's about you follow the rule about keeping your feet on the floor." Hazel tried to sound casual as she grabbed Finney's coat belt, which was untied and slipped free.

"What I want"—Finney turned and reclaimed her belt—"is to go up, up to the sixth, Women's Lingerie. Then I want to come down, down, stopping on every floor. Last is the jewelry counter. If I have twenty-seven minutes I'm going to use them."

Below the girls, the black-and-white-tiled ground floor of Sterling's Department Store spiraled around the square jewelry counter, so that from Women's Lingerie, looking over the railing, Hazel knew she would feel an urge to jump. "Women's Lingerie it is," she said, taking Finney's arm and heading for the elevator.

The folding metal door of the elevator closed, cagelike, behind them. In the red velvet interior the air was warm and close. The elevator operator hummed along with Bing Crosby's Hawaiian Christmas song, which both Hazel and Finney hated. Jerry Hamm, that was the name of the man sitting on a stool in front of the elevator's controls, but Hazel didn't acknowledge him, nor did he look at her. He was a patient of her father's, and there were countless rules of conduct that applied to meeting a patient in public, or at his job. Finney knew him, too, of course, but she ignored him, leaning against the back wall to watch the numbers light up above the doors.

In Women's Ready-to-Wear, in Household Goods, in Infants and Children, Finney had asked, "Do you want this? Is this on your list?" No, Hazel had answered, and no. Finally, walking toward the jewelry counter with only four minutes to spare, Finney asked, "What *do* you want for Christmas?"

"A book. I don't know, something I can keep. Nothing frivolous."

Finney took a deep breath, rolled her eyes. "I worry about you, Hazey."

"Really."

"Yes, I do. I worry that any day now you will tell me you want to write short stories or romances, and then you'll turn to strong drink."

"Will I abandon my Christian principles?"

Finney considered the possibility. "You will."

"Will I die young and tragically?"

"That's not funny." Finney ran her fingers over a dozen strands of freshwater pearls, took one off the metal rack and held it to her throat.

Hazel fastened the necklace, gently lifting Finney's hair. "This looks beautiful on you."

Finney looked in the square mirror on the counter, turned her jaw to the right and the left in a way that would have never occurred to Hazel. Finney's camel hair coat was down around her shoulders and her long neck looked more vulnerable than ever, with the pearls lying pale and imperfect against her skin. "I'm not a pearl person."

"Hmmm. What kind of person are you?"

Finney took three steps away, didn't answer.

"Anyway, what do you most want for Christmas?" Hazel asked, just as Finney stopped before a display of gold chains.

"Oh, look at this."

In a blue velvet box were two chains, each chain holding half a heart. On the inside lid of the box were the words MAY GOD WATCH OVER US WHILE WE ARE APART, and carved on the heart itself, ME FROM THEE. Hazel lifted the left half and warmed it in her hand as Finney did the same with the right.

"Do you think," Finney whispered, leaning close to Hazel, "that he will ever buy me one of these?" She whispered, it seemed to Hazel, because she had lost her voice, like a girl in a fairy tale. It was only a matter of time before a hunter came after Finney's real, beating heart, or until her legs became the tail of a mermaid, and she vanished. No, the man in question would never, never buy Finney such a necklace; the possibility did not exist on planet Earth or within the bounds of time and space. "Maybe he will," Hazel said, turning away from the display. "Your four minutes in jewelry are up, Miss Finnamore Cooper." She used the old nickname as a distraction, but it failed.

"I will be blue until I die," Finney said, sighing.

Hazel's stomach knotted into a fist, and she could taste at the back of her throat the coffee they'd had at lunch. She reached into Finney's bag and pulled out her muffler, wrapped it around Finney's neck as they walked past the great Christmas tree beside Sterling's revolving doors. "Bundle up," she said, tucking the end of the scarf into Finney's coat.

Finney smiled, said, "You do the same."

They'd grown too mature for hats, so they walked close together, heads bent against the bitter December wind, across the street to the parking lot and Albert Hunnicutt's late-model, sleek black Cadillac. Tomorrow Hazel would return for the necklace, she knew, and she would give it to Finney signed with her own name. Hazel would never pretend it had come from someone else. Finney would accept the gesture as she always had, for years and years now, as long as Hazel could remember. Finney would wear her half of the heart as if it mattered to her as it did to Hazel, and only someone who really knew her, only a best friend, would see the unease and disappointment on her face. It was just metal, after all, and probably hollow at that.

"Admit that you're a brat."

"*Captain* Brat."

"*General* Brat."

Hazel and Finney tormented little Edna until she was nearly in tears—this happened every time they baby-sat—then gave her what she'd asked for.

"I'll tell Mama," Edna said, sitting at the kitchen table, a TV dinner cooling in front of her.

"Tell her what?" Hazel asked. "Here's your Bosco. Drink it fast or you can't have it at all. It's almost bathtime."

"I'm not taking a bath."

"Tell her what, Edie?" Finney stood behind Edna, combing the girl's blond hair with her fingers.

"Tell her that a boy calls."

"It's not a crime for a boy to call and anyway he doesn't call for me. So you'd be getting Finney in trouble and you love her. Think about that."

Edna took a drink of her chocolate milk, pushed away the foil tray with her uneaten dinner. "I'm not taking a bath."

"But you are. And what about that chicken leg?"

"I'll tell Mama you smoke a cigarette once. When her and Daddy was gone."

"Yeah? Is that right, Edie?" Hazel picked up the washcloth from the edge of the sink and threw it on the table. "How about if I tell Mother about the letter your teacher sent home last week, the one I signed so you wouldn't get in trouble? How about if I tell Mother that you got caught stealing a cap gun from the Ben Franklin and I got you out of that one, too?"

Edna sat very still, one hand in her lap and the other around her Mickey Mouse Club cup. She was small for eight—almost nine—with the facial features of a much younger child. Staring at her, Hazel couldn't see at all who her sister might turn out to be. Edie's chin shook and her gray eyes filled with tears, but it was not to Hazel she apologized. "I'm sorry, Finney!" she said, jumping up and spilling her Bosco all over the table.

"Great. I'll just clean this up for you," Hazel said, using the washcloth she'd thrown at the child.

"Come here, Edie," Finney said, holding out her arms. "Don't cry, I'm not mad. You just don't want to take a bath, right? It's cold in the upstairs bathroom." Finney held her on her lap, using her sweater to wipe Edie's face. "Come on, we'll go upstairs, I'll wash behind your ears and brush your teeth and we'll call it a night. Maybe mean old Hazel will bring you some more milk." They stood and walked toward the back staircase.

"Nice," Hazel said to the empty kitchen. She dropped Edna's frozen dinner in the trash can, poured more milk in her cup. "Thanks a lot, Finney."

The arm of the record player lifted the 45 and dropped it back in place, and the needle settled into the wide opening groove. "Theme from *A Summer Place*" began for the third or fourth time, the waltzing melody washing over Hazel as if it really were another season. She and Finney lay on their backs in Hazel's bed, looking out the window at the bare winter branches, the clouds passing the moon.

"Don't you love this song?" Finney's arms were crossed behind her head and she wiggled her toes inside her white socks.

"I do." Around the room the elephants marched and the circus train faded against the gray walls. Edna's nursery had been painted pink, with dancing circus ponies in ribbons and flowers, as if Hazel had been invited to one kind of carnival and Edna to another.

"You don't mean it." Finney would be blue until she died.

"How do you know?"

Finney shrugged. Hazel turned her head on her pillow and watched Finney's eyes trace the border of the casement window. "What *do* you love?" Finney asked, still looking ahead.

I love—Hazel thought—your parents' farm and the tone of voice you use with animals. I love that you have stolen your father's cardigan and made it look like the most feminine sweater in the world. I love the way your curls hang against your neck, and how you are the one true thing I've ever known, and how if I were captured by pirates and didn't see you for a hundred years I'd still recognize any part of you, even an elbow. "I love Johnny Cash. I love the music from the war and from before the war. I love *The Steve Allen Show* and the smell of kid leather in my mother's car. Oh, and toasted marshmallows."

"That's a lot."

"The world is full of riches." Hazel settled back into her pillow. "Have you seen him lately? I mean, actually seen him?"

Finney gave Hazel a nervous glance, an unhappy smile. "My parents had gone to get some grain for the horses, and he found me skating on the pond. I was by myself, I looked ridiculous. I was wearing Dad's overcoat with the raccoon collar, the one he had his only year at Purdue, and a white hat I knitted last winter, and a yellow and blue woolly scarf wrapped around and around my neck, all the way over my chin. My skates are even dingy. I'm sure my nose was bright red from the cold."

"When was this?" Hazel couldn't keep the blade off each word, the edge that told everything about how lost she was, how scared she was to think of Finney with no need of her, carving figure eights into her frozen cow pond, which in the summer was thick with algae and mosquito larvae. And also what was under the ice, and what would happen if Finney should go there.

"Three days ago? Maybe."

Hazel said to herself, *Don't ask, don't ask,* then asked, "Where was I?" Not plaintive, not demanding. She tried to make the inquiry casual, to suggest a passing puzzlement over her own agenda, three days ago. But how could the question not contain the other times she'd asked it, when Finney had seen a movie without her, when Finney showed up at school with pale pink lips instead of coral, and where did the coral go? Where did she find the pale pink, who shopped with her? When Finney, for instance, suddenly loved "Theme from *A Summer Place*" and last week had loved "Only the Lonely"? Where was poor Roy Orbison now, with his ugly glasses and slow-dance opera?

"I don't know." Finney bit her thumbnail, seemed not to give Hazel's whereabouts on ice-skating day a second thought. "He didn't approve of me skating."

"No, I wouldn't think so."

"He asked what would happen if I fell and got really hurt while my parents were gone."

The arm of the record player lifted in hopeless repetition, and Hazel tried to keep her breathing steady. Time was he didn't talk to Finney that way, didn't suggest any tenderness. This was new, his fear, and it was akin to Hazel's own.

"What did you say?"

"I told him I'm *indestructible*. Then I skated backward around the pond twice and he stood completely still watching, right up until I skated into him and we both fell and he hurt his hip and I hurt my wrist." She raised her eyebrows at Hazel, warm with irony and in full possession of the memory. She was resurrected, the now gone Finney of three days ago, and Hazel could see the coat and hat, the bright scarf, Finney's long limbs and neck, how graceful she was for such a tall girl. There he was, too, standing on the ice, worried and angry and miserable (so much a part of his charm), watching Finney glide like a carved figure over the mirror of a music box. It would have been a moment outside of time for both of them, and then the sudden physical awakening of her body against his, the swift transport back into the rudeness of winter on an Indiana farm, the love he couldn't have. Finney's smell of sleep and tea.

"And then what happened?"

"We helped each other up. I brushed him off, he brushed me off, he kissed me once, so hard my teeth nearly went through my lips, then he walked fast away. I tried to follow him and he told me to go home." Finney blinked, her eyelashes damp with tears, and Hazel could see Finney was happy to be so sad, because *he* had made her sad, *he* had sent her away. In turning his back to her, he had told her something intimate and they shared it now, and the most Hazel could wish for was to witness it. "Do you hear a car?" Finney asked, raising her head.

Hazel sat up, glanced at the clock. Her parents weren't due home for three more hours. "We've got to clean up the kitchen and fold the laundry." She hopped around, pulling her shoes on. Finney stood up, stretched, languid as a cat. Her parents were kind, permissive, sloppy. They let her bake cookies when she and Hazel were barely old enough to turn on the stove. Nobody cared about the mess. On Sundays in the winter, after the livestock were fed, Finney's dad, Malcolm, came home and put his pajamas back on, drank hot chocolate, and listened to the radio, letting the sections of the newspaper pile up around him. Their house wasn't a museum or a testament to anything. Just a house.

"Hazey, that isn't your dad's car."

Headlights were more than halfway down the lane, and Finney was right—it wasn't the Cadillac. Hazel bent over, tied her shoes. She ran her fingers through her hair, pulled it into a ponytail, and wrapped it with a rubber band from her wrist. Finney, too, sped up, tying her shoes and straightening her sweater. "You expecting someone?" she asked.

"No. Are you?" It would be unbearable if she'd invited him here.

"Hardly. He wouldn't come if I invited him to a church social."

The car pulled up in front of the house, and in the sodium light Hazel almost recognized it. It was someone who had been there before, and recently. Yesterday?

The brass doorknob of her bedroom door was cold; the pattern of the hallway rug was a thousand eyes. Hazel turned left and Finney was behind her, humming. They went down the front staircase, passing the silvery ancestors, through the front parlor, past the wide front door with the leaded glass panes, to the side entrance with the heavy lock and the screen. Neither thought to take a coat. They walked out into a bitterly cold, windless December night just as the car pulled into one of the clinic parking spaces and stopped. A man jumped from the driver's side, shouting, "Miss Hunnicutt, where's your mama?"

Hazel and Finney stopped on the porch, squinted into the dark to take him in. "Jerome? Is that you?"

"I need your mama, Miss Hazel. Lorraine isn't doing good, she's bleeding, where's Mrs. Hunnicutt?" The young man covered the distance between his car and the porch in two long strides: Jerome Wilson, who played center for the Southside Wildcats, a local star, and Negro.

"She's at a . . ." Jerome had been here yesterday with Lorraine, that much was true, and while her father was at his Jaycees meeting. Her mother had asked Hazel to take over at reception for an hour or so, and Hazel had taken three phone messages. Lorraine was pretty, a cheerleader at the all-Negro high school.

"She's at a Christmas party at the Cannadays'," Finney said, stepping around Hazel. "She won't be home for quite a while."

"Miss?" Jerome wiped his mouth with the back of his hand. "You've got to help me."

Hazel and Finney ran the length of the porch, took the stairs two at a time. The passenger door of the old Chrysler opened with a groan, and the overhead light didn't work. Jerome reached for a flashlight on the floorboard and shined it on Lorraine. Her head was tipped back against the seat, her lips pale. Her coat was unbuttoned and her hands hung limp at her sides. She was wearing a black flannel skirt, pulled up around her thighs, and in between her legs was a stack of blood-soaked towels.

Hazel pulled her head back so hard and swiftly she smacked her scalp on the doorframe. "Finney, there are five hooks on a board next to the door leading to the clinic. On the second are the clinic keys. Unlock the inner door, then go through and unlock this door we're facing. Jerome, can you lift her?"

"Yes, ma'am." He handed Lorraine the flashlight and reached into the car, his arms so long they slid under Lorraine's knees and behind her back and came out the other side. Lorraine let out a tight breath, not quite a moan, and Jerome did the same. He straightened up to his full height, kissed her forehead, whispered something against her hair.

Lights came on in the clinic, and then the light outside the door was burning and Finney was holding the door open. Jerome walked quickly, trying not to jostle Lorraine, and Hazel ran ahead. She wasn't thinking or praying or making note; only hoping in a vague way that Edna stayed asleep and that there would be room to get out of this, somehow.

"Take her in where you were yesterday, Jerome, and put her on the examining table. Finney, I need you to call Mother."

"Do you know the number?" Finney's face was pale, her eyes bright.

"Jesus *Christ*. Try the phone book." A line of sweat ran down Hazel's neck and into her sweater. Finney turned and headed for the outer office.

Lorraine was on the examination table, nearly panting, her eyes glassy and her lips chapped. Jerome leaned over her, running his thumb over her forehead and whispering the same thing he'd been saying walking in.

"Help me get her feet in these stirrups. Lorraine, cooperate with us, we're going to elevate your legs."

"I found a Cannaday on Riley Road, is that it?"

"Umm." Hazel thought she might faint. She grasped the table and swallowed, waiting for her vision to clear. Lorraine was wearing polished saddle oxfords and rolled white socks flecked with blood. Her legs were as smooth and chilled as glass. "Yes, I think so. Tell Mother that I need her. You can say Edie's got a fever or that I have a feminine problem, whichever will get her here without my father. Make sure she understands she needs to come alone."

Finney left without another word, closing the examining room door quietly. Hazel turned the black handle that raised the stirrups and a trickle of blood dropped onto the floor. In the silence she could hear Jerome whispering, *We'll get married, we'll get married, we'll get married.*

In bed that night Hazel knew she could buy the heart necklaces or not, it no longer mattered. There were gestures stronger than vows, secrets that contained more momentum than a tall girl skating backward, and she and Finney had such a secret. In part they all—Hazel and Finney and Caroline—had become bound by the shared labor, and by Caroline's cool response (which both girls had tried to imitate), how she had unpacked the towels so calmly and given Lorraine injections of antibiotics and pain medication, then finished what she'd started the day before. No one suggested Finney leave, as if Caroline had taken Finney as a daughter in a dark hour. But they were also united by the honesty of the lawless—Finney might love any boy and never speak the words again: *I understand, I will never tell, I will never.*

Hazel slept, finally, and dreamed of a foreign place where many objects were stored. She wandered through alone, picking up things she didn't recognize, and then there was an old man standing next to her, his hair gone white, his back bent like a crone's. She remembered he had once been beautiful, and was sad for him. He handed her something—a candlestick, a broken bell, a hairbrush—and Hazel knew that it was hers to keep. She hated it, whatever it was, it felt like death itself in her hand, but she couldn't give it back and she couldn't put it down, and in the morning she was still holding it, in all the ways that matter.

By five o'clock the sky was fully dark and a light snow was falling; Claudia sat in her sister Millie's kitchen and watched the wind swirl the flakes into white tunnels. The snow fell on the barn, the new garage, the empty chicken house—all were lit up and vivid in the yellow glow of the security light.

"You're probably sitting there thinking about Mom," Millie said, taking one container out of the microwave and putting another in.

"No, I'm not," Claudia said, but she was.

"I bet you're thinking how Mom would have been snapping beans or grinding corn or whatever for dinner."

"You don't snap beans in December."

"You know what I mean."

There, then, was Ludie, standing in the warm kitchen, listening to gospel music on the AM radio, and outside there was a snow falling like this one, and Millie was probably upstairs in her bedroom, on her way to becoming the person she was now but not yet there, and Claudia was in the kitchen, with her mother.

"It's no crime to enjoy the time-saving devices of the modern world, Claude."

"I never said."

"I happen to like microwaved food, and I happen to like not having to do dishes."

Millie happened also to like not eating, although she never said as much. She was tall (but not too tall) and thin, what Hazel called Warning Label Thin, or Sack of Hangers Thin. Hazel sometimes referred to Millie simply as Death's-head, and it was true that in certain lights you could see Millie's skull as surely as if she were being used in an anatomy class. At thirty-eight she was pinched and severe; the lack of body fat, combined with years of tanning, had left her with a web of fine lines on her face and neck. She wore her hair so short it stood up straight at the crown, and she did something to it she called 'frosting'—which she would do to her head, but not a cake—so that the roots were black and the ends were a creamy orange.

Millie's two children, Brandon and Tracy, came and went from the kitchen, speaking to neither their mother nor their aunt. Brandon, a junior in high school, took a soda from the refrigerator, then went back into the living room, where he slumped down on the couch to watch TV. A few minutes later he came back and got a bag of chips.

"We're going to eat in about fifteen minutes, Bran," his mother said.

Tracy, a year younger than her brother, ran into the kitchen, a cordless phone against her ear, and copied a phone number off the chalkboard, where she'd written *TRACY + TIM 4EVER!* Claudia had never heard of Tim, and doubted she'd ever make his acquaintance.

"We're going to eat in fifteen minutes, Tracy," her mother said.

"You are, maybe," Tracy said, and slid across the linoleum in her socks, out of the room.

How could it be that everything had changed so much so quickly? There was no such world as had Ludie in it. She was the last mother to put up vegetables every year; the last fat mother who didn't dye her hair or wear pants to church; the last to sing the old hymns and maintain a flourishing garden. Claudia couldn't think of one other soul in the world who had a pawpaw tree in the yard, one that bore fruit, and that was because of Ludie. But Millie was the New Mother, no doubt about it, driving her SUV and buying everything in her life (her clothes, her furniture, her food, her pictures in frames) at the Wal-Mart. Sitting in Millie's country kitchen with her seven thousand unnecessary pieces of plastic, Claudia sometimes expected to hear a voice call out for a manager in aisle nine. Ludie had worked all day, from the time she got up until she went to bed. She cooked and cleaned and visited the sick. In the summer she gardened and hung the washing on the line; in the autumn she raked leaves and baked; in the winter she shoveled snow and made candy. All spring she drummed her fingers on the windowsills, waiting for the time to put in annuals. She was never too sick or too tired for church or to take care of her own elderly parents. But it was Millie, who did none of those things and had no other job besides, who treasured time-saving devices like nacho cheese you could heat up right in the jar.

She put the jar of cheese down on the table, and a bag of corn chips. Beside the chips were refried beans, taken from a can and microwaved, and a jar of salsa. Millie had emptied a bag of shredded lettuce into a plastic bowl; another bowl held ground beef. The back door opened as Millie was putting paper napkins on the table and Larry came in, stamping his feet and blowing on his bare fingers.

"We caught three horses, but there's two more still out there somewhere." He pulled off his wool cap, shook the snow off his jacket. His muddy-blond hair was pushed up on his forehead.

"Sit down and eat something before you take the kids to the school," Millie said, without looking at him.

"Temperature's dropping. There'll be a livestock alert by morning, I'll bet, and tomorrow it'll be too cold to snow." Larry reminded Claudia of an actor in a western film. No particular actor—just a character with a squint, and an air of indifference to his clothes, his bunk, his companions.

"Sit down and eat something, Larry, before you take the kids to the school."

"Take the kids to school? What for?"

"There's a varsity game tonight."

"So? If Brandon can't drive them, they don't need to go."

Millie continued moving around the kitchen, opening the dishwasher, putting a dish in. She had a way of moving, Claudia had often noticed, that closed a door on a conversation. "Brandon isn't driving with the roads the way they are, especially if two of Woodman's horses are out."

Larry looked at Claudia, sighed, pulled his cap back on.

"Sit down and eat something, I said. We're having Mexican Hat Dance."

"Well, I can't, can I. I have to start the station wagon. I'll eat something at the game." The door closed behind Larry, and he left in his place a pocket of air so cold it surprised Claudia, even though she'd been sitting and studying the weather all evening.

Tracy came in now wearing makeup, and boots that wouldn't keep the damp out. "Tell Dad it's time to go," she said to her mother.

"He's starting the car, Trace."

Brandon came in with his letter jacket on—a single varsity letter in golf, which Claudia would never see as a sport—and jingling the change in his pocket as if he were a man much pressed for time.

"That jacket's not warm enough for this weather," Millie said.

And right there it happened—a kind of disorientation that left her dizzy—it was December. High school basketball season in Indiana. The snow was falling, and Claudia was sitting at a kitchen table as teenagers got ready to head back to the school they couldn't wait to leave earlier in the day. She was warm and safe, but there was a kind of voltage in the air, an excitement generated by having something, anything to do on a Saturday night, and it seemed to Claudia that *nothing* had changed. If she could just get home she'd find Ludie in the living room knitting in front of the television, and Bertram in his study. This was just what it felt like all her growing-up years: December, January, February, March.

"Kids, sit down and eat something before you go," Millie said again, but Tracy was already putting on lip gloss and reaching for the door.

"We'll eat at the game." And then they were gone.

Millie watched the door for a moment, reached into the freezer where she had hidden a pack of cigarettes. She lit one and sat down across the table from her sister.

"You're smoking again?" Claudia asked. She had grown accustomed to the idea that she might spend the rest of her short life inhaling other people's fumes.

"Just this one," Millie said, inhaling hard and blowing a thick cloud out over the table. "And don't give me any crap about it."

"I won't."

"I know Daddy would be horrified." Millie dropped the cigarette into the jar of cheese and burst into tears. "Do you see? I do and *do* for them, *look* at this food on the table, and they don't even *notice,* nobody cares."

But what difference did it make, Claudia wondered, whether they ate nachos at home or nachos sold by the Band Boosters?

Millie wiped her face with a paper napkin. "You don't know, Claudia, you can't imagine what it's like to watch your perfect babies who loved you so much grow into strangers who won't even eat the food you offer them."

It was a shame, Claudia thought, that Millie wasn't one of those pretty criers, and also that she didn't see how it is the fate of every animal to watch the children walk away and disappear. She reached out and patted Millie's arm, and Hazel was right—it did feel precisely like a clothes hanger. "It's all the same," she said, without meaning to.

Millie wiped her face with a napkin. "Oh, I know you're right. They'll be fine eating there as here."

Claudia nodded. That wasn't what she meant at all. Those ball-game nights, Millie up in her room getting ready and Claudia not only prepared but thrilled to stay home, she would listen to Millie moving around, the low, scratchy insistence of her portable radio. A hair dryer. Some pink cologne that came from the drugstore. Millie wore soft sweaters and tight blue jeans, a gray wool coat that tied around her tiny waist, and a slick, fruit-scented lip gloss called Kissing Potion. She was a mess of smells and textures. Their rooms were divided only by a hallway, but it might have been the Mississippi, or one of the bright bands that divides the living from the dead. Claudia had grown too tall for her bed and for the sloped ceiling above it; her wallpaper was still gray with white cabbage flowers, Jack London was her favorite author. No teenagers would ever pound up the stairs to claim her for some mundane adventure, as they did with Millie nearly every night. At school they passed each other a few times a day, Claudia keeping close to the walls and lockers and Millie moving down the center of the hallway in her clump of friends, all in muted pastels and clinging to each other like common roses. Millie was two years younger, so they were there together for years, and not once in that time, on not a single occasion, did Millie ever meet her sister's eye. Claudia didn't consider it something to forgive. She patted Millie's arm and said, "Your kids will be fine. You'll be fine."

Later, Claudia shut her own house down for the night; checked the doors, lowered the thermostat. She carried her book upstairs, intending to try again. She brushed her teeth, hung her white shirt in the six inches of closet space not taken up with Ludie's modest dresses and winter coats. Claudia had moved into her mother's bedroom six months before, after thinking about it for more than a year. At first the move had seemed simply practical: take her mother's room, use her bed. But she'd noticed that she still hadn't cleaned out the drawer of her mother's nightstand or moved any of her belongings. It still felt new, this death, and Claudia didn't want to disturb anything in the room in case her mother returned.

Ludie's blood pressure medicine, Atacand, in 16-milligram tablets; a box of Nytol (she hadn't slept well, those last years); Doan's Pills; Gas-X; a box of light blue Kleenex tissues, looking dusty; a small green book promising *The Comfort of the Scriptures;* Dr. Scholl's corn pads:

these were the things in the nightstand drawer. On top of the night-stand was an old white porcelain lamp with a yellowed shade, and a rectangular electric alarm clock, Westclox, white plastic (also gone yellow). The clock had a slight buzz, would light up if the button on top was pushed, and kept impeccable time. Next to the clock was the item that had most fascinated Claudia as a child, a plastic disk half an inch thick, with the words NOW YOU ALWAYS HAVE A DRINKING CUP! printed on the top. On occasion Claudia took off the lid, as she had been moved to do as a young girl, so she could see her mother's six remaining aspirin, now turning to powder. The disk expanded when the outer edge was lifted, a large ring surrounding a smaller, surrounding a smaller, forming a cone, to make a cup.

Her book was open in her lap but Claudia wasn't reading, and the gun lay beside her leg, but she didn't pick it up. She'd begun to see it as a sort of *pet,* a very patient, quiet, house-trained animal who waited for her to make a decision and had no opinion either way. For certain she couldn't do it in this room, not with Ludie's corn pads right there. She couldn't do it in her childhood bedroom—she'd been happy enough as a child. Not in Bertram's study, still filled with his books and papers, his favorite radio sitting next to his desk. Not Ludie's kitchen or cellar or the bedroom she'd converted to a sewing room; not the living room, which was after all aptly named. That left a guest room, unused since the last of Claudia's grandparents died, and Millie's room. Claudia let her head fall back against her pillows and considered it—how grand it would be! How theatrical and dishonest and an enormous mess besides; she would give Millie something to think and smoke about for the rest of her life. Millie would assume it had something to do with their history, a personal message about the grief of sibling estrangement. Millie would assume it had *something to do with her,* instead of the truth: the ability to cease living had long been the only thing keeping Claudia alive. She picked up the gun and slid it across Ludie's nightstand, placing the barrel between the lamp and the yellowing alarm clock.

At 3:48 that morning, Claudia sat up, suddenly awake, her blankets and bedspread thrown to the floor. She was covered in a cold sweat and suffering from the aftertaste of a dream now completely gone. The blast of heat she'd begun experiencing was grim, and when it arrived during the day it was bad enough, but what had begun happening at night was so much worse. In the first few moments after opening her eyes she would be filled with a knowledge so diamond-cut and deep she could only assume it came to her from God alone: nothing would ever save her. That was part of the news. We are alive, she would think, improbably so, and hostages to fortune, and no matter what, no matter if we gather riches or children or the blessings of the Holy Spirit, it will end badly. We'll first lose all we love and then die, either old, alone, and in pain, or quickly, too soon, and in terror. She woke with the taste of it on her tongue, no words for it, certain that all that had kept her from seeing it before had been the curtain of estrogen hung between her and the plain facts. Some nights she would wake and think, *I'll lose Bean,* her beloved redbone coonhound, even though Bean had been dead three years already. He died over and over, those nights. She thought of Millie, walking on a treadmill in her finished basement, her bony elbows pumping at her sides like brittle machinery about to snap and cost someone an eye. She thought of Hazel sitting on the couch with her cats, watching television alone, and Rebekah, the victim, finally, of her father's rage. Claudia saw mudslides, bacteria, gigantic oiled weaponry. She saw the simpler, more certain spring, when the frozen ground would thaw and churn up objects long lost and forgotten, and the ways those objects—an old school eraser, a bottle cap, a bent spoon—would arrive like indictments (of what crime she couldn't say). Worst of all, what she realized in her sleep was so common she had taken to whispering to herself, "This is it, this is it," this is the dark night, the existential panic that had driven the human race out of caves and into pulpits. The voice she heard, speaking calm and slow, said: You might have loved, or given your life to another or to a cause. You might have had a family, or visions—none of it would have mattered in the end.

She turned on the white porcelain lamp, looked around the room, taking in its familiarity. Ludie's bed had no footboard, so Hazel had helped Claudia cover a cedar chest with a foam cushion. They'd placed the chest flush against the end of the bed, making an extension to the mattress. Eventually she would rise, open the window, let the winter air in, so cold it felt like a solid thing; she would pace, close the window, try again to sleep. While her knees (and to a lesser extent, her spine) would never fully recover from the growth spurt in the sixth grade, she felt fine this particular night. Nothing really hurt.

In Rebekah's lifetime, Vernon's schedule had rarely wavered. Weekdays he stood on the assembly line at the Chrysler plant. For all she knew, he'd been standing in the same place for the past forty years, every day since his family's farm had sold; for all she knew, his black work shoes had left a fossil-like impression in the concrete. Wednesday evenings were reserved for Prayer Meeting. Saturdays he tended to the fleet at Peacock's Mortuary, cleaning and waxing the coach, the family car, the black Fleetwood Brougham that Martin Peacock drove. He changed the oil in the cars, checked the tires. Sunday morning he rose at dawn and went to church. In the winter he turned the heat up, organized hymnals. Summers he cut the grass, trimmed the hedges. He would have done well, Rebekah thought, or at least far better, in Puritan New England. Vernon would have been the one to stuff old newspapers in the cracks in the chinking, the one to light the potbellied stove and sweep out the dirty water from boots and hems at the end of the day. He seemed to need the feeling of shoring up structures against the elements, doing it with his bare hands, and all he had now was the airtight, square brick building at the edge of town the Mission had purchased from the Jehovah's Witnesses in 1980, after the old meetinghouse had burned down.

Dinner was nearly ready. Rebekah checked the corn bread, took the cast iron skillet from the oven. The vegetable soup would be too hot to eat, the corn bread steaming. Vernon sat at the table silently, hands crossed over his plate. He had taken off his work shirt in the kitchen heat and wore only a white T-shirt and his dark blue factory pants. As Rebekah passed behind him she was struck by how clearly she could see his spine snaking up his back, pressing through the skin, the shirt; the vertebrae were close enough to touch. The Mission taught that Scripture was a skeleton. The sinew and flesh of the Body were two things: the interpretation of the Book given through prophecy, and a life lived in absolute accordance with the church's principles.

"Do you want milk?" Rebekah asked.

Vernon seemed not to hear her. He moved his right thumb over the back of his left hand, stared unseeing at the butter dish on the table.

"Do you want milk, Daddy?"

"Hmmm?" He glanced at her, his eyes bloodshot, a line of shadow around his jaw. "Yes, thank you."

There was a sort of temporary brilliance, Rebekah had noticed, that caused some men to be handsome just a moment, maybe right at the edge of manhood; later their wives wouldn't be able to recall what precisely had set up such a need in them. What had they seen in this fleshy, mottled, dull-eyed bore, or in that brute now gone to seed? Peter would probably not stay handsome, if she was being honest. His light seemed connected to his age, his freedom. He was lovely in that cabin, by moonlight or with candles burning on the windowsill. The curve of his neck and shoulders as he played his guitar was like an undiscovered coastline, and Rebekah had been the first to sight it.

She slipped silverware, a napkin next to her father's plate, placed in front of him a bowl filled with soup. He was the other sort of man. Rebekah didn't have to squint or look at him aslant to see what her mother had seen, at seventeen. His wavy, dark red hair was still thick, and streaked with white, not gray. His eyes were the green of imaginary water, not a lake or a pond or even the sea, but dream green. And everything in his face—his nose, his chin and jaw, his forehead—was so uncompromising that time couldn't change it much. He would be whittled down as everyone finally was, but until then he was like stone.

"Precious Lord," he began, not waiting for Rebekah to sit, "we thank You for this food, for the blessings of Your love and comfort, and ask that we may use this nourishment to Your greater glory, in Jesus' name."

"Amen." Rebekah pulled her chair closer to the table, opened her napkin in her lap. She was struck by a wave—not of sickness, exactly, or exhaustion, but of sadness, an unaccountable sensation. Was it the light in the kitchen, her grandmother's butcher block table? Her hand was so close to her spoon, but she couldn't seem to reach for it. For years after her mother died she'd find herself frozen, a sewing needle halfway through a hem, the bed half made, and Rebekah just standing there, unable to move. She didn't think about Ruth in those long minutes, not specifically, anyway. Her heart just turned things over, a handful of pebbles: one for the dresses in her closet (she didn't know why). One was for loneliness. This one was the piano, in tune, and this was the heavy front door of the funeral home that opened just before you could touch it.

"Rebekah?"

It was gone. She picked up her spoon, stirred the too hot soup, didn't bother answering Vernon. He did not, as a general rule, speak to her, hadn't for the past five years. She abided by the laws he established in the first harrowing weeks after she left the church, and he responded with silence. Her room was still hers, but she was to clean the house, buy the groceries, and prepare all of his meals, seven days a week. If she ate with him, she couldn't read a book or listen to the radio, nor could she talk *at* him, as she had done all of the years of her life. How strange it seemed to her now, the way she used to sit at the table and babble away, telling first both her parents everything that had happened in her day, laughing crazily over every funny thing she'd seen or heard, and later just Vernon, who didn't respond but didn't tell her to stop, either. She would tell her parents how her favorite boy cousin, Davy, could fill his cheeks with peanuts and imitate a squirrel, and as she told them she'd first laugh, and then begin to cry from laughing, and finally she'd realize she was in such a state not because the squirrel imitation was so funny but because she herself, laughing so hard, was so funny. Some days she'd even admit this, wiping tears from her face and holding her aching right side; she'd say, "Oh, lands, I am just completely out of control here," and that would make her start all over again. Ruth would say, "Well, Rebekah, I never," and Rebekah would put her head down on the table and simply weep. Eventually Ruth would start to laugh, and sometimes it went on this way all through the evening, and Vernon just watched. Ate his dinner, folded his napkin, watched them. Rebekah never would have guessed—it didn't occur to her until she was fully grown—that not everyone shared her belief that God had spared humanity its relentless fate in a single way: by making a good portion of every day *hilarious*.

Vernon, who ate everything quickly, wiping his mouth with his napkin between each bite, was finished. Rebekah realized she didn't really want to eat anything, she'd just been applying herself to the ritual. She put down her spoon and was pushing her chair back from the table when Vernon said, "Rebekah, sit."

She sat. Was there something she had failed to do? Had she salted the soup, vacuumed the hallway, folded his handkerchiefs? It seemed she'd done all those things, so what was coming? Vernon swallowed, clenched his jaw muscles, didn't look at her. Rebekah waited. She heard (not for the first time) the hum of the overhead light, the motor of the refrigerator grinding, her pulse.

"You have not," her father began, "had a menstrual period in two months." His voice was low, reasonable. He could have been on the radio, he could have been the person to announce, *This one is for all the lovely girls sitting by the phone tonight, waiting for a word from their sweethearts. The message from Woody Herman is: We "Surrender," darlings. We have surrendered.*

Rebekah could see, it seemed, the individual threads in Vernon's T-shirt, and there was a powerful light at the edge of his body, just where it became itself and not the space around it. The whole of the kitchen rose up this way, vivid and exact. She thought to say, *How do you know this?* And then, *How do you KNOW this?* But she couldn't speak. Because he was right, and she had just realized it herself as he said it.

"I assume this means you are pregnant, and by the young man who is unemployed and takes money from his parents. The young man with the guitar who hadn't called you or seen you in four weeks."

Rebekah wanted to reach across the table and take Vernon's hands, something she hadn't done since childhood. She wanted to tell him to stop talking, because she needed time to take in what he'd just told her, she needed to sit still and think about it a minute. Because he was right—there had been something swimming just at the edge of her consciousness, and for weeks when she turned to look at it, it was gone. Just a small, swimming thing. Her breasts ached and tingled, for how long now? Her abdomen felt like one continuous bruise, from her pelvic bone up to her stomach, and there was the tiredness like fainting, and how the color on a box of Cheerios had nearly made her throw up. She was stunned, and mortified. Her periods had always been irregular; it wasn't unusual for her to skip a month, but two? There had been that one night with Peter—she remembered it clearly —when she had been lying on her back and felt . . . what was it? What a leaf must feel when its stem breaks free of the tree.

"He's got a new girl now, a twenty-year-old from the college who drives a red Mustang and smokes cigarettes. He dated her while he was still dating you. Her name is Mandy."

Rebekah sat back as if something had flown too close to her face. Mandy? A college student? But how could that be, when it should have been clear to everyone that the cabin belonged partly to Rebekah, the bed, the dishes, the vanishing notes of the guitar were hers, it was *her life*? Hadn't they spoken promises to each other? She couldn't recall, and it hadn't mattered at the time; they were implicit.

"I've taken this to the Elders—"

"You told *Governance*?"

Vernon's jaw muscles flexed, relaxed. "They certainly would have known soon enough."

She saw, first, the women of the church, all of them cycling through pregnancy and nursing, year after year; the shapeless tent dresses made of rough fabric, the whispered consultations and fears. They stayed away from the men—not as a rule but because pregnancy was a sign of . . . Rebekah rubbed her forehead, she couldn't think. It was a sliver of power, narrow as a blade, and the women wouldn't share it. And it was a time to return to your mother and your grandmother. She closed her eyes, tried to will Ruth back to life, back to the table, but when she tried to picture her mother's face she could only see the Governance men.

Rebekah imagined them sitting around the folding table in the basement Fellowship room: her father; Martin Peacock in his black suit, the vest straining over his stomach; Jeb King, the cattle farmer; Jim Mason, the kindest of the Governance men; Rich Ford, who worked at the Chrysler plant with Vernon and spent all his free time hunting whatever was in season; and Pastor Lowell. Rebekah couldn't actually see Pastor—just the chair, a squatting shadow. Her father was explaining to them that his daughter, a woman they refused to acknowledge if they saw her on the street, had missed two periods. He told them this. The men considered it, the menstrual blood, the Levitical laws no doubt playing like a bass note under their prayer and conversation. And Mandy?

"You *told* them this?" A wave of anger pulsed at her scalp, flooded her face and neck. She felt it in her shoulders and hot in her chest. And there, finally, was her mother's voice: *Don't let it touch the baby.*

"No doubt you realize," Vernon continued, staring now directly into her eyes, the bright green unblinking, "that I was censured for allowing you to stay here at all after you left the Mission. The terms of that censure is private, of course. I let you stay because—"

"Because you're my father?"

"—my spirit wasn't clear."

"It's clear now?"

"You made this decision for me." His left thumb rubbed against his right hand, as he had before dinner.

"I don't understand what you're saying."

Was someone listening? Rebekah wondered. His speeches were obviously prepared, but she couldn't say who had authored them.

"When I allowed you to stay here five years ago, I invited corruption into my home. I have battled against that corruption every day. I prayed for your soul even as your damnation was certain, and as you wore your worldliness like a cloak. Rebekah"—and here he leaned forward, looked at her—"you wear slacks in my *home*. You cut your hair and walk right through my doorway, as if the laws that have guided my entire life and all of yours don't mean *nothing*. The Governance committee has threatened to remove me from office, because having you here is no different than committing those sins myself. And now."

Rebekah swallowed. She was pregnant. Peter had allowed someone else into the cabin and onto her pillow. Someone else sat with him in front of the woodstove; Peter was, maybe right this minute, telling . . . Mandy? What sort of person was a Mandy? . . . about his seventh birthday, the way his mother had made him a crown and proclaimed him King for a Day. He'd worn the crown to school, and there was so much magic in it that no one had stolen it or made fun of him or anything, they'd let him be King. And when he came home he played on his swing set, wearing his crown, and once, at the very top of the slide, he'd said to his mom, *I am happy happy happy happy.*

"Now you have stepped so far outside the fold that there's hardly anything can reclaim you. You've committed the last crimes available to you: lust, fornication, the defilement of your body and of the institution of marriage. You've broken commandments. You've done everything but commit murder, and if Ruth was alive this would surely have killed her."

This would have killed Ruth? Rebekah nearly shouted. *You* would suggest *I* could commit murder? She didn't say these things. She didn't even know what she meant by them.

"This is the decision of Governance. You may go to the home of a couple in Tennessee and stay there until the baby is born. We'll decide what to do with it later. Then you come back here and rejoin the church—you make a commitment and you live up to it. This will never be talked about amongst us or your cousins neither one. And you live here until a suitable husband is found for you."

"And if I don't want to do that?"

"Then you can no longer live in my house and you will no longer be my daughter."

Rebekah's breathing steadied. She felt perfectly relaxed, almost sleepy. There was Vernon across the table from her, the same place he'd been sitting all her life, and Ruth's chair was empty. Here was the table under her hands, the window over the sink her father had painted shut, the faucets she'd turned off and on thousands of times. Outside it was snowing again, and cold enough to kill a man. But the house was warm and dry, because Vernon made sure of it. She was pregnant, Peter hadn't called in four weeks. Her father was her family, and this was her home. Not for a moment did she think he'd change his mind. She smiled at him, her eyes filled with tears. "This is your *grandchild*. And it's Mama's, too, there is *Ruth* in this baby."

For a long, still moment he didn't move, and when, finally, he raised his hand, Rebekah closed her eyes and prepared herself. But all her father did was brush the tears off her face with his knuckles, gently, then stood, thrusting his fists into the pockets of his work pants. "Be that as it may. You have until Monday."

Long after she heard him climb the stairs and close his bedroom door, Rebekah sat unmoving at the table. She should rise, she knew, and get the dishes washed, the leftover soup put away. There was enough to freeze a quart, which Vernon could take for lunch some-time in the spring, long after she was gone and no one in his life knew the secret of Ruth's recipe. She thought maybe she should write it down and tuck it in a drawer somewhere, in case her father ever took another wife, or allowed a widow from the church to come in and feed him. The note could say: My mother sprinkled cinnamon in her veg-etable soup. She cooked rice in chicken broth, not water. She touched everything as if it were fragile. She listened when you talked and she didn't judge and she had an easy laugh, for a woman in her time and place. Resting her head on the table, Rebekah cried and cried.

Chapter 3

SUNDAY MORNING Claudia was walking from the kitchen through the living room, just passing the telephone, when it rang. She was so surprised that for a moment she just looked at it. It rang again. Millie called her sometimes, telemarketers a couple times a week, but at eight-thirty on a Sunday morning?

"Hello?"

"Claudia," Hazel said, as if continuing a conversation they'd been having for a while, "are you coming over today?"

"Am I supposed to?"

"I don't know, are you?"

"Hazel, what—what are you asking?"

"Didn't I ask it? Are you coming over today?"

"Not now, I'm going to church," Claudia said, rubbing her palm over the top of her head.

"Church?"

"Yes, you know. The Protestant Reformation, ministers, hymnals."

"I know what church is, wiseass. I just don't know why you're going."

Claudia sighed. "We've been over this like a hundred times. If you would just go with me one time and meet Amos you'd—"

"I have met Amos."

"Excuse me?"

"I have met Amos," Hazel said. "He came into the store looking for an old-fashioned bubble gum machine for one of his daughters. We chatted. We went out to lunch."

"You—when? When was this?"

"I don't know. A couple weeks ago."

"Well." Claudia was exasperated. "Why didn't you tell me? Why didn't he?"

"Minister-client privilege, I suspect."

"Did you—do you like him?"

"Why, is he your boyfriend?"

"Hazel, I'm hanging up. You vex me."

"Are you coming over?"

"No. No, I'm not coming over, because you vex me."

"So I'll see you after church?"

"No."

"Claudia, wear—bring a change of clothes, like work clothes. Something you'd wear on a farm."

"No. This is getting worse by the minute."

"So I'll see you after church?"

Claudia sighed again, resigned. "Okay. Okay, I'll be there."

They sang a song about bread, or at least that's what Claudia sang, not being much moved by Christian metaphor. Her neighbors were singing about the Bread of Life, she understood, or something involving wheat and sheaves and leaven.

Amos Townsend stood and arranged himself behind the pulpit, straightening his shirt, his black wool suit coat. He opened his notes. He started to speak, then glanced down at one of his two blond daughters sitting in the first row, and said, "Ellie—Eloise, don't chew on that pencil—give it to your—thank you." Everyone laughed, and no one glanced around for the girls' mother in order to give her the thin smile, the judgmental look so often favored in church. If she was there, Langston, she was sitting in the very back pew, nearest to the door. Claudia had sat near her on two occasions, and couldn't help but study her: the perfect pattern of her dark braid, her thinness. She'd come in after church had started, slid into the aisle seat in the back, and watched her husband all through his sermon, her head tipped slightly to the side, and a look on her face as if she were studying an exotic bird whose native habitat escaped her. Just before Amos closed with a prayer, Langston had slipped out the heavy swinging doors without a sound. But their daughters, two little blond girls, a matching set, were there every week, sitting in the front row with their grandmother, Beulah, or another adult, well behaved.

From the pulpit Amos cleared his throat. Every week he began his sermon reluctantly, it seemed to Claudia. He shifted his weight, smiled at the congregants, took a drink of water. Finally, he said, "God *is* Love." His audience waited. He said, "God *is* Love. This might be the only piece of wisdom that survives, in the end, from the two Judeo-Christian testaments. This might be the best we could do." He defined *philia* and *agape,* told them that the Greeks employed the verb *agapao* in their literature, but *agape,* the unmerited, unsolicited love God gives to the world, belongs almost exclusively to the Bible, as if the People of the Book had to invent the word and the concept at the same time. "'Beloved, let us love one another, because love is from God; everyone who loves is born of God and knows God,'" Amos said, quoting 1 John 4:7. He read from Mark 12:30–31, and Luke 11:42. Some of the people around Claudia made notes, or turned the pages of their New Testaments. Then Amos closed his own Bible abruptly. He lifted his glasses and squeezed the bridge of his nose. "But that's not the point, is it, we *know* all that already, we already *know* what the Synoptic Gospels have to say about love and sacrifice and how we ought to feel about our neighbors; for heaven's sake, we've been reading these texts over and over for our whole lives long. It's just chatter now, just background noise. We say that God so loved the world; we say it and everything meaningful or revelatory is missing from those words. The point is God *is* Love, and that could lead us to a deeper understanding, couldn't it, a sort of rethinking of the Godhead, wherein the Supreme One is in the process of becoming, the divine character remaining eternal while the temporal pole acquires experience with us, *with us.* Like love."

Amos took his glasses off, slipped them in the breast pocket of his coat. "I—that didn't really make any sense," he said, with a slight laugh. "Let me put it this way: What if God loves us the way we truly love our children, walking around outside with them and watching them eat cinnamon toast and listening to them talk to imaginary friends on imaginary telephones, and they are becoming and we are becoming with them, because all of this, this life with them, is planted in us and stays in us and it's what we know of love. But instead we huckster around, saying that we know God is love because God is omniscient and sent a son to die, and we know God is love because of Scripture. We don't say God is love because the *world* is love, because we die without it, without it we're like those monkeys who were removed from their mothers and given just a metal cutout to cling to—we might say God is a mother, God is oxygen, God is blood. No, we take the most fundamental of human principles, something that may have tripped the wire toward us evolving into what we are, and grind it down with metaphysical abstractions, and in the process make God unreachable, unknowable, unavailable, and *unlovable*." He stopped, shook his head.

"Even within our own system," Amos continued, "we can't agree on what God's love is or what it means, because there are people like Archbishop Romero—remember our workshop in liberation theology?"—there were a few nods—"who believe, for obvious reasons, that God's love demands justice for the poor and oppressed, and that working for justice is an act of love most closely aligned with the love of Christ. But Stanley Hauerwas points out"—Amos crossed his arms, nodded—"and I think he has an interesting point here, that an embracing of the story of Jesus doesn't guarantee the eradication of injustice; rather, we have to have the integrity to accept Jesus' story as our own, and to speak God's truth without corruption. Do you see what the difference is? You can look at the Christ event and see what amounts to a call for the end of suffering, an external demand, or you can look at it as an ongoing event, one that's repeated in the soul of every individual, every day. I just wonder"—Amos opened his arms and asked the congregation, palms up—"if maybe what John, that old man, meant was that when I love you, I am loving God, and the feeling, that astonishing feeling of being loved in return, is what God's love feels like. Nothing else. God has no eyes, no feet, no mouth to speak with, and this is the gift we've been given by God, our material gift. We love the patch of land we grew up on, we love the belongings we live with and touch. We love the spring and the harvest, we love snow at Christmas, and music. We love each other deeply and sometimes without reservation, and we love our children as wild animals love and protect their children, and it's all God, God, God." He was smiling, but Claudia thought he seemed a little crestfallen.

"Let's close with a silent prayer," he said, and Claudia sat silent but forgot to pray, and then everyone was shaking hands or hugging one another, the Something of Peace, they called it, and she made her way out the door.

The Cherokee started up with new energy, just a little bit of sunlight and warmer temperatures had that effect. Claudia pulled out onto Plum Street and headed out of Haddington, the radio off. She understood it, the path Amos had gotten on and where it had ended up, but there was still something so sad in it. All the way to Hazel's, Claudia couldn't shake the feeling that she'd missed something important, something she would have learned already if only she'd lived an entirely different life.

On Saturday night Rebekah had driven by the cabin, and he hadn't been there, not when she got off work at four. He hadn't been there any hour up to midnight, when Rebekah had given up and driven home so tired she couldn't discern where the shoulder of the road began. And now, all Sunday morning, he wasn't there. She had so much to do—things from her bedroom she didn't want to leave behind but wasn't sure how to pack, and the simpler problem of not knowing where she was going. This was a long shot, she knew, but some part of her believed that if she took the risk and told Peter, he would see that the only thing to do was . . . she didn't know what. He would do something.

At noon she made her decision, and drove back to the edge of Jonah, to a subdivision built in the late sixties where Peter had grown up. His parents still lived there, in the same house. Peter's bedroom looked like it had when he was in high school, and his basketball hoop was there, and in the three-car garage a 1957 Thunderbird, robin's-egg blue. Peter and his dad, Pete Senior, had restored it together. Like Rebekah, Peter was an only child, greatly cherished. She thought of the house at the edge of town as the Peter Museum for the way his mother, Kathy, had one whole wall of the living room covered with his school

pictures, an eight-by-ten of every year, right up to the graduation portrait of Peter leaning against a ladder outside the photographer's studio.

She pulled into the driveway, turned off the car. Kathy and Pete
Senior were here, and Rebekah should have reckoned on the wave of
heartsickness she felt seeing the house, the backyard. There was the
padded glider, now covered with snow, on which she'd sat with Peter
in August while his father grilled hamburgers, and the line of trees at
the edge of the yard where they'd watched one squirrel chase another,
back and forth, for thirty minutes. They'd only started dating last
spring, but all through those months she'd believed, in a way, that she'd
been redeemed. She thought her own tribe had been taken from her
and she'd been given this instead, this comfortable suburban home and
family. His parents had been warm to her, if not intimate; they'd welcomed any opportunity to have her over for dinner, or to meet Peter
and Rebekah out somewhere. They had been decent, polite. It seemed
odd to her that Peter could vanish from her life and his parents would
just go with him, that they wouldn't put up a little bit more of a fight.
When they mentioned the upcoming holidays they had always looked
in her direction, as if to include her, and yet Thanksgiving had come
and gone without a word from them.

Rebekah got out of the car and walked toward the wide back
porch. She navigated the icy steps and scuffed her boots on the welcome mat. The pale yellow curtains on the kitchen door were drawn
open and tied. She knocked. Only strangers used the formal front
door. No one came. She knocked again, saw Peter's mother approach
from the living room and look around the curtain.

Kathy opened the door. "Rebekah! How nice to see you, come in
out of this cold." She was wearing a pair of cream-colored slacks and
a dark brown sweater. Her sleek ash blond hair was perfectly cut to
accentuate the eyes she'd passed along to her son.

"Hi, Mrs. Mitchell. I was in the neighborhood . . ."

"What's this 'Mrs. Mitchell'? We settled that a long time ago.
Come in, come in." Kathy's face relaxed into a smile. "Well, it's quite
a winter so far, isn't it?"

Rebekah walked into the warm kitchen, and was again taken by
surprise. How could she have forgotten this smell, the apple-cinnamon
potpourri Kathy kept on the stove, mixed with years of dinners and

laundry? Or the magnets on the refrigerator proclaiming the "Foot-prints" poem, and I ASKED JESUS HOW MUCH HE LOVED ME, AND HE STRETCHED HIS ARMS OUT AND SAID THIS MUCH. "It's—I'm glad to be in this room again," Rebekah said, smiling at Kathy.

"Kath?" Pete Senior called, walking in from the living room. "Who was it?" He walked into the kitchen and saw Rebekah just as he finished the question.

"Rebekah was in the neighborhood," Kathy said to her husband.

"Ah. How are you, Bekah?" Pete asked, then simply stood there. Peter had his father's dark curly hair and his build, although Pete had thickened as he aged. He looked as if he'd never had his son's slight-ness, or look of whimsy.

"I'm good, thank you." No one asked her to sit down, even though there was the table and there were the benches where she'd had so many dinners. She knew where the dishes were kept, and that Kathy's spices were alphabetized not in a cabinet, but in a drawer built just for the purpose. "How have the two of you been?"

Kathy gave her a slight smile. "We've been fine. Fine. Are you— on your way somewhere? Have a big day ahead?"

"I—" Rebekah realized the room was hot, the smell of the pot-pourri overwhelming. She needed to sit down. "Can I sit down?"

Kathy gestured to the nearest bench. "Of course, I'm so sorry! How rude of me." She didn't join Rebekah there, and Pete didn't, either.

"I wonder if you know where Peter is?"

"Well"—Kathy blinked, glanced at Pete—"I do, as it happens."

Rebekah swallowed, tried not to breathe too deeply. "I need to talk to him about something."

"I see." Kathy looked down, turned the thin gold watch on her right wrist. "I wish I knew what to say."

The kitchen was too hot; the perfumed air left a chemical aftertaste in the back of Rebekah's throat. She unzipped her coat and pulled at the scarf around her neck. "Will you just—will you tell me where I can find him?"

Kathy placed the palm of her hand on her chest, a delicate gesture of consternation Rebekah had seen her make before. "It's not my place to—"

"I thought, Kathy—I thought you *liked* me."

"I do," Kathy said, sitting down next to Rebekah, "we do, very much." She took a deep breath, said, "We were delighted to welcome you as long as you were dating, but we felt it best to—you know—before you got too serious . . ."

"What are you saying?" Rebekah looked at Pete Senior. "What is she saying?"

"I'm only"—Kathy held out her hands as if to grasp Rebekah's own, but didn't—"I'm just trying to be honest. Peter is young, he has so much potential. He's going to be touring around the country starting . . . well, soon, playing his guitar in coffeehouses, seeing the sights. It's the wrong time for him to be tied down in a relationship. He needs room to grow."

"Maybe he should get a *job,*" Rebekah pointed out, her face flushed, hands trembling. "You bought his truck, you pay his rent and give him spending money. I paid for our dates for seven months, seven months of believing we were committed to each other, and he abandoned me without a word for a twenty-year-old? And somehow *I'm* not good enough for *him*? Is that what you're saying?"

"No, no, of course not," Kathy said, dropping her hands. "But Mandy comes from a very good family. They live on Geist Reservoir outside Indianapolis."

"I see." Rebekah's voice was barely above a whisper.

"Her father works for Boeing, she . . ." Kathy looked at her husband for support, but Pete Senior continued to stare at the kitchen floor. "Mandy's studying business. She's in a sorority."

"And how, forgive me for asking this, Kathy, how do you think her family is going to feel about your son and his prospects? How do you think they'll feel about a man who intends to travel around the country on someone else's money, playing his guitar in coffeehouses?"

Kathy leaned away from Rebekah. "Well, I guess they'll feel fine about it, as Peter has gone away for the weekend with them, skiing in Michigan."

Sweat trickled down Rebekah's back, and her stomach fluttered. She was aware, again, of the cloying smell coming from the stove, the way it was mixing with Kathy's department store cologne. "I hope," Rebekah said, standing up too quickly, "that Mandy is still able to ski after Peter gets *her* pregnant."

Rebekah slammed the kitchen door behind her, slammed the porch door, too. She kicked the glider just to see the snow fall from it, and when she got into her car, she nearly pulled the door closed on her own foot. She'd never been the one in her family to lose her temper; hadn't yelled at her girl cousins, or thrown things; had never understood, really, what compelled other people to such misbehavior. She understood now. Even though her heart was pounding and she thought she might have to eventually stop and throw up, she was glad she'd come. Her mind felt clearer than it had in weeks. Kathy and Pete hadn't been her replacement family after all, and she would never miss them again.

Claudia left church and drove home to change her clothes, knowing full well that whatever awaited her would be distasteful at best. During the drive to Hazel's house, she considered worst-case scenarios, and the list was long and terrifying: (a) Hazel had decided to exhume a corpse; (b) one of Hazel's cats was dead in the crawl space, and Claudia had to go in face-first, and claim it; (c) Hazel had taken up some form of Spiritual Farm Dancing; (d) she was going to trick Claudia into participating in a Carhartt fashion show.

Sycamore State University lay on the east side of the Planck River, whose sluggish current now struggled under a thin layer of ice. Claudia didn't know if it was the case with all universities, but this one had, with slow assurance, spread itself out over half of Jonah, after beginning as a discrete entity in the 1920s: a teacher's college for young women. Sycamore now boasted an enrollment of eighteen thousand undergraduates, a respectable college of architecture, a competitive nursing program, and a MAC-Conference champion basketball team. The main campus occupied a thousand acres, with satellite buildings radiating out like spokes on a wheel. The nicest neighborhoods in Jonah were those where the faculty and administration lived—a dozen streets lined with restored Queen Annes and modest Victorians.

Students took up the ugliest neighborhoods east of the river, and most of these houses were so wretched one would have thought they were inhabited by bands of wild, orphaned seven-year-olds. In the summer the yards were littered with broken-down chairs and inflatable baby pools where men in their twenties sunned themselves, drunk and half naked. In winter the streets and lawns were garbage strewn, and snowdrifts at the curb were streaked with yellow, evidence that those same men had learned to write in cursive. No area of the county made Claudia more uncomfortable, or more aware that something cataclysmic had occurred between Ludie's generation and the one currently in residence at Sycamore State. Bertram had begun working for a Farm Bureau office at sixteen; by twenty he was married and writing his own accounts. At twenty-five he opened his own branch. Now, it seemed, no one need ever grow up.

Claudia drove down the main university thoroughfare, which was lined with bars, Laundromat/billiard combinations, pizza parlors, and, in a stroke of ironic brilliance, a shop that sold surf-themed clothing. She had been expected to grow up, hadn't she? So she hadn't been encouraged to go to college or get a job out of high school; that was because her parents were worried about her, they wanted what was best for her. She helped her mother in the house and garden, she helped Bertram with his taxes each spring. In May of every year they moved the furniture out of his office on a weekend and repainted. Claudia was proficient at most kinds of home repair—she had even helped a local man repair the tuck pointing on the chimney of her parents' house. So it wasn't as if she was useless to her parents.

She turned on Glen Street toward Hazel's. Nearly every porch for the next three blocks contained furniture otherwise designated as "indoor." The exception was the omnipresent Weber grill, set up on wooden porches, inches from wood-framed houses. Claudia sighed, shook her head. What was she supposed to have done, especially after Bertram died? She couldn't have left her mother, and Millie had already married Larry. What a terrible year that had been—she could hardly think of it, even now. No one knew, or at least she hoped no one knew, that ten years ago when the Home Depot had gone in out on the highway, Claudia had applied for a job there. It was the first thing she'd ever really wanted, that job. The store manager was someone she'd graduated high school with, a man named Clarence Yoder, and she'd applied and waited and never heard from him. So she'd gone to see him, and was shocked to discover that at thirty he still resembled Sonny Bono, that no kindhearted woman had told him he had to cut his hair. Clarence had said there wasn't anything open but he'd keep her in mind. She was good, she'd told him, with her hands, and she would memorize the store faster than anyone. She'd said things she hadn't intended to say, like how she assumed a man in his position surely would have the integrity not to treat her as she'd been treated in high school. Clarence had blinked at her over the mustache that threatened to take over his face, said nothing. Claudia had even opened her mouth to say that Clarence hadn't been so loved himself in high school, had he, given that his nickname was Fifi and not because his parents were French. There was a rumor that Clarence had been caught having sex with his poodle, and the rumor was passed down to every incoming freshman class. When Millie came home as a freshman and asked Claudia if she'd heard the rumor, Claudia knew Fifi was doomed, and would do well to leave the state.

She didn't mention it, that day in his office, and it wouldn't have done any good anyway, she was certain of it now. Because he didn't call, and over the years he had hired hundreds of people in her stead, idiots and rude people and teenagers. When Lowe's opened across the highway, Claudia just started shopping there instead.

Hazel's house was a two-story cottage built in the 1930s. Only the lack of recreational furniture separated it from the student rentals surrounding it. Every few years she had a student crew repaint it an indifferent shade of yellow. She did not have a garden in the summer; she didn't put in flowers in the spring. A boy cut the grass of her small lawn and Hazel called it a day. Rebekah had asked Hazel once how she could stand to live there, how she could endure the parties and the traffic and the general histrionics of college students. Hazel thought about it and said, "I like the noise, actually. I like seeing people around. Far worse for me would be someplace like Montana." She shuddered. "I *prefer* car stereos and exhaust fumes."

Claudia parked behind Hazel's six-year-old Jetta, turned off her Jeep. She took a deep breath, dreading Hazel's fresh surprise, stepped into the street. A college student, a young man wearing a knit cap advertising his attachment to the Patriots, came around the corner, walking a young shepherd mix on a length of rope. There were bags under the man's eyes and his skin was faintly green, as if he were up far earlier than he intended. The dog bounced around on the end of the rope, slid, fell into a snowdrift, bounced out again. Claudia made brief, reluctant eye contact with the student.

"Hey," he said, a quick verbal gesture.

"Hey," Claudia said.

The student stopped in his tracks but the dog kept going a few feet, nearly pulling them both into a parked car on the other side of the street. "Duuuuuuude!" the young man said, looking squarely at Claudia. "Are you *a girl*?"

Claudia stopped, braced herself. "Yes," she said, nodding slightly.

The Patriot looked her up and down. "That's cool," he said, walking away.

Hazel's street was icy; Claudia took careful steps between the cars and up onto the sidewalk. "Yeah, right," she muttered, "it's cool."

Rebekah remembered walking out of the cemetery after her mother's funeral—it had been a cold April 17—and while everyone around her wept, they also took consolation in the belief that Ruth had become one with Jesus, that she was sitting at His right hand, His bride. But Rebekah knew long past argument that she'd seen the last of Ruth Harrison Shook; her light had gone out. She had vanished. Pastor Lowell, if she'd ever consulted him, would have called what felled Rebekah grief, and she had most assuredly grieved. She continued to. But she also was simply changed. Her mother's death changed her, as it was meant to, and while it took almost five years for Rebekah to finally leave the Mission, she began the process of leaving when she walked out of the Sycamore Grove Cemetery, and slid, her knees pressed together, into the slick backseat of Martin Peacock's family car.

Now her sewing machine and basket, along with three storage containers filled with fabric, took up most of the trunk of her Buick. Her family hadn't bothered with many photographs, but there was one album and Rebekah wanted it. She took her mother's Bible, with its battered leather cover and Ruth's name stamped in gold. The pink flannel robe Ruth died in, and which Rebekah had washed by hand and sealed in a wedding dress box; the lamp that had stood on Rebekah's nursery table; a flour sifter just beginning to rust—she took things Vernon would never notice were missing, and in this way filled every square inch of the Buick, leaving just enough room for her to drive.

When the car was loaded and the Sunday sun had tipped from its zenith, she wandered around the upstairs, all through the warm, tight rooms on the bottom floor, touching the walls, the furniture, the pots and pans. She was about to see the end of the Great Experiment, the trick of taking a notion—that of a dead and resurrected man—and turning Him into the stuff of daily life, the meat and breath and *will* of human existence. Everything lovely and kind, every stroke of luck, every moment they lived while others died, had been His work. And every toothache and untimely rain, every fall from grace or patience, had signified His absence, their failure to perceive Him standing there before them, where nothing stood. She was about to see the end of Him, and the end, too, of Vernon Shook and all her family and the whole of her past, and she felt lucky that she'd been given so much warning. There were mudslides, after all, and avalanches, and every manner of misfortune that permits you not a second of preparation before your bones break. Afterward kind people in uniforms pull you from the wreckage and tell you, gently and with hesitation, that you have lost everything you knew and loved and imagined permanent, and that hadn't happened to Rebekah. As she walked across the porch, the steps and sidewalk her father had long since cleared of snow and ice, she felt she was leaving, again, the Sycamore Grove Cemetery. She felt the same wonder and grim weightlessness. She drove to Hazel's.

Even though her car was there, Hazel wasn't home. Rebekah had the sensation that she had been afflicted with a neurological condition, one that caused her to drive past empty houses, disbelieving, then to turn around and drive past again. A sad, demented repetition. She drove out to the retirement community, Cambridge Village, where Hazel's mother, Caroline Hunnicutt, lived, but she didn't go in; she wasn't sure what she would say. Rebekah stopped, tried to imagine where else Hazel could be. Her sister, Edie, was still in jail, and even when she wasn't, she was homeless, Rebekah thought. Who were Hazel's friends? Rebekah realized with a slight shock that she had no idea; Hazel never talked about anyone outside work except her family. Wasn't that odd? Rebekah drummed her fingers on her steering wheel, stared at Caroline Hunnicutt's front door without really seeing it. Who were *her* friends, for that matter? Hazel, certainly. Claudia, maybe. Claudia didn't like her much, that was Rebekah's guess, and why should she? Almost the entire year they'd worked together Rebekah had done nothing but moon over Peter, which—even though she was still doing it—she recognized as tedious.

She drove out of the Cambridge Village parking lot, unsure where she should go. How different life would be, she thought, if she had the church, her girl cousins, the ring of history they represented. Their pale, plain hands were as recognizable to her as her own; the varying shades of auburn of their hair. Susannah was afflicted with eczema in the winter, and this weather was probably bothering her. Elizabeth had a mole just to the left of her upper lip. Right now the girls would be leaving church, heading home to make lunch. They would meet together in the early afternoon for quilting, and to share church gossip. . . . Rebekah stopped at a stop sign and didn't move. They weren't girls anymore, and she didn't know them. They were all married now and probably had children, and their world had become so unbearable to Rebekah she had traded everything to leave it.

She realized where she was, at the stop sign on One Oak. Peter's cabin was half a mile away, she had driven there automatically. Pulling away from the crossroads, she wondered what she would do if he was home. Would she try to reclaim him as she had tried yesterday, would she use the news of her condition as the final heartsick message left on his answering machine? The question was answered for her when she reached his driveway and saw that he was still not there.

Rebekah parked, let her eyes linger on the windows, the porch, the chimney. Having a baby who shared the genes of another either meant everything in the world or it meant nothing at all, she thought. If it meant everything, then Peter was not only honor-bound to share in it with her, he would want to. The event would represent for him as well as for her a stepping off into the void of adulthood, nature's penultimate cliff. If it meant nothing—Rebekah took a deep breath— then she was alone in a condition that might kill her, would certainly change her forever. If it meant nothing then the world's talk about family was just static, and all those things her culture was so enamored of—the family photographs, the reunions, the romanticizing of children—they were nothing but shields against the truth; against a wider, graver emptiness. Rebekah's eyes filled with tears. Her child, if it should actually arrive (and at this point she wasn't sure there was really anything in there—the whole thing seemed less a baby and more an idea), would be denied those lies, and didn't they all, didn't each accidental, unwanted baby in the world deserve the same falsehoods as every other?

Hazel tipped her box of malted milk balls into her palm, offered one to Claudia, who declined. Claudia drove out of town by way of a neighborhood of Section 8 housing called Westside Green. They passed the uniform brick apartment units, the grassless courtyards, and the squat blue house of a woman named Jinx, who was infamous for practicing voodoo and for kidnapping for sixty days a lover who'd tried to leave her.

"You're not a cat person," Hazel said, chewing.

"I never said that." Claudia was not a cat person. There was no part of it she understood. Hazel's house reeked of ammonia, and everything, every surface and article of clothing, was covered with fur. Five minutes in Hazel's doorway, and Claudia's pants would be plastered with hair. As soon as Hazel opened the door, Mao and Sprocket and Merlin had begun bumping against Claudia, circling her as if she were fresh tuna. And Sprocket, the retarded one, *drooled*. There was a wet spot the size of a dime on the top of Claudia's boot.

"You don't need to say it."

"Will you tell me where we're going?

"You're doing fine. I'll tell you when you need to turn."

Hazel had left her house wearing her version of Barn Clothes: stretchy denim pants, a white turtleneck under a black sweatshirt advertising a casino in Las Vegas; red-and-white striped socks with bells on each ankle, and gold lamé tennis shoes.

"Have you been to Las Vegas?" Claudia asked, unable to picture it.

"God, no," Hazel said, putting her box of chocolates in her unicorn bag. "I'm just a breath away from complete misanthropy. That would be the nail in the coffin."

"Would you like to tell me where we're going?" They were heading west in Hopwood County, past the horse farms and big Nazarene churches. A few miles more and Claudia wouldn't be familiar with the landscape.

"Did I tell you Edie's out of jail?"

"Really. You bail her out?"

"Not this time, no. The judge said sixty days, she served sixty days."

"So she called you? Where is she?"

"She's back out at the place on Cobb Creek. She stopped at Mother's briefly and called me, then disappeared in the middle of the night. She's gone back to where she came from because there'll be no twelve-step geographical cure for our little Edna, absolutely not." Hazel adjusted her feet around the plastic lawn-and-leaf bag on the floorboard, in which she was carrying what appeared to be clothes. "And why shouldn't she lift up her life the way she might hold up—I don't know, imagine something rotten, whatever suits you—and hand it to our elderly mother?"

"Caroline seems capable of dealing with her."

"That isn't the point. Edie believes she has the right to do whatever she wants. Sun in Aries, Venus in Scorpio, *Mercury* in Aries." Hazel shook her head at the treachery of the stars. "Anything she wants."

"Would you like to listen to the radio?" Claudia reached for the dial.

Hazel sighed. "Only if you can find a station that doesn't broadcast the hillbilly circus."

They rode in silence for a mile, then Hazel took a deep breath and said, "Here is what you must do."

Claudia took her right hand off the wheel and held it up like a crossing guard. "Don't tell me, don't tell me. Whatever it is, no."

"It's time for you to get another dog."

Claudia lowered her hand, squared her shoulders. "No, thank you."

"There are litters being born, and I mean perpetually, at the place at Cobb Creek, and I want you to go out there with me today to pick one out. I need to look in on Edie. You need a dog. The breeds there are primarily of the man-eating variety, meaning they are noble and in servitude to monsters." Hazel sat back, as if all had been decided.

The Jeep swerved into the packed snow at the edge of someone's driveway, shuddered to a stop. "Let me—am I correct in thinking you want me to go to the camp of a—Hazel, a motorcycle gang? In order to look at pit bull puppies when I don't want another dog, and when going there is like both of us begging to be killed? Is that what you're saying?"

Hazel met Claudia's eye without blinking. "Yes," she said. "I'm asking you to go with me because that's what you must do. You won't be killed."

"No! Hazel, we can't do this." Claudia felt tears pressing at her throat. Again and again this had happened in the year she'd known Hazel, and Claudia couldn't seem to fight back; she'd arrived at the Used World already weakened. What she really wanted to say was, *You think I don't understand astrology but I do, Sun in Control Freak, Moon in Control Freak, Ascendant in Bully.*

"But we *must.*" Hazel raised her arm to pull down the sun visor, and Claudia caught a flash of silver at the elastic waistband of Hazel's pants, which were not blue jeans regardless of how many times Hazel tried to call them that.

"Hazel, are you carrying a gun?"

"Of course I am. I always carry it when I visit Edie, wherever she's living."

Claudia pressed her thumbs against her temples. "Do you have a permit? A license to carry? A license to *conceal* it?"

"Well, yes, Claudia. I do. But if I didn't that wouldn't stop me."

The road ahead of them looked exactly like the road behind. Claudia let her head rest against the cold window, suddenly so tired she thought she could sleep right there, parked at the side of the road, filling the sharp winter air with the Jeep's exhaust. What difference did it make whether she went forward, or turned around? "What kind of gun is it?"

Hazel unsnapped the holster. "It's a Derringer."

The gun was no bigger than a deck of cards. Claudia reached out and took it, admired the mother-of-pearl handle. "Forgive me, Hazel, but if we find ourselves in danger, are you going to ask one of those fat, tattooed psychopaths to lift his shirt and point to his kidneys? Are you going to say, 'This barrel might feel a little cold, Porky, but I need you to stand still'?"

Hazel took the gun back, narrowed her eyes at Claudia. "You're right. Good thing I have the nine-millimeter in my coat pocket."

The compound at Cobb Creek had been there a long time, fifty years or more. It had started out as a migrant camp, with fifteen houses on the ten acres of land, and it had been marked by trouble for as long as anyone could remember: blood feuds between the farmworkers, a fire that took four houses and killed nine people.

After the camp was abandoned in the late sixties, it became a magnet for disaffected teenagers and later for veterans back from Southeast Asia. Now there were only four houses left standing, and in what state of repair Claudia couldn't imagine. The place had been raided eight times in the past year, three times under suspicion of the manufacture and distribution of methamphetamine. Last month it was dog fighting. The group of men who lived there now, and who were bound together by loyalty to a particular motorcycle, called themselves Legion.

Legend had it that the lane leading back to the compound was booby-trapped; some had it laced with mines brought back from Vietnam, as if ordnance were as easy to smuggle as hashish. The Cronies said the men set beaver traps, which was indicative only of their latent ability to dream in metaphor, according to Hazel. But when Claudia actually made the turn down the lane, all she found were potholes, and trees and brush so long unattended that small, bare branches scraped both sides of the Cherokee. At the end of the drive, squatting around a large open space, was the estate of Legion.

The four remaining houses were shotgun style and long devoid of paint. The porches were held up by two-by-fours, far enough off the ground that the spaces under them were used for storage. On each porch there was at least a sofa, and in some cases there was also a refrigerator and a recliner. Bedsheets hung in some of the windows, but a few were covered with Visqueen stapled right into the brittle siding.

And everywhere, between the houses and back into the trees, were vehicles, most buried under snow.

Claudia took a deep breath, turned off the Jeep. As soon as the engine died she could hear it, the barking of countless dogs, coming from somewhere behind the houses. Some of the barks were deep and threatening, as she would have expected, but the majority were high-pitched, not like the yapping of small dogs, but something more frantic.

Edie's remaining front teeth were ridged, and nicotine had stained them in pale brown lines. The three she was missing had crumbled, according to Hazel. Edie was ten years younger than Hazel, which would have made her around fifty, but she looked much older. There were deep grooves dug around her mouth, and a series of creases that pointed toward her lips, the hallmark of a smoker. Nothing short of radical surgery could have repaired the lines around her eyes, or the ruin of her hair, which was a weak brown at the inch-long roots and white-blond down to the crispy tips.

"Hazel," she said, opening the front door to let them in. "Wow. You got here fast."

"Can we come in?" Hazel asked, walking in.

Claudia followed, but reluctantly, ducking to get through the low doorway. The smell of kerosene was so dense she recoiled; two heaters were burning, one in the middle of the room and one in the doorway to the rest of the house. The living room was dim, lit only by the football game flickering from the old console television. There were people sitting on every available surface—on the two sofas, on two recliners, on an end table being propped up by phone books, and on plastic milk crates. Most barely registered their presence, but from one of the recliners a man said, "'T'sup, Hazel."

"Hello, Charlie," Hazel said, and as Claudia's eyes adjusted, she saw it was Edie's boyfriend, who was himself only intermittently out of prison. He'd once spent an afternoon—well, forty minutes of an afternoon—helping Claudia rearrange the store. They'd carried in a sideboard from Jim Hank's truck, stood around and looked at it a minute, and that was enough for Charlie, who disappeared, never to be in Hazel's employ again. Claudia hadn't realized he would be here. He was beefy and soft, and wore a long, thin ponytail and a beard. He looked violent, but the only person he had ever really hurt, as far as Claudia knew, was Edie.

"Hey, Claude," he said. She nodded in greeting.

Edie was wearing a small scooped-neck T-shirt and a pair of white jeans gone gray. She rubbed her arms, said, "You didn't have to rush right out here."

Hazel looked around at the cracked plaster walls, the curled and yellowing rock star and motorcycle rally posters stuck up with thumbtacks. "We took our time, actually." She reached in the garbage bag and pulled out a blue sweatshirt. Edie took it and slipped it on but said nothing.

"Come in the kitchen, I guess," Edie said, leading the way.

They went through a cold, damp bedroom with a set of bunk beds, a double bed without a frame, and another mattress on the floor; they passed the doorway to a dark bathroom Claudia didn't even want to consider. A second bedroom was remarkably like the first, and then they were in the kitchen.

There was much more light in this large, south-facing room, which struck Claudia as unfortunate; there was no place safe to look. Dishes and garbage were stacked so high they surely had anthropological value, and the smell in the room was overwhelming—layers of organic decay underlined by more kerosene fumes, these radiating from five-gallon containers scattered around the room. Above the doorway to a collapsed back porch, someone had painted the name Legion inside a circle in black enamel.

Hazel pulled out a rusty metal folding chair, slid a stack of dirty dishes and newspapers from a place at the table, and sat down. She did so without a flicker of distaste, as if she'd made this gesture many times before. "So I see that your friends have discovered the womblike joys of OxyContin. This would be why my garage was robbed two weeks ago, I assume."

Claudia continued to stand, not at all sure she could touch the debris on the battered Formica table, as Hazel had.

Edie rubbed her nose, pulled out a chair of her own. "Yeah, I guess."

Hazel straightened her coat, continued to look directly at her sister. "Oh, I expected them. I left an old VCR, a space heater, a couple pieces of estate jewelry out there so they wouldn't come in my house."

Edie dug a pack of cigarettes and a lighter out from one of the stacks on the table. "Big of you."

"Not particularly. Explain to them, please, that it was a one-time gesture, and the next time they show up at my house I'll end their tenure on the planet."

Edie sat back in her chair, crossed her arms over her chest like a sullen teenager. Like Millie as a teenager, Claudia realized.

"How about you?" Hazel asked. "Is synthetic heroin your rabbit hole these days?"

Her sister shook her head. "Nah, I'm not using. Just a little something to keep my weight down."

Claudia heard it, a squeak and scrabble that she assumed to be a rodent. She glanced at the dishes on the sink, but nothing moved there.

"So how did this happen?" Hazel asked. "I mean beyond the obvious."

"I don't know, Hazel. Jesus." Edie blew a stream of smoke toward the ceiling. "What difference does it make?"

Claudia's eyes scanned the room, and when she finally discovered the source of the sound, she took a step backward. In the corner, next to a gold gas stove, was a large cardboard box, partly in shadow. But plainly visible were the head, shoulders, and chest of a pit bull, solid red with a red nose. Her green eyes were so pale they seemed ghostly. A group of puppies, five or six that Claudia could see, were waking as a group and scrambling toward their mother. The dog stared directly at Claudia without moving or blinking. The dog's forehead was wrinkled, her ears cropped close to her head. Claudia could just make out a constellation of pale scars along the dog's jawline.

"Do you know the age?" Hazel asked.

Edie drew on her cigarette as if trying not to scream. "I was in jail, Hazel, if you recall."

Claudia's heart pounded, and she felt a line of sweat break out over her upper lip. She wanted to take off her parka, but was afraid to move. The dog continued to stare at her, even as the pups nipped at their mother, clawed at her soft belly.

"What about shots, what about food?"

"I don't know, I don't know, I don't *know*." Edie was speaking now through a clenched jaw.

"Claudia?" Hazel said. "Would you like to sit down?"

Claudia didn't answer, but took a step toward the sink, away from the dog and her pups. Through the window above the sink Claudia could see the other dogs, the ones behind the house. There were at least twenty, each one chained to a metal stake planted next to a blue plastic igloo-shaped doghouse. The dogs had run half-circles in the snow, back and forth, down to the frozen dirt. Metal pans were scattered around them, and most were barking so hard they were rising up onto their hind legs, the sound punctuated with small explosions of white breath.

"—the reason you give," Hazel was saying.

"No, it's the truth. Really, Hazel."

To Claudia's left was a small dark room, probably a pantry of some kind. Next to that doorway was an old refrigerator, its door held closed with bungee cords; taped low on the wall next to the refrigerator was a poster saturated with bright, swirling colors. It said, in the center, RELAX, MAN. Propped on the floor in front of the poster was a dirty plastic baby chair.

"Will anyone even notice?" Hazel asked, in a quieter, less provocative tone.

"No. Nobody cares. If there was somebody who did, they're gone."

Claudia took a step forward, praying that she was mistaken, that the chair was just another castoff.

"Charlie and me's got plans, we're thinking of heading out west for the big New Mexico rally and then staying out there. So you can see I need this took care—"

Claudia took one silent step, then another. She knelt down behind the chair, and slowly turned it to face her. The baby was wide awake, thin, blue-eyed. Claudia was no expert on the ages of infants, but she guessed this child was less than six months old. He (if it was a he) was wearing a one-piece suit, blue pants and a white shirt with blue stripes. The sleeves hit him in the middle of his forearm, the pants halfway up his calf. Tucked beside the baby's leg was an empty bottle; the streaks inside it were gray and grainy.

She heard Hazel take off her glasses and put them on the table, a sign that she was about to release a deep sigh, then smile—it was a gesture she made when she was victorious, and also when she had lost. "Charlie will enjoy his liberty for less than two weeks, Edna, and then

he'll be back in jail. You're not going to New Mexico with him, whether or not this problem is solved."

"For God's sake, it's just mean how you say things like that when you don't know nothing about Charlie nor New Mexico either one."

The baby stared at Claudia, unmoving, unblinking. She reached out very slowly and took his fist, which lay at his side. He was freezing. She could see that his diaper had soaked through, and the moisture was rising up his clothes to his chest. Now that she was this close she could smell him, too; a sharp, sick, chemical smell.

"Perhaps I don't," Hazel said. "There are many times I hope I'm wrong, actually."

Claudia saw herself, as if she were her own neutral critic, reach down between the baby's urine-soaked legs and unfasten the harness that held him in the chair. She did this as quietly as possible, glancing up at the two women at the table just as Hazel stood up from her chair and the pit bull in the corner leapt over the side of the cardboard box without a sound. Claudia put one hand behind the baby's head, which was so small she could completely enclose it, and another hand under his bottom, all the while whispering shhh, shhh, and then she had the baby against her chest and under her parka, and wasn't it amazing, she was thinking, that she had worn the Carhartt coveralls, which just happened to be waterproof. She was thinking this and not about the fact that she had someone else's baby under her coat when she saw Hazel move more quickly than Claudia would have imagined possible, the nine-millimeter out of her pocket, where it had been hanging like a lead weight, now pointed directly at the dog that was taking one slow step toward Claudia.

Edie stood up. "Hazel! Bandit! Get back on your bed!"

The dog ignored her, and Edie, in her own moment of heroism, stepped up on her chair, kicked at the clutter on the table until she found a place to stand, then came down in front of the dog, catching her by the collar just as it appeared she was about to spring. "Put that gun away, Hazel!" she hissed, furious. "You pull a gun in this house you'll get us all killed."

"You put that dog away, Edie, and come back and walk us to the front door as if nothing has happened. Then I'll hide the gun."

Claudia, shaking now, was trying to support the baby and zip up

her coat. She finally gave up and pulled the coat closed around the infant. Edie dragged the dog down the hallway to the bathroom and closed her in. Bandit hit the door in a fury, barking not in the high-pitched, almost joyous frenzy as the dogs in the backyard, but in full-throated rage. Someone from the front room yelled, "Shut that bitch up!" which earned him a round of laughter.

Edie came back to the kitchen, her face splotchy and her eyes filled with tears. "I didn't know you was coming so soon. I don't know if you should take him after all."

Claudia reached in her pocket and got out the keys to the Cherokee, tossing them to Hazel, who fumbled but caught them. "You'll need to drive, Hazel."

Edie grabbed Claudia by the arm. "Don't tell nobody where you got that baby, Claudia, I beg you. We've got enough problems out here as it is."

Hazel slipped the gun in her pocket, walked over and looked in the cardboard box. "Want a puppy, too, Claudia?"

Claudia shook her head, dumbfounded. "No, thanks."

"Edie," Hazel said, "lead us to the door now. Just act naturally."

Edie walked ahead of them through the two bedrooms, past the bathroom where Bandit was rioting, through the dim, fume-soaked living room. She opened the front door; Claudia ducked, stepped out onto the porch, and Hazel followed. The air outside was frosty, clear. Claudia took a deep breath, pulled the silent baby closer to her, and headed for the car.

"Well? What now, Hazel?" Claudia said, opening her coat and turning the baby around.

"What do you mean, what now?"

"I mean, what do you intend to do with this baby?"

"He's your baby."

Claudia coughed, covering the baby's exposed ears with her hands. "No, he isn't," she whispered. "You're insane. I don't want any part of this!"

"Well, it's too late now." The Jeep rocked from side to side as Hazel traversed the holes in the lane leading out of Cobb Creek.

"We have to take him to the hospital, or to Child Services—"

"He smells terrible," Hazel said, grimacing. She was sitting at the edge of the seat, trying to accommodate the twelve-inch height discrepancy between Claudia and herself.

"You can move your seat up, Hazel, you don't have to drive like you're ninety-seven."

"This is identical to the Jumpin' Bean situation," Hazel said.

"Wha . . ." Claudia couldn't speak the entire word. She gestured to the heavens. "What on earth are you talking about?"

"I'm talking about Jumpin'—"

"This is nothing like Jumpin' Bean, why would you even say such a—"

"How is it different, then?"

Claudia took a deep breath, prayed for patience. "For one thing, Jumpin' Bean was a *coonhound*."

"So he was of a different mammalian species. Big deal."

"AND Ernie Hinshaw didn't want him, had never wanted him."

"Exactly the same here."

"And Jumpin' Bean started coming around to my house on his own, I didn't go and just steal him off somebody's floor. And I'll remind you he was a dog, Hazel."

"As I recall, you fed him for three days running, then started letting him sleep at your house, and presto, he was your dog."

"You are crazy to be making this comparison."

Hazel turned onto the highway. She wasn't a great driver, and Claudia pulled the seat belt a little tighter around the baby.

"All I'm saying"—Hazel pointed at the lump under Claudia's coat—"is feed him for three days and then see what happens."

"Hazel, I can't take this baby home. It's out of the question. I'll be happy to go to the emergency room with you, or the police department, Family Services, anything. But I can't take him to my house."

"And why is that, just tell me why. Tell me why it's okay to toss that baby, who was obviously born into suffering and has continued to suffer every single day of his godforsaken life, into the jaws of institutional bureaucracy, and what is it exactly that prevents you from rising to the occasion here?"

Claudia stared at Hazel, stunned. "How dare you make this my problem. How *dare* you pass judgment on me because I don't want to take a stolen baby into my house."

Hazel glanced at Claudia, raised an eyebrow. "Why did you pick him up, then?"

"Because"—Claudia shook her head—"because I couldn't leave him there to die."

"What's the other reason?"

Claudia let her head fall back against the seat. "There was no other reason."

"Really?"

"I have been—Hazel, I have always been cooperative with you, I trust you. But you need to point this Jeep in the direction of the hospital, and from there we're calling the police." The baby still had not moved, and the smell rising off of him made Claudia panic; she felt tempted to grab the steering wheel, even if it meant plowing into a tree.

"Can I tell you who this baby's mother is?"

"I don't care, Hazel."

"She was that nineteen-year-old meth addict who died of exposure after passing out at the end of the lane at Cobb Creek. She had apparently been running all around the property in just a T-shirt and underwear, running for hours because she believed a gang of Mexicans was chasing her."

Claudia swallowed, turned and looked out the passenger's side window.

"Do you know who his father is?

"No, Hazel. I don't." Claudia pressed her back teeth together so hard she felt something pop in her jaw.

"That's fine, because nobody else does, either. The mother of the dead nineteen-year-old is herself in prison for check deception and embezzlement; there is no father in that case, either. Do you see what I'm getting at?"

"Drive to the hospital, Hazel, and we'll get this straightened out."

"The baby will go into the foster care system. Maybe you're familiar with the foster families of Hopwood County."

Every year there was a scandal in the foster care system; in just the past summer a family with twelve children in care had been found to keep them in cages at night. "You're being manipulative—wait, Hazel, listen to me. Manipulative is just the beginning. You're doing something illegal and involving me and that's too—"

"You picked him up and put him in your coat."

"It's *too far.*"

Hazel took the exit and approached the commercial edge of Jonah. "Do this for me, if not for him."

"I won't."

"Please, Claudia—this isn't like anything else, this is a favor I would never ask of another person in this world. *You.* I would ask it of you."

Pressing her temples, which now hurt much worse, Claudia said, "I don't have one single thing this baby needs, and I don't know how to take care of babies, I've got no instincts." She tried not to sound so furious; she tried to suppress the black rage she felt toward Hazel, toward Edie and the criminal underworld she and Charlie inhabited. They were just *animals,* she thought, before realizing that animals would never live as Edie did. "What I don't have for this situation is . . . what I don't have is everything. Everything I need is missing."

"So?" Hazel said, shrugging. "We stop by the drugstore, we go to the Emporium. It's not rocket science."

"How would you know." Claudia no longer had the energy to fight. She stared out the window at the bare, snowy fields. The baby looked straight ahead and didn't move. "Why not you, Hazel? Why not take care of this yourself?"

Hazel reached across the Jeep's center console, rested her hand on Claudia's knee a moment before touching the baby lightly on top of his head. "It's too late for me." But she didn't sound particularly sorry to say so.

❧

1964

She could look at the sky and see it for what it was, and she could look at the names of the planets and see something else. A constellation was a catalyst, pushing energy so dense it was nearly matter out into the universe while remaining itself unchanged. An astronomer could say *Saturn,* and Hazel would picture the formidable planet, its debris field; but if she herself wrote the words *Saturn in its trine position,* there was no planet at all. This was no different, she assumed, than how the word *God* is not the same as God. The word does not only not *invoke,* it barely *evokes,* or at least it seemed so to Hazel, in the grimly literal mid-twentieth century.

Saturn, that old devil eating his children. Saturn was the bottom line, the uncompromising; it had been in Gemini the year she was born and ruled over Capricorn, her sun sign. How to think about it? Hazel sat on her bed, facing the window, a book open on her lap. She tapped her pencil eraser against the pages, drumming out an uneven rhythm. Nothing was predetermined by the time of birth, and the inner light of the night sky, the sky we carry inside us, was neither particle nor wave. Nothing was predetermined, and yet. There were influences—people were born and lived inside shafts of behavior— they lived within their natal chart as if in a suit of clothes so perfectly fitted to them it seemed to match their DNA. And she had reached a point where she could meet a person and see within a few seconds their sun, their moon, their ascendant, which was nothing like foreseeing the future and everything like reading the past, what was right before her; but the present became the future, and so it was foresight, after a fashion. At Sycamore State, where she had been a part-time student for seven years, she had heard every ancient art mocked with savage ardor by the empiricists of the age, and what she was always tempted to say in response was that she was herself empirical in her assessments, because she had a hypothesis and she had tested it (tested it every day, in fact) and the results had been replicated. The fact that her professor of natural sciences, a beaky unhygienic man much enamored of mineral deposits, could not replicate them was his failure, not hers. And not the failure of the art itself.

Hazel sighed, closed the book on Greek astronomy she'd been reading. She had real tests coming up and knew she should be devoting herself to them. That natural sciences class, for instance. By the end of Christmas break she was supposed to have written a paper titled "The Dinosaurs: Where Did They Go?" but she hadn't even begun it. She was also to have developed a thesis on John Steinbeck's

The Winter of Our Discontent, and had not. She sighed again, closed her eyes.

A car pulled into the lane. It wasn't Finney, who was at this hour working at Sterling's Department Store, selling handbags and nylon stockings to Christmas shoppers.

It wasn't Hazel's father, who was no longer ever home in the evenings. Hazel couldn't remember the last time she'd had a meal with him. If she had asked (and she wouldn't), he would have reeled off his busy, important schedule: the town council meetings, the men's professional organizations, the philanthropic fraternities through the aegis of which he intended to leave his name as a legacy. In death he hoped to be far more than the general practitioner with the country clinic. He would be the decorated army surgeon, the Albert T. Hunnicutt Memorial Wing of This or That.

Maybe someone's mother was coming to pick up Edie to take her to the skating rink, or to a Christmas party in a basement somewhere, a gathering where there was bound to be frantic, preadolescent groping in a closet.

Or did her mother have a patient? Hazel got up and walked to her desk, ran her finger down her calendar. No, there was no one listed. Of course, sometimes people just showed up, desperate for advice. Caroline had grown, over the past few years, into a daunting presence, her hair streaked with white and swept up into that twist, so perfect it seemed to have been designed by an architect, or a sculptor. She was thin, severe, intolerant of complaint, nonsense, or sentiment. Hazel had three times accompanied Caroline to the Negro neighborhood across the river in Jonah, to help deliver babies when the situation had grown too complicated for the local midwife, a toothless, creaky old woman named Lulamae who was so smart she left Hazel as shy as a child. She had spoken to the laboring women with such straight indifference— *Don't scream, you aren't dying; don't tell me you can't do this, you can and you will*—that they had simply obeyed her.

A car door closed. Hazel slipped her shoes on in case she was needed, straightened her sweater. She opened her bedroom door to the sound of "A Hard Day's Night" in the hallway; Little Edna was still home. Hazel rolled her eyes, slid her headband off, ran her hands over her hair, making sure her bangs covered her scar, put the headband back in place. A conspiracy had grown up in the Hunnicutt household—one of omission and silence rather than action—to ignore Edie as much as possible and hope for the best. Hazel would never have been allowed to do, as a thirteen-year-old, what her sister took as her right. No one guarded Edie from her own worst impulses because none of them understood what to protect, what was in there. It wasn't just the knee-high white boots that puzzled Hazel and Caroline, or that Edie wasn't good in school and had so little intellectual curiosity. It wasn't even the boy-crazed nonsense she shared with the friends who all looked and dressed like her. For Caroline as well as Hazel, the problem was that Edna wasn't sufficiently serious. When Hazel combined Edna's temperament with what she saw in her chart, there seemed little chance of an adulthood devoted to either altruism or a worthy profession.

Hazel could hear her mother talking in the parlor, and then her heels crossing toward the stairs.

"Hazel?" she called. "You have a visitor."

It would be Jim Hank Bellamy, motherless boy, much loved by Caroline and Edna. He had been courting Hazel in a steady, distant way for more than a year, and he still showed up on odd nights, even though she'd declared herself unavailable. She had declared herself unlovable, unable to love in return. He had listened patiently, sitting on the down-filled settee in the parlor, fixing his gray eyes on her face with the look of an athlete about to leap a hurdle. His expression suggested that no obstacle was greater than any other, and having crossed a class barrier, having earned enough money to buy a car to drive out to her house, having braved the potential scorn of Albert T. Hunnicutt, he was prepared to wait.

She took the back staircase, clomping down two at a time so as not to look like Bette Davis on the grand front stairway.

"Hey, Jim Hank," she said, emerging from the servant's hallway.

"There you are, dear." Her mother reached out for Hazel's hand. "Jim Hank was just telling me about the weather."

"Yes?"

"It's nice." He wore his blue wool overcoat and a black scarf Finney had made him, along with a wool cap that didn't complement his coat in any way, but somehow drew out the paleness of his eyes and the length of his dark eyelashes. Anyone could see he was a handsome boy—a man now, Hazel had to admit—and worthy of all good things. "It's winter," Hazel reminded him, although she knew it was his favorite season.

"I'll leave you alone," Caroline said, tugging at the seam of her suit jacket. She still wore a skirt, blouse, and jacket every day, along with silk stockings and heels. In the clinic she wore a white overcoat, so there were layers upon layers between herself and everyone else. "Jim Hank, stay for hot cider, won't you. I'll be in the kitchen working on my reports." Her heels tapped against the hardwood as she took the long way, through the library and dining room, rather than the straight servant's hallway to the kitchen.

"Would you like to take a walk?" Jim's cheeks and lips were flushed. "It's cold, but dry and no wind."

They walked down the straight flat lane toward the road, rather than around the barn and down into the meadow. He was right about the weather, and Hazel pulled her chin down into her coat with pleasure. She slipped her arm through Jim's and rested her mitten against his coat.

"My dad got me on at the Chrysler," Jim said, looking at the vanishing point of the locust trees.

Hazel stopped, turned toward him. "What? When?"

"He found out today. It's"—Jim rubbed his forehead through his wool hat—"it's the best thing that could have happened."

"How can you say that? Good God, why didn't you . . ."

"Why didn't I what? Wait for something?"

"Yes! Wait for something would have been better by far."

Jim pulled against her and they began walking again. "I've worked for Malcolm for four years now, Hazel, trying to save up to go to school, but it's no good. And one by one all of his other hands have taken better jobs. Red and Slim are both already on the line at Chrysler, getting overtime, too. I'm the only one left and Malcolm doesn't need me full-time anyway." He took a deep breath, blew it out in a cloud. "He's cut back a lot. I think he only kept me on because he felt sorry for me."

Hazel pictured the house where Jim Hank lived with his dad, Coy Bellamy, too close to the railroad tracks and nearly up against the grain elevator. The place was small and dejected; the oilcloth curtains at the kitchen window were laced with a decade of dust and cobwebs. The inside smelled of kerosene and boiled dinners, and even though Jim kept it neat, no one had actually cleaned it since his mother died ten years before. And Coy himself was best not considered. "Malcolm doesn't feel sorry for you."

"If you say so." Jim tried to blow a smoke ring from the frigid air, but it didn't work. They were midway down the lane and he stopped, letting Hazel's arm fall. He turned and looked at the line of locusts, at the low stone walls that ran along the sides of the lane, built by four Italian immigrants who got off at the wrong train stop twenty years before and never made their way farther west. The wall had been intended to prevent the lane from drifting closed, and it nearly worked. Jim's eyes took it all in, and he looked, too, at the house, which appeared, with all the lights burning, to be a ship in the distance. "Can I ask you something?"

"Yes." Hazel put her mittened hands in her pocket.

"Do you think this place is haunted?"

Hazel took a breath, glanced at the house, the barn, the closed county road running down to the meadow. "Honestly?"

"Honestly."

"I think it *is* haunted, but in the future."

Jim tilted his head, gave her a slight smile. "You'll have to clarify your answer for the judges."

She scuffed the toe of her snow boot at the hard-packed dirt and gravel of the lane, thought about what she meant. The house, the outbuildings, had been born as surely as anything else. They weren't fluid like the land, the tumbling stones in the Planck River. The assemblage of property was under the influence of its genesis, just as Hazel was, as Jim Hank was. "One afternoon," she said, "in the summer, I was walking right here, on my way to pick up the mail, and—it's hard to describe, but the light was very strange, and I stopped and held my arms out and I felt this . . . is there a collective noun for . . . a *mutiny* of spirits, let's say. It was all around me, like the air was thick with it, and . . ." She stopped, unable to say the rest. She had seen, in flashes, a woman in a white nightgown crawling across a bed like a cat. She'd seen a man standing in the corner of her nursery, wearing a dark suit and turning the handle of an eggbeater, colors spinning out of it and filling the room. She had seen a year, if one can witness such a thing, when many animals would die; there would be raccoons and possums lying fetal at the bank of the river, and one white cat hanging dead from a rafter in the barn.

"And?"

"And"—Hazel reached out for Jim's arm again and they continued walking—"I realized that what is true of every place is true of this place. What has already happened is nothing compared to what will."

They walked in silence until they reached the end of the lane, and Jim Hank gestured for them to sit down on the low wall.

"Does it make you angry," Hazel asked, "that you work for her father and you might never get to go to college, and Finney gave up that scholarship?"

Jim blew out through his lips, a chuffing sound like a horse, or a tiger. "Honestly?"

"Honestly."

"I'm not angry that she gave up the scholarship, or that I didn't get one, nothing like that. I feel like if Coy Bellamy is your dad, the DAR isn't going to be lining up to pay your way to school." Jim reached into his pocket for a handkerchief. "But that she gave it up for . . . I started to say *love*. That's what she says, isn't it? I can hardly stand it that she gave it up for *him*."

"Ha." Hazel's laugh carried no mirth. "She gave it up for him. And now she's working at Sterling's as a shopgirl, watching the door on the off chance he'll come in. That he'll call. Which he doesn't, by the way, not very often."

Jim turned to her, took her hand. "Would you say, Contestant Number One, that Miss Finney is haunted?"

"Oh." Hazel flinched, pressed her other hand against her forehead. "I would say . . ."

"She will be?"

"No. I would say that *we* are."

They looked at the sky, the deepening night. Jim Hank offered Hazel his handkerchief and she touched her nose, watery from the winter air, with it.

"You'll not change your mind," he asked, but it wasn't a question.

She turned to him. In the light of the moon she was prepared to appreciate him as more than what he was, which was less than what she wanted. The bones of his face cast their own shadows, and she admired him, admired the way he let her look at him so openly. It had not always been so between the two of them, who had grown up together, and from two different worlds. "Tell me how to change my mind," she said, with anguished sincerity.

Jim took his handkerchief back, wiped his own nose with it. "If I knew that," he said, *"I'd* have given up on *you* a long time ago."

They didn't talk on the walk back to the house; nothing had been started and nothing had been finished. When they reached the parlor they smelled the cider from the kitchen, and from upstairs a thin ribbon of Nag Champa, the incense that in the years to come would permeate Edna's walls as the dancing circus ponies faded.

With a sudden intensity, as if she saw it clear for a second, she drew a line there, in the centre. It was done; it was finished. Yes, she thought, laying down her brush in extreme fatigue, I have had my vision. Rebekah finished the last lines of the novel and put her head down on the table, praying she wouldn't make more of a fool of herself than she already had, weeping silently through the last two chapters. She didn't know why every book Hazel gave her made her cry so. When, two months ago, she finished *The Member of the Wedding,* she'd told Hazel it had made her suicidal.

"I'm sorry to hear that," Hazel had said.

"No, in the good way."

"Ah, wanting to die in the good way. I feel better."

On the cover of *To the Lighthouse* a woman, mostly in shadow, looked out a dark window at the sea. Other people, Rebekah was convinced, could read this book without weeping because they were . . . she didn't know what. Culturally inoculated, maybe. No one said to them that the world itself was a lie and a prison, and the only thing worth imagining was the blight of Golgotha, the carcass on the cross. One sob escaped Rebekah, a sharp intake of air, and she made herself think about something other than Mrs. Ramsay and Virginia

Woolf. There were dishes all around her folded arms—the dirty plates from her early dinner—and an empty coffee cup, an empty coffeepot. The after-Sunday-evening-services crowd had come and gone from Richard's Diner and there was still no answer at Hazel's house. Rebekah had called her at least a dozen times from the pay phone just inside the front door. God only knew what the waitresses thought she was up to. They'd let her sit at a table undisturbed for almost four hours. She'd eaten two meals, gone through at least half a gallon of decaf. She'd had two glasses of milk, an orange juice, and had gone to the bathroom upwards of twenty-five times. No one asked her how long she was going to be or if they needed to call her social worker. Why hadn't she befriended these women before now? Rebekah wondered. She'd been coming in for lunch for years; she'd been polite, the waitresses were polite to her. Once in a while she'd ask about someone's children, or if Wanda was over the flu, but mostly she kept to herself. If she'd only been different, if she'd been open to them, she could have asked any one of these women for a place to spend the night and they'd have invited her home, she was sure of it.

Rebekah had counted on Hazel; she had *assumed* Hazel, and now—there was no way to disguise it—Rebekah was homeless. She was amazed at how blithe she had always been about such things as homelessness, what happened to people when their mistakes and bumbling caught up with them and they were cast into exile. *One paycheck away,* it was a phrase she'd heard on the news any number of times, and while she had recognized that it applied to her in some way, it didn't apply to her at all. Because her life wasn't predicated on any paycheck, not ever before.

She raised her head, wiped her face with a napkin. In the five years she'd been working she'd spent very little money, so she could go to a motel if she needed to. It was the idea of a motel that scared her; the one nearest the store, for instance, rented rooms by the hour and there was often furniture floating in the pool. And it would have been another first, staying in a motel alone, as a thousand things had been and continued to be, and she didn't want to do it. She wanted to go home, wherever that was.

* * *

There were two men in the booth in front of Rebekah's. She had been so consumed with first the novel and then her own problems that she'd been able to block out their conversation for the last forty minutes, but now it began to filter in. The man facing her was in his forties; he was wearing a blue seed cap advertising Monsanto. His skin was sun damaged and his eyes were pale. She tried not to look too closely at him, afraid he'd mistake her curiosity for a different kind of interest. The man facing him was also wearing a seed cap; his was red faded almost to pink. He seemed a normal size, at least from behind, but there were two folds in the back of his neck that made Rebekah's stomach flutter.

"D'jew hear what them granolas is up to over at the college?" Blue Seed Cap asked his friend.

Red Seed Cap sighed, as if his life were one long chain of grievances, each link a shenanigan committed by someone over at the college. "Naw. What this time?"

"They're picketing at the Wal-Mart. Jeannie seen 'em when she was there today. They're saying Wal-Mart and Meijer and all them stores out on the highway has killed the downtown."

"Jonah has a downtown?"

"It's all gays over at the college, you know that, right? And Clintonites. If you interview for a job over there you get just one question: Do you enjoy"—Blue Cap leaned toward his friend—"*ass sex?*"

Red Cap snorted in his coffee cup.

"Must be offerin' a Ph.D. in whining is all I can say. 'Ooooh, bad corporations ruinin' my liberal fun! Bad Home Depot for robbing customers from Public Hardware!' As if free enterprise don't apply to everyone equally."

"You said it." Red Cap nodded.

"Them falling-down termite holes downtown has failed because of the laws of the jungle, nothing else. 'Oooh, save our history, save our pretty buildings!'"

Red Cap shook his head, poured himself more coffee. "It's pitiful."

"I wished I'd been there with Jeannie, I'd'a said, 'You show me a place downtown where I can get new tires for my truck, bullets for my rifle, and a six-pack of briefs all at once and I'm there. Oh, and don't forget the popcorn and Slushie I'll need on the way out the door.'"

Red Cap laughed, blew his nose on his napkin. "No Slushies downtown that I've ever seen."

"That's because downtowns are stupid."

"Downtowns," Red Cap said, giving his punchline a pause, "are *gay.*"

Rebekah and Blue Cap exploded with laughter at the same time, Blue Cap for one reason, Rebekah for another. She was imagining the men chasing each other through Wal-Mart in their underwear, trying to insert plastic toys in each other's rectum. And during the chase they would be offering up for public consumption their brilliant social commentary: Red lights is gay! Cats is gay! Books is gay! Green vegetables is gay! The men laughed at each other and at Rebekah, who was way past being able to control herself. They saw her as an ally, and in a way she was: she hadn't laughed this hard in quite a while. Red Cap turned around to look at her, and as she wiped tears from her face with her napkin, she tipped her own imaginary seed cap to him.

As the men passed Rebekah's table on their way out, Blue Cap casually reached out and picked up Rebekah's check. "It's on us," he said, smiling at her. "Our wives never laugh at *nothing* we say."

Rebekah parked her car behind the storage unit, in the most isolated space in the lot. "This is insane," she said aloud, her hand on the overnight bag she used to carry to Peter's. She stepped out of the car and locked it; the night air was biting and darkness fell so early this time of year. With each step she took she tried to recall better Christmases, like the year her mother made her a Pollyanna doll in a red gingham dress with white lace trim. In the last box Rebekah opened was a matching dress for her. There was the year of the ice storm, when the electricity went out while they were at Aunt Betty's, and she and the girl cousins sang carols to their parents by candlelight.

For one long moment Rebekah couldn't remember the key code to the back door, even though she'd entered it every day for years. After hours the door required a key and a code, and the same code was entered in the alarm system just inside the door. She closed her eyes and let her fingers rest on the number pads, and it came back to her automatically. Something very important, she had never asked what, happened to Hazel on the Fourth of July, and that was the security code: 0704.

The Used World Emporium in the dark, in the days before Christmas. The alarm system beeped its warning and Rebekah disarmed it by its own light. She closed the door and leaned against it, her heart pounding so hard she had to bend at the waist and take deep breaths to keep from throwing up. She was terrified. She hadn't reckoned on being scared, although she should have, and would have anticipated it if she hadn't gone completely insane. Spend the night *here*? Might as well try to sleep in a pen with psychotic clowns. She leaned against the door and the vastness of the space bore down upon her like a weight. This half of the store was in near-total darkness, relieved only by the blinking of the Christmas lights at the entrance to the breezeway. The lights came on and there was a flash in the vanity mirror in booth #37, a flash of light but also of shadow. Rebekah couldn't move, not even to open the door and run screaming to her car. To her left, deep within those black aisles, were the rocking horses with their glass eyes and decaying hides; there were dolls with human hair, dolls with *teeth;* there was the old telephone, which had not rung but might yet ring.

I have to go, I have to get out of here, Rebekah thought, without taking a step. She was afraid to blink, afraid to turn her head. Nothing like this had ever happened to her; she had been afraid as a child sometimes, but that fear was not the same species as this. She knew she was standing in a cavernous space and that what had crippled her was a congregation of inanimate objects; she knew, intellectually, that the mannequin (the *mannequin*) in the Costume Shop had not moved, would not move. She also knew, intellectually, that it was moving.

Time passed; the Christmas lights blinked off, on. Above her the fans thrummed and there were slight noises everywhere: clocks ticking, the gurgle of a drain, dolls grinding their teeth. Rebekah stood frozen.

Hazel came out of the drugstore carrying two huge bags, which were so heavy she gave up and dragged them. Claudia knew she should get out and help her, but felt justified in staying put, since the baby's dia-per had soaked right through the waterproof Carhartt's. It had been quite a feat on his part, but he had succeeded.

"I asked a matronly sort in the store what I should get, I told her I was going to a baby shower for a new adoption, and she said at six months he needs formula and cereal. So look, I got this formula you just pour in a bottle." Hazel poked through the items in the larger of the two bags in the backseat.

"Could you close the door? You can tell me on the way home."

"And I got cereal with bananas in it, and a bowl that heats up, and a baby spoon. Also some bibs. Here are diapers, twenty-four for now but I can get more tomorrow, and here's zinc oxide since he's bound to have diaper rash. I got a pacifier, a digital thermometer, baby wash, baby shampoo, a sponge thing you lay him on in the sink, baby towels, a baby brush, though I notice he doesn't have much in the way of hair. I got a pack of onesies—that seems to be some sort of little underwear thing—and a nightgown, tiny little nail clippers, look at this. Here's a six-pack of bottles with cartoon characters on the side, quite cute. This is a thing you strap to his wrist and he can shake it like a rattle."

"Hazel, please get in the car and close the door."

Hazel closed the back door, slid into the front seat. "He needs, in this order, I think, food, a bath, clean clothes, a good night's sleep, a visit to the doctor, and more stimulation. He needs to be held a lot, according to the chubby woman in the drugstore."

"Let's get home, then."

"And he needs a name."

"Hazel, I am not I am not *I am not* keeping this baby."

Hazel pulled out of the parking lot, irritating four other drivers in the process. Humming, she ran the first red light she came to, then rubbed her hands together and glanced at Claudia. "What an adven-ture we've embarked upon!"

Claudia had never seen her look quite so happy.

After they had discovered that the baby could indeed scream like a normal child, which happened all through the diapering process; after they found that he could eat far more than they would have thought, and instantly throw it back up in an impressive, far-reaching arc; after he kicked and flailed and howled over being given a bath (he was, as Hazel predicted, bright red from stem to stern, and he had cradle cap); after they had gotten him powdered, onesied, wrapped in a blanket and asleep, Hazel left, saying she'd be back as soon as she could with a crib and everything else Claudia could possibly need.

Claudia held the baby in Ludie's old rocking chair, the one in the living room next to the window, and rocked, hummed a low, slow version of "Michael Row Your Boat Ashore." Tears had dried in his pale eyelashes, gathering them up like the arms of starfish. He hiccuped periodically in his sleep, and sometimes his mouth trembled as if he would cry again, and Claudia couldn't tell if he was heartsick or exhausted or ill in some way not indicated by her new thermometer. She didn't know how to care for someone who couldn't speak, who couldn't give the slightest information about what ailed him. What if he was ill and Claudia missed it? What if he was dying? She pressed her nose and face against his head, which now smelled like baby lotion. His hands were gathered up in fists on either side of his face, and she slipped her pinkie finger inside his hand, which opened up just a little, then squeezed, and Claudia knew she was in the worst trouble in her life.

Rebekah had to pee, and in fact could imagine herself peeing like a racehorse for five or six solid minutes. But not even that, not even a physical emergency was enough to cause her to move. She realized she was going to die this way and it would be a source of great embarrassment to Hazel. STUPID GIRL, SLIGHTLY PREGNANT, DIES FROM FRIGHT AND A BURST BLADDER; HAZEL HUNNICUTT "EMBARRASSED." So not funny. Her eyes had adjusted to the darkness and what had formerly been the curved backs of beasts became again a Turkish rug draped over two sawhorses and a console stereo from the 1960s. It hardly mattered, as under the conditions the truth was as scary as the illusion.

A car pulled into the parking lot, and Rebekah's scalp tightened, causing her ears to lift slightly. She strained to hear with the same intensity a dog would give to distant footsteps. There was a car in the parking lot, and this, finally, broke Rebekah's paralysis. She fell on her knees below the level of the window, then remembered the door didn't have one. She stayed on her knees anyway, as she felt slightly faint, and curling up in a ball took pressure off her bladder.

The car door opened and closed with a muffled whump. The heavy door between Rebekah and the parking lot prevented her from hearing whether the visitor had keys, but she could hear the sliding door on the storage unit grind up on its metal track. Rebekah was scarcely breathing and still her pulse hammered in her ears. Something in the storage unit toppled; something else was scooted across the concrete floor. Whoever was out there wasn't trying to be quiet.

After a few minutes the storage unit door was lowered on its tracks. The parking lot was silent just long enough for Rebekah to hear footsteps heading for the door she had her ear against. She turned and ran toward Your Grandmother's Parlor, leaping over a low bookcase she knew impinged on the aisle just slightly, changed her mind and turned around, leapt over the bookcase a second time. She ran as fast as she could toward the bathroom, slipping around its entrance just as the back door opened with a metallic groan.

Damn damn damn damn, Rebekah whispered—the only swear word she was comfortable with—trying not to panic. The bathroom was an enclosed space in the middle of the store; it had not a hint of a window and was as dark as a bank vault. Hazel kept a bucket and mop in the corner, but the room was small enough that if the bucket had rolled out even a few inches, Rebekah was bound to trip. Who could be here? It wasn't Hazel, who had said dozens of times that she'd gouge out her own spleen before she'd visit the Used World at night. It wasn't Hazel, it couldn't be Claudia, because . . . it just couldn't be. Claudia would no more raid her workplace than rob a bank. And no one else had keys.

Rebekah hadn't reset the alarm. She smacked her forehead; she hadn't reset the alarm. But how could I have? she thought, justifying herself; I was catatonic and had lost the use of my digits. She steadied her breathing, tried to discern whether the intruder noticed the absence of the alarm. There was, it seemed, a heavy pause between the closing of the door and the turning on of the middle bank of lights.

Standing in the bathroom made Rebekah realize even more urgently that it was pee or die. Pee, or *die.*

The intruder moved down . . . it sounded like the left-hand aisle, the same aisle Rebekah had originally chosen. What sort of a person would rob an antique mall? A desperate man of taste, someone hoping a Mission-style mule chest would help him finally complete his bedroom ensemble? More likely it was a run-of-the-mill drug addict; the newspaper had reported only yesterday that an estimated 40 percent of the county's unemployed were addicted to methamphetamine, which the editors had called a Rural Plague.

Rebekah felt for the stall door and was able to slip around it without moving it. The door was on a spring that complained heartily when sprung. Please please, she thought, let there be toilet paper, if there isn't any toilet paper it's my fault, as I am the one who's supposed to change it—and there was some. Rebekah found the end of the roll and lifted it, unwinding a few feet, which she lay on top of the water in the toilet bowl. So far so good. Now she had to get her blue jeans unbuttoned and lowered without making any noise.

There was a crash from somewhere near the Nostalgic Kitchen; it sounded like a wooden bowl falling on the concrete floor. After the first noise, all sorts of things either fell or were tossed, which Rebekah took as a sign. She sat forward on the toilet seat, trying to hit the front of the bowl, one of Peter's tricks for using the bathroom silently. Of course she wasn't a boy and didn't have perfect aim, and also as soon as she began she wasn't entirely in control.

From the intruder came the sound of . . . was that a *drill?* A power screwdriver? Was a robber actually taking the time to dismantle furniture? He made a loud grunting sound, as if he were trying to lift something heavy. Rebekah heard the sound of the dolly, with its one crooked wheel, being pushed toward the back door; the man took one load out and came back for a second. She was going to live, Rebekah realized—this was almost over. The mannequin wasn't going to kill her, neither her heart nor her bladder was going to burst, and the little clump of baby cells she was carrying around would get to grow one more day.

Before he closed the back door behind him, whoever had come and taken apart a display also turned off the overhead lights, casting

Rebekah back into the cavelike, paralyzing darkness. She scooted around the bucket and mop, zipping her blue jeans and muttering *damn damn damn damn*. Once outside the bathroom she could hear the car start and drive away. *I ran to the bathroom,* Rebekah said to herself, *I can run away from it.* But after only three steps her legs felt leaden and her eyes darted back and forth at the shapes made once again diabolical. *Go, go,* she said aloud, *you have to get out of here.* Such terror couldn't be good for the little bean pod, she was certain, and for the first time she tried to think of the mess she was in as containing *two,* even if one of them was, so far, nothing more than two gigantic eyeballs in a shrimp. That was enough. Rebekah sprinted past the NASCAR display, the entrance to the breezeway where the Christmas lights twinkled, and to the metal back door, stopping only long enough to grab her overnight bag from where she'd dropped it beside the low bookcase. Her hands trembled as she pushed in the security code, but she had the presence of mind to make sure she had her keys before she opened the door and let it close behind her.

With the baby asleep in the middle of Claudia's bed, surrounded by pillows, Claudia and Hazel had spent forty-five minutes putting up the crib Hazel had brought back from the Emporium. Claudia kept eyeing the new crib mattress Hazel had picked up at Babies "R" Us, wondering if it would be entirely wrong to just put the mattress on the floor. In the whole time they'd been working on the crib, Hazel hadn't brought up that she had just done something she swore she'd rather . . . Claudia couldn't remember what. Something about her spleen.

"So?" Claudia finally asked, irritated that she had to.

"So, what?"

"So you went into the store at night and you're still alive. How did it go?"

Hazel put down her wrench, looked puzzled a moment. "I don't know that I would have gone through with it, but Rebekah was there."

"What? What was she doing there?"

"I have no idea. Her car was parked behind the storage shed, way back in the corner next to the delivery truck, and she'd dropped her overnight bag just inside the delivery door."

"Did you ask her what she was doing there?"

"No—all the lights were out, so I think she didn't want anybody to know."

"Wait." Claudia lowered her screwdriver. "Did you *see* Rebekah?"

"I didn't. She was in the bathroom the whole time I was there."

"Hazel, good Lord! Do you even know if she was all right?"

"She's all right." Hazel reached in and tightened a bolt she'd put on and taken off four times. For some reason they kept putting the sides on backward, which meant that Claudia couldn't push the release bar with her foot, thus lowering the side rail. Why she needed to lower it was still a mystery. "I waited in the parking lot at Richard's until I saw her come out and leave."

Claudia leaned back against the trunk at the end of her bed. No one in her right mind would choose to traverse the Used World alone, after hours, just to go to the bathroom. "What—what do you suppose that was about?"

Hazel shook her head. "Couldn't tell you. Hand me that L-shaped thing."

Claudia let the subject drop. Rebekah was impossible for her to grasp, anyway; she was like a creature fallen to Earth from some distant planet. She didn't even know what solar system Rebekah would call home.

Two hours and an entire cycle of feeding, vomiting, screaming, and sleeping later, Claudia could say they'd made headway in meeting the baby's needs. They'd figured out how to put the car seat, dusty from the storage unit, in the Cherokee, and they'd set up the changing table (which had seen better days) with diapers, changing pads, baby wipes, powders, and unguents. Hazel had unfolded something called a Gymini—a red, black, and white quilted pad with two arches crossed over the top, from which dangled animal shapes and rattles and crackly things. This was for the stimulation part of the baby's needs.

"Sheesh, that's it for me," Hazel said, stretching.

"Wait—what does that mean?"

"It's ten o'clock, it means I'm going home. To my house. And my sad sad cats."

"I don't—" What she wanted to say was that she couldn't possibly be left here alone with a stolen human infant. "You could stay, I've got all these empty bedrooms and—"

"Claudia, you have to spend your first night alone with him sometime. It might as well be tonight." Hazel looked around for her purse, headed toward the stairs.

My first night alone with him sometime, Claudia thought, her head in her hands. Somehow this was really happening to her, even if only for a night or two. Hazel insisted and Claudia acquiesced, and where before that had always seemed like a relatively simple plan, now Claudia could feel the sinister undertow of obeisance, the lunacy in surrendering one's will to another. "Wait!" she said, following Hazel down the stairs. "I have an appointment in the morning and I don't want to miss it. You'll have to keep the baby, and also we haven't talked about work—tomorrow's Monday and we both need to be there, have you thought about these things, Hazel?"

"Indeed I have," Hazel said, looking around the living room for her purse. "I'll be out here tomorrow morning bright and early, and I'll take the baby to my mother's for the day."

Claudia swallowed. "Your mother's?"

"Do you have a problem with my mother?"

"No! Of course not, it's just that she's . . ."

"Old?"

"Well."

"She's eighty-three. I don't know if that's old anymore."

"I know what you mean."

"Mother is very healthy and strong, regardless of her age, and she adores babies, which is more than can be said for either you or me."

"But what if he . . ."

"Listen to you!" Hazel looked up at Claudia. She wore an expression of such satisfaction that Claudia itched, momentarily, to slug her. "Worried about a baby you claim not to want! That is so cute."

Claudia crossed her arms, glared. "I would be worried about any infant I thought might be in jeopardy. That doesn't mean I would want to *steal* him or dress him up and pretend he's my *own*."

Hazel spied her purse next to the couch. "Yes, that's fine. Keep telling yourself that. But I'll remind you that earlier today—this very day—that same baby was a scant three feet from a box filled with gasoline-soaked rags."

Claudia felt the color drain from her face. "He was?"

"He certainly was." Hazel pulled on her gigantic sleeping-bag coat and a red hat trimmed with white fur. She looked very little like Tuesday Weld. "Bright and early," she said, walking out the door.

Claudia locked the dead bolt, the chain. She waited for Hazel to drive away, then turned off the porch light and the sodium lamp that lit her yard all the way to the road. She rested her head against the cold pane of glass at the top of the door a moment, and headed back upstairs.

The baby was asleep in his crib, on his new yellow sheet, under his soft blanket and a mobile that played Brahms's Lullabye while giraffes and elephants and koala bears danced around on strings. Claudia couldn't imagine how much this had cost Hazel. For now the baby was sleeping and Claudia was alone again, on a winter night like any other, or she could pretend it was so. His bed was right there, only a few feet from her own, and between the sighs and ticks of the radiator, she could sometimes hear him breathing, or she could see the sad little swimming gesture he made with his legs, like a marine creature out of his element.

Claudia sat watching him a long time, half afraid to move or leave the room. What if he awakened and she couldn't hear him? What if he knew he had been kidnapped, and woke up afraid? What if Legion suddenly roared into her driveway, all of them fat and dressed in black, like a squadron of locusts? She'd brought this fear up with Hazel earlier in the evening, who had left behind not only an entire layette, but also a loaded, unregistered .38 she'd confiscated from Edie the year before, and which Hazel claimed to have forgotten to take out of her car. A simple weapon for street criminals. Claudia was not to use her own gun in the event of an emergency, Hazel insisted, because if the .38 was fired, Claudia would have no problem insisting that the gun belonged to the assailants, and that one of them had turned it on his brother, as such people were wont to do.

"But I would have gunshot residue . . ."

"Wash your hands, change your clothes," Hazel had said, waving away the possibility of crime scene investigators.

"But there would be—"

"Don't worry," Hazel had told her. "They're all too busy rubbing their itchy noses and listening to the ringing in their ears to wonder where that baby's gotten off to."

"How did this happen?" Claudia had asked—asked herself as much as Hazel. "This morning I was one person, my normal self, and now I have an unlicensed handgun and a strange baby, and I'm actually talking to you about what statement I should give the police if I'm attacked by a motorcycle gang and shoot a couple of them? Explain this to me."

Hazel had shrugged. "What a difference a day makes, huh?"

Claudia studied the sleeping baby and sighed. She looked around her bedroom, her mother's room, and it was filled with all this foreign stuff, these objects she'd never lived with before, had no understanding of. It was like a nightmare of proliferation, or time-lapse photography, one of those dreams where mushrooms grow too fast. In one scene: her life. Minutes later: her life teeming, unrecognizable to her.

She stood up finally, and put on her pajamas. Her knees and hips ached, and her shoulder blades and neck, the places she carried tension, felt as if she'd been moving boulders all day. She got into bed, wishing she had hot chocolate, tea, something there beside her, wishing she'd remembered to eat. *A Prayer for Owen Meany* was on her bedside table, waiting for her. She picked it up and read the three epigraphs, the last of which was by someone named Léon Bloy: *Any Christian who is not a hero is a pig.* That was as far as she got before falling asleep.

⏰

"Rebekah?" Peter didn't look surprised to see her. He looked . . . wary? Sad? He held open the storm door, gestured for her to come in.

She would have to work at keeping her thoughts straight; all she wanted to do was sit down in front of the woodstove, in which a fire was struggling to get going, and take in the room, the crisp cedar-and-woodsmoke smell that permeated the cabin. Rebekah used to carry that smell on her hands to Vernon's house and to the store. She wanted to study Peter, the slight sunburn on his nose and cheeks, the way one side of his hair had been flattened down by his ski cap. Of course they needed to talk, she wanted to talk, but she would be happy just to be. For a little while, even if only a few minutes, she could pretend this was her cabin, as she used to pretend she lived here with Peter.

"Sit—here, Beckah, let me move this stuff." He walked past her and picked up his duffel bag, on which two chairlift tags were hanging by metal clips. "I was out of . . ."

"I know."

"Right." He gave her a rueful smile. "My mom. The Minister of Information."

Rebekah sat down on Peter's futon couch; the cabin was starting to warm up and she felt sleepy. Peter carried his duffel bag into his bedroom, went into the kitchen, and began making tea. He didn't need to ask if she wanted some (she did) or what flavor she preferred (mint and chamomile—he already knew). She was flooded with a sense of well-being all the more potent for what had preceded it; this day had been like driving too fast over a hill that could make a car go airborne.

The tea was done and Peter was back in the living room so quickly Rebekah wondered if she had, in fact, dozed off for a few minutes.

"It's hot," Peter said, handing Rebekah her favorite stoneware mug.

"Thank you. Peter, we need.—"

"Beckah, are you pregnant? Is that what you meant by what you said to my mom?"

Rebekah blushed furiously, put her cold hands against her face. "I haven't been to the doctor yet, but this morning I used one of those stick—"

"A home pregnancy test?"

"Yes, and it made a plus sign so fast it seemed to be in neon."

Peter sat back against the couch, closed his eyes. "I guess I don't need to ask if—"

"If what?"

He wouldn't look her in the eye. "If there's any chance that someone else is the father."

Rebekah was uncertain what she should do with her body, her face. Would a normal woman scream, commit an act of violence? All Peter was saying was that she had experienced one relationship and he had experienced another. His disappearance, his college student, and now this question—he was outlining for her, because she'd been too blind to see it, who she had been to him. She took a sip of tea, calmly. "No, there's not a chance."

Peter nodded, rolled his own mug between his hands. He finally looked at her and winked. "Sure it's not Claudia's?"

Rebekah gave him a steady look, and not as if she found him funny.

"I'm sorry," he said. "It was a cheap joke." He took a sip of tea; his own favorite was Red Zinger. "No chance of an abortion, I guess." Peter said this with a tone of resignation bordering on the theatrical.

"No," she said, shaking her head. "No chance of turning back time, either."

"Sweetheart," Peter said, taking both of Rebekah's hands in his and turning her slightly toward him, "I don't want you to go through this alone, I really don't. I don't know what it means—I can't think . . ." He pulled one hand away and ran it roughly through his hair. "I can't get my mind around it."

"I can't either."

"I want to help, I do, but—did Mom tell you about the tour? Rebekah, this is so important to me, I should have done it years ago. I feel like, like if I don't do it now I will have missed my chance and I'll never know if I could have been—"

"I understand."

Peter sat back, looked at Rebekah with such intensity she felt a familiar heat start at the back of her neck and travel down her spine. "You do?"

"I do. I do understand." She meant it. Even though she had been raised knowing she would never have a career, much less a vocation, she had recently been able to see that life gives you openings both false and true, and that one of the measures of genius is knowing which doors to walk through and when.

"It's going to be so great," Peter said, taking her hands again. "People underestimate these do-it-yourself tours but they can really create a groundswell of support for an unknown artist. Green Day sold something like forty thousand—"

"I don't know who that is."

"No. Well, it doesn't matter. It's just . . . I see a real chance here, Rebekah. And I know I'm really young, maybe it could wait—"

"Aren't you twenty-six?"

Peter nodded, sipped his tea. "Yeah, like I said, I know I'm young, but—"

Rebekah tried to pinpoint when twenty-six had become young. Imagine, she thought, someone questioning Vernon's manhood at twenty-six, when he was working sixteen hours a day trying to save his family's farm, when he had a wife who couldn't get pregnant and he was waiting on a call for the ministry.

". . . some towns I know ahead of time where I'm going to play, other places I'll . . ."

In fact, Vernon wouldn't have taken kindly to being called a "boy" at sixteen, and maybe not at six.

". . . a few covers, maybe ten altogether, and I'll alternate them in different towns so I don't get tired of them myself. Listen to this, I just learned this on Friday—no, on Thursday I learned this." Peter was up and grabbing his guitar before Rebekah could say anything. He sat back down beside her and tuned it up and there it was: a Martin D28 and a whole lot of hours Rebekah had worked for Hazel to purchase it. She counted on her fingers, squinted her eyes. More than two hundred hours, actually. Peter began playing a series of sweet, bouncy chords, sang: *I could while away the hours / Conferrin' with the flowers* . . .

She'd only seen *The Wizard of Oz* once, but would always remember it. Peter knew how to choose that kind of song, the one that touched his listeners without hurting them. Although in truth, Rebekah didn't know who his audience was. As far as she knew, she was the only person who'd ever heard him play. That had been the case until Mandy, at least.

She clapped when he finished; told him the whole thing was wonderful, that people would love it. He sat back down next to her, talked a while longer about the music industry, its level of corruption. He knew he was entering a den of vipers, but what choice did he have, really?

"You should do this if it's so important to you."

Peter's eyes filled with tears, and he put his arms around her, drew her close. "Oh, thank you, thank you, you are so great to see it this way."

"Can I ask you a question?"

"Shoot." Peter stood up with his guitar, uncomfortable.

"Will you tell me what happened? Why you stopped calling me?"

He didn't answer for a long time. The guitar was put away, the pot was put back on the stove for more tea. Finally, he rejoined her in front of the woodstove. "I don't want the truth to hurt you."

"Nothing could hurt me more than—"

"Okay, the truth is that we were just dating, you know? Like I said, I'm young, I don't want to be tied down. You seemed perfect because you didn't ever ask for anything. I've had"—Peter shook his head—"girlfriends who were just *on me* all the time. Where had I been, where was this relationship going, on and on and on. You never asked those questions."

"No, I didn't."

"We just had a good time; we were friends, weren't we?"

After he'd offered her a slinky nightgown ("This isn't mine," she'd had to tell him); after they'd brushed their teeth in the usual pattern— Rebekah first, carrying her overnight bag into the bathroom, Peter following; after they'd settled in and Rebekah had grown used to the hard futon sofa, she heard Peter begin to snore in the other room, lightly.

She looked around at the cabin in the faint light from the woodstove. It wasn't the same place she had loved, and she wasn't the same person who had loved it, so she tried to see it that way, as the museum of another person and another time. She wished she were still that other Rebekah, or that she could find the Peter who loved her. Without them she was hopeless. She was asleep before she knew what had hit her.

Chapter 4

"THAT WAS A FOUL, I'm quite certain," Amos Townsend said after Claudia had smacked the ball out of his hands. He'd been dribbling toward her with a casual ease that left the ball unguarded on the up bounce.

"I didn't touch you," Claudia said, dribbling twice and taking a sixteen-foot jumper. "Ten to four."

"It was foul in other ways. Can we take a break—how's that go again?" Amos moved his hands around in meaningless semaphore, as if trying to remember how to make the letter *T,* for time-out.

Claudia retrieved their water bottles from the corner of the court, handed Amos his. He was bent over, hands on his knees, gasping for air.

"I'm dying," he said. "Why aren't you dying?"

"I don't know," Claudia said, surprised. She was a little tired, a little hot, but mostly she felt great. "Maybe it's this court." It had been impossible for Amos to find an available gym in December in Indiana, so he'd gotten the use of the indoor court at the Nathan Leander Church of the Nazarene, which was carpeted. A full-size basketball court inside a church, stretched end to end with low-pile indoor/outdoor carpeting.

"Maybe carpeting makes it more Christian."

"It is hard to keep up with all the rules." Claudia bounced up and down, keeping her knees warm and loose.

"I thought you hadn't played in years." Amos took a drink of water, wiped his forehead on his T-shirt.

"I haven't. This is easier than moving furniture all day, though."

"Well," Amos put his water bottle down, stretched. "It's actually easier than writing sermons, too. It's probably too late to become a professional, huh?"

Claudia looked at Amos, who probably hadn't even seen a basketball game in more than twenty years. He was six three to her six five, both of them over forty. Amos still believed they were giants. She tried to imagine them standing next to Yao Ming or a half dozen other really tall people. "It's too late in many, many ways," she said, passing Amos the ball.

They played another thirty minutes and Amos rallied at the end, but not enough to beat her. The final score was 30–22. After they'd returned the basketball to the closet, where there was a great deal of sporting equipment ("There is much about the Nazarenes I do not know," Amos had remarked), they changed in their respective restrooms and met in the snack bar, which had coffee, soda, and juice machines, and two more machines filled with chips, cookies, and microwave popcorn.

"I don't know if I can go back to your church after this," Claudia remarked, sitting down with a grape juice and bag of peanuts.

"We're inadequate. I never knew." Amos came back to the table with a cup of coffee and a giant cookie. "I looked around, but I can't find the tanning beds."

Claudia coughed, nearly choking on a peanut. He was right. Other places combined coffeehouses and bookshops; Indiana was probably right on the verge of putting tanning beds in evangelical churches. "The one nearest my house is called A Place to Tan."

"I like that, it's to the point." Amos stretched his legs out, rested them on an empty chair. "It would be easier if everyone would just admit they're depressed. A lot less skin cancer that way."

"Is everyone depressed?"

"I've always thought so. Maybe I'm wrong. Are you depressed?"

Claudia shrugged. "I don't think so."

Amos studied her a moment, weighing, or so it seemed, his next comment. He took a sip of coffee.

"Are you?" Claudia asked, uncomfortable.

"I am not . . . unaware of the human condition, and I'm fairly clear on my own. Given those facts, it only follows that one would be—concerned." He gave Claudia a sheepish look, as if he knew he'd taken an end-run around the question. "I think everyone, from the beginning of recorded time, has been depressed. It just follows. Jesus says in the book of Matthew, "You are the salt of the earth; but if salt has lost its taste, how can its saltiness be restored?" That's *some* kind of loss He's talking about. The Beatitudes are meant to comfort the poor in spirit. Maybe that's all I am, maybe all you are, the poor in spirit."

Claudia watched Amos, expecting him to add something but he didn't. "You say those words and all I hear is static. We've heard them so many times they no longer mean anything."

Amos let his head fall back and hit the wall. "Oh, when a man's flock turns against him, and using his own words, no less."

"I don't really mean it."

"No. Well, you're a better person than I, if you don't." He drank his coffee, continued to look bemused. "Want to tell me what's new in your life?"

Claudia ran the palm of her hand over the top of her hair. "Not much." Was she allowed to lie to her minister? "Not a lot. I mean— something has happened, but it's not that big a deal."

"Oh?"

"I have a—someone has come to stay with me."

"Is that a good thing?"

Claudia shrugged. "I don't know yet. Maybe. I doubt it. It's too soon to tell."

"You've lived a solitary life for a while now."

"Yes, since . . . since Ludie died."

"And that was comfortable for you?" Amos broke his cookie in half and offered it to her.

"It was," she said, nodding. "It makes me realize you never know when someone or something is going to appear. I mean, it happens on television all the time—a fifty-year-old woman finds out she has a twin she never knew about, or a brother resurfaces who's been gone for decades. I'd never thought it applied to me."

Amos looked shocked. "Can I tell you something?" he said, leaning toward her.

"Yes."

"This is completely confidential."

"I assumed it was."

"Well, yes—what you say to me is confidential, because I'm your minister. But you aren't obligated to keep my confidence."

"Okay."

"My wife, Langston. She had a brother who disappeared thirteen, fourteen years ago; they've never heard of or from him in all that time. Recently she got a call from him."

"You're kidding." Somehow her baby robbery already paled in comparison.

"Nope." Amos dropped the last of his part of the cookie in his mouth, wiped his hands on his gym towel. "He was cautious, didn't tell her where he was, but he sounded, in her words, as if he's thriving. I've never"—he swallowed, looked down at the table—"seen her the way she was right after that phone call." Amos laughed, and Claudia saw the slight shine of tears in his eyes. "She's the moon and the stars to me; I thought I knew everything about her. And yet I'd never seen her unreservedly happy before. But she was that night, after she finished yelling at me because of my primitivism. Oh, and for causing her to live in the wasteland of Haddington, where we still don't have caller ID."

"So she could have seen his phone number."

"Maybe," Amos said, using what Claudia guessed was the same tone he used with his wife, "unless he called from some other city or from a pay phone or using one of those whatsits you can get in a gas station."

"A phone card."

"Exactly. I told her that her brother might not have even called if we'd been living some place more sophisticated. It was his faith that we wouldn't have a real telephone that allowed him to contact her in the first place."

"Good argument."

"Thank you. It worked." Amos swept his cookie crumbs into his empty cup. "I didn't mean for us to talk about me. That wasn't very professional. Tell me more about your own visitor."

Claudia looked at him, thinking how funny it was, all those years of Ludie's ministers, men pedastalized (perhaps even coffinized) and kept distant from their humanity. Claudia had assumed that's what it meant to choose the profession, or that it was a prerequisite for choosing it—the warmth in the pulpit that could be faked if necessary, the blameless cold reserve in person. But here was one, a minister who had taken on his task like any other craftsman, and Claudia loved him. She loved him simply, like a friend or kindred spirit, as one loves one's peers. "Next time," she said. "It may come to nothing, and anyway, your story was more interesting." She handed him back the other half of his cookie, rose from the table, and threw away the plastic bag from her peanuts. The Nazarenes, she noticed, did not recycle, so she slipped her juice bottle into her gym bag. "But thanks for talking with me."

"My pleasure," Amos said. "Come back any time."

"Get—we're gonna have to turn it—get your end straightened up there," the man said. His face was nearly purple with exertion, and his WWF cap had been knocked crooked, revealing a hat-shaped dent in his forehead.

Claudia didn't say, she would never say, that she had suggested they tip the love seat a long time ago. It was a sleeper, with a single bed built in, and awkward. Right at the very beginning she'd said, "We ought to turn this on its side," not like a woman who'd just beaten her minister in basketball, but as a polite suggestion from someone who worked at the place and moved furniture every day.

Rebekah passed the open delivery door, carrying something into booth #42. Claudia got just a glimpse of her. In fact, all morning Rebekah had moved through the store like a ghost, a blank expression on her face.

The Undertaker. That was the character on the man's hat, Claudia recognized him now. One of the Cronies was fond of him, too. She had no idea what any of it meant, what this character did or why. She turned the couch into the position she'd originally suggested, squatted under her side of it, and lifted. The Undertaker lifted his side and backed out the door into the freezing, bloodless day; he breathed heavily and didn't meet her eye.

A black Ford F150 was waiting with the tailgate down, and the man puzzled a moment over how to get the couch into the high bed without a ramp. This was what he'd bought such a gigantic truck for, right? Claudia wanted to ask. The bed liner was unscuffed. It seemed the man could lift the couch no higher. Claudia didn't tell him that if he put his end down, she could easily take care of it. She stood there, letting him make his own decisions. She knew what he looked like under the barn coat and black sweatshirt; his arms were the size of hams, but not strong, and his belly and chest were weak and white. After a lifetime of being a healthy farm specimen of a boy, he'd become a reclining, television-watching, soda-drinking captive to the modern time-saving conveniences, and he was under the weight of a piece of furniture he could hardly lift with a woman who was at least six inches his superior, and Claudia remained silent.

He put his end down. "You got a ramp, a dolly?" Lifting his cap, he wiped a line of sweat off his forehead.

"They're in that shed," Claudia said, putting down her end. This would be the first time she used them today. "I'll be right back."

After they'd loaded the couch and covered it with plastic, she asked the man if he wanted to take the ramp home with him. He shook his head, said, "I'll get my boys to bring it in," as if they weren't just like him, as if they weren't the New Sons. She imagined them at home right now, a ranch house on the highway, playing video games and eating Doritos out of the bag, the room dark. It didn't matter what age they were—twelve or twenty-seven—that's what they were doing. For just a moment she saw something flicker on the Undertaker's face, a grimace or a twitch, as if he'd seen it, too. He slammed the tailgate shut, took his keys from the pocket of his relaxed blue jeans. "Thank ya," he said, walking toward the driver's door.

☎

Rebekah pulled the red dress over the mannequin's head, trying to make the unnaturally high and pert breasts fit in the space provided for them. If she made an adjustment one way, the neckline was too deep; if she repaired the neckline, the nylon fabric slipped off the mannequin's plastic shoulders.

"Well," she said, humming along with Sammy Davis, Jr., singing "Christmas Time All Over the World." She pulled the dress up, pulled it down.

"Rebekah?"

She turned and there was Peter's mother, a vision in her traditional winter palette: cream, cinnamon, and rust.

"Kathy?"

"I don't mean to bother you at work." Kathy reached out for the cheapest of the holiday dresses, a concoction of bows and inorganic fibers.

"That's all right," Rebekah said, allowing the red dress to fall in an awkward way. She looked at Kathy's straight, structured hair, the delicate blond streaks, and unconsciously reached up and touched her own tangled, untended curls. "Are you . . . shopping?"

"No," Kathy said with a nervous laugh, glancing at the other shoppers. "No, I wanted to apologize for what happened at the house. It was an awkward situation and I'm afraid I . . . well, I didn't mean to hurt your feelings in any way."

Rebekah swallowed, fought back tears. "That's all right. I'm sorry for the tone I took with you, too."

Kathy waved the memory away. "You had every right." She reached into her purse and took out a tissue. "I also want to tell you something."

"Okay." Rebekah didn't know whether to hope or take a step backward.

"My husband and I have been talking. . . ."

"You mean Pete Senior?"

"Pardon?"

"You said 'my husband,' as if I don't know who you're talking about."

Kathy pressed her lips together, looked down at the floor. "*Pete* and I have been talking and we realize that you must feel very alone right now." She waited for Rebekah to reply, but the understatement had left Rebekah speechless. "I don't know anything—I wouldn't presume to know anything about your financial situation—but we were hoping we might make a helpful gesture, just something to—"

"I can't take money from you, Kathy," Rebekah said, shaking her head. A painful blush began at her chest and worked its way up her neck. Worse and ever worse, what she might have to endure over the next few months.

"It isn't much," Kathy said, reaching again inside her purse. "Just enough to help us all resolve this. We know"—she took out her wallet—"that this was an accident on your part as much as on Peter's, that there was absolutely not a hint of malice or entrapment or anything like that, we're certain."

"Resolve this?"

"Pardon?"

"You said 'resolve this'?"

Kathy unzipped her wallet, counted out six one-hundred-dollar bills. "I spoke to someone," she said, barely above a whisper, "and this will cover everything, including a Xanax before and a painkiller during. We wanted"—she slipped her wallet back in her bag and dabbed at her eyes with the tissue—"we wanted you to be as comfortable as possible. To have everything you need." The money, folded in half, was pressed into Rebekah's palm. She looked down at it, looked at Kathy's face. Kathy's eyes were half filled with tears, as if she had meant to cry but forgot.

"I can't—"

"Oh, please let us do this," Kathy said, covering Rebekah's hand with her own. "Please. I feel it's the least . . . and then we can call it a day and remember one another fondly. This doesn't"—she leaned her head close to Rebekah's—"this does *not* have to be the end of the world, sweetheart."

Rebekah pulled her hand away, and the money fell to the floor like confetti. She couldn't blame them, couldn't hold it against Kathy and her husband. She bent down and picked up the cash, refolded it, and pressed it back into Kathy's hand. "It isn't. It isn't the end of the world. But thank you, anyway."

Kathy pinched the bridge of her nose as if a violent headache were coming on, turned, and left without another word.

"Did you move things around in number fifty-one?" Hazel asked, when Claudia got back to the counter.

"I did, but we should call Bennett and tell him with the love seat and corner hutch gone, I can only do so much."

Hazel nodded, continued arranging the vintage watches on the white velvet display. She carefully tucked each price tag under each face so customers had to ask her to remove a watch they were interested in if they wanted to know the price.

"Does Rebekah look all right to you?" Claudia asked, picking up one of the self-published books Hazel had stacked on the counter.

"She's a little short for my taste."

Rebekah moved in and out of Claudia's sight in booth #18, Barbie knockoffs and action figures in original packaging, where she appeared to be dusting. Claudia saw a flash of red hair, a pale hand. "I'm wondering if there's something wrong with her."

"You mean other than having grown up in a cult, outside civilization?"

"Yes, other than that. I think she's sick. Have you noticed how pale she is?"

Hazel raised her eyebrows, glanced at Claudia. "Well, she's the damsel in distress in this story, isn't she? She could hardly be tan and athletic." She slid the watches back in the larger display case, sat down on her stool. The black canvas tote bag she pulled off the shelf had a cowgirl on the side and the legend, spelled out in the cowgirl's spinning pink lariat, KNIT HAPPENS. "Rebekah's basic problem is that her sun is in Pisces, and Venus is in Pisces, putting it in its exaltation. The Love principle in its highest evolutionary development. But no moderation. The first time I looked at that child I heard Aphrodite's bells ringing at the edge of the foamy sea, if I may say so."

"Maybe she has the flu," Claudia said, tapping her fingers on the counter.

"Maybe the flu, or maybe it's because she has a Cancer ascendant and a moon in Cancer—a triple water sign, that one, the big whammy. No earth to stand on, no fire to fight with. Gives her great depth, a rapport with the Universe, but leaves her open to addiction, alcoholism, and emotional instability."

"Do you think I should ask her? If she's all right?"

"I think you should ask her if she needs some Virgo. Virgo in her last three houses would suit that child fine. Alas, we cannot change the stars. We can only change ourselves. Now you, Miss Claudie, have an enviable natal chart. Sun in Virgo, moon in Capricorn, Scorpio rising. An interesting little triad, there. Rebekah could definitely use a piece of what you have."

Rebekah appeared, disappeared; her hair would suddenly shine out from between two pieces of furniture like the sun breaking free of clouds. Was there something different on the surface of her? She was wearing blue jeans that were a little tight—that was unusual, but she walked in them as she always had, like a person who had spent the first twenty-five years of her life in dresses. Rebekah's loose white sweater was pretty, her hair a shock against it. All day her skin had been flushed—there was a red circle on each cheek the size of a silver dollar. And when she'd arrived for work, flushed from the cold air, her green eyes had been too bright. She was feverish, that's what Claudia suspected.

"The air is a bit disturbed around her, I see that," Hazel said. She put down her yarn and reached under the counter for a book she kept there, *The Complete Book of Dreams,* published in 1934. The glue on the spine was gone, and rodents had gnawed the corners of the cover; Hazel held the thing together with rubber bands. She opened her reading glasses and rested them on the bridge of her nose. "What did you dream last night?" she asked Claudia as she scanned the table of contents.

Claudia felt a catch in her chest, just a glancing knock, and then it was gone. "I . . ." She remembered something, what was it? The middle of the night. The clock on the bedside table, the curtain in the window—she'd awakened and looked at these things, which gradually grew in focus and became familiar again. Why? "I dreamed . . ." It had something to do with Millie, something Millie had said. "The basement—I've been dreaming of the basement lately." She had walked down the stairs, through the living room, dining room, kitchen. She opened the cellar door. In some dreams Ludie stood at the sink, scrubbing potatoes or scraping the grubby skins off carrots. The cellar was a cave, consistently cool and damp. The steps were rickety, with open risers, and condensation dripped from the lead pipes snaking through the ceiling. There were cobwebs and mice. Sourceless flashes of light reflected off Ludie's jars of tomatoes and pickles and beets. Claudia opened the cellar door, reached out for the pull string connected to the bare bulb above the stairs, and leaning toward it was an act of faith. It hung in complete darkness, and could be grasped only by a practiced gesture of leaning forward and praying. The cold, earthy smell rose up and—what did she seek there? And would she go down?

Hazel looked at Claudia over the tops of her glasses. "The basement? Could you be less original?" She ran her fingers over the *B*'s in the table of contents. "See, Mr. Allen doesn't even include a listing for basement, that's how much everyone knows what it means."

"Try cellar."

"Cellar—ah, here. Three different places he puts cellars. Basement must have not yet entered the lexicon in 1934. Here—under Love Dreams he writes:

> The condition and contents, as well as the odor, govern the significance of this dream.
>
> A wine cellar portends marriage with a person of gambling instincts or one in a hazardous occupation.
>
> A cellar well stored with foods, canned foods, fruits or vegetables, is an indication of success in business or love, or both.
>
> A musty cellar indicates disappointment.
>
> Being unable to get out of the cellar foretells that you will find yourself beset with difficulties of a serious nature."

Hazel looked up at Claudia. "Dear Mr. Allen. This is what I love about him—no danger of being shocked in his icy depths." She turned to a chapter further in the book. "In Good Luck Dreams he writes: 'A well-stocked cellar, whether with food, wine, or coal, is a presage of contentment.' Is there coal in your dream?"

Claudia thought about it. "Not that I can tell. But you know, it's a basement, so it's dark. And coal is coal."

"All true. And here's what he says in Strange Prophecies, Warnings, and Bad Luck."

"I hate this chapter."

"Don't we all. 'A cold or damp cellar is a portent of bad news from a relative who lives at a distance. If you dream of being locked in a cellar, it is a presage of illness.'"

"One has to wonder who edited this book," Hazel said, turning it over in her hands. "Because what's the difference between not being able to get out of a cellar, and being locked in a cellar?"

"What is the difference between Love and Strange Prophecies?"

"Indeed." Hazel put the rubber bands around the book, slipped it under the counter. "Interesting how the world has changed, isn't it, Miss Claudie," she said, returning to her knitting. "Basement doesn't mean the same thing as cellar. One is like the dark muck of the unconscious, and the other is more like a pantry, it seems to indicate bounty."

There was Rebekah, walking down the breezeway and disappearing from sight, bountiful and sick. "I was thinking about something like that at my sister's the other night, about how it isn't just that my mother is gone, everything that made her what she was is gone, too. Ludie was more like a cellar."

"And you're a basement?"

"No," Claudia said, shaking her head. "I'm not a basement." But she knew as she said it that she was at least partially wrong. The difference between herself and Ludie was that there wasn't a basement *inside* Ludie; there were jars of tomatoes, each fruit glowing like a red planet, and shelves for holding the jars. There was a barrel filled with sand where she kept carrots crisp all winter. But in Claudia there was the doorway, the black steps, the lunge into emptiness.

"You didn't know everything about your mother," Hazel said, pulling out a length of yarn.

"I know I didn't."

"You only know yourself in relation to her."

"I know, Hazel."

"You're just telling a story called Ludie. You've made up a character who stands in a spot and fulfills certain needs and is rounded by your perfect imagination of her."

But, Claudia wanted to say, what about how her worn-out bras cut into her back, and I could see it through her dresses? What about her heavy ankles, and the way she loved to smooth out fabric, run her hands over tablecloths and quilts, it was heartbreaking. What about the way she left my father's study untouched and kept the radio off for a year after he died? I wouldn't put those things in the story of Ludie, if it were mine to tell.

"You're ignoring me," Hazel said.

Claudia rubbed the sleeve of her sweater over a smudge on the countertop. "That's because you're just a story I'm telling called Hazel."

Hazel dropped her knitting, leaned so close to Claudia that she could see the copper edges of Hazel's otherwise faded brown eyes. "That's *right*. Now look busy, Rebekah is about to come around the corner. We don't want her to know she's the only one who does any work around here."

Rebekah came around the corner, her hands empty. She seemed to have been crying, or sneezing. Between the dust motes thickening the air all through the building, and the cigarette smoke of the Cronies, Claudia considered it a wonder they weren't all hauling around oxygen tanks.

"Do you mind if I go get something to eat?" Rebekah asked. She sounded exhausted, Claudia thought.

"What? And leave us here with this crowd?" Hazel said, glancing around at the four or five people in the store.

"I'm just going across the road to Richard's. Do you want anything?"

Hazel and Claudia both said no; Red and Slim arrived as Rebekah slipped out, and within seconds had removed their coats and were smoking, staring off into space, silent. Neither of them could ever remember a dream.

"Hazel," Claudia said, exasperated, "there is something wrong with her."

Hazel pushed the yarn down farther on the needles, pushed up her glasses with her shoulder. "Yes, there certainly is."

"Well—why didn't you say something?"

"Say what?"

"I don't know, maybe 'Rebekah, are you okay?'"

"But she isn't okay, you can see that much."

"How about, 'Rebekah, *what* is wrong with you?'"

The older woman busied herself counting stitches, or pretended to, then said, "But I know what's wrong with her. I'm not going to be the one to decide when she talks about it."

Claudia raised her palms in a gesture of helplessness. "If you know, tell me, Hazel."

The door opened, and a couple from the local college came in. They were both pretty and well dressed, and could have been brother and sister. In a glance Claudia guessed that she taught art history/women's studies, something like that, and he was an architect. Hazel smiled at them, gave them a friendly nod. She whispered to Claudia, "You're no Pisces, but you should be able to see what is made manifest before you. It's not *magic*. Look at her with the devotion you give to the past, Claudia—try that and see what happens."

Claudia tugged her cuffs out from under her sweater, sat up straighter. "You're not very likable sometimes."

"Alas," Hazel said with a shrug. "'Tis true."

Rebekah passed the front window, head down and shading her eyes against the reflection off the snow, which was painful even inside, where Claudia turned on her stool to watch her. She stood. She generally hated standing. The Cronies glanced at her, as they always did, went back to discussing a certain NASCAR driver, whom they had concluded was too pretty to be trusted.

Her hips and knees had begun to stiffen from the basketball game, but she wouldn't limp in front of the men. She repeated to herself the words she'd used since the sixth grade: The ground is made of glass, and I'm just gliding along. She pulled her feet forward rather than lifting them, a slight adjustment that prevented her from rocking back and forth. By the time she reached the door, the stiffness was receding. "I'll step outside and make sure her car starts," Claudia said to Hazel's back, as if the car not starting were something that worried them all.

This is how it is, Rebekah thought: Your life is like a pool and you are small inside it. The walls are so high and far away you don't know them to be walls, but if you could reach them, you couldn't climb them. And all that you know fills up the pool, there are your people and your things, all the conversations you've had, your souvenirs, the whole of your history, and not once, not one time does it occur to you that everything is held there by a thin membrane over a hole. How often does it happen, to how many people, that whatever is covering the drain slips, and everything swirls away and vanishes? It happens in natural disasters or vast crimes. She would have thought those were the only times. But it had happened to her, and was continuing to happen, minute by minute. She lost her mother when she was eighteen, and that death had carried with it the hint of Death; Rebekah had seen, standing next to Ruth's casket during the day of calling hours, and at the funeral the next, that there was a chasm she'd walked beside but never noticed before, and everything, eventually, falls in it. But when she left the Mission, she lost things she hadn't even known she'd miss. She'd gone from having seven aunts and uncles and thirty cousins to being shunned—not one had spoken to her in five years. The sweet old women of the church, the men with their breath mints and pocket combs, the singing and potluck dinners and weddings and baptisms: gone. The Faith that had been a body slung over her bones: gone. Little wonder, looking back, that she had stayed in her father's house and held fast even to his silence and reproach, because this, she thought, this ringing in her head that overwhelmed her ability to plan or save herself, was the sound of the last things disappearing.

The parking lot was so bright Rebekah had to close her eyes against it, and even then she felt the tears clinging to her eyelashes and freezing there. A gust of wind knifed under her coat as she dug in her pockets for her keys. She had missed them before today, of course, all those relatives and friends; she had missed them every day for five years. Some days it was her aunt Betty, Vernon's older sister, who was quiet and smelled like lavender powder. Rebekah wouldn't have guessed there was much there, but time had opened Rebekah's memories of her aunt like a book, and in it she saw moments of perfect sweetness and safety. Aunt Betty had let Rebekah spend the night anytime she wanted, and she'd taught her to sew, to make a Scripture Cake. She could make flowers out of construction paper, and a Christmas tree from the Sears catalog. Rebekah could no longer remember Aunt Betty's voice, as if all their time and all of Betty's kindness had been played out in silence. She missed her cousin Davy, of course, because it's a rare boy who will let the whole world laugh at him.

Today, right now, it was five of her girl cousins she missed: Magdalene, Susannah, Elizabeth, Etta, and Virginia. They had been born within three years of one another, Magdalene and Susannah to Vernon's sister, Margaret; Elizabeth and Etta were sisters of Davy, children of Vernon's brother, Everett; and Virginia was Aunt Betty's only daughter. Rebekah had been the youngest of the girls, the smallest, the most treasured. They had been as close as sisters, and shared sisters' joy and derision. Someone was always getting pinched. Someone else got too much cake or her mother had made her too fancy a nightgown.

Rebekah sprayed a little rubbing alcohol on her door lock, from a bottle in her pocket. Her key slipped in and turned. Once in the car and out of the wind, she tipped her head back against the seat, felt herself collapse inside her coat. She was too tired to start the car, she had to pee, she needed to eat before she got sick.

One night when they were all staying at Magdalene and Susannah's, Elizabeth, who was braver than the others, told them that she had accomplished her mission. She had gone to the public library in Hopwood under the pretense of a project for the church school, and while there, she'd read and photocopied everything she could find on the movie version of *Gone With the Wind.* How had they become obsessed with that one film? Who first mentioned it, and how did it catch on? Elizabeth had the photocopied microfiche pages of magazines and newspapers rolled up and tucked behind her dollhouse in the closet. They'd stretched out on the floor, passing the pages back and forth by flashlight, listening for Aunt Margaret's step on the stairs, any sign that they were being too quiet, and would be caught. Because they never knew what sort of sin they were committing until it was too late, until the fathers had gathered with their verdicts and the girls had to guess how to take it. Looking at a picture in a magazine of a movie star in a dress was obviously not the same sin as watching a movie, which none of them had done or could imagine doing. But looking at a secular magazine was a sin in itself, and admiring women who wore makeup was quite a bad sin, and lying about one's business at the library, where their parents didn't like them going anyway, was dangerous. And now here they were, on the floor in the closet when they should have been either in bed or doing something wholesome. They were looking at a secular magazine about a movie, and there was Vivien Leigh in her makeup and gussied-up hair and shocking ribbed bodices, and there was Clark Gable, whose name they now knew.

"You should have seen the real picture, her eyes was the prettiest blue I've ever seen, and black black hair and red lips," Elizabeth said, tracing Scarlett's face with her fingernail.

"Could we read the book?" Rebekah asked. "What color was this dress?"

"Green, I think, green velvet. I can't believe you can't see the colors—they were so bright it seemed like they'd come right through this ink."

"What happens in this movie?" Magdalene looked through the pages for some sort of story line. "Do you know what happens?"

Elizabeth shook her head. "It's in the War Between the States, and it's something about Scarlett's dresses, and a staircase. There's a big house, and a fire. This is Rhett Butler, and I don't know if he's bad or good. They go to Atlanta, Georgia, and somebody has a baby and somebody else's baby dies. Then there's a potato. Oh, and slaves."

"Is there such a real thing as slaves?" Rebekah asked, not really expecting an answer.

"I wonder what Uncle Vernon would say, he heard you ask that question. Wasn't the Hebrew peoples slaved in Egypt? Didn't Moses lead them to the Promised Land?" Elizabeth hit Rebekah on the upper arm, hard.

"I know all that," Rebekah said, "but I mean for real."

The pages stopped turning. Virginia looked right at Rebekah, "What do you mean?"

"I only meant—"

"Because remember how you said last week at the school prayer meeting that either there was dinosaurs in the Garden of Eden or else God left them skeletons in the dirt as *a practical joke*?"

Rebekah stared at the carpet, her eyes and cheeks flaming. She had made this mistake so many times recently she'd lost count, sometimes only in her mind, but plenty of times out loud. She was embarrassed, and also afraid she was about to start laughing, because she could see a little wrinkled-up man with white hair roaming around the earth, burying dinosaur bones and laughing into his cupped hands, saying, "This'll *really* confuse them."

Etta, who had the greatest authority because she was the most pious, finally spoke. "It seems that Satan is working in you, Rebekah Anne."

Rebekah crossed her arms on the floor and let her head fall on top of them. Her shoulders began to shake, and when they heard her crying, her cousins folded up the pictures of Scarlett and Rhett and knelt on the floor around her.

"Don't cry, Bekah," Susannah said, patting her shoulder. "We'll hold you up in prayer right now, won't we," she said to the other girls, who agreed. "We'll drive these thoughts out of you and leave you cleansed."

Rebekah held out her hand as if asking them to stop, and what her cousins saw was her humility, her knowledge that she was broken and unworthy of God's love. They persisted, and began to pray in unison, a murmuring of similar voices, pleas they'd learned in infancy. (Lord we ask that You heal our sister Rebekah please ease her sinning heart she is small and weak Lord and the powers at work in her are strong.) Rebekah let her tears fall on the carpet. She was racked with laughter. She hiccupped, arched her back to take the pressure off her aching stomach muscles, let the laughter out in a gasp. She was seeing herself as a snow globe; everything between her shoulders and her hips was rounded glass. Inside was a long table in a flame-lit room, and an array of coins and iron tools. Sitting on a little stool at the table was Satan, the goat-footed elf, hammering out broken toys and muttering to himself. He was just a small thing, sly and old, and he was *sick* of working in Rebekah, he wanted to go *home* and have a chicken pot pie.

In the car, Rebekah's head dropped toward her shoulder, and then she was lying down on her side. She was dreaming of Magdalene's closet, the feeling of the carpet against her elbows. She was with her cousins in the dollhouse, sitting on the perfect furniture and holding a tiny teacup. "I'm pregnant," she was telling them, "and I need your help, I don't know how to do this." They stared at her, unspeaking. Rebekah looked down into her glass belly, where now there was a baby sleeping in a crib, its face turned from her. "See?" she said, pointing at her stomach. "It's in there, just like I thought. But I don't know what it *means.*"

She woke and looked around. She was still in the car, which was bright and warm; no, the car wasn't warm—she was under a heavy quilt, the

one that hung over the quilt rack in #32. It was a Wedding Ring, red and white, Amish. Every stitch was perfect, and it was signed *Frances Massey Odom, on the Occasion of her Marriage to Wilder Odom, June 15, 1914.* Rebekah felt as she had as a child, when her mother gave her paregoric for toothaches or sore throats and tucked her into bed, and the sheets and blankets, even her skin felt like heavy soft fabric, like she was wrapped in hot, dark velvet.

There was no way up. She could open her eyes briefly, but they closed again. She drifted out onto the hot, sleek sea, floating. The girl cousins were gone and Rebekah was alone on the sidewalk in front of her house, in some long-ago autumn. In truth it was the season of the believers, and Rebekah still was one, so she could stand there, under the maple tree. There was a clan and she belonged in it, and when the fold was gathered she would go.

We believe that the ways of God are hidden, she was saying, that He hideth our souls in the cleft of the rock. We believe in deliverance and salvation, the Holy Spirit, Baptism, prophecy, the gifts and fruits of the slain. We believe in the Blood of the Lamb. She lost track of what they believed, but it began with God creating the earth in six days, and by that they meant six o'clock, seven o'clock, and so on. And God, Jehovah, Yahweh, God of Thunder and the Mountains, was the One True God Who presided directly and immediately over All. If the wind blew a leaf across the sidewalk, God had made the leaf and God had sent the wind, and the pattern by which the leaf moved was known, preordained by God. And they believed that God had left a wrench in the works that required a Son to be formed not out of clay and breath as Adam had been, but by the act of impregnating a virgin, a young girl, and sending her to marry a widower, and that baby was the Messiah. Far away in Bethlehem. What was prophesied in the Old Testament was made Flesh in the new, a perfect, unbroken line from Adam, Abraham, Moses, and David to Jesus the Nazarene. The Hebrews said that the Messiah would come, and He would be of a certain lineage, and all of that came true. And there were the Gospels, which were books but because they had been dictated by God were also living things and not objects like a clay pot or a sink but a living thing that was in fact more alive than the life of Rebekah herself. The Living Gospels told the story of Jesus but they also contained Jesus and

when they were spoken or when they were read or when the Bible was just lying around on the table still they were alive, not by meat but by Spirit. And this Jesus, the Word, was crucified by the Jews, by the Sanhedrin, and for this and many other reasons they had ceased to be the Chosen People. Rebekah, the girl on the sidewalk, didn't know Jewish people actually still existed; she thought they only lived in first-century Palestine, as dusty and unlikely as anyone walking down an ancient Middle Eastern road. And then it all happened so exactly as the Bible said, that He rose again and appeared unto the five thousand and preached His message. But His message was not the Prophecy. The Prophecy began with Paul. It started with women not talking in church, and women not wearing pants or jewelry or being allowed to cut their hair, and husbands as the head of the household and the family as the body of the church. No one wore wedding rings but men could wear watches and men could cut their hair and shave. And men received the gifts of the Spirit and maintained the offices of the ministry, they were slain by the Spirit and spoke in tongues, one man receiving and another man interpreting the message. The same sounds were repeated quite often in the Spirit, it seemed to Rebekah, who watched the leaves tumbling and circling in front of her. The men said: *lahobaytaylayseeweedwahdumsaylay.* Spoken with the tongue fluttering. But no matter what the first man said, the interpretation was always the same: Lord, You are telling us that some here tonight have not accepted Your power, grace, and majesty, have not seen the wonder of Your works and the glory of Your face, do not know the peace that comes Lord from just inviting You into our hearts. And those who have not accepted You are afraid Lord and they should be afraid because we are living in the Last Days and You want to tell us that these are the Last Days, Your signs and wonders are everywhere apparent and You are telling us to come to You, to open our hearts to You and to sign our name on the Holy Register before the One arrives Who will usher in the monstrous Last Days and leave behind the fallen sinning remnants of this world, while we the saved and purchased flesh for Your flesh will ascend directly into Heaven and will watch from above as a thousand years of toil, pestilence and death rule this earth, we are Your bride Lord and wait for You. We wait for You.

Rebekah remembered the days of her childhood and teenage years

as if they were one long day; she remembered sitting in the pew in the gingham dresses Ruth made for her, her cotton slips, her hair brushed up high over her forehead and sprayed with Aqua Net, then held back in a headband, pastel to match her dress. She sat in the hard pews with her cousins, and they knew better than to swing their feet or whisper, but they sometimes wrote notes or drew pictures on the mimeographed church bulletin. They sometimes got so bored they let their heads fall from side to side as if to distant music. She wore white socks and black patent leather shoes. Her cousins dressed the same. From a distance they all looked alike, except for Rebekah's red hair. At the front of the church Pastor Lowell would be preaching the Second Coming, Revelation, the End Times. He would say that the ark of the covenant was buried beneath the Dome of the Rock, sacred to both Jews and Muslims, and the only way for Christians, the rightful owners of the ark, to get to it would be to start the final War, in which the Jews and the Muslims would kill one another over the site. Our job as Christians, what the blessed Savior is calling us to do, he would say, is to start the War, and the only way to do it is to penetrate the deepest reaches of government and the military, if not by election or enlistment, then by conversion and by force. Christ is waiting! he would yell, and the men in the church, stone-faced and heavy-jawed, would flare their nostrils and whisper Amen, while the women moaned, rocked back and forth. How painful it had been for Ruth, Rebekah knew, to have Him so close, to feel Him just on the other side of . . . what? What divided them from their heart's desire? Only these events, this reality, which was acting as a shield. The time had come, Pastor Lowell would shout, for the Horsemen of the Apocalypse, the Rapture, the rule of the Antichrist; until the first switch was thrown, the Prophecy of the Bible could not be fulfilled. The pastor would grow flushed, he'd perspire, and the tempo would rise until the organist had joined in, and the congregation would be slain, and in the end there would be a laying on of hands and an altar call and all manner of people on the floor, and through it all Rebekah and her cousins sat in the hard pews, bored and restless and sometimes swinging a foot. She didn't hear what they were saying; she hadn't heard it. And then five years ago, out of the blue, she heard it.

She sat up in the car, weak as if a fever had broken. The worst of the snow glare was gone, and in fact the day was diminishing. There were so many problems to solve at once, each of them acute: She had to go to the bathroom immediately. She was going to throw up. The quilt was tangled up around her legs and over the steering wheel and the gearshift, and it was worth a thousand dollars and she was about to throw up on it. The car was cold, and her hair was damp with sweat. As soon as she opened the car door, the wind plowed in and put things in order; she slid out, folded the quilt. Seeing her shoes on the parking lot made her think she'd been dreaming, but whatever it had been was gone.

After the store closed Rebekah had dinner at Richard's and then did something she'd never done before—she drove to the mall alone.

It was mayhem there, just what she should have expected. There was no place to park, and when finally, after circling the parking lot for fifteen minutes, she found a spot the farthest possible distance from a door, she should have given up and left. She couldn't accept such defeat. The air in the parking lot was so cold and there was in the air a sort of chemical aftertaste; her eyes watered and she felt sick before she'd ever gotten inside.

She entered at the JCPenney end and couldn't believe the crowds. She fought her way inside, unwinding her scarf, unbuttoning her coat as she walked. There was no reason for her to be where she was, she realized; the mall was just someplace warm she could pass the time before dealing with the question of where she would sleep.

The lighting was aggressive, and everyone looked older than they were, and defeated. She passed an athletic shoe store so bright she had to look away, and a candy store stocked with dozens of different kinds of brightly colored jawbreakers and jelly beans. She strolled into a crowded record store but didn't recognize anything advertised, so she backed out after a few seconds. There were movies she could sit through but she didn't want to, and there were restaurants she could while away the evening in, but she was both exhausted and restless and no option felt right. She needed to be carrying something to nibble on—she'd realized she couldn't let herself get hungry at all—and something to drink, so she stopped at a kiosk that sold soft pretzels and lemonade and bought one of each. The girls working behind the counter were interchangeable with a hundred other such girls she'd seen in the mall; their hair was processed, streaked, and perfectly straight; their eyebrows were plucked in two nearly invisible arches, and they talked with a strange nasal accent it took some moments to realize was in imitation of black girls.

While Rebekah was being waited on at one window, a girl very like the girls behind the counter was ordering two lemonades at another. They were all friends, it seemed, because they were asking her about her love life, or about a date she'd recently had. Rebekah glanced at the girl beside her, but no—it was impossible to differentiate her from the others. She was very thin, and her blue jeans were so low Rebekah could see her sad hip bones. She was wearing a tight white shirt that stopped at her waist and a short coat made of rabbit fur. Rebekah caught a glimpse of a ring in the girl's tiny belly button. In another time she most certainly would have been pegged as a prostitute; here she looked like any other high school senior.

"I'm in looooove," the girl said, leaning over the counter toward her friends.

"Oooh, she's in love," one of them answered.

Another said to Rebekah, "That'll be two sixty-eight," in her faux ghetto accent.

"Girl, you always say that." It came out, *Girrr, you alway say dat.*

"Yeah, I mean it this time."

Rebekah smiled at the girl in love, at her tiny pants and at the exposed stripe of stomach, so foolish in this weather, then took her lemonade and her pretzel to the park benches that formed a square around a plastic tree. Sitting with her back to the kiosk, Rebekah sipped at her drink, watched people shuffle by her, miserable with packages, dragging their screaming children. She wished she had a book but was also glad she didn't have to endure another *To the Lighthouse,* or something even more painful. It was fine just to sit.

The skinny girl in love passed her, walking toward the other end of the mall, hand in hand with her beau, who was now drinking the second lemonade. They were holding hands and swinging them back and forth between them. It took Rebekah a minute to realize what she was seeing—the dark curly hair, the blue down-filled coat, Peter's hiking boots. She stood, dropping the bag with her pretzel in it. There was Peter, walking without shame through the mall, hand in hand with a child prostitute who most assuredly was Mandy. Rebekah saw stars, she had to put her own cold hand on her forehead to keep from shouting at them. When she'd left his cabin this morning, Peter had said nothing about seeing her again before he left on his coffeehouse tour, just after Christmas. He'd made her breakfast, treated her kindly, as he would any friend with whom he had such a history. He'd not mentioned the pregnancy again, had not again suggested he wanted to be there with her or for her.

She watched them until they were out of sight, then reached down and picked up her trash. Hazel would surely be home by now.

The door opened and Hazel stood there, a little out of breath and dressed in a red Mickey Mouse–as–Santa sweatshirt covered with cat hair. She said, "Rebekah, didn't I just see you? Come in, what are you doing abroad in such cold weather?" She gestured to the book-strewn, bleak living room, where Merlin, Thackeray, Mao, and Sprocket all waited to descend on Rebekah like a rumbling fur blanket.

"Hazel, I need . . ." Rebekah began, slipping out of her coat, unwinding her scarf, "I need to talk to you and to ask you a favor."

"Okay. Sit."

Rebekah chose the couch, and Hazel sat in the armchair next to the small table where she kept her knitting, her Diet Faygo, and the *TV Guide.*

"I've had a falling-out with Daddy," Rebekah began.

"*What?* With that sweet, reasonable man?"

"Stop it. And I need some place to stay, just temporarily."

Hazel bit her lip, stared down at her lap.

"Hazel?" Rebekah leaned forward, rested her hand on Hazel's knee. "What's the matter?"

"Nothing, nothing," Hazel said, shaking her head as if to clear it. "It's just . . . this isn't the right place for you. That's all."

Rebekah felt a wave of heat start in her stomach and work its way up her throat, ending finally with her face and ears. "Why not?"

Hazel looked at Rebekah with an odd directness, unusual because Rebekah had come to recognize Hazel only by the distance between what she held out in offering, and what she held back. "Do you know that our lives don't exist, really—or, that's not exactly right, we exist but only as a story and we are the ones who tell it? I used to have a friend, this was a long time ago, who would ask me, 'So do children decide they're going to die in a house fire? Do babies *tell a story* in which their parents beat them to death?' And the answer is no, of course not, telling the story of your life requires will, and openness, and very often Nature overwhelms our narrative with a narrative of her own."

"What does that have to do with me staying with you?" Rebekah swallowed back tears, tried to sound as if they were having a normal conversation.

"I don't think"—Hazel reached over and took Rebekah's hands—"I don't think your story is best told by doing that. I know I interfere too much, and I dominate the tales around me, but"—she waved away the charge—"that's just how it is, it shouldn't have been given to me to see quite so clearly if I was expected to be passive."

She had offended Hazel in some way, Rebekah concluded; she had mortally angered her father, and her boyfriend and his parents considered her both a colossal mistake and a fool. Rebekah could say nothing. There, lined up before her, were the strata of legitimacy from which she was permanently excluded. For twenty-three years as a member of the Prophetic Mission, she had been exiled from the wider population of her peers; having left the church, she belonged nowhere. And now she was to be a mother without property, stability, or a mate. She couldn't think fast enough to understand it, how she had become the person an entire church despised, a father would renounce, and no parent would want her son to marry. Hazel didn't want her to spend even a night in her home.

"Can I just use your bathroom, then, before I go?" Rebekah asked, the words so tight in her throat she sounded twelve years old.

Hazel nodded, and Rebekah turned and walked through Hazel's bedroom into her large, well-lit bathroom. She looked in the mirror, shocked to see the bright contrasts of her hair, her eyes, her blushing cheeks and ears. Everything in the room was generic: cream-colored wallpaper patterned with dark green strips, a matching border with maroon flowers and dark green stems. The shower curtain matched the wallpaper, the rugs matched the shower curtain, and the small plastic trash can matched the rugs, all of it inexpensive and purchased as a set. Then Rebekah saw them, between the toilet and the wall, two litter boxes side by side, and a slotted spoon used to clean them. She saw them and the persistent, sharp smell hit her at the same time, and before she'd even felt herself move, she had the toilet lid up and was sicker than she'd been since childhood, the upending, turned-inside-out, unstoppable force of vomiting that was similar to the anger she'd felt at Peter's parents' house.

It was over in less than a minute. She managed to go to the bathroom and clean up the mess she made; she splashed water on her face, straightened her sweater, and walked back out to the living room.

Hazel was already standing, and she held her arms out to Rebekah in a gesture she'd never made before. Rebekah allowed Hazel to hold her, more for Hazel than herself, and said, "You're right, I can't stay here."

"You should go to Claudia's," Hazel said, patting Rebekah's back, and as soon as she said it, Rebekah knew it was true.

The baby had gone to bed like a normal little person for the second night in a row. Claudia was grateful, but she would have stayed up with him all night happily, would have been peed on by him and cleaned up after his mighty vomiting, so happy was she to see him emerge safely from Caroline Hunnicutt's. His day there had worked out well; Caroline lived in the part of the retirement home still designated 'independent living,' so she had an apartment and plenty of privacy. But she also had nurses just a bell away—she and Hazel paid dearly for their attention—and once they'd gotten wind of the baby, Caroline had a steady stream of visitors vying for a chance to take care of him. Hazel couldn't have chosen a better place than an assisted living facility, given the abundance of nurses who were flat tired of old people and their problems.

He wouldn't sleep long, two or three hours, before needing a bottle, which made Claudia wonder (with fresh horror every time) what his nights had been like at Cobb Creek, where he had spent them, and how much he had been ignored. She had just closed the Irving novel and was staring out the window at a scattering of stars when she heard a car pull in the driveway. Without a second's hesitation, she rolled off the bed, pulled the .38 out from under the mattress, and slipped out into the hallway, turning off lights as she passed them.

She took the stairs two at a time, landing on the edges where they were less likely to complain. The ache in her back, in her legs and hips, was completely gone. Her heart had sped up in a pleasant enough way, and she wasn't thinking much of anything at all, just picturing the doors, the locked front door, the locked kitchen door, were there any windows they could get through, how much time did she have?

Claudia couldn't see the car through the narrow window at the bottom of the stairs, so she crept down silently, expecting the men to swarm up and surround the house, like a fat SWAT team. Maybe they'd fallen asleep waiting for someone to lead them.

A car door opened, closed. Claudia turned and pointed the gun at the front door. She'd expected to be overwhelmed by the moment, but the weapon actually felt small in her hands, natural. At first it had seemed she was thinking quite clearly, and then not at all, and in a split second she realized she was clearly *not thinking,* and that wasn't like her. She lowered the weapon and looked through one of the three panes of glass at the top of the door. There was Rebekah's car right in front of the house, and rising up from the porch, Rebekah's small white hand about to knock on the window. Claudia threw open the door, turned on the porch light and the overhead light in the living room at once. Rebekah stood with her hand in the air, her green eyes wide, her serviceable navy peacoat unbuttoned.

"Rebekah, my goodness"—Claudia waved her in with the gun— "come in, come in, it's freezing out there."

Rebekah stepped inside, glancing at the gun, and then at Claudia in her old man's pajamas and chenille sweater, and it seemed to Claudia that something passed through Rebekah's body, starting at the top of her head and traveling down to her stomach. Rebekah threw back her head and began to laugh. She periodically tried to say something, she would point at the gun or at the pajama pants and say, "I'm sorry—" and then she'd double over, sometimes actually snorting and once issuing a sound that was surely a guffaw. She made her way over to the couch and lay down, opening her coat and wiping her eyes with her scarf, and Claudia followed, sitting in Ludie's rocking chair.

"I can explain about this gun, Rebekah," Claudia said.

"Oh please don't," Rebekah said, pulling her knees up to her chest. She stopped laughing a moment, then began again, saying, "Oh my God," waving her hand in the general direction of Claudia.

Things might have gone on like this all night, except that the baby woke up with a wail, and Rebekah stopped. She sat up and looked at Claudia, who rose and headed for the stairs.

"Claudia, is there a . . . are you baby-sitting?"

"No. No, not really."

The baby, when Claudia reached him, was on his back, his blanket thrown aside, his arms and legs pinwheeling in fury. In repose he was a bit elfin, but angry he looked like a furious little Secretary of Defense. Claudia leaned over the crib, rested her hand on the top of his head, just to feel it. He stopped crying, but began gnawing on his fist. His diaper had soaked through, so she moved him to the changing table, removed the diaper along with his nightgown.

"Claudia?" Rebekah said from the bedroom doorway.

"Oh, Rebekah—help me, would you? His sheet's wet, there are dry ones in that laundry basket. I think we're using the wrong-size diaper."

Behind her Rebekah was silent a moment. Claudia heard her step in, slip off her coat, drop it on the bed. "Whose baby is this?" she asked, lowering the crib rail.

"He's mine. I guess."

Rebekah nodded. "You're not sure?"

"I'm not sure yet. He's mine for now, anyway." Claudia studied the baby, who studied her in return, sucking his thumb. Sometimes he took a deep, shuddery breath, as if he weren't quite done crying. By the time Claudia had him in clean pajamas, the crib was ready.

"Can I hold him?"

Claudia handed the baby to Rebekah; he grabbed her hair and

tried to eat it. She handled him so competently—the way Ludie had been with babies—that Claudia felt like a lumberjack. "Are you, have you known a lot of babies?"

Rebekah tucked her hair into the collar of her sweater. "Oh, lots. Our church was filled with babies, and I worked"—she thought— "twelve? thirteen years in the nursery. What's this fella's name?"

"He doesn't have one."

"I see. He probably needs to have one soon, then, and he should eat again before he goes down for the night," Rebekah said.

"Should I—"

"Why don't you—"

"I'll go—"

"Great. I'll stay here with him."

By the time Claudia got back upstairs, Rebekah was lying on the bed with the baby, letting her hair fall on his forehead, tickling it down his face. He wasn't just laughing, he was making an odd sound—a sharp intake of air, and then an "Ooooo" as he expelled it.

"Guess who's back, Mr. Buttons?" Rebekah said to the baby, kissing his nose. He made a sound in his throat like a baby raccoon.

Claudia handed Rebekah the warm bottle.

"No, you feed him," Rebekah said. "I'll just watch."

She hadn't been self-conscious with him yet, really—there hadn't been time—but now Claudia felt as if she might actually hurt him. She picked him up, settled him on her lap.

"Here, raise him up some, cradle him against you." Rebekah guided Claudia's arms into position and tucked the baby into them. "Remember, babies like to drink a bottle as if they're nursing, it's the comfort they crave as much as the milk. He's heavier this way, so why don't we put these pillows under your arm, there, like that? See?"

"Yes. I get it, thank you."

"I'm actually here to ask you a huge favor," Rebekah said, looking at the baby. "I wonder if you'd mind if I stayed here for a little while."

"Stay here? Really?" Claudia asked, nearly dropping the bottle. "There are *four*—I'm not kidding—four empty bedrooms in this house. Just choose. You can choose two if you want. Millie's bathroom, well, it *was* Millie's bathroom, hasn't been used since she got married, although my mom and I long ago chipped away the crusts of perfume and hair spray and I don't know what all, so it's actually quite nice in there now. And you know I've got, well, my mom had this amazing kitchen, in the summer you can sit at the table and see the garden and her pawpaw tree, and also the little English gardening shed my dad built for her, all three things."

Rebekah lay down on her side, tucked her coat under her head. She smiled sleepily at Claudia, at the baby, said, "I remember pawpaws. Nobody has those anymore."

Rebekah didn't choose Millie's room with its own bathroom, but Claudia's old room under the eaves. She couldn't have said why, really. There was something about the sloping walls, the gray wallpaper, the plain white coverlet on the bed that made her feel less homesick. On the low bookcase next to the bed were Claudia's favorite books from high school, her Jack Londons, the Hardy Boys, all of Nancy Drew. There was a series of books by Albert Payson Terhune, who wrote the Lad and Lassie books. Here was *The Bronze Bow,* and *The Witch of Blackbird Pond*. Rebekah ran her finger over the spines, imagining a childhood with these books. She had learned to read with Bible stories, and then the Bible, and had finally graduated to what these days was called 'Christian fiction,' or as Hazel referred to it, 'by Oxymorons, for Oxymorons.'

She wanted to study the rest of the room, but her body was closing down in a way she couldn't get used to; she had no say in the matter. Claudia had made her a peanut butter sandwich and a bowl of soup, and Rebekah had eaten and eaten, had two glasses of milk, and only stopped because she was too tired to swallow. While Rebekah washed the dishes, Claudia carried all her things in, carefully setting the odds and ends in a line in the foyer so Rebekah could put them where she wanted in the morning.

Rebekah's own pillow was on the bed. She pulled back the quilt, the old, soft sheets, which were freezing, even through her nightgown. Rebekah had the sensation the bed was moving; when she opened her eyes it stopped. Just before she fell asleep, she realized again that she was pregnant, and that it was something she could, from this moment on, begin to dwell upon. She rested one hand on her abdomen, and was stunned to feel, in the place her stomach had always dipped between her hip bones, a solid, hard thing, like the edge of a cantaloupe. It was in there. It wasn't leaving, not for a long time. And somewhere, deep in that darkness, a heart was beating as fast as a hummingbird's, right below her own heart, which wasn't broken, wasn't breaking. It was just beating.

Part Two

For as soon as I heard the sound of your
greeting, the child in my womb leaped for joy.

—LUKE 1:43–45

Chapter 5

"I USED TO BE a believer, I was. Some time ago."

Amos nodded. "Used to be. But you're back in church."

"Right, I—"

"Not that it means anything, necessarily. Being in church. There are as many reasons for showing up as there are people in the pews. Or as many reasons for not attending, as the case may be."

Had she been a believer? She had attended the Jonah Christian Church with her parents right up until her mother's death, a rural church with an unobtrusive theology and little in the way of graven images. The pews made predictable protests each time the parishioners sat down or stood to sing. The stained-glass windows along the south wall were just two colors—milky white and tangerine in alternating panes—so the light in Claudia's memory was dusty and gold. The pews, the worn brown carpet, the broken-backed hymnals, the light. She could still see her parents' hands gripping the pews in front of them as they rose to pray, the skin becoming marked with age, the fingers knobbed and angled. Sunday upon Sunday morning passing and gone.

Amos cleared his throat but said nothing more.

From Nativity to Crucifixion, Christianity was a club into which Claudia had been born; she hadn't needed to apply or beg entry. Ludie told her, *This is how it is, this is who we are,* and it became true, and Claudia had been safe there, all things considered. Even after she had grown past the point of acceptability everywhere else, even when, at eleven, she was taller than all the women in the congregation, no one stared or turned her away. But none of those things were the same as faith.

"I don't know what it means, to be a believer," Claudia said.

"No?"

Had there been a moment of suspension in her life when all that was actual, tangible, had fallen away and she had seen something in the remaining darkness? And what would one see in that instant anyway? What had it felt like to believe in Santa Claus or an imaginary friend? Claudia tapped her foot on the floor of Amos's office, tried to remember not Christmas morning itself, but the feeling of belief. It had been . . . it had felt as if a wide array of needs was about to be met all at once, this desire, that emptiness, all swept away by wrapped packages and plates of cookies. And when the belief was gone, what was left—what seemed to be left for most adults—was the unending labor of re-creating the myth.

"What happened was . . . it was a couple years before my mom died, and we were in church during the Easter season, I don't remember the exact Sunday. I wasn't listening to the minister—Bill, we called him Pastor B.—I was making a grocery list or something."

"You'd stopped listening to him."

"Years before. I'm not sure I ever listened to him, actually. He just said the same things over and over, year after year, I'm sure the same things I could have heard in any mainstream Protestant church anywhere in the country. Over and over."

"John 3:16."

"Exactly. But on that Sunday I tuned in just as he was saying it's impossible to deny the historical proof of the Resurrection and what it means for humankind. Those were his words."

Amos tilted his head, pushed his glasses up. "What . . . historical proof?"

"Right? I approached him after the service, something I never did ordinarily, and asked him what he meant and he said, 'Why, the evidence in the Bible, my dear.'"

Claudia and Amos were silent for a moment.

"That's too bad," Amos said.

"Which part? That there is no historical proof, still?"

"It would have been nice."

She hadn't felt, in the instant Pastor B. revealed his argument, a crashing disbelief, no temple falling, nothing grandiose or tragic. It was more as if she'd been standing uncomfortably in one room and she took a step sideways and was now standing uncomfortably in another. In the first room she nominally belonged to a group—the congregation of the Jonah Christian Church—and to a larger world, and to a history. Then she didn't belong anymore. The hardest part was Ludie, how to continue living with Ludie and not let her know. Her mother's faith was simple, innocent; if told that the stories in the Bible were true and there was proof, and the proof was the Bible itself, Ludie nodded, stood, sang "Blessed Assurance" in her flat contralto. Then she went home and baked a meat loaf.

"There are lots of ways to talk about, to think about the Resurrection," Amos said, "and all kinds of ways around the damage of our childhood religion."

"I know. I didn't mean to suggest that you're *all*"—Claudia made a gesture meant to encompass the whole of the clergy—"so circular."

"I just wonder"—Amos picked up a pencil, put it down—"if there was some other reason, other reasons you might have left the Jonah Christian Church."

"Like what?"

"I don't know. You tell me."

High on the wall behind Amos's head the black hands of a clock ticked forward; Claudia heard herself breathing in time with it. There had been other reasons, he was right.

"Last full day of work before Christmas," Claudia said, standing, "and a Saturday besides. I should get over there."

Amos stood, too, offered Claudia his hand.

"Thanks for talking to me," she said.

"My pleasure. Come back anytime."

The sofa, circa 1880, was one of the best pieces Claudia had ever seen pass through the Emporium. The burled walnut was as smooth as glass. Some of the grain looked like caramel being poured hot from a pan. A pew construction with fifteen walnut slats so strong they might have been steel, with a rare double-lyre pattern in the back. Even the fitted cushion was beautiful, a heavy red and gold brocade with two match-ing bolsters tied with red ribbon, like rare candies.

Claudia didn't know the man who delivered it; he was in a white step van that advertised nothing—no antique dealer or service. He was middle-aged and silent, wearing a gray wool coat and matching driv-ing cap, obviously not a local. The only question Claudia dared ask him was if the sofa was French. He replied, without looking at her, that it was purchased in a French market but was Swedish in origin.

They carried it all the way back to the Parlor, where its elegance was jarring. The man left without another word. Claudia stood look-ing at the available space, but there was no part of the Parlor that wasn't of a piece. What happened in that room was a Saturday after-noon in Queens or Baltimore, a family gathered together to listen to news of the war on the radio, sons too close in age wrestling on the threadbare Oriental. This was not a room that held a double-lyre sofa.

Behind Claudia someone whistled; she turned to see Rebekah walking up the aisle.

"It's something, isn't it?"

"Would you even dare *sit* on that?" Rebekah asked, running her hand over one of the arms.

"It was made for sitting, I guess."

"How do we know? Maybe it was meant to be just . . . spectated."

"Like a museum piece? Maybe." Claudia straightened the bolster at her end.

"Well, since its original purpose is forever beyond us, let's go ahead and sit on it."

"You first."

Rebekah sat. "Hmmm," she said, leaning back. "Surprisingly com-fortable." She patted the cushion beside her. "Give it a try."

Claudia eased herself down beside Rebekah, but the wooden slats made no sound at all. "My God, the Swedes."

"Where did it come from?"

"A French flea market."

"No, where did Hazel get it?"

"She said she found someone on the Internet who needed to divest himself of a few fine articles. . . ."

"In a hurry."

"Exactly." Claudia leaned back. Rebekah was right—it was comfortable. "In a hurry. You wouldn't so much want to sit on it to watch a Jimmy Stewart movie, though, would you."

"Not so much."

"Okay, let me ask you this." Claudia turned to Rebekah, continuing a game they'd been playing for the five days they'd lived together. Claudia would pick up an item Rebekah had brought from Vernon's house and ask her the story of it; Rebekah in turn would ask Claudia to find something in her house that was similar. Narrativewise. Claudia had seen Ruth's flour sifter and shown Rebekah Ludie's. She had seen a chipped bud vase from the only time Vernon had given Rebekah flowers, when she had scarlet fever, and she'd held some of the clothes Rebekah had made over the years, creations so strange, the combinations of fabrics so . . . *unlikely,* that at first Claudia hadn't known what to say. Three days later she couldn't stop thinking about them.

"Tell me about that wooden box you keep on the dresser."

"Tom Smith and Sons?"

"Yep."

"Well." Rebekah took a breath, squinted into the distance. "Terry, the first boy who ever courted me. He was a foster son of one of the elders, he was sixteen, I was fifteen. He began his courtship by leaving a dead king snake on my chair at the church school."

"Very romantic."

"I failed to see the beauty. I ignored him for a year, and in that time he"—Rebekah held up her fingers to count off—"broke his arm trying to impress me by jumping a fence on one of Davy's horses. He wrecked his father's car, driving and talking to me through the window as I walked down the street. *And* he was hit in the thigh by a round of BB's while singing 'O Holy Night' under my window. Pellets fired by my daddy."

"He was serious."

"Apparently so. He joined the army, and the night before he left he made one last gesture: he gave me an antique box that had belonged to his real mother, and in it he placed part of a poem and an incisor from a black bear. And just like that, I opened it, I saw what was inside it, and I fell in love with him. Looking back the snake seemed . . . you know, magnificent, something like that. I kept reliving the moment with the horse, seeing his front feet clear the fence, one of his back legs get caught. And in my vision of it I did *not* laugh so hard Davy's mother had to make me lie down on the bed. I was a very different sort of girl."

Two customers walked by, a young couple in matching camouflage jackets. "What happened? In the end."

Rebekah sighed. "I never saw him again. He was sent to Korea and he married a seventeen-year-old local girl. He never came back to Jonah. You can look in the box when we get home."

"What was the poem?" Claudia asked.

"It was by e. e. cummings. I can only remember the first line, 'your homecoming will be my homecoming.'"

"Cummings? You Pentecostals never cease to surprise."

Rebekah sighed again. "Terry. He was a rebel in his way. He found the poem in the library, which is where we got all our contraband." She rubbed her palm over the brocade cushion. "Very nice upholstery."

"It is."

"You"—Rebekah turned and looked at Claudia—"know more about me than anyone ever has."

Claudia blushed, looked at the floor. Rebekah, Claudia knew, loved crisp food and glass doorknobs; she disliked wind and open-backed stairs. She was a morning person and enjoyed the winter, she had a beautiful singing voice and her two smallest toes on each foot were webbed. She had, for years as a child, dreamed she was a twin, and that her brother had died by drowning. She even knew her brother's name: Samuel. Claudia knew about the girl cousins, and how for one summer they had all pretended to be married to the Apostles. "Well"—she cleared her throat—"I'm sorry to say you're the only person I've ever really known."

"Really? The only one? What about your sister?"

"Millie?" She might have known Millie briefly, when they were children, but that time was distant and fast fading. "I knew *of* her."

"Your dad? You loved your dad."

Bertram, much on Claudia's mind of late, had been unknowable to women, and probably to other men. What she treasured of her father now was not any communion they had shared, but just the memory of him in his study at night, writing up policies and reports as he listened to high school basketball on the little black radio with gray knobs. "Yes, I did love him."

"Okay—look: you had to know Ludie. Nobody could have known Ludie more than you did."

It was true that she could have recognized Ludie blindfolded, by the smell of her powder, the smell of her *comb,* or by her odd tuneless humming in the garden. She would sing a few words (*while the dew is still on the roses*) and then hum more. There was nothing about her mother Claudia didn't know, nothing she couldn't have predicted, and yet . . . "It's not the same, what I'm talking about with you."

"Do you know"—Rebekah looked at Claudia, eyes wide—"this is the longest we've talked in the past five days without mentioning the baby?"

Just like that, there was the shock, the low, rumbling anxiety. Where was the baby? She had a baby. Mornings Rebekah moved through the kitchen like a waitress, fixing larger breakfasts than Claudia would ever have made on her own. She made cereal for the baby and got him to eat from a spoon, which Claudia still couldn't convince him to do, and she handed him Cheerios one at a time in his bouncy chair. (He dropped them, mostly.) Every day she put him in his high chair, and he slid sideways and stayed there, like a tired old man on a train, until Rebekah said, "Enough of that, Buttons," and lifted him out, resting him on her hip as she cleared the table.

Where had she put the baby? He was with Caroline. Claudia should wear a little bracelet printed with HE IS WITH CAROLINE. Was someone going to come for him, was she going to have to kill someone, would she go to jail? "My stomach just somersaulted."

"You should try to get over that," Rebekah said, tipping her head back against the rolled wood. "I'm tired."

"Okay, the baby. The baby reminds me that I got an afternoon appointment for him and for you with Dr. Gil; this is the last day he's going to be open until after New Year's, so you have to go."

Rebekah raised her head. "When did you say?"

"This afternoon."

"I'd rather not. And also we shouldn't leave Hazel here alone, it's going to be busy."

"Do you realize how long we've been sitting here, leaving Hazel alone? And we get to make it up to her this evening; she needs us to pick up some things downtown."

"Still. I'd rather not."

Gil Parker's office was still in the one-story brick building he'd moved into in the early 1970s, when it had seemed a good idea to abandon everything attractive for anything else. The waiting room hadn't changed at all: there was a metal sculpture on the wall of three men (the three Greek physicians whose names Claudia could never remember); fake-wood paneling; and a corner devoted to faded plastic toys and copies of *Highlights* and *The Bible in Pictures*.

"I don't like doctors," Rebekah said as Claudia held the door open for her.

"Have you ever even seen a doctor?" Claudia whispered.

"There was a doctor in the church, thank you, who took care of our ailments," Rebekah whispered back.

"Where did he get his medical degree, in a vision?"

"You're mean. I don't like *secular* doctors."

"You might have to make adjustments," Claudia said. The sleeping baby, dressed in a fat, fuzzy snowsuit, weighed, it seemed, two hundred pounds in his car seat basket. A hard plastic runner ran from the doors to the front desk to keep the snow and salt off the carpet. Claudia stepped on it and felt again a tilt, a seesawing dissonance in her chest: the smell of the building, the runner, the metal sculpture. How could she come to terms with it and keep coming to terms with it, that she would lose all she loved and everything familiar to her, if now and again she stumbled into a room unchanged? As if it were possible to keep the room unchanged?

Gil's wife, Judy, was still behind the reception desk, as she'd been all of Claudia's life. Now that Claudia was past forty, Judy had finally ceased calling her A Long Cool Drinka Water. "My goodness, you brought the whole battalion."

"Judy, this is Rebekah, and this is . . ." On the drive over, she and Rebekah had gone through a list of their favorite names, but hadn't settled on one. "Oliver. Oliver James. James was my dad's middle name." Claudia's face turned scarlet. She reached up and tugged at the neck of her sweater.

"Hello, Rebekah. Claudia, take that baby's hood down and unzip his suit before he overheats. And go sit down while I tell Gil you're here." Judy typed something into the computer and began printing out a form. "I saw Millie the other day at the Home Depot, she looks like a dadgummed Biafran. Whose baby is this, now? He belong to you, Rebekah?"

"No, he's . . ." Claudia reached out for the diaper bag on Rebekah's shoulder. Tucked into a zippered pocket in the front were the official papers, signed by the baby's thirty-eight-year-old maternal grand-mother from her semi-permanent residence at the women's prison in Indianapolis, transferring guardianship from herself to Claudia Mod-jeski. Signed by Hazel's attorney, Harold Piper, and a nearly senile judge who frequently lost to Harold at the back-room poker game at the Top Cigar and Lunch. Official papers. "He's mine, actually."

Judy stood, peered over the counter at Oliver's sleeping face. "Con-gratulations, then." She looked back up at Claudia and raised a single eyebrow.

"I'll bring in the birth certificate as soon as I get my copy."

"That's fine. Oliver, you say?"

Claudia nodded, then watched in fascination as Judy wrote *Oliver Modjeski* on a piece of stiff paper and slipped it into the colored tab of a manila folder. Just like that.

"Did he"—Judy looked back at the computer screen—"come from a foreign country?"

Rebekah let out a small laugh and headed to the waiting room.

"You could say that," Claudia answered.

Judy took two clipboards off the wall beside her, handed them to Claudia. "Fill one out for the baby, have your friend fill out the other."

"I told you, he was my father's best friend," Claudia whispered, even though there wasn't another soul in the waiting room. As she talked she rocked Oliver's car seat with her foot.

"I know, but how old does that make him?"

"Let's see, he was a couple years younger than my dad, and he would have been, this year—Gil's probably seventy-seven."

"Oh Lord."

"Rebekah, you have to see a doctor. The baby has to be vaccinated. Gil is where we have to go."

"We were never vaccinated," Rebekah said quietly, looking away.

"What did you say?"

"Nothing." Rebekah smoothed out her blue jeans with the flat of her hand, as Ludie would have a tablecloth.

"You did so say something."

"I only said that we were never vaccinated, the church doesn't believe in it."

"Well, that's just—" Claudia stopped herself. "My guess is that you'll have to have some shots, too, then. I don't know how it works."

Rebekah sighed. "I'm uncomfortable."

"I understand that."

"And also, I've never had, what do you call it. An internal exam."

"So it will be a day of firsts. Where's the diaper bag?"

"It's under my seat. I really don't want to do this."

Claudia rocked the car seat, pushed up the sleeves of her sweater.

"We could just get back in the car and you could take me home," Rebekah said. "I'll take vitamins, whatever you want." She shifted in her seat. "I'm uncomfortable."

"I know you are."

"Between my hip bones, really low, I keep having this sharp, muscular pain. It's like a stitch in my side, only spread all the way from one side of my abdomen to the other."

"You should tell Gil."

"Or you could take me home and I could have a nap."

Claudia tapped her pen on Oliver's intake form. She didn't know much about him, but she'd filled in her address and phone number. The date. Her insurance information—she'd need to add him to her policy.

"Also I'm worried about leaving Hazel alone for the afternoon. It'll be busy."

"Can I ask you something? Why does Hazel hate your dad so much?"

"Whew." Rebekah took a deep breath, blew it out. "They met once, when I had a cold—let's see—about three years ago. Hazel stopped by with some medicine and soup. I didn't really want to let her in the house, because I was afraid he'd come downstairs."

"Why? What would he have done?"

"Oh nothing, really, it's just that he's not very skilled at, um, disguising his contempt for people outside the church."

"Nice."

"Well, he has his standards."

"So what happened?"

"Hazel insisted on coming in; it was sort of odd. She's not really the type. I brought her into the parlor, because I couldn't very well say no, she was trying to take care of me. And Daddy came downstairs just like I was afraid he would. They shook hands and I could see him taking her in, her hair, her clothes and jewelry. She was wearing that ring she has that's the head of a goat."

"She's a Capricorn."

"Right. That one. He was sort of chilly at first and then just before she left—she was only there a couple minutes—he said, 'I understand you dabble in astrology and the dark arts now, Miss Hunnicutt.' My heart near stopped beating."

Claudia gave a little whistle through her teeth.

"Hazel said, 'You've heard that, have you?' smiling at him as if they were friends, or as if he were a complete fool, it was hard to tell. Daddy said, 'I know plenty about you.' And then Hazel looked as if she got a little bigger, you know how she does?"

Claudia nodded.

"And she said, 'I know a fair piece about you, too, Mr. Shook.' She wasn't smiling anymore, and the air in the room felt—it reminded me of the scene in that movie, what was that movie again?"

"I'll need more to go on than that."

"It doesn't matter. So then Daddy, who's never been sassed by a woman a day in his life, says, "I'm of a mind to come to your house sometime in the night and *burn* all your books about astrology and devil worship. That's what I might do.' Hazel laughed, said, 'If you ever step foot on my property, or touch anything I own, I'll be forced to shoot you through the heart like the common criminal you are.'"

Claudia shook her head. "But what did *that* mean?"

"I don't know. Daddy turned bright red, his hands gathered up into fists, but he turned and marched straight upstairs and slammed his door and Hazel laughed all the way to the car."

"I can picture that."

Gil's nurse, Patti, stepped out into the waiting room and called Oliver's name. Claudia stood and picked up Oliver's seat, said to Rebekah, "Fill out your form while I'm back there."

Rebekah picked it up and sighed, took a peanut butter cracker out of her pocket.

Gil tipped his head back so he could see through his reading glasses. "You don't know his birth date?"

"Not—" Claudia shook her head. "I haven't gotten his birth certificate yet. I had to put in a request at the courthouse and they're going to send it to me. So no."

"Well." Gil made a notation in Oliver's chart. "I would put him at five, six months. Either way his weight is low, and his head circumference is in the thirtieth percentile, so our first priority will be nutrition."

Claudia held Oliver on her lap, her hands wrapped around his chest. His rib cage felt tiny, breakable, as if she were holding a rabbit. Gil consulted a small book, put it back in his pocket. He breathed noisily. He seemed healthy, hale, but Claudia knew he'd cut his patient load to almost nothing, and that he'd wanted to retire for more than a decade. It wouldn't be long before he was gone, taking Judy with him, and then Claudia would have to face moving on to Gil's young replacement, someone who knew nothing of her and had never even met Ludie or Bertram. She lowered her face, smelled the top of Oliver's head.

"Claude?"

"I'm sorry—I'm listening."

"I'm sending home this higher-calorie formula. We'll start his vaccinations today and you'll call me if he has a reaction—a rash, a fever above a hundred, vomiting, or diarrhea. Call me at home. Now, you've brought a friend"—he shuffled through some folders—"Rebekah?"

"Yes. She's pregnant, she's not married, she chose the absolute worst insurance plan from Hazel's HMO. Her deductible is more than most people would pay for a car. Is there . . . could you just charge me for her co-pay and whatever her insurance doesn't cover? She doesn't need to know."

Gil removed his glasses, sat back in his rolling chair. He slipped the glasses into the pocket of his coat, let his hands lie loosely in his lap. The baby squirmed, arched his back, still unhappy from being awakened from his nap. Claudia turned him around and raised him to her shoulder as Gil sat passively studying her. He seemed to be considering the situation, and in no hurry to make a pronouncement; she had forgotten this element of his personality. He took a deep breath and said, "I don't want to go through a pregnancy and deliver a baby, Claudia."

"I understand."

"I am elderly and tired and I want to tend my garden."

"I know."

He rubbed his eyes, watched her bounce the grizzling Oliver. "I could recommend a wonderful ob/gyn clinic right here in Jonah."

Claudia nodded. She wasn't the pregnant one, she wasn't the person who should care, but as soon as she pictured Rebekah walking into a big, cold clinic, cycling through eight different doctors who would never know her, she felt sick.

"We could compromise," Gil said, his shoulders still drooping, his eyes watery. "If Rebekah will agree to see my new partner in the clinic, Dr. Mehta, when I'm not here, and if she'll agree that he might be in charge of her delivery if I'm too tired to get up, I'll take her on as a new patient. But." He raised a finger in the air. "After the baby's born you have to promise me that you and Oliver and Rebekah will move over to Dr. Mehta and let me die in peace."

Dr. Mehta. The light that contained Claudia's history flickered, dimmed. But she agreed.

Is your mother living or dead?

Rebekah looked at the question twice, trying to imagine how her pregnancy was dependent on its answer.

Dead. Cancer.

Is your father living or dead?

She thought, Well, what is the truth? She checked Dead and felt a momentary burst of guilt and joy.

What is the date of your last menstrual period?

Rebekah fanned herself, tried to remember, but all the months, all the occasions ran together as one. She wrote, *Mid-October?*

Are you sexually active?

I was. *Yes.*

Have you been diagnosed with or are you at risk for any of the following: herpes, gonorrhea, syphilis, chlamydia, AIDS?

She imagined Peter in the living room of the cabin, his arched back and laddered chest, how everything had been so new. She left the question blank.

A nurse, who was nice—she was round and powdery-smelling, and her hair was cut in a strange sort of bob that made her look daring—led Rebekah to a lab at the back of the clinic and directed her to step up on a scale. "You weigh one fourteen," she said as Rebekah stepped down. "Perfect for your height."

"Thank you," Rebekah answered, grateful to have gotten something right.

The paper gown opened in the front and Rebekah clutched it closed against her chest. She was naked underneath it, sitting on a strip of paper, a second paper exam sheet over her lap, and crying. None of this was *right,* she couldn't make it right in her mind that she would be so dishonored and humiliated. She had been raised to believe in the body as belonging to God, hers connected to the wider body of the Church, and she could even recall once when she fell jumping rope and Ruth had comforted her by saying that Jesus felt it, too, the raw scrape on her knee, and had tears in His eyes for her. But in the wide world and certainly here, in a doctor's office, she was more like a side of beef marked into quarters and about to go under the saw's wheel.

Nurse Patti came in with a blood pressure cuff. "One-ten over sixty." She pulled tissues out of a box, pressed them into Rebekah's hand. "Are you scared he's going to hurt you?"

Rebekah nodded, then shook her head. She couldn't stop crying. "A little, but really I just don't think I should have to be here this way, and I'm cold, and I have a sense that the whole experience, the whole pregnancy, is going to be miserable like this and I won't have any say, I'll just have to endure it. I shouldn't have to sit here naked like this."

The nurse folded the blood pressure cuff and slipped it into her pocket. She sat down in the doctor's chair and rolled toward Rebekah. "*A*, you aren't naked, and *b*, you're sitting there now because you were naked someplace else. And if you ever thought you'd escape with your dignity intact, you missed a lot of facts for a woman your age. You're right about how it's going to get worse, so I'd suggest you talk yourself into some courage here at the beginning."

Rebekah wiped her face, sat up straighter. They weren't the exact words Ruth would have used, but they would do.

"Okay," Rebekah said, taking another tissue. "Okay, I'll do that."

Dr. Gil came into the room and looked at Rebekah's chart. She could see right away that he was kind and well-intentioned, and he couldn't help it that he was tremendously old and that his hands were purple and brown. But all Rebekah could think of was that he was about to remove or move aside her pieces of paper with his very old hands, and so while he was talking to her and asking her questions, showing her diagrams of what he was about to do, she cried quietly and tried not to look at his skin.

"Lie back, dear," Dr. Gil said, and Nurse Patti handed her another tissue. Rebekah lay back, and he said, "Scoot down toward me. Scoot again. One more time," until Rebekah was certain she was going to slide right off the end. Her embarrassment was now so acute, she could scarcely catch her breath. Patti moved over and stood beside her, took Rebekah's hand. Dr. Gil was rolling from the cabinets to the little tray on which there were instruments and gloves, asking her to repeat the first day of her last period, said it was okay she didn't know, wondered how long she had been acquainted with Claudia, wasn't that Oliver a little pistol? Finally, when the dreaded speculum was revealed and the water-soluble jelly had been produced, the clear gloves snapped on, Dr. Gil said, "It might help if you visualize something or some place that makes you feel better, and to stay there in your mind until the exam is over. It makes the time pass faster, and it's good practice for labor and delivery. You don't have to say anything—the place is your secret."

Rebekah nodded, wiped her eyes. The place is your secret. Peter sitting across from her at Richard's Diner on a Sunday morning; Peter on any given Sunday, waking beside her, the still-strange feeling of liberation and well-being she experienced each time she realized she didn't have to go to church. Not going to church in winter, in freezing rain; not going to church when her throat was slightly sore or when she was just tired. Not going. She tried to make one of those her secret place but they vanished before she could really see them. Instead, she remembered a moment from a few months before, when Red had said something cruel about Claudia, something Rebekah didn't at first catch. He hinted that she might actually be a man, and Hazel, who had continued reading throughout the conversation, looked up as if as an afterthought and said, "Well, boys, everyone has a secret. Isn't that right?" All three Cronies shut up, coughed, looked away, and Hazel had gone back to her book as if nothing had happened. Dr. Gil touched Rebekah's skin with the speculum and it was cold; she flinched and he stopped, asked her to try to relax her thighs.

Red had been right that Claudia had a secret, but he'd guessed incorrectly. It happened Rebekah's first morning at Claudia's house, four days ago. Claudia had just stepped out of the shower and Rebekah opened the bathroom door without knocking; it was an accident—she didn't share a bathroom with Vernon and wasn't used to being careful. It was a dark morning and the lights above the mirror were burning. Claudia was standing on one long leg on the bath mat, with the other propped up on the edge of the tub. She was bent over, drying the tops of her toes, when Rebekah walked in, and instead of saying anything, she just straightened up to her full height.

"Are you okay?" Dr. Gil asked. "I'm taking a swab here—you won't really feel it—for some tests."

Claudia's shoulders were as broad as a man's, straight—not sloped like Rebekah's own. Even just standing there holding a towel, not lifting a chair or exerting herself in any way, the muscles in Claudia's arms were dense and defined, slick with water and dark like the cool skin of something just pulled up from the sea. She stood completely naked, the towel at her side, and the Cronies would never have guessed this: her breasts were as high and full as those of a girl half her age. A line of water ran between them, down the plane of a stomach long and flat, contoured. Rebekah's eyes, tracing that surface, seemed to fall for whole minutes, until she reached Claudia's hip bones, their protective curve, and then there was the length of her legs. Her thighs looked as if they'd been carved out of wood, and her knees were pronounced, covered with small scars. Water ran down Claudia's shins, past her calf, toward the feet she'd been trying to dry.

"Okay. I'm just going to palpate your uterus manually now," Dr. Gil said, as if it made sense. He pressed against her abdomen and stared into the distance, measuring something he couldn't see. When he was finished he snapped off his latex gloves and stood beside Rebekah, gently easing aside the paper gown. He ran his fingers over each breast, as if playing the piano, and pressed under her armpits. It had been the look on Claudia's face that most amazed Rebekah, a look she'd never seen Claudia give anyone. What had it been? Not fear or shyness or anger at being interrupted, even though Rebekah guessed that no one had ever seen Claudia completely naked as an adult.

"Yep," Dr. Gil said. "There's a baby in there." He reached for his prescription pad, wrote down the name of a prenatal vitamin, talking as he wrote about folic acid and iron and calcium. He said based on her rough estimate of her last period and the internal exam, he'd put her at ten weeks pregnant, at term on July 23. Rebekah gathered the paper sheet around her, answered his questions: No, she didn't smoke or drink alcohol, didn't like fast food. Yes, she was tired and nauseated, but manageably so. He told her to come back in a month and they'd listen to the baby's heartbeat; he handed her a stack of pamphlets on nutrition, sex during pregnancy, when to call the doctor, and all the while Rebekah was seeing Claudia's expression. Bemusement, that was part of it. Her face seemed to say: *Here it is.* Later she had walked out of the bathroom wearing a white dress shirt, a sweater vest, and a pair of dark brown corduroys, and no one looking at her could have known.

"Congratulations, Rebekah," Gil said, offering her his hand.

She took it, grateful suddenly, even fond of him, "Thank you," she said.

"You should go to T.J. Maxx," Red said. "The wife gets everything there, clothes and dishes, and now she's started bringing home food I've never heard of before."

"Food you've never heard of before?" Slim asked. "And it came from a clothes store? Has she tried stuff from the bait shop? The automotive center?"

Jim Hank gave his wheezy, painful laugh. "What kind of food have you never heard of? Is it Martian? Canadian?"

Red said, "All right, you tell me, then: what's a caper? If your wife brung home a jar of capers, what would you say that is?"

Slim and Jim Hank sat back, considered each other.

"I can't say I know what a caper is," Jim Hank said.

"Never come acrost one myself," Slim said.

Claudia looked through the phone book, writing down the name and address of the now closed secondhand store from which she and Rebekah said they'd go retrieve a few things. "Do you know which part of Elm this is?" Claudia asked. "One twenty-two B? Is that before or after Walnut?"

"The two of you don't interest me much anymore," Hazel said, pulling her necklace, a heavy gold Celtic cross, out of Oliver's mouth. "You were fine for a while, but now I only really love the baby."

"Sam's Club is where you ought to go, Slim," Red said, pointing at his friend with the red tip of his cigarette. "You could get your tires and also twenty-four rolls of toilet paper and a gallon of mayonnaise, all at the same time."

"What—what would I do with a gallon of mayonnaise?" Slim asked, raising his hands in the air as if begging for mercy. "Open a school cafeteria?"

"You'll be all right?" Rebekah asked Hazel, wrapping her scarf around her neck. "He's had a dose of Tylenol, just in case, and there's more in his diaper bag. We probably won't be long."

"I'd like to keep him for the evening, if you don't mind," Hazel answered, lowering Oliver into a playpen they'd brought up from the back. She wound the mobile hanging crookedly above him and it began to chirp out a show tune. "We're taking Mother out for dinner. He cheers her considerably."

Claudia folded the address and phone number of their destination and put it in her back pocket. "She's feeling down?"

Hazel cleared her throat, looked for something under the counter. "Well, Edie has disappeared with Charlie."

Claudia froze. Oliver blew spit bubbles and rocked from his left side to his right.

"It seems he missed a few meetings with his parole officer, failed to pay child support on that thirteen-year-old he's got in Hopwood. Oh, and he borrowed a neighbor's truck in the middle of the night without mentioning it as such."

"Did he return it?" Claudia asked without really knowing why, as it couldn't be considered the issue.

"He traded it to his dealer, who was arrested while driving it. So there's a warrant out on Charlie for, oh, sixty-two different things, plus his dealer will kill him dead every day for the rest of his life if he finds him. There are a few reasons for old Charlie to lay low."

"And Edie went with him?"

"We have deduced. All we know is that he's gone, she's gone." Hazel settled in with her knitting, took a drink of grape Faygo. "This makes our mother sad, for some reason."

"Children," Red said, lighting a cigarette. "It don't matter if they're good or bad, they break your heart every time."

On the drive downtown, Rebekah wanted to ask Claudia what it meant: was it good or bad that Charlie and Edie were gone? Should they be more scared for Oliver, or less? But Claudia wasn't talking. She drove with grim determination, chewing her lip. They drove through older residential areas, once lovely and now given over to student housing; past the Queen Anne that used to be known as the House for Wayward Girls; past the bus station and a hairstylist's called Family Beauty. Claudia turned left on Walnut Street and from there it was one empty building after another, some with the names of the businesses still inscribed on the facades, some stripped completely clean.

The light was fading, and the empty buildings began to resemble tombs. They passed the shell of the magnificent Sterling's Department Store, which Rebekah had been in only once as a child. She could still recall the ornate interior of the elevator, and the elevator operator, a small man with a smashed nose and prominent chin who'd complimented Ruth on her hair and made her blush. The ceiling soared straight up through five floors, and on each floor you could look over a rail to the hypnotic black and white tiles of the entrance. They had gone to find a birthday present for a woman in the church—who was it? Someone slightly grander than the others. Ruth and Rebekah had been so out of place among the scarves and gloves, the silk blouses and crystal, that finally Ruth had said, near tears, "I'll make her something," then refused to ride the elevator a second time. They had gone straight to the Ben Franklin at the edge of town and bought some gingham in an autumn print, and Ruth made the woman an apron with a pumpkin for a pocket. Rebekah tried to imagine what was inside Sterling's now, the abandoned display cases, the fallen plaster, air unmoved for years. She pulled her coat closer, and Claudia said nothing.

"It was amazing the place lasted as long as it did," the man said as he led them inside what remained of Second Chance Furniture and Collectibles. "I'm Myles," he added, shaking first Claudia's hand and then Rebekah's.

"Were you the owner?" Rebekah asked, studying him as if he were an apparition. Myles was tall, black, densely built. He wore a charcoal gray suit and a black overcoat, along with a dark gray fedora and a gold hoop in one earlobe.

"No, no. I own the building, but the store belonged to a young couple who've already left town. You can see they took the wheat and left the chaff."

The storefront was dirty and smelled of stale cigarette smoke; the few pieces of furniture remaining were cheap and worn—bunk bed frames, sofas and recliners that had been cheap when new and now were shiny with grime and age. There was a stack of mattresses leaning against the wall, and a bouquet of halogen floor lamps gathered in the middle of the room, the sort that heat up to three thousand degrees and routinely incinerate whole apartment complexes.

"Whew," Claudia said, walking toward the back.

"What are we here to pick up?" Rebekah asked, trying to imagine Hazel purchasing any of this kindling. "It can't be much; she told us we didn't need the truck."

"No, it's just some boxes, and a trunk I've got set up on a handcart. Even the trunk isn't worth anything; it's pressed paper, like the kind a kid might take to college."

"Wha—what would Hazel want with it?" Rebekah put her hands in her pockets, shivered slightly.

Myles shook his head. "Couldn't tell you. You want me to roll the trunk out? It doesn't weigh much of anything."

"No, we'll do it," Rebekah said, watching Claudia load the last of the boxes in the backseat of the Jeep, parked half a block away. She rolled the handcart most of the way down the sidewalk, where Claudia lifted the trunk as if it were empty.

"Thank you, Myles," Rebekah said, returning the cart to him. "It was nice of you to meet us here at—you know, this hour. And all."

"Nah, my pleasure. I'll be glad to get this place cleaned out. It's on the market, if you know anyone who's interested in buying property in a ghost town."

"Maybe you should hold on to it, turn it into a tourist attraction," Rebekah said, turning as Claudia walked up beside her.

"It was a pleasure meeting you," Myles said, taking Rebekah's hand. He turned to Claudia. "And you, too, sir."

Claudia smiled, said, "Likewise."

1968

It was the year the cat arrived. In the late summer: Hazel had been at the kitchen sink, cleaning up her dinner dishes, complaining (inwardly, as no one else cared) that the slate sink, original to the house, had been designed for midgets. It made no sense to her. The ceilings all soared, and the fixtures were so low Hazel had to bend over to reach the dishes she was washing. And the house had been built when *Lincoln* was president.

"I'm going, and don't think you or Mother neither one will stop me." Edie was sitting at the table, flipping through the novel Hazel had been reading with dinner. Edie wasn't reading it, merely looking for all the scandalous bits.

"Leave my book alone."

Edie read a section, whistled. "Hazey, I didn't know you had it in you."

Hazel turned and threw her wet washcloth at Edie's head. "You're too young to even understand what you're reading. Put it *down.*"

Edie caught the washcloth, tossed it back good-naturedly. "'I am Myra Breckinridge whom no man will ever possess.' It doesn't *sound* sexy." She closed the book, sighed. "I'm going is all I'm saying."

Hazel straightened her back, spoke to the wall in front of her. "I wouldn't stop you. I wouldn't even try to dissuade you. I think it's the perfect place for you, maybe the *only* place for you."

"But not for you. Because you're old. And ruined. You're ruined by living here with Mother and Daddy, living as their slave person, and you can't see the truth when it's right in front of you, you can't see what's beautiful nor true either one."

Hazel turned and looked at her sister, considered an act of violence involving the skillet from which she was trying to wash out the remains of her grilled-cheese sandwich. Edie had one leg tucked up under her voluminous patchwork skirt, and she was twirling a length of blond hair.

Hazel put the skillet down in the sink. "Edie," she said, pulling out a chair and sitting down across from her sister, "you are seventeen years old."

"Nearly eighteen."

"Actually, no. You're seventeen. Go to San Francisco if you wish. Attend this Be-In or Wallow-In or whatever it's called. Take your place among the unwashed. But don't tell me I don't understand the counterculture because I choose to live like an adult."

"Who gets to say what's adult? That's the question you ought to ask yourself."

Hazel rested her head in her hands. "Adults determine what is adult, and nature determines it, Edie. Listen," she said, leaning toward her sister, who only periodically made eye contact with anyone these days, and rarely with Hazel, "have you read the Port Huron Statement? Do you understand what the Marxists are arguing, or what's at stake with the Cuban revolutionaries? Do you in any way, Edie, understand that dressing a certain way and smoking pot until you're blind *is not the point*?"

"I understand that I want to be free and I believe in Love. Isn't that the point?"

"Hello, girls," Caroline said, walking through the door that separated the kitchen from the clinic, studying a patient's chart. "I trust you've eaten."

"Can I fix you something?" Hazel stood, still watching Edie. Maybe it was the nature of their relationship, or perhaps there was actually something unique in her sister, but Little Edna was not transparent. Her stubbornness was so complete it seemed a form of stupidity; her resistance defied reason in the same way certain animals would rather drown or die in a fire than allow themselves to be saved.

"No, thank you, dear, I'll . . . what is that?"

Hazel followed her mother's gaze and saw a cat sitting by the radiator. He looked first at Caroline and then at Hazel with eyes the color of pumpkins. He was young, black, with a white blaze on his chest. A slight underbite revealed his pink lower lip.

Edie had risen from her chair, was leaning over the table. "That's not one of our barn cats."

"How did it get in?" Caroline walked back through the kitchen door, glanced at the outside entrance. "The door to the outside is closed."

Hazel walked toward the cat, careful not to alarm him. He watched her, blinking slowly. He yawned. She knelt in front of him, held her palm flat a foot above his head, as she'd seen Finney do, and the cat sat up on his hind legs like a squirrel, stretching out his long neck until his nose bumped Hazel's hand. Hazel lifted him up, settled him into the crook of her arm, where he curled up, purring. He was thin, long-legged, probably hungry, but his nose was cold and wet and his eyes were clear.

"He came in on his own," Hazel said, rubbing the top of his head with her nose.

"Well, put him back out," Caroline said, looking back at her chart. "Your father doesn't like animals anywhere near the clinic, and certainly not in the house."

"He came in on his own," Hazel said again, not looking at her mother. "If I put him out he'll just come back in."

"Hazel?" Caroline's voice was chilled, with a slight edge of confusion. "I asked you to put the cat outside."

"I heard you," Hazel answered, scratching the underside of the cat's chin, causing him to close his eyes. "But this is my cat, and I'm keeping him."

"I beg your—"

"This is Mercury, this is my cat, and I'm keeping him." Hazel turned and headed toward the servants' staircase. "Edie, open a can of tuna and put it in a bowl for me. Bring some water, too. We'll be in my room."

"My sister *disobeys,*" Hazel heard Edie say behind her. "Far out."

By December 23 of that year, Edie was long gone—swallowed up in the great experiment. First they heard Berkeley, then Haight-Ashbury, and finally word reached them that she'd been spotted on a commune in Vancouver, using the name Karma. Hazel knew it might be Edie in Vancouver, or it might be someone who looked like her, given that *everyone* that year looked like her.

True to his name, Mercury came and went without the permission of anyone, Hazel included. She could close him in her room while she was working, and come up between patients and find him gone. Later he would reappear on the front porch, scratching behind an ear or rubbing a paw over his eyes like a sleepy baby. He had grown, become dense and languid, loved only Hazel. When she walked down the lane to the mailbox, he walked behind her like a dog; when she spoke to him, he appeared to listen. Hazel felt herself becoming foolish, becoming that sort of woman, the one who never leaves home, who is bound forever to her mother and to her mother's secrets. Hazel loved the cat, she understood, too fiercely, he was too much her companion. Nights when he went to bed before her, she could slip in beside him and he would conform to her, and in this way—the warmth, the fit, the drowsy lingering in the mornings—the years with that cat were the closest she ever came to a good marriage. And yet she would have denied him his liberty had there been a way to do so, had he not been so peaceably defiant, a magnanimous animal, a credit to his species. Caroline and Albert said nothing. They had lost one daughter already.

In the beginning, working alone, Caroline had not known how to keep records of her individual patients. She was not by nature a deceitful person, and when Hazel joined her, she had been surprised to find that Caroline had more or less told the truth in the charts of the women she saw after hours, even though most of them used false names. Hazel decided to create a code known only to herself and her mother, and to transcribe her mother's charts into it before burning the originals in the fire ring beside the barn.

Why keep records at all? Caroline had been elusive on the subject, and Hazel suspected that her mother's professionalism was, in this case, a liability of destructive proportions. She had spent hours begging her mother to do away with every trace of her work, but Caroline was firm. Hazel consulted her father's books on the code breakers of World War II to invent the system she would use, and only when it was complete did Caroline admit that she intended to donate the records to an appropriate medical research library, perhaps to Indiana University Bloomington, at the end of her life or at such a time as they might be used to better understand the past.

Caroline took cash from the women if they offered it, but asked for nothing if nothing was offered. The money went into a safety-deposit box registered in Caroline's and Hazel's names jointly, out of the way of the government, the husband, the father. Left alone there, the money grew and grew.

Patient # 47281, Elizabeth J. Smith, 1414 Skylark Drive, Jonah. Birth date: 10/30/48. Height: 5'5", weight: 132. Pulse: 72, blood pressure 112/70. Temperature: 97.8. Patient complains of persistent lower back pain following the moving of heavy furniture week prior. Muscles tender but no visible injury. Suggested alternating hot and cold packs, pain relief ointment. Showed patient exercises to strengthen lower back and prevent repeat occurrence. Phone consultation if necessary, no follow-up appointment made at this time.

Every number, every word—even the vital signs—were a code for something else, and only Hazel and her mother knew what it was. And Finney. But Finney would never tell.

Her parents had gone to the Elks Club Christmas party, an event wherein the men, Hazel imagined, flushed with county power and whiskey sodas, moved in a parade of self-congratulation, stuffed into their best suits like meat in casing. The women stayed at the tables, smoking, making daring pronouncements about the men, their marriages, their disappointing children, all of which would be regretted (or forgotten) the following day. And at eleven o'clock something happened—or maybe it was eleven minutes past eleven—there was an Elk call, a silent thrill in the blood, that caused all the men to stand and chant their Elk oath. This was the part that baffled Hazel: the swearing of an oath to anything, to anyone, when the truth or reliability of such an act could not be trusted even at the moment of its issuance. There was no such thing as 'Elk,' and thus no possible reason to swear fealty to it. The men were not pledging themselves to one another, as the slightest downturn in fortune or small-town propriety could cause a man to be exiled without hesitation. Albert's reasons for standing at the sacred hour and repeating the primitive mantra were clear—he would do anything, he had already done everything a man could do, to proclaim the real estate of Hopwood County his fiefdom.

It was Caroline whom Hazel least understood; Caroline, who was, in her way, the most subversive person Hazel had ever met, and who was, on a steady basis, subverting the moral code her husband seemed to embody. Caroline never shirked what her community declared her duty, and every year she attended the Elks Club Christmas party in her elegant black dress. She locked the holiday pearls around her throat, touched the upsweep of her hair for reassurance, and went gliding out the door into the dark and cold anticipation of the soul's nativity, lying, lying, lying.

Or maybe she wasn't lying. Maybe Caroline's honesty, which seemed incontrovertible in all other situations, was at the heart of this story, too, and Hazel could not read it. The Elks Club, the Cardinal Golf and Country Club, the awful Cannadays in their new, sprawling ranch house: this grim world of commerce and conformity and the Jaycees' Prayer Breakfast—maybe Caroline was up to something genuine in those places, and was not worthy of Hazel's latent contempt. Or so Hazel hoped.

Hazel lay on the bed in the husk of Edie's nursery, idly watching the only television in the house. There had been one Christmas special after another: *Mr. Magoo's Christmas Carol,* followed by *Cricket on the Hearth,* and then the new one, *The Little Drummer Boy.* What Hazel needed was either the mindless spectacle of *Shindig* or *Laugh-In,* or *60 Minutes.* She heard a peculiar sound, the sort that might be coming from inside one's own head or might be coming from some distance. She sat up, listened more closely. Nothing. Beside her, Mercury slept curled in a ball, one paw hooked over his cheek, covering his left eye against the television light. The noise came again, and Mercury raised his head. Hazel stood and turned off the television. Something was coming down the lane, but without lights and with no motor. As Hazel slipped on her shoes she heard it: a tinkling, or singing. No— there were no voices.

She turned right in the hallway, took the formal staircase two steps at a time, causing the portraits of the elders to quake. In the vestibule she wrapped her neck in one of Finney's scarves, pulled on her hat and coat, stepped out onto the porch.

A team of black horses was headed toward her in the moonlight, their necks heavy with bells. They were pulling, with artful ease, a black sleigh over yesterday's snow. Hazel closed the door and walked down the steps as the driver of the sleigh pulled back on the reins and the horses stopped. Jim Hank leapt to the ground, wearing his peacoat and a top hat, and Finney jumped out behind him, bedecked in a moth-eaten prom dress, her father's ratty old fur, and a hunter's cap with earflaps.

"Merry Christmas!" Jim Hank said, bowing beside the horses, whose muscles flickered beneath their skin.

Hazel covered her mouth, felt a sheen of tears grow cold on her eyes.

"Merry Christmas, Miss Hazey May!" Finney clapped her mittened hands together. "We did this for you, for Christmas!"

They were like children, and Hazel, too, felt childish, unhinged. The night was starlit and beautiful after yesterday's tree-creaking snowfall, and she was breathing in the air, the scent of the horses. Her eyes traveled over the feminine lines of the sleigh, the light glinting off the bells and the formal tack. "How did you do this?" She reached out and rested a hand against the neck of the nearest horse, who raised and lowered his head.

"I rented it from Trockler's Mortuary!" Jim Hank seemed barely able to stay in his skin. He ran his hands over the sleigh, patted a horse on the rump. "I rented it for you. Finney and me were thinking"— Jim looked at Hazel with the shyness she thought he'd overcome years earlier—"that maybe we could ride down the Old Road and around the meadows, to say Happy Chris—Happy Holidays to you, you know."

Hazel held out her hand and let Jim Hank take it, and for the rest of her life she would remember snapshots of that night, the edges of herself against the air, the horses so graceful they might have been mechanical. But she would remember nothing as clearly as that moment, her hand in Jim Hank's worn leather glove, the way he helped her into the carriage and Finney slipped in the other side, the way the three of them were warm and happy, pressed against one another. The horse's hooves measured out their music against the ground, and Hazel and the two great loves of her life were moving away from the house, past the corncrib, the flatbed wagon, turning past the fire ring and the barn where the ghost of her cruel pony thrashed against his stall. They were at the top of the curve and Hazel could see all the way to the bottom, the horizon where the line of virgin timber rose up and up against the sky. She followed the birch tree to the top without thinking, and saw the owl there, not leaping off the branch like a man who had convinced himself he could fly—just sitting there. Then Jim Hank cracked the reins and they were heading down the road and toward the open meadow, and beside her Finney began to sing.

Chapter 6

THE BIRTH OF A SAVIOR. Every year Claudia turned it over in her head—that strange, compelling story—but could never get far. Things weren't what they appeared to be in the tale, of that much she was certain. An illegitimate son, born to a young girl in a barn. The way the stars aligned, as they do for all of us, and the three foreign men who arrived, bringing both treasure and embalming fluid. Death in life—that seemed to be what the story foretold far more than the promise of resurrection. Maybe there was some occult wisdom there, a snakelike understory that wound its way into our consciousness and wouldn't leave. Not the miracle of birth; not the bastard son that rises to change the world; not those things. It was the fascist king, the tyranny of the tax collector, the exile, the baby born to die. Because the rest of it? The singing of hosannas in honor of the Messiah's arrival? In what way—and this was something Claudia had wondered for a long time now—in what way was humanity changed by the murder of a Nazarene carpenter? In what way were we saved? As far as she could tell, life and suffering and desire continued precisely as they had always been. All the crucifixions on all the hills of the world could not alter the most elemental facts.

But this was Christmas in America, if one was adult and had a family. Claudia sighed as she pulled out of the parking lot of the mall. She recalled, wistfully, the last years with Ludie, and then alone, when the holiday's only claim on her was a brief dinner with Millie's family on Christmas Day. Millie and Larry would chew on some grievance; the children would be silent and sullen and vanish from the table as soon as possible. And then Claudia would be allowed to go home, where there was no tree, no Santa knickknacks, no inflatable snowmen.

Now she had a backseat filled with gifts and twinkle lights. She had dug through the basement until she found the old tree stand and the boxes of ornaments that dated all the way back to the earliest days of her parents' marriage. This morning she and Rebekah sat on the couch and took them out of their tissue wrappings, studying each one. Claudia hadn't remembered them as so delicate and interesting, but to Rebekah they were priceless; not merely as relics of Claudia's history but as the symbol of something Rebekah couldn't name, something she had sorely missed. Vernon had forbidden it all, of course, the whole secular mess, and Claudia was beginning to understand why.

She sighed again, thought of the money spent, the time in the mall. She drove past the Used World, where the lights were out and what was to be sold this season was sold and gone.

Even if the image had been created by an advertising firm—no matter what kind of lie it might have been—when Claudia drove home in the crepuscular light that Saturday in December from last-minute Christmas shopping and saw her house lit up like a ship on the dark sea, and knew that Rebekah and Oliver were in there, warming every room, Rebekah likely gliding around the kitchen floor in her socks to Glenn Miller, Claudia felt a joy all the more powerful because it was tenuous. There were no words spoken between them, no promises, not even a glance at a calendar. Rebekah had asked to stay for a while, until she got her bearings, and while they talked and talked, late at night and first thing in the morning and all the way to work and all the way home, neither of them ventured a word about the future. At work Claudia watched Rebekah open and close suitcases, polish mirrors, disappear for an hour or more in the back. There was nothing in her movements Claudia could read. And when, daily, Claudia was called to help empty a truck or rearrange a booth, she listened for Rebekah's laughter, which she could hear above all other sounds, as if it occupied its own airwaves, a frequency that bore Rebekah's name.

Any day now she could be gone, and with her would go not just this daily happiness, but the baby. That other baby, the strange creature, was more real to Claudia, she knew, than it was to Rebekah; for Rebekah it was also a condition. But Claudia imagined a person, just a person like Oliver, who was in there doing what people do while they bide their time—swallowing, breathing, thinking. Soon it would begin to suck its thumb. Claudia blinked, pulled into her driveway, got out of the car and looked at the house. The tree tied to the top of the Jeep was dusted with snow; she left it there.

She stepped into a cloud of heat and steam, a fire in the fireplace, music from the kitchen (Sinatra this time). She took off her coat, her scarf, and hung them in the closet, hoping to be quiet enough to catch Rebekah unaware at whatever she was doing. Oliver's Gymini was open on the living room floor, his toys scattered around it. His swing sat silent; the blanket and stuffed rabbit in the playpen looked as if he'd recently gnawed on them. Claudia walked through the living room, past the stairs, past the door to Bertram's study, the guest bathroom, an unused bedroom, and into the hot kitchen.

Rebekah was at the stove, stirring a dark soup and singing "It Was a Very Good Year." She was wearing a forest-green dress with short sleeves and little gold buttons; Claudia had never seen it before. Rebekah's hair, thicker and longer than two weeks ago, was gathered up in a big barrette; she was barefoot. Oliver wore only a diaper and a pair of blue socks, riding on Rebekah's hip and clutching a wooden spoon he periodically waved in the air like a sword. Claudia wanted to say something casual but found herself tongue-tied by the scene—this woman in her kitchen, dress straining against her new curves, the creamy smoothness of the baby's back, his shoulder blades moving like vestigial wings.

"Oh, look who's here, Mancub," Rebekah said, breaking the spell Claudia found herself under. "Take him, will you? I think he's wet, and also put something on his chin, some Vaseline or something—he's drooling so much I'm afraid his face will get chapped."

Rebekah cocked her hip so the baby was raised up. Claudia reached out for Oliver, who reached out for her, and as her hands closed around his naked chest, Claudia noticed Rebekah's own chest, which shone in the heat. A blue vein bisected the smooth, white expanse where her right breast just began to swell.

"What are you making?"

"Beef stew with carrots and potatoes. A spinach salad. There's bread in the oven."

"It smells wonderful." Claudia turned to head upstairs and change Oliver.

"Your sister is coming over."

Claudia stopped, turned back toward Rebekah. Oliver tapped her on the head with the spoon. "I'm sorry—what?"

"Your sister is coming over."

She hadn't told Millie a thing about Oliver, about anything, really, had even spoken to her sister a couple times on the phone while hold-ing the baby and failed to mention him. That she was now caught had nothing to do with Rebekah and was entirely Rebekah's fault.

"I don't understand how this happened."

"She called. On the phone, the way people do. I answered and invited her over for dinner."

Claudia took a deep breath, closed her eyes. Oliver hit her on the head again. "Did she ask who you were?"

Rebekah checked the bread, slipped the pan out of the oven and onto a cooling rack. "No, when I answered the phone, she said, 'This must be Rebekah.'"

"Oh Lord."

"Oh Lord is right. How long did you think you could keep this all a secret, Claudia, in a town like Jonah? For all I know, there's been an announcement in the *newspaper*: TALL WOMAN, PREGNANT HOLINESS GIRL, STRAY BABY. Hopwood County is probably on fire with talk."

Claudia walked back into the kitchen and sat down at the table, overcome with dread. "How long did I think I could keep it a secret, a good question. I don't know. Longer than this." She pulled at the collar of her sweater, realizing how hot it was in the room.

"My feelings would be hurt, too, if I was your sister."

Claudia shook her head. "You have no idea. You don't know her." She wanted to point out how lovely everything was, how lovely the whole rest of the evening would have been if just she and Rebekah and Oliver were going to be there together for dinner. They would have eaten, given the baby a bath, decorated the tree still tied to the top of the Jeep. After the baby was in bed, they would have gone into the living room with tea or hot chocolate, reading and talking until they were sleepy. She wanted to ask Rebekah to consider that loveliness, and then to remember it when Millie was there. The distance between how nice it would have been and how ugly it would actually be was another measure of how long Claudia hoped to keep her life a secret.

"Well, it's too late to do anything about it now. She'll be here in twenty minutes."

Claudia sighed, stood, hoisted up Oliver, who was rubbing his gums together and making a *yang yang yang* sound.

"Also I wouldn't have pegged you for such a coward," Rebekah said, rinsing the spinach in a colander. Even with her back turned, Claudia could tell Rebekah didn't mean it, that she was squinting up her eyes as if she'd said something mildly funny, but Claudia didn't answer. A coward. Rebekah didn't know the half of it. Claudia climbed the stairs feeling the whole of her weight on her knees and ankles, and with each step she recited in her mind things she was afraid of. Green eyes, green dress, red hair, blue vein.

Claudia changed Oliver's diaper, dressed him in a blue one-piece decorated with red trains, brushed his hair with the baby brush until he looked like something in an Easter basket. She put him in his crib and turned on his mobile, then lay down on her bed. Downstairs, Rebekah set the table, filled water glasses. Claudia heard her move into the living room and begin picking up the baby's things. Rebekah was tired, Claudia knew, and washing the spinach had probably made her queasy, as she was having a hard week where anything with leaves was concerned. Who would have guessed that textures could make a woman vomit? Just two days ago Claudia had offered Rebekah a set of flannel sheets, and Rebekah had touched them, then run for the bathroom.

I'm punishing her, Claudia thought, but couldn't get up and stop doing so, surprised to find herself furious. Her house had been invaded, her life had been entirely co-opted by a woman who might not even stay, Claudia didn't know from day to day which might be the last, and now she was going to have to endure a wasted evening with a sister who had never been a sister to her and had never come to dinner before.

Oliver's mobile played "Rock-a-Bye Baby," tinkling out the tune that had grown so familiar it seemed to represent all babies, babyhood, the universe of infancy in a few measures. Claudia sat up and looked through the bars of Oliver's crib; she could just see him, above the bumper pad, grasping his own feet and rocking from side to side. He was blowing spit bubbles, his new favorite game. Oh, she was mad at Rebekah all right, and she didn't want Millie in her house, there was all of that, but probably she should also face the other thing that had sent her up the steps and onto the bed, the thing that had lifted a dark wing and brushed her memory. She had been recalling, out of the blue and persistently, moments in the sixth and seventh grades; whole days of junior high school; an encounter with her gym teacher; an overweight girl named Trisha who'd once cornered Claudia in the restroom. Something in the seventh grade. Something in junior high. The gym teacher, who had pushed Claudia at basketball until Claudia couldn't play anymore. Trisha. Amos had asked her: Was there any other reason she had ceased to be a believer, had one day found herself *apart* from the simply faithful of the Jonah Christian Church? She awakened to a handful of images tossed, confetti-like, onto the day's screen, and she considered them as she drove into work and took care of Oliver and in all ways acted as if nothing were amiss. A ragged, sick feeling had entered her body, and she knew it wasn't the flu or her diminishing hormones. It was something she would have denied existed if anyone had asked her six months earlier—it was nothing but the truth barreling toward her faster than she could move out of the way. This happened in books and movies, any time a certain level of drama was called for, but it didn't really happen in Jonah, Indiana: a character reads a letter, or is told in the hospital that blood tests have confirmed that her father couldn't be, et cetera, or a man sees the leaves falling one autumn and recognizes that his entire life has been a lie.

Downstairs, Rebekah was opening, then closing, the oven door, and dishes were being moved around. Claudia lay back down, heard again Hazel asking her, two days ago, why she didn't have any close women friends.

"I do, Hazel, obviously."

"Who? Who, then?" Hazel put a sticker on a stack of Mikasa bowls, priced to sell.

"Duh, *you,* for one, and Rebekah, for another."

Hazel nodded. "Who besides us? Who before?"

Claudia thought about it, but couldn't answer. If she couldn't count Ludie, and she assumed Hazel wouldn't let her, it was indeed the case that Claudia had lived her life virtually friendless, tucked into the shadow of her parents and the safe house they'd made for her. She'd lived it in books, and in Ludie's garden, and in the infrequent, unreciprocated gestures toward Millie and her children.

Hazel shook her head, looked down at the dishes. "It's an old wound, I'm guessing, the risk of such relationships."

Claudia had walked away, hadn't denied or confirmed anything. She strode heavier than she meant to back through the breezeway, past the new corner booth that sold nothing but NASCAR collectibles still in plastic, grinding her teeth. Hazel just *said* things, it was a trait of hers Claudia couldn't get used to; Hazel didn't even try to imagine the effect they would have, or whether they were appropriate. Claudia walked all the way to the Parlor, turned around, and walked back.

In the sixth grade there had been a piece of paper . . . what had it said? Claudia had written something on a piece of paper and her teacher, Mrs. Nelson, had found it in her desk. Ludie was called, there were hushed meetings, and the whole incident disappeared. She'd wanted to burn the note, pictured herself burning it, but probably that hadn't happened. Probably Mrs. Nelson had thrown it away. Then in the seventh grade, there it was again: a teacher, a piece of evidence, Ludie's calm hand setting things in order. I was in love with Sarah Jackson, Claudia thought, stopping in front of the glass-eyed rocking horses. I was in love with Sarah Jackson, and I wrote it on a piece of paper and slipped it into my desk. I didn't mean anything by it, I just wanted to record the information for myself so I could see it.

She had been in love with Sarah Jackson in the seventh grade and all through high school, really, that's what Claudia recalled, standing transfixed in the glare of the rocking horses, and what she thought about lying in bed waiting for her sister to arrive. Sarah had been plain and bookish, the smartest girl in the class. She hadn't curried favor with the teachers, didn't care about being popular—she seemed to live privately and inside her head. She wore glasses with lavender frames, and she treated Claudia just the same as she treated everyone else: as if she were invisible. At lunch she sat alone reading Isaac Asimov and Ray Bradbury, and in high school she took up piano. She developed a hunched-over, neurotic walk that Claudia found endearing. Claudia had not pursued Sarah, hadn't given herself away. Some part of her must have realized (she suspected now) that nothing but heartbreak lay down that path; that if she had somehow forged a friendship with her, that's all it would have ever been—a partial life, a not-enough.

And Trisha. She kept her hair cut as short as a marine's, smoked in the parking lot, and walked like a wrestler. She wore black concert T-shirts stretched over her massive frame, and she was always looking for someone to fight. No one understood what she wanted, whether it was to vent her rage, to prove something, or to actually get hurt. There they all were, the faculty and administration, the students of the Midwest. They had no psychological vocabulary, and no experience outside the razor-straight lines of their county, and in every class there was someone like Trisha (someone like Claudia, she now realized), a vexing atypicality: a girl too thin; a boy who, every day, threatened to kill his stepfather. There had been curly-haired Kevin, who wanted to stage Broadway musicals, the girl whose arms were covered with self-inflicted cuts, and to a person the teachers had just tried to get them through the system and out the double doors before they blew up or expressed themselves irrevocably.

Trisha had cornered Claudia in the girls' restroom. Had she pushed her? Claudia remembered how the other girls at the sinks had vanished without a sound, and how she had hit her elbow on the towel dispenser. Trisha was the height of Claudia's stomach, her glasses were smudged—as soon as Claudia started to remember it, she remembered every detail. The T-shirt that day, faded, frayed around the neck, was KISS *Love Gun*. Claudia had never hit anyone; she had, in fact, worked very hard to keep her body separate from all other bodies. She remembered the breathless near-panic as Trisha got closer and closer to her, the sharp heat rising through Trisha's shirt. Trisha was going to hit *her*, or worse.

"I want to ask you a question," Trisha said. She had a grinding voice, already affected by cigarettes. "I *said* I want to ask you a question."

"Well, then"—Claudia cleared her throat—"ask it."

Trisha lowered her head, looked up at Claudia like a bull about to charge. "Will you go to the prom with me?"

What had Claudia answered? She had no idea; she could no longer imagine the horror she must have felt, the black implications of the question. She said . . . whatever it was she said, and Trisha's eyes filled with tears, and then she punched not Claudia but the towel dispenser, breaking two of the knuckles of her right fist. Everyone had fled the restroom, but by the end of the school day the news had spread far and wide, and that night at dinner Millie had tortured her by talking obsessively about the prom, who was going with whom and wearing what, the theme song, the colors, finally saying, "Have you ever thought about going to the prom, Claudia?" In a moment all the more shocking for its rarity, Ludie had picked up a dinner roll and thrown it directly at Millie's face; it had hit her in the forehead with a satisfying, doughy thunk.

Claudia had remembered it all over the past few hours, a thousand separate moments that told her who she was, or who she might have been if she'd paid attention, if she'd been braver. I could have moved away, she thought, imagining a place where it was okay to be both so tall and in love with Sarah Jackson, but of course she couldn't have moved away and there was no such place. She sat up, watched Oliver shake his bunny rattle, pull it furiously into his mouth, chew on it a moment, then shake it again. Her hips and hamstrings had begun to ache; she'd lifted a dresser wrong, or set it down wrong, something.

She stood up slowly and walked toward the crib. Oliver watched her with a look of such concentrated happiness she nearly laughed out loud. He seemed to have forgotten all about her in the ten minutes she'd been out of sight, and now he was re-creating her, building himself a great big trustworthy toy, like a lion hidden in the back of the closet. If she'd moved away she would never have found him. He frowned, kicked his legs and swung his fists while also making a spit bubble—everything required such heroic *effort*. Claudia slid her hands under his head, his bottom, and lifted him up to her chest. He turned and began sucking on her cheek. Rebekah called this kissing but really it was something else, a desperate little remnant that made Claudia's throat tighten with sadness.

She held him, amused him with the black and red jingle-bell worm, and tried to imagine what she might say to Rebekah, or even to Millie. She was what she was and she loved whomever she loved, and none of that was making her so angry. What infuriated her was simply that she had, out of the blue and surely against the wishes of all the Millies everywhere, been given what everyone else expected as a birthright. The world belonged to other people; it belonged to the Death's-heads in their SUVs, to frat boys, to the fat women in the gas stations who stared at Claudia as if she carried a plague. It belonged to evangelicals and morbidly narcissistic politicians. No one had ever said to her—and it pained her to realize that she included Ludie and Bertram in this failure—no one had told her that the brand-new, perfect, everyday world was hers, was Claudia's as much as it was anyone's. No one had ever even hinted that there might come a day when she would open her front door to Sinatra and Rebekah Shook, a blond-haired baby on her hip, bread in the oven, and it would be hers to have and to hold, at least for a little while longer, at least for tonight.

She changed her mind about the train suit, and dressed Oliver in his clown pajamas, adding the little nightcap with the fuzzy ball on the end, and decided that if and when the moment arrived, the moment Millie criticized her or made fun of her, or raised an eyebrow at Rebekah's unmarried, fatherless condition, Claudia would simply lift her up by her cheap clothes and carry her out the door. Claudia wouldn't need to say a word to her sister, she'd just pick her up and deposit her outside, locking the door behind her, and then she'd sit Rebekah down and explain to her that her whole life had been a lie, but it wasn't going to be anymore. That's what she would do.

The doorbell rang and Claudia jumped, scaring Oliver, who puffed out his bottom lip as if he would cry. Claudia bounced him a moment, listening. She heard Rebekah turn down her music, walk from the kitchen down the hallway, through the living room. The front door opened with a vacuum sound from the weather stripping, and there was Millie's pointed voice, right on time. Claudia couldn't hear what they were saying, so she stepped out of her room and stood at the top of the steps. Rebekah laughed; Millie said something. Claudia took a few steps down, then a few more, until finally she was in plain sight.

"People are talking, you know how people talk, I was in the Pizza King with Tracy yesterday and I heard someone say . . ." Millie dropped two shopping bags filled with wrapped gifts, took off her coat and tossed it on the couch. Claudia took the last few steps down, still watching Rebekah.

"And then someone from the PTA Daisy Chain—well, it isn't really a *gossip* Daisy Chain, it's for snow days—called and said she'd heard Claudie was living with a woman *and a baby boy*." Millie glanced at her sister and Oliver, turned back to Rebekah. "I said, '*Please.* Claudia Modjeski will have a baby when I grow wings and take to the—'" Millie looked back at Oliver, taking him in, and shouted, "I have a nephew!" startling everyone. She raised her arms in the air as if declaring a touchdown. "When Sheila Hopkins asked me at the Aldis today was I aware of what was going on in my parents' house, I said, 'I most assuredly am, Sheila Hopkins, are you aware of what goes on in the backseat of your Grand Am?' in a way that put the squash on that conversation. I have a nephew, give me that baby," she said, crying and reaching out for Oliver. "Oh, I'm just a mess, I know it, but you can't imagine what this means to me, you can't imagine how awful it's been for me to think that all I had left was my own stupid husband and those children, Rebekah, you can't imagine what teenagers are like, what it feels like to have to go on every day taking care of and being all nice to people who despise you, who wouldn't give you the time of day if they had enough money and someplace else to live. And then when I found out about you, and about little Oliver here, I waited and waited for Claudia to call and tell me herself, but finally I couldn't wait. What was I saying? Oh, when I heard about you and Oliver I just cried and cried, well I'm crying now, aren't I, I am such a *mess,* because I suddenly realized there was *hope* for me, because even though Mom and Daddy are dead and I can't stand one single person who lives in my house, I still have a family, there's a new family in town, and if anyone will do it right it's Claudia, I'm sure you already know that, Rebekah, but she will do this one hundred percent right because that's how she's always been." Millie wiped her eyes on her sleeve, kissed Oliver's head again and again. "Claudia, it's a good thing you've got your shoes on because I about cleaned out the baby section of Wal-Mart today, you better get out there and start hauling it in. If I guessed wrong on any of the sizes, just keep those things for the next one, Rebekah, come over and sit down and tell me how you feel and when you're due. I had such a terrible labor with Tracy I thought I was going to die, I finally said to the doctor, 'I am dying and you won't admit it, you bitch!' And poor Gil, he just told me to breathe."

Claudia would have gone on standing there, dumbstruck and staring, if Rebekah hadn't given her a nudge toward the front door. As she stepped outside she heard Millie say, "Show me—does it hurt right here? Because that's probably—"

She let down Millie's tailgate and there it all was: a new battery-operated swing. A new bright blue playpen in a box. Bag after bag filled with diapers and formula and bottles and little socks. Claudia took a deep breath, began to shoulder the plunder. She didn't know anything about anything, that's what she was figuring out. Poor, poor Millie. All the poor sisters of the world.

"Mom liked the green glass closer to the top," Millie said, directing Claudia in the hanging of the ornaments. "No—Claude, land's sakes you can reach all the way to the top, could you hang it a little higher, where Mom would have wanted it? Like I was saying"—she turned back to Rebekah, who was rocking Oliver—"I only married Larry because we'd had sex in high school and he convinced me I was ruined. *Ruined* was the word he used. I believed him. I mean, we were this couple, and at Jonah High people get started early on this mating business, as you know it comes from being around farm animals all the time."

Claudia glanced at Rebekah, who raised an eyebrow in reply. Claudia shrugged.

"And Mom and Daddy did not say one single word, not one, to stop me. You'd have thought they'd at least suggest waiting, but no— they pushed me right out the door, glad to have me gone so they could devote all their time to Claudia, who was so much their favorite it wasn't funny. Was not funny. Of course I'm over all that now."

"I wasn't their favorite, Millie. I was just here."

"Oh, remember this one? Rebekah, did you look through this pin-hole here, holding it up to the light? There's a miniature nativity scene in there, this was the one I liked absolutely the best. I should have thought to ask for it years ago, I just love it."

"Take it now," Claudia said, standing next to the tree, waiting for the next order.

"No, no. I won't take it now. If Mom had wanted me to have it she'd have given it to me, wouldn't she. And the other thing is that after I was married, especially in that first year, remember that apartment, Claudie, where Larry and I were living, I think it had been a gas station before? It was terrible, I was always afraid to light a candle for fear the place would explode. Evenings we would sit on that ratty couch and watch an old television that didn't hardly get any channels and we didn't have anything to say to each other, not one single thing. Sometimes I'd get so lonely I'd just show up here during dinner and of course a place would be set for me but no one ever asked, 'Millie, why do you look like this, why are you so miserable?' Because that's not our way, to ask and maybe save someone from a life of utter and complete joylessness, no, we just politely look away and keep our counsel. I would sit at the table and watch Mom and Daddy and Claudia interacting so nicely and I would think if only I could have what Claudia has, if only I'd found a way to get that. Here, Claudia, put this special one close to the front. Remember how Mom would want to take it down when company came to let people look through the little hole."

"Mil, don't you want to go outside and start smoking again?" Claudia asked, placing the ornament where she was told.

"What do you mean?" Rebekah said from the rocking chair. "What do you mean about if you could only have gotten what Claudia had?"

Millie rubbed her hand over the frosted spikes of her hair, shocking Claudia with familiarity. When had *that* happened? When did they both begin making that gesture?

"Whew, well, it's hard to describe."

"I feel like you're going to try." Claudia reached in the box, pulled out a red and silver ball, faded now and flaking its metallic shell.

"She just"—Millie looked at Rebekah as if the two of them were alone, which was fine by Claudia—"she was so self-contained and nothing got into her, nothing. It was as if . . . as if she lived on her own planet and nobody bothered her there, and everything there was orderly and clean and without . . . you know, disruption. Her car was always clean and her clothes were always pressed and she moved . . . as if she was just gliding over ice."

Claudia was leaning down for another ornament, and stopped midway. "What did you say?"

"I said you just glided past the rest of us. You never reacted to me or my life. I'm not complaining or anything, I'm saying I envied you, especially after the kids were born because God knows my own life became such a tangle and I could never get anything done and everything *right* seemed, you know, just out of reach. But not with you, Claudia."

The three women were silent, but Claudia could hear Millie's voice still ringing around the room, nearly four decades of an ignored monologue.

"Everything with you was always right. Now, this one goes near the bottom of the tree so his little legs hang down," Millie said, holding up a dessicated fabric Santa with a porcelain face. "Yes, like that. Oh he's a sad one, isn't he but Mom couldn't throw such a thing away now, could she."

1969

But where is the angel for the top of the tree?

Hazel and Caroline had looked through every box, uncoiled every string of dead lights. They had found a strand of tinsel so scraggly neither could recall its purchase; they'd found the missing baby Jesus from the plaster nativity set, gone three years now; they'd found the evidence of mice below the tree skirt. But no treetop angel.

On the east side of the wide hallway were three mahogany doors side by side. Standing before them, Hazel could see how they might appear in a dream: identical but for what was behind them, and what that was the dreamer couldn't know until she'd opened one and it was too late. Awake, and in the bright daylight of Christmas Eve, they were just doors: one to the bathroom, one to the linen closet, one to the attic.

She opened the attic door, turned on the light to the hallway, which stayed dark even on the brightest days. The stairwell walls had gone unpainted perhaps the entire twentieth century; their color, streaked and flaking, was not one Hazel could name. It was a muddy yellow and it lacked uniformity, as if the original owners had mixed the remnants of two or three other colors together, without regard to the results, in order to cover raw plaster. The stairs, the same fine wood as the front staircase, were covered with dust. Nancy, their current housekeeper, obviously never ventured through door number three.

Six steps up, a landing, a turn, seven more steps. At the top Hazel turned and there it was. The ceiling was twelve feet at the peak, six feet on the dormer ends, above the windows with the large fans. The attic stretched the width of the house, as big as a ballroom. To her right was the place Albert had intended to build an entire village for model trains, if only Edie had been a boy. To the left was the nook, hidden behind an old batik blanket, where Edie used to bring her boyfriends to smoke pot and talk about overthrowing the government with mass levitation. Behind Hazel, stacks of waxed cardboard boxes, two hundred or more, containing medical records, invoices, journals Albert intended to read but never quite got around to. And everywhere, in front of the boxes and in place of the model train village, was the story of her family's life, told in objects.

A birdcage, a child's wheelchair, a set of crutches: these were left from the previous owners. A dressmaker's dummy, a broken sewing machine, a wobbly hat rack. Here was a metal pole run between two beams, on which hung her uncle's clothes, zipped up in a cloth bag and saturated with mothballs. Boxes marked *Edna's Things,* packed up by Nancy when it seemed they would never see Edie again. A high chair that doubled as a potty chair, its decals of dancing teddy bears faded. Hazel rubbed her arms in the cold. She picked up the high chair and moved it across the room, closer to the wheelchair. She leaned the crutches against the bags of Uncle's clothes. She straightened the dressmaker's dummy, scooted it back until it caught a shaft of sunlight, and moved the sewing machine close enough that someone could really sit there, sewing, then stand and make adjustments. She found a stool, its cane seat shredded, and slid it in front of the sewing machine.

A breath crossed her shoulder. Hazel stood up straight, looked around. The room was bright, dusty, but nothing moved. She took a step toward the corner where the Christmas boxes were stored, and she felt it again: a sigh, a stirring. Her palms began to sweat and she rubbed them against her blue jeans.

Nancy hadn't left any stray boxes when she carried the decorations downstairs. The angel must have been separated from the others last year, after the ritual dismantling of the tree.

Hazel blinked against the light, against the slight aura on the edge of the high chair. A child's wheelchair. She closed her eyes, felt herself falling, but when she opened them, looked around, she was still standing. She moved her eyes and they jerked from object to object, as if the attic were the set of some stop-frame animation, a gothic *Little Drummer Boy*. She knew enough from working in the clinic to realize she might be having a seizure; she might be having a stroke, although it was unlikely. Getting downstairs was best, but for the moment she'd need to sit down.

The rough planks of the attic floor had been swept, but were gritty and had a charred smell. Hazel went all the way down, resting her cheek against the back of her open hand. She was fine and conscious, had access to all the usual nouns. The picture of an apple in her mind conjured the word apple, and when she wondered if the attic had ever burned she saw a fire and thought the word fire, so she hadn't had a stroke. But if she tried to lift her head she felt it again, the overwhelming, sweeping sense of falling that caused her stomach to drop. Sweat ran down her back, soaking her bra strap. Head down then, she thought, and eyes closed.

She was not dreaming. She wasn't dreaming because she knew where she was and she knew why she had decided to lie down on the attic floor. The board beneath her palm was threatening her with splinters; her right hip pushed painfully against a key in her pocket. She could picture Edie in her bedroom watching television, speaking to no one, and she could even conjure up Edie's new, peculiar scent: it was a funk, in both ways. Edie had come home not right—scarred and depressed and smelling bad. She talked ceaselessly about making her way back to British Columbia, where the shreds of a commune were still trying to make a go of growing hemp and eating nothing but what fell on the ground. Food that volunteered, they called it, and Hazel knew if she could remember that, she was conscious.

But why, then, was she also seeing another world as clearly as if she were there? She was thinking her own thoughts about her own life and time, and watching something else unfold against her closed eyelids in clear, manifest detail. There was a man. Jack Lynch, he was black Irish and his mother used to call him Black Jack. He lived in a shed at the edge of a cemetery . . . it was the Wilbur Wright Cemetery, about half a mile away. In it was the lone Civil War grave, of a settler who'd gone back to Georgia to fight for the Confederacy. Jack was the groundskeeper, Hazel knew, he ran the three cemetery dogs, and they lived together in the shed, under a magnificent spreading tree.

A hanging tree, a Lynching tree. Black Jack was tall and thin, a shuffling man with big hands and a cockeyed, lined face. He was a couple degrees past handsome and into ruination. She watched him leave the cemetery—a moment ago it was daylight, but darkness fell in seconds as Hazel watched—and walk down the road that curved in front of the graveyard. The dogs followed him, silent: a wolfhound, a shepherd, a block-headed terrier. They followed him a quarter mile or so, then turned and ran back home. They made no sound, but Hazel could hear Jack's boots on the gravel: scraping, insistent.

He passed the old woods—wait, Hazel thought, those aren't there anymore. That acreage had been cleared for hay. He put his hands in his pockets, whistled, pulled out a comb and ran it through his hair. He turned onto Hazel's road, kicking along in the gravel. Before the road was paved, she realized—it was still the County Road. So that was what it looked like.

He was coming there, to her house. Hazel tried to open her eyes, to raise her head, and her vision swirled as if she'd had too much to drink. When she lay back down, the scene had changed and Hazel was studying a girl of nineteen, Marguerite Henrietta Post, someone Hazel felt she knew but in the way she knew a virus was incipient or that a coming storm would bring with it a high wind. Marguerite's hair was strawberry blond and she had a mole on the side of her neck. Her mother was buried in the Wilbur Wright Cemetery and that was where she met him, Black Jack. Marguerite's father was a judge, he was Teutonic and coldhearted, worse than Albert Hunnicutt but similar. And corrupt, where Albert was not. Marguerite was sitting in . . . she was sitting in Hazel's room but it looked very different; the walls were papered black and covered in a pattern of hand-painted blooming peonies. But Marguerite's bed was in the same place as Hazel's, facing the window. She sat in a rocking chair, wearing a long gray dress. Her mother was dead; her father was ill with tuberculosis and mostly out of his head.

Hazel saw Marguerite growing older, and fast, a speeding past of hands and hair and silk, then back again to where she rocked, nineteen, in Hazel's room. Marguerite's room. Her hands rested on her abdomen. Jack was in the lane, it was the middle of the night, Hazel could see him from above, as if from the veranda, and there were animals—rabbits and mice and all manner of small things—running away from where he stepped. The animals were fanning out and away from him and Marguerite was inside waiting, her father delirious, his pillowcase flowered with a spray of blood.

Hazel rolled over on her back, taking the weight of her head off her hand. Marguerite had called him but Hazel couldn't imagine how she did so; in what language, along what conduit? Marguerite wore gray but all around her was blackness, a miasma of damage. Hazel had never seen the likes of her before. Or she had, but couldn't remember where. Marguerite lifted one hand from where it rested on her stomach. She winced, and brushed the hair away from her forehead, which was perspiring . . .

. . . and Jack slipped in through the unlocked back door, sleek as Mercury. He stopped in the kitchen, where things were very much the same as now, the same low, misbegotten sink, the same stone floor, except it was dirty, there were dishes piled up everywhere. They had even let leaves blow up against the cabinets and the pie safe. He rummaged through the bread box, found something and ate it. In the butler's pantry, which had been wrecked, he pillaged the last of the Judge's brandy, tossed it on a pile of unmarked bottles in the corner while Marguerite—

—drew in a deep breath and wiped her forehead and there they were: two thick scars, branching out beneath Marguerite's hairline. The window was open (it hadn't been a moment before) and the owl leapt off the sill and circled the room.

Hazel didn't know what the bird wanted; she had never known, but Marguerite did, and she barely glanced up as the draft off his wings moved her hair. Or Hazel had known but refused to bite. A bite. She could see Marguerite's mother's grave, silver in the moonlight. Dead ten years, since Marguerite was nine, a hard age for girls, an in-between. Marguerite suffered as her mother suffered, similar to the way her father was suffering his own way out of life, and perhaps it wasn't all that strange, Hazel thought, the experiment of Family gone so radically wrong: mother dead, the hanging judge dying, the daughter with her black heart panting now in the nursery. The owl flown and Black Jack creeping up the stairs, tiptoeing down the wide hallway, his arms outstretched for balance, not touching either wall.

Together they delivered the baby. Hazel didn't see this part, but she could have written it if asked, she knew the script as well as anyone. The greatest violence the human species knows, worse than tumbling off the bridge at Remagen, worse than being trampled underfoot by wild horses; she had seen the souls of women fly out through their mouths in the depth of it and later they were changed. They did not recover although they claimed they did. The affluent took the ether from the mask, delivered in the amnesiac twilight they were blessed to be able to afford. Better, Hazel believed, to forget the entire thing and take what you are handed, even if it's the neighbor's baby, even if it grows up to be a stranger. It was the poor, or the outlawed like Marguerite, who endured it in a long, blind panic and recalled it with spite.

The baby was a girl. They placed a coral bracelet on her plump right wrist, a tiny band handed down through many daughters. Her profile was flawless, the nose and chin, the downy forehead, her eyes closed and her black lashes resting on her cheeks. Amazing to Hazel how we all arrive in a bloody fog but soon enough look like nothing but love; she was love itself, the round bottom and belly, the ten toes as small as pearls, the mouth opening in a kitten's yawn, so helpless.

Jack placed his daughter on newspapers in a small trunk. He closed and locked it, then opened the third mahogany door in the upstairs hallway and climbed the attic stairs—Hazel could hear him coming. He crossed the floor as quietly as he could, stepping over her, and even in his day the attic was filled with older things: a spinning wheel, pieces of a loom, burlap bags advertising the Jonah Mill. He moved aside a part of the wall, right behind where Caroline kept her Christmas decorations—Hazel had no idea those boards moved—and placed the little trunk back in a small crawl space next to the dumbwaiter. There were the workings of the pulley, the hemp rope guaranteed to last two hundred years wrapped around the steel wheels. A simple, timeless arrangement.

Jack slid the boards closed, brushed his hands together, stood. Hazel waited for him to leave but he hovered above her, leaned over her. He lit a cigarette and Hazel knew then she was—

"Hazel?"

She opened her eyes and Edie was leaning over her, smoke curling around her hair and up toward the ceiling. Her eyes were dull, her skin dusty over her fading tan.

Edie sat back, stretched her legs out, took a hit off a crookedly rolled joint. "Mama said you were up here doing God knows what, I said leave it to Hazel to get completely sucked in by all that crap and forget what she'd gone up there for. I said leave it to Hazel."

Hazel sat up, rubbed the back of her head.

"You sick?"

"No." She could move her eyes without the jerkiness. She wasn't falling. "Are *you* sick?"

"Sick and tired, maybe. Rather die than stay here, that's for sure."

"There's a box," Hazel said, pointing with her thumb to the corner, "behind those boards. They move."

"Yeah, well, there's also a box sitting right in plain sight, like an attic would have."

Hazel turned too quickly, felt her vision dim. There it was, the green box the angel was kept in. She stood, walked over and picked it up.

"This was, coming back here, what you might call a last resort if you know what I mean. Things had gotten hairy, a couple people had taken a dive and Mad Dog, he ran the place, was mad at me over something I didn't . . ."

A whole colony of dead flies littered the windowsill but she gripped it anyway, squatting down beside the dumbwaiter. She reached out and touched the three boards, expecting them to still feel warm from Black Jack's hand.

". . . I was trying to tell him—man, this is no way to get where we're trying to go, this My Stuff Your Stuff drama, if something of mine is laying around and you need it, take it, be free! It ain't as if I hadn't done the . . ."

Hazel pushed lightly against the boards and nothing happened. Exhale, she told herself, seeing the first gray dots of dizziness. She pushed again and the three boards moved as one, an inch or so and Hazel stopped, sat down. In that open space was a darkness so complete she would have to call it *pure,* something she had seen once before, inside a man's mouth, behind his missing teeth. A townie who brought his daughter in to Caroline one afternoon. The daughter was twelve. The midwife in town, Lulamae, knew crawl spaces, Hazel guessed. Caroline, too, for that matter, although in a different way.

"Haze? What are you *doing*? What's back there?"

She turned toward her sister, who sat in the sunlight, encased in her own brand of innocence. Smoking. "Nothing," Hazel said, sliding the doors closed.

"Are we putting up this retarded angel, or what? I'm thinking I need to get good and drunk if it's going to be Family Power Hour at the Hunnicutt Asylum."

Hazel laughed, stood, and brushed off her jeans. "You carry the treetop to Caroline, be the hero."

"Well"—Edie stood, stubbed her joint out on the floor—"it'll be the first time, won't it?"

Edie went down the steps before her and Hazel paused, hesitated before looking back. Everything was perfectly normal, if in better order. It made sense, didn't it, the high chair, the wheelchair. The dressmaker's model and the useless sewing machine. The crutches for the Uncle, his suits waiting for him, zipped up tight and hanging beneath the eaves. Small animals radiated out from under Black Jack's bootfall, and the bird swooped, just an owl and her kind, calling the Earth *Mother.*

"Admit it."

"Admit what?"

"Say it out loud: say, 'I was entirely wrong about Millie.'"

"I wasn't *entirely* wrong about Millie."

"Say, 'I don't know a thing about my sister.'"

"You don't know a thing about your brother, either."

"True enough."

They lay on Claudia's bed, staring at the ceiling.

"Is Oliver ever going to fall asleep?"

"Eventually he will."

"What's he doing?"

Claudia listened. "He's singing. No, now he's spitting."

"Isn't he tired? I am so bone tired I'd like to die."

"He'll fall asleep soon." Claudia rubbed her fingertips over the bedspread, glanced at Rebekah, who was wearing a pale pink nightgown. She looked like herself, and also she was like a form, like the idea of a woman. Claudia wanted to tell her how she could have been a photograph in a book, but couldn't find the words.

"This reminds me of a slumber party," Rebekah said, yawning.

"Really? Slumber parties are this boring?"

"I'm not bored." Rebekah brushed her hair back from her forehead, let her arm fall above her head. "Slumber parties were fun, we had them all the time. Except that my cousins always fell asleep before me and I would be the only person awake for what felt like ages."

"Why?" Claudia turned on her side, watched Rebekah's face in profile.

"I don't know," Rebekah said, shrugging. "That's just how I was." She paused, listened for Oliver. "Is he asleep?"

The baby was silent, then began spitting and kicking his legs again.

"No. I swear he'll fall asleep eventually. Millie jumbled up his schedule. Also she's too loud." Claudia pulled the bedspread up a little higher around her waist. "Can I tell you something?"

"Sure." Rebekah sat up, resting her weight on her left elbow.

"Something has . . ."

Rebekah's eyes were the green of a fern—of a fern seen from a distance, hanging on the porch of someone Claudia didn't know. That's how everything felt suddenly, as if she were passing a house she

admired and there was a garden, a garden enviable by Ludie's standards. Claudia could see how fine it all was, how lucky she was to be
passing by before the morning mist was burned off by the sun, but
that's all she could do—walk past. It wouldn't work, what she was
about to say.

"What?" Rebekah pressed her hand against Claudia's arm, and it
seemed easy for her, this physical emphasis. "What's happened?"

"Nothing, nothing. I don't mean to be dramatic, I've just come to
realize something. I should have known it a long time ago, or probably I did know it and turned away." Claudia shook her head. "It hardly
matters one way or the other."

Oliver, who had been quiet for minutes, suddenly let out a startled
wail, as if waking from a dream.

"Yikes," Rebekah said, covering her heart with her hand as Claudia jumped up, saying, "I'll get him." She was tangled in the bedspread
and nearly fell.

"Claudia, you're going to break your—"

"Take the end of this, then I'll unwrap—"

By turns they freed her, and Claudia made her way to the crib,
where Oliver had become so distressed he'd kicked his blanket up over
his head. "What a problem," Claudia said, uncovering him and lifting
him up, his little body still such a surprise in her hands. How could
something so insubstantial bear within it Oliver's nature, his character,
everything that would compel him into adulthood?

"Don't forget," Rebekah said from behind her, sleepily.

"Don't forget what?"

"Don't forget what you were telling me. As soon as he's back down
I want to hear it."

Claudia lay Oliver on his changing table, tapped his pacifier against
his chin until he grinned at her and opened his mouth. "Okay," she
said. "I won't forget."

By the time Claudia had changed Oliver, given him the rest of his
evening bottle and rocked him back to sleep, Rebekah was also asleep,
her lips slightly parted, a ribbon of hair out of place and covering one
eye. Claudia sat down beside her, pulled the blankets up over her
exposed shoulder. She reached out and slipped the strand of hair off
Rebekah's face, tucking it behind her ear. The tip of Claudia's finger

brushed Rebekah's skin, just barely. She sat that way as long as seemed right, then went downstairs, turning off lights behind her.

It was Christmas Eve, and there were gifts to place under the tree, Rebekah's cookies to put on a plate by the fireplace. She left a note beside the plate that said *Rebekah and Oliver have been very, very good this year,* then she lay down on the couch with a blanket and slept without dreaming, the lights of the tree playing over her face like fireflies.

Chapter 7

REBEKAH DIDN'T WANT to go to church, and she had tried to make it clear that she didn't want to go, had vowed to never enter a church again, but somehow Claudia hadn't heard, or else she was ignoring her. It had been a long time, a long relief of a time since Rebekah had risen earlier than she'd wanted to and frantically tried to find a missing skirt, a pair of stockings without a tear, her Bible, the tortoiseshell barrette Vernon approved of. Oh, it was all idiotic. Fine, Claudia loved this minister and loved the church, and insisted that he was nothing like the ministers of Rebekah's lost youth. That was probably all true. She seemed to think, Claudia did, that Rebekah didn't want to go because she'd been traumatized by the Mission, as if they'd made her participate in a Full Gospel Sex Ring with goats down in the basement Fellowship Hall. In fact, Rebekah didn't want to go because taking her to a safe, liberal, kind-hearted hour of worship would be like taking a cheetah out of the zoo and back to the savannah for a visit, but she would only be allowed to see the home she was stolen from through a window. Through the grimy window of a tourist's van. That's what it would be like.

"Rebekah? What are you doing?" Claudia called up the stairs. "I think I got that dried banana off Oliver's face." She paused. "Rebekah?"

"I'm sitting on the bed! I'm not going!"

Claudia climbed the stairs and walked down the hallway toward Rebekah's room. "Why are you just sitting here? If we don't leave now we'll be late, and Oliver is about to fall asleep in his swing. What are you doing."

"I don't think I should go, because look, I don't have anything to wear, I'm too fat for all my dresses, and if I have to wear panty hose even for an hour I will slit my own wrists." Rebekah felt near tears again; she'd already cried twice this morning, once because she'd dreamed of Peter on a swing set—he was swinging too high and scaring her, and she kept asking him to stop, to come down, but he just smiled and went higher—and the second time because standing in the shower she realized she'd gotten everything wrong and was now living such a weird life her sweet mother wouldn't have recognized her. And she was quite happy, which only made her cry harder.

"This is a Church of the *Brethren,* not the Junior League fashion show, Rebekah, nobody cares what you wear. And remember opening gifts this morning? I got you some new clothes?"

"But I'm crying about that, too, because I couldn't make the thing I wanted to for you."

"You know that means absolutely—"

"Also I always thought I'd be a great pregnant person, I thought I'd be a natural. And pretty about it, and romantic. But I hate it, it's terrible. I feel every minute like I have the flu, I'm exhausted and sick and my breasts ache, and look how swollen I already am, my fingers look like fish sticks."

"Talk to Gil about it this week. You have an appointment on Wednesday."

"What's Gil going to say, I mean really? That he'll get me out of it somehow, that I don't have to see it through to the end? Claudia, why on earth do you want to go to church anyway? It's Christmas Day, we could have a nice lunch, invite Hazel. We could go see a movie, take a walk, something."

"We can do all those things anyway. And you don't have to go. I mean it, you don't have to go."

"Well, do you want me to go or not?!?"

Claudia took a deep breath, sat down on the bed. "Tell me what you want me to say."

"No! You have to figure it out yourself."

Claudia thought about it. "I'm leaving in five minutes. All of your clean laundry is right in that basket. Your new clothes are on your chair.

You may go with Oliver and me, or you can go back to bed. Your choice."

Rebekah fell down on the bed, pulling a pillow over her face. "You're mean, Claudia Modjeski! You are mean to me, and I'm not going."

On the way to church Rebekah noticed that Claudia listened to an AM gospel station; so this was what she did when she was alone, on a Sunday. They heard the Oak Ridge Boys sing "On the Sunny Banks"; Don Rigsby's "Love Lifted Me"; the Nelons' "O for a Thousand Tongues"; and a song that activated Rebekah's newfound weeping gene, Merle Haggard singing something with the line *Come home, come home, it's suppertime.*

"What's that song called?" she asked, wiping her eyes.

"'Suppertime.'"

"Ah."

She was on her way to church again after so many years, the building and hour that contained a thousand conspiracies and dramas, to listen to a man tell her that what was right before her eyes was not true, that it did not, in fact, even matter. It mattered enough to destroy; that was all. Its import was as an obstacle, a stumbling block. Rebekah watched it go by: the winter fields, the stark sky, a hawk descending.

"You're going to church with me," Claudia said.

Rebekah stared at her a moment, at Claudia's sharp jawline, her perfect, burnished skin, the streak of rose that blushed along her cheekbone. Vernon had seemed to think that Rebekah had fallen as far as a woman could, and so had she. But it had turned out that the few square feet of the planet she lived on were gravity-less, full of bottomless surprises. Unmarried, pregnant, in exile, and now living with a woman and her rescued child. If they had their way, the men who meant to rip away the screen of reality, the men who meant to devour everything, everything—on the dark day they finally seized the reins, she knew she would be the first to go. They would be the first: Rebekah, Claudia, Oliver, and the little alien. The lithe, red-haired, beloved child of God, lovely little Pentecostal Rebekah Shook, had become the enemy of both the temple and the state.

"Well, as it turns out," she said to Claudia, "I'm going to church with you."

The church was bare, not as if anything was missing, but as if nothing had ever been there. They were slightly late and Oliver was asleep; Rebekah held him as Claudia hung up their coats. The vestibule smelled so familiar, but she couldn't decide what to call the smell, or what it was made of. Filling, and emptying out—that was part of it, the comings and goings of people driven to congregate and talk it over. It wasn't a home, it wasn't an institution, it was merely a space standing still and waiting.

Claudia took Oliver and pushed against one of the double swinging doors, which sighed open on a well-oiled hinge. There were thirty or so people gathered in front of them on the old wooden pews, all completely silent, including the few children. A clock ticked so loudly in the expectant air that it made Rebekah's heart speed up. The only concession to the season were two red poinsettia on either side of the altar. She followed Claudia to a place at the end of a pew midway down the aisle, and was surprised to find herself embarrassed without knowing why. She'd ended up wearing the last pair of black slacks that fit her, but that wasn't it; everyone was dressed plainly. She was pregnant, which amounted to wearing her sex life on her sleeve, but she'd mostly gotten over fretting about it.

The minister stood from the short pew where he'd been sitting behind the altar and approached the podium. "Good morning, friends, and Merry Christmas." Amos Townsend was tall and lanky, handsome, severe, but with a warm voice that carried a trace of irony? Chagrin? The congregation answered him, and Amos pushed his glasses up and held his hymnal out the length of his arms.

"I wonder if we can start today by singing my favorite Christmas hymn, 'The Friendly Beasts'? It's on page one forty-two of the blue hymnal, the modern one. My father"—Amos lowered his hymnal, nudged his glasses again—"used to refer to every modernization of the church as Peter, Paul and Jesus."

Rebekah made the hiccupy sound of an abbreviated laugh—her Peter had *loved* Peter, Paul and Mary—which in turn made everyone around her laugh, and then she was even more deeply mortified. At the Mission, with its One Strike policy, she would have been out the door and pleading for mercy.

She watched Amos bounce up and down a little as the piano started, although the opening chords were stately, not bouncy. Not hymns, not hymn singing, she had no desire for that. She didn't want to hear them again, not "Power in the Blood" or "The Old Rugged Cross," none of them. This, she wanted to say to Claudia—could have just turned and said to her in front of everyone—is what I do not want and am allowed to be free of. The small congregation began to sing:

> *Jesus our brother kind and good*
> *Was humbly born in a stable rude*
> *And the friendly beasts around him stood*
> *Jesus our brother kind and good*

Each verse was from the point of view of a different animal, the donkey, the camel, the dove. The song ended:

> *Thus every beast remembering it well*
> *In the stable dark was so proud to tell*
> *Of the gifts they gave Emmanuel*
> *The gifts they gave Emmanuel*

Rebekah pressed her fingertips against her eyelids, tried not to cry. Well, it had been a lovely song, she was never right about anything, and her little peanut-shaped alien had heard it. That had been what she dreaded the most—the notion that the baby would be infected with the language of her father; that it might know even before greeting the world that it had been responsible for the death of an innocent man two thousand years ago. Lambs, slaughter.

There was the familiar sound of thirty hymnals closing, being slipped back into place. Beside her Oliver slept on Claudia's shoulder, sometimes making a little snoring sound. Amos waited a moment, cleared his throat. "In every other church you'd be hearing about the Nativity right now. Maybe you'll be disappointed not to hear that story today. But you know"—he looked at the ceiling, seeming to search for the right words—"I'm just a little tired of it."

Rebekah began to feel queasy, and pulled a saltine cracker out of her pocket, trying not to make any noise.

"I'm tired of the television specials and the songs. I'm not even talking about the secular, commercial part; good heavens, everyone is sick of that, and sick from it. I'm tired of the Archangel and Herod and Joseph the Widower. I don't want to talk about a virgin birth or the Three Wise Men. Is it just me, or is there something in that story you can't get your mind around?"

Rebekah froze, the cracker halfway to her mouth. Oh yes, she certainly knew the story of the Nativity. She, like all of her cousins, could quote Luke 2:1–20 in its entirety, and also she didn't understand it.

"It's—I'm not sure what I want to say, even though I've been thinking about it for a few weeks now." Amos tugged at the cuff of his white shirt absently. "All I know is that what we're told to read there is not what I read. It is the story, after all . . ."

. . . of a child born to die, Rebekah thought, glancing against her will at the sleeping Oliver. If she knew he was the Messiah, if her faith in that proposition was uncompromised, her life would be an unhappy one indeed. And so would his.

". . . of a child born to die. So, with all due respect, and I mean that, I'd like to talk to you today not about how the person of Jesus was born, but why; in the same way that on the anniversary of Einstein's birth we talk about how he changed the world."

Rebekah closed her eyes, felt something like a trapdoor open beneath her. Pregnancy had had one unexpected effect, one she had never heard mentioned in the literature. Her memory had become vibrant, crystalline. She remembered events full of body and color and scent. Now, sitting in church beside Claudia and Oliver, whose lips were pressed in sleep into a little squash blossom, Rebekah was also sitting on the couch holding a shoe box she'd found in the coat closet. She had been looking for scraps of material; she wanted to make dresses for her dolls. The box was in her hands, dusty, the texture displeasing. It had held her father's work shoes, was blue, faded to gray. Here was the couch beneath her, the exact color and weave; here the oval braided rug that slid if she ran on it. Rebekah took the lid off the shoe box and found her baby book, which she had never seen before, the book that celebrated her birth. She opened it and nothing was written there. Nothing. Not even her name. She turned every page just to make sure, her heart growing more steadily unsure, and at the very back she found a black-and-white photograph, someone she didn't recognize, and then her mother was upon her. The only time Ruth ever struck Rebekah, and it was across the cheek with a wet dish towel. By the time Rebekah lowered her hand from the stinging surprise, the box and her mother were gone.

". . . where we read, 'In those days John the Baptist appeared in the wilderness of Judea, proclaiming, 'Repent, for the kingdom of heaven has come near.'"

Matthew 3:1–2, Rebekah thought. Repent. There was a number one hit from the Prophetic Mission. She was constantly being told to repent, to beg forgiveness for her sins; she was first admonished at the same age other children were being shown a toothbrush for the first time and told of Mr. Cavity Man.

Amos looked up. "*Repent* in this case means, literally, to 'return,' an important Judaic concept. It signifies, oh, more like turning around and going back to something, back to the original covenant, the one between the Hebrew God and the Israelites. The writer of Matthew is saying that because the kingdom of heaven has come near—and remember that phrase, it has 'come near'—because of its nearness, whoever reads this document should return to the original promise."

There—there was something familiar; the nearness of God, the maddening sensation the Mission had that He was *right there,* and the only thing keeping them from instant and complete unity was sin. And what of you, little Rebekah? A question posed to her in Hazel's voice. Rebekah *was* the failure, the sin, at least she had become that for her father. But as a girl? She had not understood it—she just thought God was everywhere and it was simple, really. Vernon, the Governance men: they understood the divide.

Amos said, "Later in Matthew, um . . . 13:10–12, we're told, 'Then the disciples came and asked him, "Why do you speak to them in parables?" He answered, "To you it has been given to know the secrets of the kingdom of heaven, but to them it has not been given. For to those who have, more will be given, and they will have an abundance, but from those who have nothing, even what they have will be taken away.'" When Jesus says, 'To those who have, more will be given,' He's talking, I think, about a certain kind of insight, what my father used to call a leading. He's not suggesting power or privilege, certainly not wealth. If he is, I've chosen the wrong profession." There was polite laughter, a shuffling in the pews. "The kingdom of heaven, the king- dom of God—it's the cornerstone of Jesus' ministry, and the subtheme of the entire New Testament. Again, it's a Judaic concept, but that goes without saying; it's as if someone talking about Indiana were to remark on what Indiana has in common with America. Remember that the Hebrew people believed that the Messiah would be a king—he would be a person who had harnessed immense political force. So the king- dom of God meant one thing in that context, and it means something different coming from the carpenter from Nazareth. I—" Amos shifted his weight, cleared his throat. "I don't mean to take any kind of polarizing stand here, but it behooves us, I think, to remember that the 'Church' as an entity, the Roman church and many Protestant con- gregations, still pray for the conversion of the Jews. But Jesus wasn't appropriate as their Messiah—not according to their scriptures, and certainly not given their condition. He failed them. He failed them in Roman-occupied Palestine; they didn't need a wandering magician, a powerless, poverty-stricken philosopher; they didn't need His philos- ophy. They spoke of one kingdom, and He spoke of another."

He failed them. Rebekah wanted to hold up her hand and ask Amos to stop, stop, she needed to write this down; she needed a doughnut and a nap. She wanted to think about it for a few days and then they could all get back together and go on with the sermon. He failed them. A chill passed over her arms, across the back of her neck. All that *anger* in the Mission! All the anger in Rebekah, for years. For so long, from the moment He died! the church had been saying He was coming soon, He was coming for those who knew the Way, the Truth, and the Life. But where was He? If only she had the guts to walk up to her father, even to call him on the telephone and say, *Daddy? Maybe He failed you.*

"We've talked before about the shift between the First and Second Testaments from the historical to the metaphorical; from the Law to the Spirit. The Hebrews sacrificed animals, the Christian community believed Jesus' sacrifice was the final one necessary. So, too, with the kingdom of God. For the Jews, God seems to have been as present, as real, as anything else in creation. To paraphrase Martin Buber"—a number of people laughed aloud, as if Amos paraphrased Martin Buber with some frequency—"there was a time when God spoke; it seems He speaks no more. God spoke *directly* to Noah, to Moses, to Abraham. The kingdom of God *was* Egypt, it was Babylon and Zion, the desert, because it was the covenant God had made with the Chosen People; a living, active, demanding deity. But by the age of the Synoptic Gospels, the King was silent; His emissary had been sent and killed; and the kingdom in question had become the stuff of parables. In Matthew, Mark, Luke, and John, God speaks *through* Jesus, Who is speaking through the writers of the books, and we are receiving them in translation from the language of the occupiers in which they were written. And now we are told that the Kingdom of Heaven is near, that it's here, that it's coming, all at the same time. I wish I knew what that meant."

Rebekah sighed. Poor Vernon. Amos was right, and simply so: God spoke, God stopped speaking; except, of course, in the little drywalled box that held the Prophetic Mission, where the cruel, the stupid, the kind and good alike believed that they were the conduits for the direct revelation of Yahweh. And the kingdom of heaven . . . she closed her eyes and could see the phrase standing like a sentry in the Old Testament, then sailing through the New as if on wings. It is near, it is here, it is coming soon. Her King James Bible—purchased for her at birth and with her name inscribed on the cover—printed the words of Jesus in red, and Rebekah could see herself lying in bed at night in her white gown, skipping everything but that red text. She had been told that she loved Him. She had been given no choice but to love Him, and so she had, with her eyes and her hands and her mind. What *He* said—His words, not the words of the apostles, not their acts or their demands—what He said sometimes rose right up out of the onion-skin pages, not like speech but like a thing; what He said rose up with mass and definition, and if she didn't stare directly at it, if she turned away just slightly and concerned herself with the moon, the dusty valence over the window, she could feel something touch her in the hollow of her throat.

"The Kingdom," Amos continued, polishing the lenses of his

glasses with a handkerchief, "is, for some, the Church. The Church is the kingdom of heaven and the world is not, and the Church becomes the status quo. Everything Jesus said, everything in the biblical tradition, is then used to uphold the status quo, because that's what it means to enter the kingdom. But when the Kingdom is seen as transcendent, or beyond the Church, there is a call to revolution, in defiance of old customs and conventions. That's where we get the Jesus I find more attractive: the radical overturning the money changers' tables, the man who, in fact, turned everything upside down, the Jesus Who is not on the side of any empire or principality, but Who is concerned with outsiders and sinners and the sick."

Oliver sighed, squirmed, went back to sleep.

"I think," Amos said, putting on his glasses and taking a deep breath, "not that you've exactly asked me what I think, but I believe that the Jesus we have come to know spoke in parables because there is no other psychically adequate way to address the human condition, and that while it seems that what Jesus is saying is that the Kingdom is like a naked singularity, a trick of physics, it's equally possible He's saying you have to choose. What you choose determines the life you live, quite simply. If the Kingdom of Heaven is here now, and that requires from you a fearful clinging to the status quo, then that's who you are and what your life meant. If it's ahead somewhere, and out of reach in this lifetime, you will spend your days accordingly. For me— I speak only for myself now—the Ineffable, the Eternal, the Kingdom of Heaven seems to be inbreaking in our lives all the time, every day. I think it's here, just beside us, and if we turn our heads we'll enter in. I think all kinds of people, especially dogs and Buddhists, have gone in ahead of us, but there's always another chance. The Kingdom of God is a door perpetually opening, and it makes me, as dear Emerson said, 'glad to the brink of fear.'"

Rebekah blinked, tearful. She knew what he meant. She had been that glad.

Amos closed his Bible, centered it on the podium. "You must be tired of me saying it, but God is Love, and the doorway is Love, and the Kingdom of Heaven is Love. And not *because* of the birth of Jesus, but it's one of the things He was born for. So. Merry Christmas, all of you, and may your new year be, as they say, bright."

* * *

They stood, and were instantly surrounded by people who took Rebekah's hand and told her their names and wished her a happy holiday, and again and again she heard Claudia say, *This is my baby,* including to Amos, who cupped Oliver's head in his palm and shared a look with Claudia that was intimate, a benediction.

"It's about time," Millie said, getting out of her car.

Claudia closed the door to the Jeep, took a deep breath. The weather was lovely, it was Christmas. She remembered a time when she would have come home from church alone, looking forward to lunch, and there would not have been a chance in the world that Millie would be lying in wait.

"I haven't seen you for so *long.*" Millie reached into Claudia's backseat and began unfastening Oliver's car seat, all but pushing Rebekah away.

"We saw you *yesterday,*" Claudia said, trying to keep the desperation out of her voice.

"You didn't see me today."

"It's true," Rebekah said, nodding. "We haven't seen her yet today."

"I stopped on the way home from here last night, the Wal-Mart was open late, and got Oliver some new clothes and shoes. McDonald's is making baby clothes now and they are just totally precious."

Claudia started toward the front door, stopped. "God in heaven."

"What? What did I say?"

"McDonald's baby clothes? What, are they dipped in lard? Addictive?"

Millie opened the back of the Explorer, took out a large plastic bag. "You always did have a critical spirit, Claudia."

"I don't think criticizing a fast food empire is a reflection of my spirit, Millie."

"Do you want to have lunch with us?" Rebekah asked, opening the front door.

"Besides," Millie said, unbuttoning her coat, "what's so wrong with

McDonald's? I practically raised my children on that food and look at them. Neither one is an ounce overweight. It's *protein,* Claudia, and *potatoes.* They weren't given little cigarettes with their Happy Meals."

"We could stay here or we could go out. I think the cafeteria at the mall is open today. Do you want some iced tea, Millie?"

"And everyone's always going on about working conditions, I hear that all the time on the news, about working conditions at McDonald's and Wal-Mart. You tell me where the black people are supposed to work if we closed down all the McDonald's like the hippies and the save-the- planet people would have us to do? Last summer Brandon had a job at that local hardware store, couldn't hardly get any hours. If there were extras they went to the owner or his son. But next summer Brandon's going to work at Wal-Mart and his schedule will be his schedule, no questions asked. And again I ask you, what about the black people. We have to put them somewhere."

"I could heat up the chicken and dumplings we had last night, or we could go to MCL."

Millie began taking clothes out of the bag, stacking them up expertly on the couch, and removing their tags with a pocketknife. "Who drives a white car?"

Claudia closed the door to the coat closet, turned and looked at Millie. "No one I can think of. Why do you ask?"

"I'm going to go change Oliver," Rebekah said. "Decide about lunch while I'm gone."

"There was a white car in the driveway when I got here," Millie said, gathering up the little plastic T shapes she'd cut off the tags.

"Who was driving it?"

"I'd rather go to MCL, personally. Rebekah is a great cook and all, but chicken and dumplings sounds a little heavy to me. I'd like to have some Jell-O salad."

"Millie," Claudia said, sitting down next to her on the couch. "Who was driving the car?"

"Well, I don't know, it was in your driveway, and also as I got out of my car and started to walk up to it, they drove away. Whoever it was."

"Claudia?" Rebekah called down the stairs. "See who's pulling into the driveway."

I am beset, Claudia thought as she opened the front door.

"Oh great, it's Hazel," Millie said.

"Who is it?" Rebekah called.

"It's Hazel," Claudia yelled back.

"She has a *dog* with her," Millie said.

"She has a dog with her," Claudia yelled up the stairs. She watched as Hazel struggled with a blur on the end of the leash. It leapt from the front seat to the back and forward again, then tried to jump out the open door.

"Maybe we'll get lucky and she'll strangle it to death right here before our eyes," Millie said, leaning closer to the window. "You should tell her not to bring it in; Mom would never allow animals in the house."

"It's you who won't allow animals in the house, don't blame it on Mom. You might remember Jumpin' Bean."

"How could I forget, it was always Jumpin' Bean this and Jumpin' Bean that."

"Good Lord, Millie."

"Well, excuse me, but a, fleas, b, filth, c, animals. They belong outside."

Rebekah came down the steps with Oliver, who'd been polished and fluffed and didn't seem nearly so angry as he'd been by the end of the drive home. "I thought you said Hazel was here."

"She's struggling with a dog out by her car," Claudia said, watching Hazel.

"A dog, huh? Here, take him." Rebekah handed Oliver to Claudia, who handed him to Millie, and walked out the door toward the conflagration of animal and puffy coat. Claudia watched her, surprised again by Rebekah's ease. Claudia herself had stood there pondering the situation, but Rebekah just strode right out and set to taming all the savage beasts. "But *why* does she have a dog, I wonder," Claudia said.

"Why anything with Hazel," Millie answered.

There was a transfer of leather at the back of Hazel's car, and then Rebekah was being dragged forward, right toward the front door, by a massive-chested, red-nosed, ear-disfigured . . . *"Bandit?"* Claudia said, stepping out the front door and closing it behind her.

"Look what I've got!" Rebekah said happily, although her right shoulder seemed in danger of being dislocated. The dog changed course and headed down the driveway.

"*Bandit?*" Claudia said, staring at Hazel, who refused to meet her eye.

"He is *strong*," Rebekah said as she disappeared behind Millie's car.

"It's a she," Hazel said, still not looking at Claudia. "Merry Christmas!"

The front door opened and there was Millie, now without Oliver, her hands on her hips and an expression on her face like an old fisherwoman. "Is that some kind of pig? What is that? Is that a pig on a leash, Hazel?"

"Millie," Hazel said, giving her a wave. "Always lovely to see you."

"Why did you bring that dog?" Millie asked.

"Yes, Hazel. Why did you bring that dog?" Claudia took a step forward so that Hazel had to look up at her.

"It's sort of a story. Can we go inside?"

"You're not bringing that dog inside," Millie said, shaking her head, as Rebekah was being towed across the yard toward the door.

"Why not?" Hazel asked, now putting her fists on her own hips. "What's it to you?"

"Well, if I am not mistaken, that is some sort of pit bull, Hazel Hunnicutt, and there is a baby in this house."

"Oh, oh, how silly of me. She's a pit bull, so let's just smear Oliver with condiments and tuck him in a bun."

"Excuse me," Rebekah said as Bandit pulled her past Millie and into the house.

"You can't pretend I'm wrong, Hazel, I read the news."

"You do? Then who is the Majority Whip?"

Claudia cleared her throat. "What I'd like to know is—"

From inside the house Rebekah yelled, "Claudia! Come quick!"

Claudia ran past Millie, terrified that now, of all times, Millie would be right about something and little Oliver would be missing an arm. What she found was Oliver in his swing, laughing madly and turning his head back and forth against the swing's seat as Bandit licked him with a tongue the length of an ironing board. Oliver was laughing harder than Claudia had ever heard him, a deep, physical sound that carried in it a premonition of the boy he would be.

"Look at this! It's like they know each other," Rebekah said, her face flushed.

"They . . ." Claudia swallowed, barely able to speak. "They do." Hazel, too, must have felt how sad it was, that this was what Oliver had—not parents or photographs, no baby book or engraved silver cup, no one guarding the story of his birth and first year as if it had been the Nativity. He had this mangy, scarred, brutalized animal, his companion in the kitchen at Cobb Creek.

"I can't tell you how I disapprove of this," Millie said, sharpening all of her angles.

"I went out there, you know, Claudia," Hazel began.

Claudia looked at her and saw it on her face, the wet cold, the garbage, the empty plastic chair facing the psychedelic poster on the wall. How would she ever tell Oliver the truth? Where would she say he had come from? "And?"

"And mostly everyone is gone. There were a couple people asleep in the living room. There has been some . . . attrition among the pets."

"I see."

"The pups are gone, and Bandit was chained to a radiator in a back room. You can see that she's gone a bit thin." Hazel's words were clipped, her tone aimed not at Millie but at Claudia alone; she was trying to tell a story by leaving all of the details out.

Bandit was certainly thin. She seemed to have lost muscle mass over her spine, and her hips were rising up, as clearly defined as an anatomical model's. More alarming were the calluses over her elbows, as if the skin had thickened to keep the bones from breaking through.

"I couldn't leave her there."

"Of course you couldn't," Rebekah said, bending down and pulling Bandit away from Oliver's swing by a thick, stained collar.

"I stopped at the store and got fifty pounds of dog food, bowls, this leash."

Claudia gave Hazel her most level look. There was nothing, really, to say: she couldn't have left the dog there to die. And what came next, that Hazel couldn't take her home because of the cats, was also true.

"I'm wondering . . ."

"You should leave her here with us, shouldn't she, Claudia?

Couldn't we keep her for a while, just until Hazel figures something else out? I've never, I was never allowed to have a dog at home—"

"You *cannot* have that dog here, Claudia, around the baby. It looks like a disease on legs. It will destroy the house and—"

"I think," Hazel said, "and of course you're welcome to disagree, but I think this is really the best place for her. Claudia, look at me."

But she didn't need to look at her; Claudia didn't need to have her fate outlined and read aloud. What Hazel wanted didn't matter; what Millie said was irrelevant. That Rebekah wanted the dog was a point on the ledger. The only vote that counted, at least today, was Oliver's. His new swing moved forward and back with a soft ticking sound and he himself was still, his eyes fixed on that battered, cinder-block head. Bandit watched him, too, her mouth opened all the way back to where her ears would have been, her eyes as clear as bottle glass. The dog and the baby studied each other as if the war had ended and a noble country had offered them repatriation. It would be exhausting, and she might live to regret it, but Claudia was that country. She blinked, let out the breath she'd been holding, then walked out to Hazel's car to bring in the food, the bowls, another bed.

❧

1970

She awakened every Christmas morning to gifts she did not need and smiled politely, thanking her parents, telling them again—as she had the year before—that the sweater was just the right color and size, the scarf would look lovely with her new coat. Later in the day her mother would find occasion to sneak up to Hazel's room with a stack of new hardcover books, each one wrapped in accordance with its gravity or mirth. Caroline had no time for fiction and she was a society unto herself; Hazel, too, stood guarded and apart, so that the books on the bed in their gold foil and sprigs of mistletoe were like smoke signals sent across a mountain range, between neighbors so distant they could not see one another at all.

Hazel and her mother worked together in the silence of complicity, together as a sort of corporation, and for Albert when their own work was slow. And it often was—sometimes weeks would go by without the frantic phone call or the veiled letter from A Friend. There were trends, if Hazel would take the time to see them. Of course they were cosmological: as above, so below. The heavens moved, the oceans boiled, and tectonic plates ground against each other. She didn't chart the events, but someday she might, she told herself, seeing the possibility of a life's work: a hypothesis that would marry the Ephemera with medical records, final proof that the universe was Female and sick of Her condition. Something was waiting there, in that idea, but Hazel never looked directly at it; she only glanced.

And in the afternoon of Christmas Day—for how long now? for as long as she could recall—she would go to Finney's house to exchange gifts with her. There was more pleasure in one of those afternoons than in all the Christmases with Hazel's own family combined. Hazel delighted in watching Malcolm fall asleep after dinner, tipped back in his recliner in front of the television: just that. A man who could be sated by nothing more than turkey and the gift of new socks. Janey bustled around the clean kitchen in an apron, usually in her battered house slippers, baking Christmas cakes that sometimes fell. What a treasure they were, these people for whom cakes collapsed, sleepy, normal people who worked hard and loved their daughter, and knew how to take a holiday off and spend it. They *spent* Christmas Day, like a bonus check or a tax return, while at the sterile Hunnicutt Clinic shoes were always worn; sleeping was a private activity conducted only at night, in a bedroom; and everything was hoarded— money and joy alike.

Last year and this year were different, and Hazel mourned the change even as she was driving toward it. At four o'clock the day was near fully dark, and Hazel was heading not in the direction of Malcolm and Janey's farm, where she had spent so much of her life, but toward Jonah. Hazel pictured the farm and it was summer there. She and Finney were driving a tractor back to the farthest southern lot to check on a mare and her colt. Or it was evening and the four of them were in the family room watching television, eating pizza off paper plates. Three cats from the ever-changing population were there with them, sitting on the back of the couch. Or there was a snow-storm, and Malcolm had just come in from the barn, saying, "The lights are out from Dan to Bathsheba," which Hazel knew meant a long, long way.

The gate to the front yard at Finney's farmhouse was crooked and wild roses grew up on either side of it in the spring. Janey had once owned a rabbit named Persnickety. Malcolm had, in 1957, hit and killed a silver fox and never forgiven himself. Hazel drove on Christmas Day, tried to quantify how much she knew of them, how much she remembered, but there was no end to it. Recalling Finney's life, Finney's family, was easier than recalling her own.

She drove past the high school and through the downtown; crossed the river and wandered through back streets to the mill houses along the railroad tracks and close to the grain elevator—the neighborhood known locally as Shack Town. Jim Hank had grown up here, but had saved his money and gotten out when his father finally died from drinking. Jim lived downtown now, in a small apartment above a shop that sold sewing machines.

In this light the houses were an indistinguishable gray; most seemed to have no paint left at all. There were no driveways here, or garages—just yards in which snow-covered, hobbled old trucks rested on blocks, and children's bicycles had been left to rust. The scene was even more dispiriting come spring, when the disguise of snow was gone and the mud and ruts were revealed. There were dogs, too, Hazel knew, shivering now in dark doghouses. In spring they appeared, dragging tow chains so heavy they sometimes became embedded in the dogs' necks.

This. This was where she now lived, the tall, graceful, starry-eyed skating girl, Finney.

Hazel walked with care up the precarious front steps, which canted to the left and were slick with mud and ice. The yellow bulb in the outside socket lent the porch a jaundiced air. Through the cheap, gauzy curtains in the front windows Hazel saw Finney's shadow move between two doorways in the center of the house, but when Hazel knocked, Finney was right there, waiting.

"Come in! Come in, Hazey May, and Merry Christmas." Finney kissed Hazel on the cheek, squeezed her hands.

"Are you expecting company?" On the small dining room table were two glasses, and an open bottle of wine.

"Just you, nutty girl." Finney took Hazel's coat and scarf, draped them over the arm of the sofa, a faded blue monstrosity with scarred wooden arms.

Hazel tried, as she had tried for the past eighteen months, not to look too closely at the home Finney had chosen for herself, for which she would forgo the comfort of the farm and her parents. It was right—she knew this—for Finney to leave home, no matter where she ended up, much more right than Hazel's decision to stay put. But the reason Finney moved when she did stuck in Hazel's throat like a bone; she couldn't get past it.

She had to hand it to Finney—she'd worked at the place gamely. There were brightly colored pillows on the cast-off sofa and chair in the living room, and scarves draped over the two lamps. She was going for a gypsy look, and had achieved it, as gypsies undoubtedly loved nice things as much as anyone else, and made do with what they had. It wasn't the decor that bothered Hazel, it was that Finney had chosen an atmosphere so shopworn and desperate. Shack Town was the end for most everyone who lived there, it was the dank bottom of the barrel. Finney was surrounded by alcoholics, by women in their twenties who'd already lost most of their teeth to their fathers' pliers. The children were hollow-eyed and prone to violence. Finney could have chosen a hundred different places, all of them an improvement, but she knew only one place where no one, not one soul, cared what her neighbor was doing.

"Sit down, let me pour you some wine." Finney gestured to the Formica table, and a metal chair with a bright yellow cushion.

"It's four in the afternoon," Hazel reminded her.

"But it's *Christmas.*"

"Fair enough."

Finney's hair was still cut in her signature style, but it no longer shone as it once had. She spent four mornings a week at the 10th Street Diner, serving up eggs and coffee and red-eye gravy in a fog of cigarette smoke and grease. It was all she could do, she'd once told

Hazel, to get the smell off before she went to her regular job at Sterling's. Some of the women she worked with gave her disquieting looks when she passed, though no one said anything outright.

"It's Mogen David," Finney said, pouring. "Not what Caroline would serve, I'm sure."

"Caroline loves you."

"I know—I'm sorry. I love her, too."

"Have you seen your parents today?" Hazel took a sip of the wine, licked her lips to hide any expression she might have made at the taste of it.

"Oh. Well."

"Finney, for God's sake."

"There was a chance he might drop by. He didn't say when, so I was afraid to leave. You know how it happens that you walk out the door for just a moment and the phone call you've been waiting for comes right then?"

"No. No, I don't know, because I don't stake my life on telephone calls."

Finney took a deep drink, blotted her lips on a cloth napkin. "I don't want us to fight."

"Neither do I."

"He doesn't come right out and say it, but I think there's a possibility, I think he may be considering leaving her when he's never thought about it before."

"He will never leave her."

"They don't sleep together anymore, that's what he told me, not even in the same bed."

Hazed sighed. "He's lying."

"No, no—their lives are completely separate. It's more like a contract he's fulfilling."

"That isn't even remotely true."

Finney drank the rest of her glass, poured another. Hazel rested her hand lightly on top of her own glass to prevent Finney from giving her more.

"We have a deep emotional bond, Hazel. I know you don't believe it, but it's impossible to put into words and impossible to get over."

"Clearly. You have wasted, Finn, *ten years* of your life. You can call it a deep emotional bond or mental illness or prison, you've still wasted it."

"I don't consider that time wasted." Finney sniffed, sat up straighter. Her second glass of wine was half gone, although Hazel had not seen her drink it.

"I never would have thought you could be this person."

"You don't love me anymore." Finney's eyes filled with tears. "You are the last friend I have and you don't love me either, anymore."

"You know why you have no friends. You know perfectly well what the reason is. Most of your friends couldn't even bear hearing about it anymore, this ghastly story you keep repeating and repeating, trying to convince everyone, trying to convince yourself."

"He's not who you think he is."

"Is that so?"

"I know you consider him . . . sinister in some way, cruel—"

"You left out dishonorable and manipulative."

"—but when we are together, when it's just the two of us, he's so tender. I know because of him what it feels like to be *loved*. When I'm in his arms I am loved and that's an amazing feeling, the only thing that matters."

Hazel blinked, looked down at the table.

"Can you say the same? Can you say you have ever felt loved?"

I felt loved by you once. "Do you know what this is, this argument you offer? You have somehow come to believe that there's such a thing as 'love,' such a thing as a *feeling* that is also an a priori truth, rather than an invention by the courtly poets. And you've got movies and music and books *confirming* for you that romantic 'love' is the highest good and it's what everyone is seeking and should be seeking. But it's a meager justification for what you've traded your life for. If there is any such thing as that sort of love, as opposed to the perfectly obvious and real love between parents and children, between friends, this ain't it, Finn, and you damn well know it."

Finney let her head fall to the table and she began sobbing. "I know you're right, I know what I've done here is awful and there's no justification for it, none at all. It makes me hate myself." She wiped her face with her napkin, leaving a smear of mascara on one cheek.

"Then stop."

"I try." Finney cried harder but was still able to pour herself another glass of wine. The bottle was nearly empty. "I've tried two thousand times. He gets ready to leave and I know he's going home to her and to his life, which everyone thinks is one thing and only I know the truth—"

"No, I also know the truth and so does Jim Hank: he's a fraud and a charlatan who has not only fooled you, he's fooled an entire community."

"—and I say to him, I scream at him, 'Just don't ever come back! You're killing me and I can't take it anymore! You're *killing* me!'"

Hazel could, alas, picture the scene: the disordered bedclothes, Finney flushed with drama while he stood before her, silently getting dressed and planning his return to his real life.

"Sometimes I even stick to it, I don't answer the phone or the door and if he comes into the diner because I won't answer him, I get someone else to take his table. He doesn't dare ask for me. But then something will happen, a week will go by, once even two weeks—"

"You talk as if I don't remember those two weeks. I remember them the way one would remember time spent as a *hostage*."

"—and I ran into him by accident. By accident, Hazel—"

"I was *there,* Finn."

"—at the gas station and our arms touched"—Finney rubbed her upper arm—"here, they touched here, and if we hadn't been in public we'd—"

"Do stop. Please."

Finney drained the wine, pushed the bottle aside with a practiced gesture. "I'm beginning to think he might not *always* be honest with me. There have been moments."

"So you've said."

"He talks about her sometimes and I get the feeling he's not telling the whole truth, it's just a sensation in my gut, I get sort of sick and fluttery just to hear him say her name. His mouth forms the word and I feel like his mouth belongs to me and another woman's name should not be in it. I told him not to call her by name anymore, I said he could refer to her as That Person, but he refuses. I think sometimes he doesn't even listen to me." Finney's chest and cheeks were bright red from the wine. There were dark circles under her eyes and her fingernails were chewed down to the quick. She reached for Hazel's full glass and Hazel said nothing. "Sometimes I follow him at a distance, when I have a day off I sometimes just follow him the whole day. I would give up the whole day just to see the back of his head in front of me, or in the summer to see him rest his arm on the open window. He has a scar on his left arm shaped like an arrow. I drive and I sit in the parking lot waiting for him to come out of the hardware store or the bank, I think about the first time I ever saw him and I can remember *everything*. I was so young but not too young, I was exactly the right age to see him."

Finney had begun to overenunciate all sibilant consonants, a sure sign that she was working overtime at staying upright and conscious. Hazel had heard it before—a few times, now that she thought about it.

"I—" Finney stood quickly; the blood drained from her face and her chin quivered. She ran with an awkward, tilted gait the few steps to the bathroom, slamming the door behind her. Within seconds Hazel could hear her, and she closed her eyes in sympathy. There was nothing worse than being sick that way, nothing. Hazel herself had never consumed enough alcohol to vomit, but she imagined it would be even worse than the flu, because she would know she'd done it to herself, as Finn was doing it to herself.

Hazel stood, took the empty bottle and the wineglasses into the spare, damp kitchen. Finney was trying to grow herbs in a little kitchen garden on the windowsill, but everything looked thin and barely alive. She washed out the glasses so Finney wouldn't have to face them in the morning, threw the bottle in the trash. In a drawer that only opened halfway, Hazel found a hand towel, which she soaked with cold water and took with her to the bathroom.

She didn't knock. Finn was on her knees in front of the toilet, her head down on her forearms. She was breathing heavily; panting. Hazel knelt behind her, laid the cold towel across her neck just as she began throwing up again.

"I didn't eat all day."

"I understand."

"I should have eaten, I thought if he came I'd leave afterward and go home and Mama would feed me."

Hazel pulled off Finney's flat shoes, put them in the closet, then unbuttoned her blue jeans and pulled them down. It wasn't easy; Finn neither fought nor helped. She lay on her back, completely still and staring at the ceiling. She wore beautiful underwear, probably something she'd gotten at Sterling's—white silk with lace inlaid on either hip.

"You might have to—Finn, you need to sit up just a minute so I can get your sweater off."

"My bra, too, I can't sleep in a bra." She didn't move.

"You're going to have to sit up a minute."

Hazel wrestled her out of everything but her panties, and Finn lay back, exhausted.

"You have to stay with me tonight, Hazey, you have to." Finney was crying, but easily. She made no noise and didn't draw attention to her tears. "You don't know how lonely and heartsick I am all the time. If I didn't have two jobs I don't know what I would—"

"It isn't night."

"Excuse me?"

"I said it isn't yet night. It's only five-thirty in the evening."

"No, it's very late. It's very late, Hazel."

She sat on the edge of the bed, making phone calls. Malcolm and Janey first, to say that Finney wouldn't be coming over because she was ill and in bed. They were sad, and confused. They'd been confused about Finney for years. Hazel barely made it through the conversation without bursting into tears herself.

She called Caroline, who seemed a bit perplexed that Hazel wasn't home; she hadn't noticed her daughter's absence.

"Enjoy yourself, dear."

"Mother, will you make sure Mercury has food and water?"

"I will if I remember," Caroline said, before hanging up.

Hazel expected to turn around and find Finney asleep, but her eyes were wide. "I'm going to borrow a nightgown, okay?" Hazel asked.

"They're in the top drawer. Take whichever you like."

Hazel chose the longest and most modest, which was still more revealing than anything Hazel had ever owned.

"Please, you're going to stay, aren't you? Please don't go."

"I said I would."

"I'm afraid you'll change your mind."

"I won't."

"Please come get in bed with me, my teeth are chattering."

"You aren't wearing any clothes."

"I'm freezing, please come get in bed with me. You aren't going to leave, are you?"

Hazel pulled back Finney's old crazy quilt, a second blanket, a sheet, and slipped in beside Finney, who was indeed shivering.

"I'll stop talking about him now," Finney said, turning on her side and facing Hazel.

"Good."

Finney was studying her, and Hazel felt the gaze travel over her like a fever. She closed her own eyes, she would not return the look. The bedroom was so quiet she could hear every movement of their skin against the sheets. Finney moved an arm up, up. A cold hand—just the right amount of cold—rested on Hazel's cheek.

"Hazey," Finney whispered, now very close to Hazel's face. In the bathroom Hazel had helped her brush her teeth and still there was the wine on top of the toothpaste. The smell of the wine was abiding, as if Finney had been working on it a long time. Finney's breath was nothing at all what it had been when they were growing up. Her skin, too, smelled different.

Hazel opened her eyes just before Finney kissed her, and saw that Finney was crying harder—late crying, it might be called—just tears flowing steadily, ignored. Her lips were chilled, the hand that had been on Hazel's face was now resting in the curve of her neck. Finney kissed just the corner of Hazel's mouth, light, lightly, then took Hazel's bottom lip between her teeth. Tears dropped onto Hazel's face and ran down toward the pillow, and it took a moment for Hazel to realize she was crying, too.

"This is what you want, isn't it?" Finney spoke quietly into Hazel's mouth. "This is what you've always wanted."

Hazel couldn't answer. She was stunned to discover that she could *feel* the shape of Finney's mouth; the Cupid's-bow top lip she'd only ever seen, she could now feel with her own. When did she begin kissing back? Later she wouldn't be able to separate the moments, one from another.

"Everyone else is gone, so disappointed with me." Finney moved her hand across Hazel's shoulder. "But you stay."

"I stay."

"Because you're in love with me."

"No, Finn."

"Yes, you are. You are devoted to me in a way he'll never be." Finney was crying harder now, speaking between small gasps. She moved her body closer to Hazel's, closer still, until her breasts were pressed against Hazel's own. Hazel couldn't breathe; she felt her chest expanding and contracting, a flutter there that was perhaps fatal. What if this was how she died? How could it be explained? Her body was turning to liquid, water spilling over hot stones. Finney's hand traced the contours of Hazel's face.

"There it is," Finney said, choking on tears, every other word a supreme effort, "there's that old scar."

"It's an old scar." Hazel reached up for Finney's hand, gently pushed it away. "You're drunk." What she meant was this can't happen, it will ruin everything, I will lose you completely.

"I've been drinking all day." Finney's hand returned to the nape of Hazel's neck. She pressed her fingertips into the hollow place there and Hazel felt it in her feet.

"I know."

"I forget what I was saying." Her hand stopped moving, went limp against Hazel's shoulder.

"You were saying you need to go to sleep." Hazel tried to dry Finney's face with her thumb.

"No, that's not it." Finney's eyes closed. She tried to open them but couldn't. She was silent for a minute, maybe two. In a long-ago winter, standing in Janey's kitchen, Finney had told Hazel that if she wanted to know how long two minutes really was, she should try stirring cake batter that long with a wooden spoon. "I was saying I love you, I love you so horribly, I wish this were our bed and that you lived here with me."

Hazel froze. She listened to her heartbeat, allowed herself to feel the inrushing of possibility, hope rising up like the back of a whale. "You want me to live with you?"

Finney buried her face in the pillow in a gesture of pain Hazel had seen many laboring women make. "Of course I do," she said, hiccupping around another sob, "it's what I've always wanted. I want you to *myself,* I want you to leave her. I want you to *leave her.*"

Hazel closed her own eyes, took a deep breath. She rolled over on her back, looked at the ceiling. Beside her, Finney continued to sob, resting her head now on Hazel's shoulder. "Lift up," Hazel said, "and let me put my arm behind you." Finney curled up against her side. Her skin was hot now and the sheets felt sticky even in the drafty, cold bedroom. Hazel said nothing as Finney's sobs faded into a tremor and her breathing grew shallow. She lay unmoving, staring at nothing, the taste of Finney's mouth still on her lips. She would stay a little longer, and then she would slip out of bed and get dressed and go home. She would escape from Finney's bed just as he would, and dress quietly the way he would, even though it was Christmas Day and he had never bothered to come, and Hazel had.

"I feel like I've been drinking." Rebekah pulled the afghan more closely around her feet. She was stretched out on the couch, periodically pressing her fingers against her temples, trying to stop a headache. Bandit was on the floor in front of the couch, asleep on her side. She seemed exhausted, partly just from eating.

"Millie does that to me, too. Drinking, or brawling in the tavern where I did the drinking."

"We have a dog now."

Claudia rested her head against the rocking chair, sighed. "It seems that way. Do you want more hot chocolate?"

"No, I just want to lie here. Remember we got up this morning and it was Christmas, and then we went to church? This is still that same day, but doesn't the first part seem so long ago?"

"It *was* a long time ago."

"Claudia, I want to tell you something before I faint."

Claudia looked slightly alarmed, but said, "Okay."

"Since my mother died, I've never . . ." Rebekah paused, considered her next words. "I've never felt so safe is what I'm trying to say.

I was afraid all the time with my dad, imagine that. I was afraid from the moment he walked in the door until he left for work again, and really I was afraid even when he wasn't there because he was going to be there eventually. And I didn't belong in that house anymore and he didn't want me, but I was raised to be helpless. I didn't—I couldn't figure out how to begin. After I met Hazel, she saw that right away, the fear I had that living in the world was too much for me. She told me to pretend, from the moment I woke up each day, that I only had one thing to do, just one. First it was brush my teeth. And when that was done I'd have just one more thing to do. I spent the first year I worked with her literally doing one thing at a time, like a stroke victim."

"You're very competent now."

"No, you're very competent. I—I don't think I've changed all that much. I see people on television, women living alone in Manhattan or London, going to work every day and navigating what looks to me like a terrifying maze, and I know I could never, ever do it. I would die of shock, like a rabbit in a trap. I don't want to be the sort of person who forever needs to be taken care of, but."

"But maybe you need to be taken care of."

Rebekah sighed. "It's a sad thing to have to admit. You, though. That's what I'm trying to say. You have been better to me than anyone has ever been, and I will never forget it. I'll build my life around remembering this kindness you've shown to me." She'd never meant anything as much, and then she heard a car in the driveway.

Claudia remembered the sound of a tree going down in a storm when she was a teenager, the way it had whined in an almost human voice, on and on, until it finally snapped. Rebekah was saying something that was that storm, or she was marshaling its energy for the future. There was, in Rebekah's gratitude, the promise to file Claudia in Treasured Incidents, which was the opposite of the promise Claudia wanted to hear. She didn't even need a vow; a vague understanding would do.

Bandit heard the car first. She sat up, immediately alert, her poor butchered ears unable to move or signal anything. Headlights washed across the wall behind Claudia, who stood up and looked out the window.

"It's probably Millie," Rebekah said from the couch, her eyes closing. "Or else it's Hazel with . . . I don't know, a peacock? An entire family of Vietnamese refugees?"

It was a white car, probably the person who had been there earlier in the day. Claudia couldn't see who got out, so she waited at the door until there was a knock, tentative and unrevealing. Bandit didn't bark, just stood watching the door.

"Who is it?" Rebekah asked, standing up. Claudia looked back at her, looked at Rebekah in her pink nightgown and the new robe Claudia had given her for Christmas, the flush of her cheeks that meant she was sleepy. Then she opened the door to Peter, who had his hands in his pockets and was half turned away, so that when he turned back to them it was as if he were offering his face as a gift. Claudia had not remembered him as so pretty, but he was: his eyelashes, his lips, his black hair. He offered both women an innocent shrug, as if to say, *What are we going to do about me?* Behind her she heard Rebekah take in a breath, then steady herself before saying, "Peter, what are you doing here?"

He took a step in—Peter took a step into Claudia's house before she had invited him—and he smiled at both women. Oh, of course, Claudia remembered now; there was also that smile. "Hey, Beckah," he said, and in his every gesture, the nuance of his voice, there was a knowledge of Rebekah, a claim to her, and that old tree on Claudia's land snapped and fell to the ground.

Six Months Later

Chapter 8

JUNE WAS A COIN TOSS. It could be a paradise, like today, seventy degrees, only the occasional white puff of cloud against a clean blue sky; the sort of day that had made Claudia wonder, as a child, where the blue of the sky came from, when air has no color, no matter how high you go.

She and Amos were walking down the gravel alley that was the outermost edge of Haddington. On one side of them were backyards and flower gardens, clothes hung on lines, and swing sets. On the other side were cornfields, hundreds of acres.

From a distance they must have looked like two very tall men taking the measure of an estate, which was the only reason men in the Midwest ever walked anywhere. They walked to where the horses got out, and they walked to the place they thought they'd someday build a new house. But strolling down the wide alley at the edge of town was not the business of men.

"Even being aware of it myself," she said, "has made me realize how diminished my status is."

"Your status," Amos said, nodding.

"I mean, just at the social level, I am at the lowest ranking in this society."

"Not the lowest, surely."

"I've been thinking, what if PBS wanted to make an after-school special about how hard it is for a child to go visit his father in prison? Republicans would grumble because any depiction of the poor is not

Family Value friendly. Because it doesn't depict the pretend ideal family. It's possible—barely—PBS would be able to sneak it in."

"I agree."

"But imagine if PBS wanted to make an after-school special about an intact, employed, *Christian* family headed by two lesbians or two gay men."

"It couldn't be done."

"*That's* what I'm saying. Lesbians are lower in the hierarchy than maximum-security prisoners. Murderers, rapists, you name it, they are higher."

They walked in silence a minute or two, Amos so distracted by what Claudia said he twice almost walked into an overhanging branch. "What makes you believe in this hierarchy," he asked, "and who controls it?"

"I believe in it because it's right in front of us all the time."

"And who runs it?"

"I don't know, Amos." Claudia sighed. "The same people who run everything."

"But couldn't you . . . isn't it possible to ignore it, to refuse to grant a *tottering,* if you ask me, social structure such power?"

Claudia turned to Amos, smiled at him. "Where are you on it, do you suppose? On this abstract list."

Amos laughed, pushed up his glasses. "Fair point." They reached the end of the alley, where one of the farmhouses original to the town had been torn down to make way for a double-wide, and turned around. "You're saying you understand Rebekah's decision."

"Yes," Claudia said. "I always did. No one would choose this, given the option."

"So for her it was a choice, you think, and for you it isn't."

"For me it isn't, as it turns out." Claudia ran her hand over her hair. "Although I haven't lived any differently, it was just, it was only her. As for Rebekah, we'll never know. Well, that's not right, exactly. She *did* choose, so I do know."

Amos kicked a rock by accident, looked at it as if it had leapt out of nowhere. "There is just stuff *everywhere,*" he said, shaking his head. "I'm reminded of a conversation I had a few years back with a man in a diner, an ordinary guy from Ohio. He believed the Second Amendment was not up for discussion; hated feminists—he thought they were funny, I mean; didn't love, shall we say, minorities. Didn't like paying taxes, hated liberals—hated all Democrats, actually. His pet issue was inner-city welfare mothers, for some reason. I asked him if he'd ever been to an inner city and he waved me away with disgust. Like visiting a zoo without any cages, he said. All these welfare mothers were crackheads and whores who had babies just to increase their monthly subsidies."

"Guess where this guy is on the hierarchy."

Amos nodded. "Afraid so, yes. Not only were these women robbing him of his hard-earned money, they were tipping the population balance, so that soon the minority population of the United States would be higher than the white. And then good-bye civilization. He'd had this idea, a revolutionary idea, he thought, to develop these mobile spay/neuter buses. Have you seen those, where you can take a dog or cat?"

Claudia stopped walking, turned and looked at Amos, who didn't stop. She took one long step and rejoined him.

"He said the government should drive the bus into the worst, most crime-ridden areas of any city. Gather up the whole neighborhood, men, women, teenagers. Offer them a thousand dollars cash, on the spot, to be sterilized. They sign a waiver, you give them the money, snip, move on to the next block."

"Just . . . okay, just to start with, where does the money come from?"

"I asked him that, and he said that at least half the taxpaying population of this country would willingly contribute to a fund for that purpose, maybe more than half. I said to him, 'What if the thousand dollars was spent on alcohol and drugs? You surely don't want to contribute to the *drug* trade.' He said the drug trade is someone else's problem and he didn't care how the money was spent. I told him that he had to admit—there is no way around it—that denying a person his or her fertility is to deny them what we've always seen as a fundamental human right, and is fascistic in the extreme. But, he said, he wouldn't be depriving them of anything. No one would *have* to take the money, no one would *have* to have the procedure, it would all be entirely voluntary. Nothing like fascism."

Claudia was silent.

"I finally said, but how could he get his conscience around the obvious? Those people have *nothing*—even their most basic needs are not being met. Many are addicted to drugs, many have probably never held a thousand dollars at one time in their lives. To offer them money for any part of their bodies, any part of their future, is coercion. And to render people sterile by coercion is evil, plain and simple. It is evil."

"I'm guessing he wasn't swayed."

Amos shook his head. "Of course not. I asked him if he fancied himself a Christian and he said he was a lifelong in-the-pew-every-time-the-doors-were-open Baptist. I asked him to imagine, then, what Jesus would think of his proposition. He laughed out loud. Jesus, he said, had his own way of dealing with taxes, didn't he?".

"Am I supposed to see"—Claudia rubbed her forehead, where the trace of a headache was blooming—"that I'm not at the bottom of the hierarchy?"

"No." Amos stopped, looked out at the midday sun on the field beside them. "All I'm saying is that if you are, then Rebekah was coerced."

Claudia turned away from him, looked out at the same field he was studying. "I see people like me everywhere now, I guess that happens whatever your condition is, and they're all married with children. They're fighting tooth and claw against what their neighbors would think about them, would *do* to them if they knew the truth."

"Do you consider those people to be cowards?"

"No. No, I don't. They're just doing the best they can, like everyone else. But they all look so miserable and out of place. They stand out like a misplaced piece of a jigsaw puzzle. I can't imagine what it costs them to live that way."

Amos and Claudia turned onto the side street that would lead Amos back to his office and Claudia back to her car.

"They're saying rain tomorrow," Claudia told him.

"I heard. Rain is good."

"Rain is fine, yes."

Rebekah lay on her back, which she wasn't really supposed to do, and looked at the sky through the living room window. Now in her eighth month, she looked like an exhibit at SeaWorld. A lump the size of a grapefruit rose up against her skin—the baby's bottom. Sometimes an elbow revealed itself, or the flat sole of a foot. When the baby had the hiccups, Rebekah's entire midsection jumped rhythmically. All of it was hilarious, or would have been if it weren't so weird. Whose idea was this, anyway? Who would think that the best way to propagate the species would be to grow a new one inside a used one? She imagined a white-coated scientist in a laboratory saying to another, "Yeah, yeah—that's a good idea. Let's put it in . . . what part isn't doing anything else? And it'll be too big to get out? Perfect."

She turned on her right side, causing the baby to turn and kick her in the kidneys. Lying on her back was amusing in a sideshow sort of way, but lying on her side actually allowed her to breathe. Her heartbeat settled; the day was lovely, even looking at it through a window, although the window itself left a great deal to be desired. She had remembered Peter's house as rustic and romantic, but once she came back she saw that it was actually just shabby. The cabin had been cold all winter, and was now damp and hot and growing mold. His window was dirty, and the trim was missing from the top of the frame. The ivory curtains were streaked with dust, and hung as if they'd never been moved, as if the wind had never touched them. The first few months she'd lived there Rebekah had cleaned every day, believing she could turn the place around, and had been defeated at each turn. Everything was the same: the dim bathroom in which giant tree roaches and wolf spiders were regularly found; the grotty aquarium; the spice rack with its evidence of mice. When they were dating, Rebekah had imagined living here, and had seen the two of them as pioneers of a sort—she'd seen them baking bread and cooking fresh fish on a grill (she'd never thought about who would actually catch the fish)—practicing a daily authenticity made plausible by the cabin, the trees, the isolation. But everything in this house was a prop, just a thin backdrop to a story that wasn't even interesting.

Poor Peter. His do-it-yourself singer-songwriter tour had not been a success; the people who booked such acts hadn't been impressed with his repertoire. "Not," Rebekah had asked him on Christmas night, "the song about the tree house?" No, he answered sadly. "Not the one about Pumpkin?" Pumpkin had been Peter's childhood schnauzer. *And when we buried Pumpkin dear / I knew at least he'd reappear / in this same patch come autumn / some fine year.* They hadn't loved the telegraph song, the flashlight song, or the one about umbrellas.

He'd totaled his truck in Kentucky, and when he called his parents they discovered he'd let his insurance lapse. He signed the truck over to a wrecking service and flew home on a ticket his parents bought him. All of it—the rejections, the wreck, the flight to Indianapolis— had taken five days, and in that time Mandy, the twenty-year-old college student with the bright future, had taken up with a tattoo artist from Fort Myers, Florida, and gone south, leaving Peter heartbroken.

Rebekah lifted the dirty curtain so she could see more of the sky. A slight breeze touched her arm, even though the window wouldn't open; the *problem* with the *cabin* (a phrase she found herself saying to Peter nearly every day) was that there was no solid division between the inside and the outside. She hadn't always spoken to him in such a way, she hadn't said things like how much she *hated* the kitchen drawers or how dearly she wished he would clean out his *stupid* fish tank, or could he possibly *bother himself* to bring home some milk? She and Peter had been fine for the first couple of months, given that she wouldn't allow him to sleep in the same bed with her and he didn't protest, and knowing, as Rebekah did, that Peter had come and claimed her because his parents, after Rebekah had refused their offer of an abortion, had threatened to cut off his allowance if he didn't. They were fine playing house as long as she was still working and supporting them and he stayed home and did whatever it was he did all day. They kept up the veneer of preparing to be a family even though Rebekah had already lost two—the family of her childhood, and her life with Claudia and Oliver—and it was loss of the latter that had finally cleaved her spirit as cleanly as a lightning strike but she never said so. She never told Peter that Claudia was so distant to her at work Rebekah had given up trying to talk to her, and that she only got to see Oliver when Hazel arranged it. She swallowed that grief and spent Sundays with Peter's mom and dad, who punished her with their *rightness,* with the way they fit into the life of Jonah, Indiana, regardless of how narrow the space they were given. While Rebekah was still working Peter even mentioned marriage, knowing that marriage would have been a species of salvation for her, a belonging, finally. She said she'd think about it, and neither of them brought it up again. In the evenings she cleaned and cooked and he played on his computer and sometimes built a fire in the stone fireplace, and things were nearly what she had dreamed of when she used to dream of Peter.

But things had changed when she went into preterm labor and was placed on bed rest. She received disability insurance but it wasn't enough. It also turned out she could no longer clean and cook every day and Peter was not inclined to do so himself, and even though he was less inclined toward gainful employment, he weighed the evils and took a job in the sporting goods department at Sears, the noon-to-closing shift. The store closed at nine; it took an hour for him to get his deposit ready, and for the shelves to be restocked. In the beginning she waited up for him, mostly because she'd nearly gone insane from all the authenticity of the cabin, and she needed to hear a voice that wasn't the television or the radio. More and more often she was asleep by the time he got home, although she always remembered to make up his bed on the futon. If she got up to go to the bathroom, she would find him sitting in the dark living room at the computer, sending instant messages to Mandy in Florida. At seven in the morning, when Rebekah could no longer sleep, Peter would rouse himself from the couch and go to Rebekah's bed, getting up just before work every day. In this way they lived in the same house, but not together.

Rebekah sighed and tried to sleep but her eyes kept opening without her permission and her hips against the hard futon ached so badly they felt broken. When she walked it seemed she was walking on a broken pelvis, too, bones grinding against bones like the graphics in an arthritis commercial. Was it a Tuesday? Tuesday was a good deal like Monday, or Wednesday, for that matter. In fact, the only different day was Sunday, which Peter spent with his parents. Rebekah had gradually withdrawn from the visits and dinners, citing exhaustion. Kathy came to see her sometimes, and always brought a gift for the baby. There was no animosity between them, just an unspoken agreement built on common sense. Sometimes on a Sunday, Hazel would stop by with Oliver. It was such a brief time—a couple hours at most—and each time Hazel was there, Rebekah saw precisely how much she had missed, what was gone of his life already and would never be reclaimed. He had been just a sprite when she left, and now he was a strong, almost stocky towheaded boy. A little Viking.

She turned over, with difficulty, to her left side. Today was not Sunday, so there was no Hazel, no Oliver. No Claudia. Rebekah's eyes stung, and she took a deep breath, trying not to cry. Claudia had never called her, not one time. She'd never come to see her. As far as Rebekah knew, she'd never inquired after her, didn't care how she was.

Rebekah moved to her bed, where she lay on her side and thought about Claudia. She told Hazel some things, like how often she dreamed about Claudia and the content of those dreams, but there were other things she didn't say. She didn't say, for instance, that sometimes she awakened in the night, her mouth dry and her heart skipping around in her chest, because she harbored an irrational, overwhelming fear that someone else was living in Claudia's house. She would lie in the dark and feel first the fear and then a sweeping sensation of jealousy she'd never, ever known before. It was not what she'd felt when she heard about Mandy and Peter, not at all. That had been mostly confusion, shock—a domestic threat. This was something else; this was a *monster*. Every week she found a way to ask Hazel, in a roundabout way, whether Claudia and Oliver were alone at the house, and every week Hazel said of course. Who else would be there? Each time she asked, Rebekah both wanted to know and did not want to know, all at once. There was a pause in the air between the asking and the answer, and in that pause was a thrill. She couldn't explain it. She did know that more than once she'd imagined someone—someone not at all like Rebekah—cooking, or walking down the stairs with Oliver, and Rebekah simply killed her. It was impossible, she would tell herself in more lucid moments, that she was dreaming of killing anyone, even a nonexistent person. Impossible. And yet the feeling didn't go away, month after month—the fear and dread and the grisly violence remained right on the surface of her consciousness. Alive: it was a living feeling, and when it came Rebekah felt herself sit up, wake up, her bruised bones thrumming, her senses sharp as knives.

She opened her eyes. In front of her was Peter's dresser, the top of which was littered with his belongings—loose change, scraps of paper, souvenirs, she didn't know what it all was. Yes, she did: it was irritating, that's what. And there was his guitar, propped up on a cheap stand in the corner, getting dusty. He never played it anymore, claiming he needed privacy in order to compose. She had imagined, during their conversation on Christmas Day, spending evenings in front of the fire, the light flickering, Peter singing. If she was honest, and why not, she didn't have anything else to do, she'd somehow put Claudia and Oliver in the scene, too; they had been in the background, enjoying it with her. There was nothing she wouldn't have shared with them, including her miraculous reconciliation, her Great Love returned to her.

Maybe she would go out and sit on the porch, try to take a walk down to the mailbox. Her sciatic nerve was pinched; the long ligaments under her abdomen were in constant pain. If she stood up too fast she fainted. But standing up gradually gave her time to look down at the bedroom floor, something she usually avoided doing. There were gaps between the cheap pine boards, wide enough for hair and dirt, even coins, to collect there. Kathy had painted the floor an institutional blue-gray that had worn badly, become more depressing than the unfinished boards themselves. The nylon area rug Peter had put next to the bed was unraveling. All manner of debris, even dead leaves, were gathered in the corners and against the baseboards. Rebekah put her hand over her eyes, took deep breaths. Something very bad had happened, and she was unable to think about it clearly. All the clues were here, but her mind was so sluggish, her motivations and desires were so distant from her they might as well have belonged to a stranger.

In order to stand, she had to believe she remembered how. She argued with herself, was persuasive, and the next thing she knew she was standing. Rebekah had imagined, back in the mythical, unpregnant time, that she would never waddle as most pregnant women did. She would never waddle, she'd never dress stupidly, she'd never complain. Today she wore a gigantic flannel nightgown Hazel had brought home from the store. There was a hole under one arm and the hem had come out. Without socks or shoes, the floor was clammy, gritty, but she had a hard time reaching her feet without help.

Rebekah took a step forward, moaned involuntarily, then waddled back into the living room. Peter's fish fought the good fight in their dirty aquarium, and right next to the struggling real fish, animated underwater creatures swam through a black, clean sea on the screen saver on Peter's computer. Rebekah sat down at the desk, touched the mouse, and the fish disappeared, leaving behind the text of Peter's last conversation with Mandy. This happened every day. The first time had been an accident; Rebekah had been cleaning and saw her name. She turned away without reading the exchange. But the second time it happened, she realized Peter wasn't just careless—it didn't matter to him if she read what he wrote at night.

Peter referred to her by name, or by the initial *R*. Rebekah had spent most of an afternoon trying to figure out who was speaking, and what on earth they were saying. They seemed to employ a language invented by three-year-olds. Today's conversation went like this:

Luvrboy614: whats it like
Panda7892: hot sunny
Luvrboy614: hot is nice
Panda7892: when r u coming
Luvrboy614: ?
Panda7892: !
Luvrboy614: I told u
Panda7892: 2day is margaritas at Cactus Charlies b there by 5 or
    else
Luvrboy614: else wut
Panda7892: like that time in Indy
Luvrboy614: !
Luvrboy614: I WISH

On and on they went, for hours every night. The thrust of their dialogue, if it could be said to thrust, was that Luvrboy had gotten himself in a trap (Mandy's words); Panda was doing some 'dancing' in addition to just generally enjoying existence; life would be perfect if they could only be on the beach together, drinking strong alcohol and getting good tans. Today there was this little philosophical blip:

Luvrboy614: wut i miss most about u is u r feral
Panda7892: wuts that mean
Luvrboy614: like a wild animal

Panda7892: screw u

Luvrboy614: sigh

Neither Peter nor Rebekah ever mentioned Mandy or Florida or Happy Hour at Cactus Charlie's. Their conversations were always innocuous, there was never any confrontation. When he came through the front door, or if Rebekah called him at work to ask him to bring something home with him, he always said, "How ya doing, kiddo?" in just the way he'd always talked to her. Sweet. He was a sweet man, and she got it—she understood that he was always kind and cooperative, and he always did exactly as he pleased. Kathy had told her that when Peter was in elementary school, she would send him to his room to do his homework, and an hour later he'd come out with his baseball bat or a comic book. She'd say, "Homework done?" And he'd say, "It sure is," with a smile so convincing Kathy didn't check, and the homework was never done.

Rebekah sat back, sighed. She needed a pillow behind her back but couldn't have one without getting up and going to the couch. There was another letter, an actual letter she'd been carrying around unread for three days since she'd found it tucked under the windshield wiper of her car on Sunday. That night she slid it under her pillow, but found that having it there wasn't conducive to healthy sleep, so she'd moved it into the book she was reading. Yesterday and today she'd carried it in the pocket of her mammoth nightgown, and taking it out she discovered it had bent to the shape of her thigh and the flap had come unsealed. On the front was her name written in her father's handwriting. She recognized it as she would a photograph of him. She took out the folded pages of lined notebook paper, put them back. Just looking at them, the awkward way they'd been arranged to fit in the envelope, made her sad. What could cause a man like Vernon Shook to put pen to paper? She closed her eyes, tried to imagine him sitting at the kitchen table, so full of . . . what? There was nothing there, no anger or sorrow or regret. She could see the table, exactly as she'd left it, but not her father. And not her father writing. What made her finally take the letter out and smooth the crumpled pages on Peter's desk wasn't curiosity—she was too tired to care, really—but the thought that someday she'd have this to tell Claudia in person. Oh, by the way, I got a letter from my dad. Claudia would look up from what she was doing, or she'd turn from the kitchen sink, and say Really? And then Rebekah would take it out of her pocket, just like she had a few minutes ago, and Claudia would accept it, smoothing it out on the counter at Hazel's, or next to the toaster at home, just as Rebekah was doing.

> Dear Rebekah, I bet you didnt expect to get a letter from me, you know I am not much of a writer as I had to leave school too soon to help grandpa on the farm. Now Rebekah there are lots of things you dont know and I am not about to tell. Times before you was born and like and we could have been a different family if things had worked out different but their not. This house is sure not the same as it was, I come home of an evening and its quiet. The Bible tells us we will be change in the twinkle of an eye and I look toward that day when I will see your mother again and others I have love. But this is not a sermon, it hurts just to hold a pen so long I dont see how Pastor does it. I thought I was to be called up to the ministry, I was sure of it but there was something so heavy on my heart and the Elders couldn't forgive although God will take it up with me on that glorious day ALL will be forgave. Was a long dark time I forgot Gods will not mine be done. Keep that in your mind Rebekah about Gods will when I say this next part. I know you arent any more living with that woman thank the Lord, though one day I seen you at the grocery and my heart about stopped as you had that baby, I thought how could that be him so soon. Now you are back with that other one and whatever you are thinking about him you are wrong. Pastor says nothing pleases the Lord like one of His own comes home. You may recall Cyrus and Penny Jester, well they have been marry 9 years and never blessed with children. If you keep your child he is hell bound there is no more to say. We have all of us prayed and prayed over it and Pastor says the Jesters can have your baby and we will make him new as an angel. I counted and no when your time is and I will come right to the hospital and take that child from the arms of Satan to the heavenly kingdom of god, this is what I want to give to you as last things from
>
> Your father,
> Vernon Shook

Rebekah folded the letter and placed it back in the envelope, her hands shaking. White stars danced at the edge of her vision. She ran her finger over her name written in her father's hand. If she had one wish—no, that never worked—if she could wish something, it would be to see Ruth as a girl. And what if Rebekah were able to say to Ruth, *don't, don't marry him, he will eat away your spirit like a cancer,* would she do it? Would Rebekah sacrifice the finely calibrated puzzle of her own genes? Her red hair, which was Vernon's, after all; the set of her jaw? And would Ruth, knowing how the story ended, listen to her?

She started as if she'd been sleeping, looked around at the bleak accommodations. She owned nothing, having left all of her belongings at Claudia's, even her sewing machine. She owed nothing. There was a possibility, vague and fearsome, just at the edge of her consciousness, but she couldn't reach it. Standing up from the desk chair was easier than from the bed, and soon she was on the couch, an old musty quilt wrapped around her. A fever was rising in her like a velvet curtain on a silent film, blocking the pain in her back and in her legs just long enough for her to fall asleep. Outside the sun was promising and the world was new; the trees, the soil in the fields surrounding the cabin awoke, and the baby, too, awakened but as if to thunder, and turned over, then turned again.

"Are you going to get one of these?" Hazel asked.

"I'm sorry?"

"You're stopped in front of the rawhides, I thought maybe you were going to get one for Bandit."

"Oh. Sure, yes. Pick one out."

In the child's seat of the grocery cart, Oliver wrestled with his restraint. When he became angry enough, he pounded on the back of Claudia's hands with his fists. He called her Ma, which made sense, and Hazel, Neem.

"Get the chicken-flavored one. She'll like that." Hazel lifted her glasses and read the label. "Is this what it claims to be, a raw piece of hide?"

Oliver had nearly figured out the clasp on the restraint when his

fingers slipped off. Furious, he bounced up and down in the seat, rocking the cart.

"Whoa, Bamm-Bamm," Hazel said, reaching in her bag for something to distract him. She pulled out a wooden boat, which he instantly stuck in his mouth. "If pieces of that show up later, don't blame me. I wanted to bring the zwieback."

"It turns to cement when it dries."

"We would cross that bridge," Hazel said, tossing the chicken-flavored bone in the cart. "Maybe we should give Oliver a rawhide. Like the kind for puppies?"

Claudia could see the grocery list she'd left on the counter, could see the first three items: milk, diapers, baby food. They went without saying. What came after? Subtle things like poultry seasoning and ChapStick. But not those. She tried to concentrate on what was before her, but she was in the pet aisle, which meant birdseed and cat litter on one side, laundry detergent and bathroom cleaner on the other. Was that it? Laundry detergent? She tried to picture the shelf above the washing machine, couldn't remember anything about the last time she'd washed clothes.

"Hazel, why am I here?"

"To know God, love Him, and serve Him in this world, and to be happy with Him forever in the next."

"Was I out of something?"

"I don't know, milk, diapers, baby food?"

"What did I say when you called? I said I have to go to the grocery store to get . . . you say the rest."

"Yes, I wasn't really listening."

Oliver pulled so hard at the strap around his waist, one end nearly came dislodged. He looked up at Claudia and showed all eight of his teeth, the way dogs will when they're happy, or before they bite. He cried Mamamamama, holding his arms up, pleading for freedom.

"He's very manipulative, this one," Hazel said. "Less like a Gemini than—"

"Was it animal? Vegetable? Was it food or something else?"

"—an Aries. But that would mean he was born much earlier than the date on his birth certificate."

Claudia glanced around the store. She was too distracted to try to complete this errand, and the only sane thing to do would be to go

home and when she got the list, come back. And that would mean enduring the countless difficulties of getting Oliver into his car seat, out of his car seat, all over again.

"Let's head this way, shall we?" Hazel asked, heading toward Frozen Foods and Dairy.

"Eggs!" Claudia said, as soon as she saw them. "That was one thing, eggs. There was more, but that's a start."

It was June 25, more than a month after Ludie's traditional day to begin spring cleaning. Claudia meant to abide by the ritual, even though the parts of the house she used got cleaned all the time. This morning she'd started in her old bedroom, at that end of the upstairs hallway. She stripped the beds of the sheets Rebekah had slept on, and hung the comforter on the line outside. She took down the curtains, cleaned the windows, vacuumed behind the radiator, checked the closet. Nothing there to speak of, besides linens and some old winter coats. She polished the desktop, blew the dust off her books. She had closed the door behind her.

"Perhaps you were thinking of making peanut butter cookies," Hazel said, checking the eggs for secret breaks.

That was it—Claudia saw the whole list. Baking soda, that was the subtle thing she'd needed. She wrapped her hands around Hazel's head, smashing her puffy hair, then leaned down and kissed her on the forehead. "Thank you, thank you." Oliver waved, made his kiss-face, said, "Bye-bye, Neem. Bye-bye."

"Do you want to come in?" Hazel asked, stepping out of the Jeep. "The cats would love to see Oliver."

Claudia laughed, picturing poor Sprocket the last time they were there, tearing through the house with his tail tucked between his legs, fleeing from Oliver, who was giggling madly and doing his Frankenstein run, yelling, "HEE key key key key."

"Thanks, but I should get these groceries home."

"Okay," Hazel said, turning as if to close the door. "You know . . ." She turned back. "You could just go out there. It wouldn't hurt anything or anyone, and maybe it would be best if you, well, told her that you'd seen Peter—"

"Hazel, stop," Claudia said, holding up her hand. "I'm not driving out there."

Hazel leaned in over the passenger seat. "He is not your rival, Claudia. You absolutely must make that clear to yourself. He. Is. Not. Your. Rival."

Claudia took a deep breath, glanced in the rearview mirror. "There's someone coming, I need to get out of the street."

"There's no one coming. Do you remember where he lives?"

"Of course I do, and I'm not going out there. If he isn't my rival, who is?"

Hazel threw up her hands with relief, as if someone had finally given the right answer to a vexing test question. "That's the point! No one is! You have no rival! Please think about it, Claudia."

"I have thought about it," Claudia said, refusing to meet Hazel's eye. If Peter wasn't her rival, why had he stolen her happiness, and why was he careless with it? What could it mean that she'd seen him twice now after not seeing him for months, the first time carrying suitcases out to his white car late at night (she'd just happened to be driving by, it was an accident, really, Oliver was feverish and wouldn't sleep, so she'd done what mothers have done since the invention of the automobile—she strapped him in the car and turned up the radio and before she knew it, she was on One Oak Road). They were going somewhere, she'd thought at first; but why was the cabin so dark? Maybe they were leaving very early in the morning. But where could Rebekah go that required so many suitcases, as pregnant as she was? The next morning Peter's car was still there; Rebekah's, too. And then two days after that, Claudia had gone to Sears for new tires, and while wandering through the store with Oliver she'd heard Peter's voice. She turned a corner into Sporting Goods and saw him talking on the phone, his back to her. She couldn't make out the words, but could tell he was upset. With his free hand he rubbed the back of his neck, then leaned against the wall as if he were dizzy.

"There is something you're not—" Hazel straightened up, looked at the blue sky, squinted. "Where are the sane people is what I want to know. Claudia, look at me. Don't you feel this heaviness in the air? It isn't just summer, it isn't barometric pressure or anything like that, it's . . ."

"What? What is it, then?"

"It's *change,* Dim. There is wild change afoot, and you must be brave enough not only to endure it, but to embrace it, to make it your own. I thought," Hazel said, "I thought you were the most courageous person I'd ever known. I trusted you with a baby and a dog and a pregnant woman."

"Listen," Claudia said, leaning toward Hazel, "I have risen to every challenge before me, and for you to suggest otherwise is both cruel and a lie, and you are *not* the author of a story called Claudia, so please back away from this car before I say something I regret."

Hazel's face gave nothing away until just before she closed the passenger door. It was then Claudia saw, just fleeting, Hazel's look of supreme satisfaction. Hazel turned quickly and walked toward her house.

Claudia drove away in such anger she actually left the top layer of her new tires on the street, and from the backseat Oliver clapped and said, "Wheeee!"

1971

In the fifteen acres that separated the house and the road, thousands of dandelions had come up in the bright green grass. Hazel was grateful that her mother was too practical and busy to care about such things as dandelion eradication, which was a popular pastime in Indiana. The ideal Hoosier lawn was rolled into a perfect horizontal plane, and there was grass. Nothing else. The grass was kept quite short and nothing was ever done *on* the lawn, like dining or croquet. Exhibit only, no touching.

Hazel walked down the lane to the mailbox. Mercury zipped in and out of the grass, chasing imaginary mice. It was one of those days she could barely keep from singing; just standing in a landscape so infused with color, so radiant and warm, felt transcendent. There was no possibility of harm. For the moment, all that was unseen remained so, and let her be.

She had been too early for the mail; no matter. It only meant she would get to go check again, later. She turned left on the old county road and headed for the barn. The apple trees in the small orchard, gnarled and gargoyle-ish as they were, still blossomed and produced fruit, imagine the luck. Mercury dashed under an abandoned flatbed wagon, peered out at Hazel as if they were playing hide-and-seek.

She reached the barn and slid the door open on the rust, just a foot or so, enough to poke her head in.

A dream. It hit her as a physical sensation, and she recoiled. She had been in the barn with a crowd of people; the barn was dark but there seemed to be a spotlight on the drama: a black horse had fallen into a hole in the floor the size of a grave. It had fallen on its back and it was thrashing, panicked. No one, it seemed, had any idea what to do. The Night Mare. Wait, wait, that hadn't been a dream. Hazel pressed her hand against her eyes. There had been a crowd, too, gathered around the fire ring, throwing art into a tall fire. *Maybe* it had been a dream.

She took a deep breath and leaned through the opening in the barn door. There was Edie, sprawled out on a full-size mattress placed directly on the dirt floor. She was still in her clothes from the day before, half wrapped in an old comforter, and sound asleep. Beside her was her new boyfriend, Charlie, a thin, handsome criminal type, probably not smart enough to pile rocks, and currently homeless. Albert had put his foot down, said Charlie could sleep in the barn and shower once a day in the basement. Edie had replied, "Because we're all so brainwashed by Procter and Gamble to believe we have to shower *every day*." Hazel shook her head. Edie was amusing in her way, but life was about to pick her up in its jaws and shake her like a rag doll, shake her until she was boneless and pliable, even though she was in love. In loooove. Hazel closed the barn door, walked back to the house.

There was a note on her desk in reception in Caroline's hand, *Call Finney*. Hazel dialed the number of the diner and one of the other waitresses answered, this one the Kentucky-bred toothless woman named Shug who worshiped Mac Davis and said her dream in life was to see him in a pair of 'tight white pants.'

"Shug, it's Hazel. Is Finney around?"

"Hey, Hay-zel," she said, drawing out the first syllable the length of a city block. "She's here but she ain't in good shape. I'll see can she come to the phone."

No one answered for a long time. Finney was in bad shape. That could mean any number of things . . . no, actually, it could mean only one thing. Finally, after a few minutes, Finney picked up the phone, said hello in a voice thick with tears, ragged from smoking and crying. "Can you come over here?"

"I'm on my way." Hazel walked back into reception to tell her mother she needed to leave; Caroline wouldn't have cared. The schedule was light today, probably because of the fine weather, and anything Hazel did, Caroline could do just as well. Instead, Hazel ran into her father, who was stepping out of his examination room.

Albert was balding—only a silver fringe of hair was left. He was monkish in other ways, too: in his faith in his cause; his discipline; his belief that it was his own constancy and dedication that bound the chaotic elements of the world. He was tan from golfing with his peers, and he was immaculate in every element of presentation: his clothes, his glasses, his hands. He wrote with a Mont Blanc pen, wore leather shoes from a village in the north of Italy that custom-made them for him from a model of his foot he'd had cast when he was there.

"Hazel, good—I need you to look up Horace Greg—"

"I'm sorry, I can't. I just came back to tell Caroline I have to run out for a moment."

"Run out where, during the working day?"

"There's a crisis."

"Oh, a crisis. I assume it is of the emotional rather than the natural-disaster variety. An emotional emergency that requires you to attend to it immediately. I assume this would be your friend 'Lucy' again." Albert's voice never changed. He never sounded sarcastic or angry, which made him all the more formidable.

"Actually, it appears Lucy's appendix has burst."

"You've used that one already."

"Alas, she was born with two."

"What are you, thirty years old now?" Albert turned and walked away, his face finally giving way to derision, and Hazel grabbed her keys and left. Albert could not get to her with anything short of a loaded gun.

"Sixty-two," she called after her father. "But thanks."

Finney was sitting at a table in the corner of the diner, a worn-out round one that didn't match the rest of the restaurant's furniture. The table was reserved for the staff; they ate there, read the paper during breaks. Finn was just sitting, a coffee cup in front of her, a cigarette burning in the already overflowing ashtray. Hazel sat down across from her.

Finn's mouth was swollen from crying, her lips chapped, and her nose was red. Her eyes were as swollen as if she'd been stung by a bee. Her hair was dry and brittle, the cut shapeless. When she picked up the cigarette her hands were trembling, and Hazel saw that her fingernails had been stripped or chewed away.

But then there was her collarbone, the delicate cross-tie above her ribs, and the white hollow of her throat. They were pristine, the bones of the perfect girl she had been. Those were the things Hazel wanted to save, those hidden places that were still so fine they seemed *virtuous*. He had not destroyed them yet. Hazel believed—some part of her believed—that if he could be made gone, and oh more than once had she imagined putting a gun to *his* head, Finney would be reborn. She would shake the ash off her wings and begin anew.

"I'm pregnant." Finney said it dispassionately, her eyes never leaving Hazel's face.

Hazel slowly closed her eyes. "You said you were careful."

"I was. I was careful."

"So there'll be a star in the east on the blessed day?"

"Don't, Hazel, please—"

"I'm sorry. I'm sorry, it's a shock. That's all."

"Imagine how it feels from where I'm sitting."

"How far along?"

"Twelve weeks."

"*Twelve weeks?* Finn, how long have you known? That's barely enough time for an—"

"Shhh!" Finney looked around desperately. "If anyone here heard you say that, we'd end up in jail."

"What, then? When do you want to—"

"He says I can't."

"You can't. He tells you you can't. This is what I'm hearing you say." Finney stared at the tabletop.

"I think I can imagine all the reasons why," Hazel said, spitting out every word as if drawing toxins from a snakebite. "Don't even tell me his 'moral' position. I'll run screaming into traffic."

"Actually, there's a reason you don't know." Finney wiped her face with a shredded napkin. "He wants me to give the baby to him. And to her."

For a moment Hazel couldn't speak. "I'm sorry," she said. "My mind just ceased functioning."

"Yeah, well," Finney sighed, "join the club."

"Where is he going to say the baby came from?" Hazel whispered as an older couple walked past them to pay their bill. "A bulrush basket?"

"He's already told her the truth. He told her last week, as soon as I found out."

He had told her, his helpmate, the sinless one, but Finney had waited a week to tell Hazel.

"And what does she say?"

"He said at first she was suicidal and threatened to leave him. She threatened all sorts of things. He told her to do what she needed to do, he wouldn't protect himself."

"A bit late for protection, yes?"

Finney ignored her. "She gradually calmed down. She's a very practical woman—"

"No kidding."

"—and now she's pleased. She's looking forward to it. A baby is a baby, she said to him, and they will never have another chance."

"Have you made up your mind?"

Finney's face contorted as she tried to keep from sobbing, "I don't know what to do. I am just completely lost."

Hazel's own eyes filled with tears, and all of her anger dissipated. This was Finn, after all. "What If," she said, smiling across the table at her friend, "you found yourself pregnant and didn't know what to do?"

Finney looked down at the table, shaking her head. "I guess I

would protect what remained to me. I'd make a plan, and then I'd make a plan B."

It only took one phone call, one conversation over coffee, and three days. Hazel and Finney met Jim Hank at the courthouse, Finn in a long flowered dress, Jim in his one good suit, Hazel in a green silk cocktail dress she'd found in the attic. Finney and Jim were married by a trollish little man who dressed like Elvis Presley and called them by the wrong names. Hazel had remembered flowers for both of them, and all the elements of the something old / something new business. Finney remembered nothing but the necessary papers. And as they walked out the front door of the courthouse, Hazel reached into her bag and showered them with confetti, all of the perfect little circles left behind by the three-hole punch on her desk. She'd been saving them for years without knowing why.

There were five bottles of champagne in the refrigerator at Jim Hank's apartment, and there was a cake from the local bakery on his counter. While making the arrangements the three had been careful not to mention Finney's parents, who were already heartsick by what felt like the loss of their only child. Finney would tell them she was married, she assured Hazel, as soon as she could figure out how.

She promised Hazel, too, that within the week she would decide about the baby, and Hazel had promised in return to honor her decision, regardless. All of those vows had been difficult to make but would be far harder to uphold, and both of them knew it.

In Jim Hank's spotless, bright apartment, Hazel opened the champagne as Jim put on music. He had eclectic taste. They listened to Sarah Vaughan, followed by The Association, Duke Ellington, the Beatles, and the Bee Gees. Hazel and Jim got rip-roaring drunk, the drunkest by far Hazel had ever been. Finney drank just one glass of champagne, watching the other two with amusement. Hazel and Jim Hank cut the cake drunk, they danced drunk, for a bizarre thirty minutes they played charades drunk, until Hazel realized she simply couldn't remember who or what she was supposed to pretend to be no matter how many times she looked at her little slip of paper with the words written on it.

Hours passed, or maybe no time at all, Jim and Hazel laughing until

Hazel had to lie down, and suddenly Finney stood up and said she had to go home. Hazel and Jim looked at each other, neither able to focus well; both knew why she was leaving. But there would be no recrimination on this, their wedding day, so they kissed her on the cheek and let her go. She slipped out the door, and as intoxicated as they were, they could see she was relieved.

The arm of the record player dropped onto a new album: Julie London. "I love this record!" Hazel said, not quite certain it was true.

"So do I," Jim said solemnly. "Hey, Hazey! Can I carry you across the threshold?"

"Yes, yes, what a splendid idea."

They stumbled out into the hallway and Jim swept her up into his arms as if she weighed nothing. "I wouldn't have been able to do this with Finney near so easily. That girl is tall."

"Not near so easily," Hazel agreed.

They hummed the bridal march as they stepped through the door, just as a song Hazel was sure she liked began to play. "I love this song!"

"So do I." Jim smiled at her, bowed, lowering an imaginary hat. "Miss Hunnicutt, could I invite you to spend the night with me on my wedding night? As I am far too drunk to drive you home and your company is so welcome?"

Hazel curtsied in return, nearly lost her balance. "Yes, you may certainly invite me, Mr. Bellamy, and I would gladly accept."

They collapsed on the couch, their shoes scattered, plates and glasses all over the table, and sang along with the song they both loved. *Two sleepy people by dawn's early light, and too much in love to say good night.*

Chapter 9

IF PETER DIDN'T get to Florida soon, Mandy intended to move in with a boy she'd met at her former boyfriend's tattoo parlor. In her own peculiar parlance she described him as a sk8 rat. Rebekah found herself worrying over Peter and Mandy as if they were characters on a soap opera to which she was devoted.

It had been days since Mandy had made her threat, or at least it seemed to have been. Rebekah couldn't tell one from another: the day Peter asked if she had a doctor's appointment and she couldn't remember; the day someone knocked at the door, then went away; the day Peter felt her head and asked her to take some Tylenol. Maybe they had all happened at once. She had been on the couch for a long time; she could feel that she hadn't washed her hair or changed her nightgown since . . . and there was the problem of the baby, who was so big and moved so much. Sometimes it put the soles of its feet (or that's what it felt like) against her rib cage and stretched out, pushing its head against her pelvic floor. She didn't know why, but that maneuver flattened her lungs until she sometimes lost consciousness. It was too hard to get up, that was the problem; the second she stood, her heart rate tripled but the rest of her felt like a falling elevator, and twice she had come to back on the sofa, her feet on the floor. She dreamed constantly—or something like dreaming—of her cousins, Davy especially, and of her mother threading a needle or studying a patch of wild strawberries, her hands in the pocket of her apron. In desperation she took to telling herself, *This isn't real,* and that would last until the baby thrust a knee into one of her vital organs, and even in her current state she could not deny that pain was real. Sometimes she would open her eyes and see Peter hunched over his computer screen and she would think there was something critical she had to say to him, there was a plea she had to make, for herself or for the baby. If for you the Church is the status quo, she might have said, you will do anything to uphold it. But when she opened her eyes again, he was gone, and just when she'd remembered the words: Mary and Elizabeth. John the Baptist. John whom Jesus loved. Cyrus and Penny Jester, never so blest. It stirred, the flickering self of Rebekah, and took calculated note: She hadn't eaten. She couldn't recall using the bathroom. When she opened her eyes, a field of stars burst at the circumference of her vision, and she was just able to turn her head long enough to look at the telephone, which was across the room on Peter's desk, next to . . . next to the place his computer once sat. She needed to reach the telephone, but not Peter's—she needed the black phone in the parlor of Hazel Hunnicutt's Used World Emporium. She saw herself there, her right index finger poised over the green metal address book. All along she believed she'd call (if she called at all) a past so distant that the act of retrieving it would restore to her all she had lost. But when the moment came, she scrolled down to *M* for Modjeski, and dialed the number she already knew. The past fell through her fingers until she stood empty-handed in the present, waiting for Claudia to answer.

In his crib Oliver enacted his new naptime drama: shaking his head and saying nuh nuh nuh, napping was out of the question and he would appreciate it if Claudia would behave herself and set him on the floor. He shook his head, then rubbed his face and nose so hard she was surprised he didn't hurt himself. He lay down on his back, pulling up his flannel blanket and rubbing his nose with that for a while, and reached for his favorite animal, which Hazel called a squeaky duck but which Claudia believed to be, oddly, a Canada goose. He sucked on its orange foot a moment, draped its long neck over his eyes, and within seconds was asleep.

She left her bedroom reluctantly and went downstairs to the big entryway closet; this was the place she should clean next. She had dreaded tackling it for so long the dread had assumed a life of its own. It was in here that she'd placed all the things Rebekah hadn't come back to claim, and probably the hour had come round to box those things up and ship them to Peter's. She got as far as grasping the door-knob, just as she had half a dozen times before, and then somehow the door was open and she was staring at Rebekah's clothes. There was her green sweater, her green dress, her blue jeans draped length-wise over a clothes hanger. Claudia took a step forward, reached out and lifted the sleeve of the sweater as if inviting it to dance. There was the smell of her, faint and vanishing, the sage soap, the buttermilk bath salts. Claudia breathed in, even though she knew with every breath she took she was eliminating the last traces of Rebekah in the air. She ran her hands over everything, as Ludie would have done in a fabric store, then took out the rusted flour sifter of Constance Ruth Harrison, studied it a long time, set to work. Outside, the rain began in earnest.

1971

Hazel could only imagine the road Finney had taken to reach her decision, as she refused to talk about it. Awake nearly all night, every night since the wedding reception, Hazel herself could have written a book about Finney's choices, where *A* began and where it would lead; the loss inherent in *B*. She made up a *C* that didn't exist, and for good measure a *D* wherein everyone was happy.

Jim Hank and Finn would arrive at seven, after Albert was safely out for the evening. Edie and Charlie had taken Charlie's motorcycle to the newly opened StarLite Drive-In. Hazel and Caroline didn't speak as they moved around the kitchen, making tea, cleaning surfaces that were already sterile. Their silence—the mother and daughter— had a vocabulary of its own; it expressed relative degrees of symbiosis or irritation.

Now, for instance, Hazel knew her mother was wrestling with a particular nameless angel. The angel wasn't Hazel's and she didn't consider her mother's conversation with it her business. But she wondered. If Caroline was afraid, there was something to be afraid of. If Caroline was nervous . . . Hazel felt a fluttering in her stomach. But neither said a word, so that when Jim and Finney rang the bell to the clinic, Hazel and her mother walked out with shoulders squared, completely confident, and comforting.

Hazel could hear Jim Hank pacing outside the closed door and she wanted to tell him to stop but didn't.

"You know what happens, dear," Caroline said, inclining her head toward Finney's, rubbing one of her icy hands. "I've given you something to help you relax, and you can breathe through this mask if you feel any pain." Caroline smiled at Finn, who was crying, crying as she always cried, her chin trembling. "I don't want to frighten you, but this might be a little harder than usual; you are farther—"

"I know."

"You're absolutely certain it's what you want to do? Because I'm happy to talk with you about the alternatives if . . ."

"No. Yes, I'm sure. No alternatives."

"All right, then."

Caroline began scrubbing her hands and arms at the sink in the corner.

"Hazey, I'm terrified."

"I know you are." Hazel sat on a stool at Finney's waist, facing her. She would stay there until Caroline was finished.

"You don't understand; I think he knows. I think he knows what I'm about to do."

"Finn, he doesn't know. He couldn't. You didn't even tell me or Jim until yesterday."

"He said something last night on the phone, I hadn't expected him to call." Finney's hands were shaking so hard they appeared to leap off the table. "If I wait for him to call he doesn't and this one time, the one and only time I don't want to hear from him—"

"You need to calm down." Hazel pressed three tissues into Finney's

right hand, then took Finney's left and held it between her palms, trying to warm it as she might a small animal.

"He asked me about my 'young man.' He asked if I would be seeing him again soon. I told him I didn't know what he was talking
about, but he wouldn't say any more about Jim."

"He does *not* know you're married. There's no reason for him to
suspect it."

"They publish the applications for licenses in the legal section of
the paper, Hazel! Anyone could have seen it."

"Does he strike you as the type who would look to see who was
getting married?"

Caroline lifted Finney's right foot, still in a white sock, and slipped
it into the stirrup; then the left. "Scoot down, Finn. A little more—
that's better. Okay, one more time."

"I can't *stand* this, I am so humiliated." Finney turned her face away
from Hazel, who had never seen her look even half so miserable.

Caroline patted her on the knee. "All right. We're going to begin
by—"

"Don't tell me! Don't tell me anything."

"That's fine, then."

"And now, Hazey, I don't need to be married, because of . . . this.
Jim Hank would have given me the ground to stand on if I'd decided
to raise it myself, but now. He did that for nothing."

"Jim didn't do it for nothing. He did it for love, just like in the
movies."

"He"—Finn's eyes widened and she winced, then relaxed—"he
said to take care of his baby. He said he would be watching me. I asked
him, 'Why would you be watching me?' and he said really smoothly
that he'd said he'd be watching *out* for me."

Hazel could see the drugs working—Finn's hands had gone slack
and her eyes were a little unfocused. "You feel all right?" Hazel asked.

"I'm fine, I can't feel . . . much of anything at all. I'm not crying,"
Finney said, sounding surprised. "I've stopped crying."

"Well, look at that." Hazel rubbed her arm. "And all it took was a
tranquilizer. A bargain."

"A bargain."

Caroline whispered to Hazel, "Come here a moment." Hazel

rolled her stool over by her mother. "Place another pad under her, please. Do you know"—Caroline lowered her voice even more—"if she has any medical condition, a clotting disorder, for instance?"

Hazel's heart jumped. "No. No, why?"

"She's bleeding more than she should be. I think we should hurry."

Hazel's hands were shaking as she pulled out the drawer, grabbing three absorbent pads and slipping them under Finney. There was more blood than usual—not enough to be called an emergency, not unless it was Finney.

The clinic doorbell rang. Hazel and Caroline tried not to show their alarm, but Finney was saying, "Who is it, who could be here? Caroline?"

"Finney, you need to lie still. Do not move; it's probably a patient. Jim can take care of it."

Hazel looked toward the waiting area. "Does that door lock?" she whispered.

"Yes," Caroline said, not looking at her. "It's like the lock on Albert's office door, you flip the anchor-shaped—"

She could hear Jim talking to someone, raised voices. I need to lock the door, she thought, but Finney wouldn't let go of her hand.

"Hazel, don't leave me!"

"Finn, let me go one second. Just a second."

Jim shouted, "I said no. I said no you can't, she's *my wife*."

There was a terrible sound, a blow textured with bone, audible even through the door. "Dear God," Caroline said as someone fell to the waiting room floor.

Hazel looked at Finney for a split second before pulling her hand away roughly. Finn's face was so white it seemed translucent, and her lips were pale blue. Hazel couldn't stop, couldn't think about what she was seeing, she had to lock—

—the door flew open, slamming against the wall behind it. Caroline and Hazel jumped, nearly screamed.

"Stop what you're doing to her, stop!" And to Finney, who was hyperventilating now, "Get up. Get up, I said!"

Caroline was reaching behind her for a scalpel, as if that would save them from the crowbar, which bore, on its hooked end, a shock of Jim Hank's hair. "You need to leave this room immediately. I'm calling the police. Hazel, get the phone, please."

"Oh, you're going to call the police? And tell them what? What you do here, what you've done to her?"

"Vernon," Finney sobbed, reaching out to him, "please please, I'm afraid." Her feet were still strapped in the stirrups, and even through the mayhem Hazel realized there was blood dripping on the floor.

"We need to ignore him," Hazel said to her mother. "We have a problem here."

"Ignore him? *Ignore* him?" Vernon swung the crowbar just shy of Caroline's head, shattering the door of the cabinet beside her. Caroline and Finney both screamed, but Hazel felt very calm, felt time slowing down to a crawl. She reached out and, as quietly as possible, released the strap that held the left stirrup secure.

"This is *my* baby, this is a human life, you are the *worst*"—Vernon's face was flushed nearly purple—"God-*damned* monsters who ever lived. Get up!" he screamed at Finney, who now was wailing. She lowered her legs and tried to sit up.

"No, Finney"—Caroline's voice broke—"no, dear, you can't possibly move, stay right there. Sir," she said, turning to Vernon, "I understand you have a grievance, but if you move her she will die."

"Then she deserves to die!" He was spitting with rage. "She is trying to kill my baby which the Lord has promised to me and she's trying to kill it, it's *mine*."

Finney sat up but could go no farther. Vernon pushed past Hazel, knocking her against the sink so hard a bright tune sang up her spine. He pointed the crowbar at Caroline as he reached under Finney's legs and lifted her up. It looked effortless, his carrying her, even though she was such a tall girl. Finney said nothing, just wrapped her long arms around Vernon's neck and rested her head on his shoulder.

Vernon carried her through the doorway, stepping over Jim Hank as he crossed the waiting room. And then—the strangest of apparitions—Albert was coming through the door of the clinic, just taking off his hat and smoothing his hair. Vernon bulled past him, nearly knocking him off the steps.

"Excuse me!" Albert yelled. "What are you doing with Finney?" He stepped into the waiting room, where Caroline was kneeling over Jim Hank, pressing her bare hand against his head wound to try to stop the bleeding. "What in the name of—Caroline, explain this, please."

"Daddy, we've got to follow them, *please.*"

"Get in the car," he said. "Caroline, call an ambulance for Jim; that injury is beyond us."

"I know." Caroline's voice was weak. "I know it is." She picked up the phone just as Albert and Hazel reached the clinic door. Hazel glanced back, a pillar of salt, and she would never forget the look on her mother's face, never—not if she lived until the end of time. It was the look of a woman watching the village burn, the walls of her own home crashing in the blaze.

"Hello?" Claudia was sitting on the edge of her bed, peeling off her wet socks.

"I'm so glad you're home."

"Me, too—it's crazy, what's happening outside."

"Are you busy, though?"

"No, not now. I just helped Millie carry in some groceries. What I mean is I carried in all the groceries while Millie stood looking at the boxes of Rebekah's things, sobbing."

"Millie's there? Good, because—"

"Millie's always here, Hazel."

"I just tried—now don't panic, but—I tried to call Rebekah and the phone's been disconnected. So I called—"

"The phone's been disconnected?"

"—Peter's parents and they said they spoke to Peter three days ago but haven't heard from his since then. Pete Senior said he had no idea why the phone would be off."

"Go on." Claudia pulled out her sock drawer too hard and with one hand, and it came out crooked and stuck. She reached in and grabbed the first pair she could find; she pulled them on, stood, and walked in circles.

"I called Sears and they said he was taken off the schedule as of two or three days ago, the guy I talked to couldn't remember."

"I can't find my—"

"Claudia, be careful driving out there, the roads are—"

"I know, Millie told me."

"I'll find you."

Claudia grabbed a dry shirt, tossed it on the bed. And for no reason she understood, she reached up into the shelf above the closet and took down the box that held the Colt .44. "How will you know where we are? Where will you be? WHY don't we have cell phones, why?"

"I'll find you, Claudia. I have something to take care of and then I'll find you. We don't have cell phones because we can't be two places at one time."

"That's ridiculous," Claudia said, hanging up. She ran down the stairs.

Hazel stopped at the end of the lane. The rain was coming down so hard, and in such blowing, twisting sheets, that everything outside the car shimmered indiscreetly, as if in an aquarium. She got out, ignoring the way she was instantly soaked. The hood of her raincoat kept the water off her glasses long enough for her to find the right key. She turned it and disengaged a lock so large it could have served on a pirate's ship. The heavy chain fell to the ground, and Hazel dragged it behind the stone wall.

"Nice," she said, hearing the squelching sound she made in the driver's seat. She drove down the potholed, battered lane, the honey locusts towering on either side of her. The grass in the front acreage was kept cut by a neighbor with a tractor, primarily so that Hazel didn't face lawsuits, but no one mowed the area right in front of the house, and the grass and weeds there reached, in some places, Hazel's head.

She parked in her father's spot, the one closest to the house. Nature doesn't intend for us to be out in rain this hard, Hazel thought, but she wasn't sure why. No thunder, no lightning, just countless gallons of water falling on us, and we run from it. She walked at her normal pace up the front steps, turning away from the formal entrance, which was boarded up (the only way to protect the leaded glass panes), to the one door or window that could still be opened. The screen door was gone and there was nothing in its place, just the gaping hinges, and the original door—the mahogany with the carved scrolls and leaves—was gone, too. Hazel had propped it up against the wall in the dining room when it had to be replaced with what stood in its stead now: a solid sheet of green industrial steel. No window, no mail slot. You either had the key or you didn't get in.

For so long Hazel had believed there was nothing more dangerous than the past. Then she'd seen the future and realized, oh the past isn't so bad. Mostly a lot of junk back there, stuff no one should have ever kept. We hold on to the strangest things, and long beyond the point they serve any good. She stepped inside the library, turned on the light. The electricity was still on, that was good. Every couple of years the power company had to come out and investigate an outage; once, Hazel herself had gone back to check the fuse box and discovered a squirrel head down inside it, his body slithered around and between the fuses, still clutching the live wire in his fried paw.

Left alone, a house develops its own smell—it will not hold yours forever. Hazel knew how quickly this happened. Standing here now, she could not have guessed at the richness the air used to carry—floor wax, lemons, laundry, her mother's L'Air du Temps, the disinfectant from the clinic, all the various subtexts of Edie's life, too. Now the place smelled like wet plaster, mold, slow decay.

In the library the stained-glass doors still ticked open on their tracks, although the shelves held no books. How it came to be that there was stuff on the floor (there was *always* stuff on the floor), Hazel couldn't imagine. Pieces of cardboard, empty bags, dirt, leaves, enough twigs to build a new tree—it all just grew there. She kicked her way into the parlor, turned on that light. No down-filled sofa, no floor lamp with the milk-glass globe. *Get rid of it,* Caroline had told her in the hospital, *get rid of it all, I don't care how you do it.* The light at the top of the staircase revealed just how much mysterious stuff can accumulate in the corner of each step, too. Quite a bit. And what was this tangled up with the leaves? *Fur?*

In the wide upstairs hallway there were no longer any eyes to open and close, tell her if she'd gone right or left. That rug had been one of the first things she'd carried out; she'd rolled it up and driven it to the space she'd rented for almost nothing, an empty building that had once been a tractor tire store. The first few trips she drove her car, taking the lightest, smallest pieces of furniture. Then she realized that Jim

Hank's truck was still right there, parked right where he'd left it, and he wouldn't be needing it anytime soon. Things went more quickly after that.

She took her flashlight out of her belt, shone it in the bathroom. Yep. A bad leak around the window. She'd get the boys to come out, shore that up. Edie's room was the worst, for some reason. The teenagers and hunters who'd briefly taken over the place, before Hazel had realized she'd need to board up the village to save the village, had gravitated toward Edie's room so naturally it may as well have been Stonehenge on the summer solstice. They'd torn down the wallpaper, dragged in an old mattress, written on the walls. She always assumed Edie herself, Edie and Charlie and their bumbling militia, had been among the vandals, but she'd never caught them. All she knew is that when the boards and the steel door went up, Edie and Charlie somehow found Cobb Creek, and the break-ins had stopped. "I'm homeless!" Edie had yelled at her, how many times over the years? "And that's my home, too, and it's empty—I should call the law." Hazel laughed at Edie, pitied her. And Edie never pushed, not really. She knew instinctively that whatever lay on the other side of pushing Hazel too far was bad for all God's children, and she must have known that it *wasn't* hers, too. At the end of the day—and they weren't there yet, but dusk was surely falling—it was all Hazel's. The whole disaster.

The key to the lock on the nursery door slipped in and turned easily; she'd been wise to buy a good one. She opened the door, stepped inside without turning on the light. It wears off, it wears off after a while, that's what Caroline told her. Your mother or your father dies and the first time you walk past his favorite chair or pick up her hairbrush, you think the planet has spun off its axis. And it hurts every time you walk past the chair, if you leave it there, *every time* until one day you don't notice it at all and you're sitting in it talking on the phone. The gray walls, the elephants marching, the braided rug. I don't care what you do with it, Caroline had said, I will not live in a crypt. Practical, her mother. Hazel stepped into a cobweb, brushed it off her face. And she had been obedient, yes. Sold everything in the clinic to a new GP just opening his practice (except for a couple things that she kept in the storage place and would not sell). There was so much money, savings accounts and insurance policies, money to burn if handled right, and Caroline and Hazel knew how. Even here, her own room, she'd carried down to the truck the toys and rocking horses Nanny used to arrange for a different sort of little girl; the bookcase with her favorite books; her desk, her rocking chair, her clothes. Caroline didn't know—didn't need to know—this: the iron bed, still turned to face the window, made up in its white coverlet.

The light in the room was silver, it flickered as rain poured down the casement window. Hazel took a step toward the bed, jarred by the sound of her own breathing. For the first fifteen, twenty? years she'd come out every few months and wash the linens on this bed. Once a year for the coverlet, even though nature itself seemed to avoid the room; the windows stayed true, no wildlife had found a way through the ceiling or up through the closet floors. But it had begun to seem, even to Hazel, strange to care. No one was hurt if she did it or didn't do it, and one fall afternoon, during the time of year she usually tended to the house, she looked at herself in the mirror, gave a shrug, skipped it.

Now, approaching the bed, she wondered if she'd been wrong. It wasn't . . . the coverlet wasn't as she'd left it, it seemed dingy and mussed, as if someone had sat down on it. The rain fell so hard on the slate roof above her it sounded like marbles being dropped on the house. Hazel sat down. The bed groaned beneath her in its usual way. She felt dizzy—closed her eyes—this bed, she thought, stayed right here, just like this, with no purpose since the last night I slept in it, not knowing it would be the last. It just waits.

And there, too: the sweater tossed casually across the bed. The first time she'd done it, Hazel had to pretend she'd just taken it off, that she was changing for dinner or to go out with Finney and Jim Hank. She pretended to take it off and toss it on the bed, pretended to turn to her closet, which was, of course, completely empty. The next time she did it, it was easier; she skipped the fantasy of dinner and went straight to the tossing and the closet. Then no fantasy, and finally no closet. Not her sweater. Finney's. Well, not even Finney's—it had begun life as Malcolm's cardigan, but Finney had worn it for so long it had become hers, just the same way Jumpin' Bean became Claudia's dog, or Oliver belonged to all of them. No one knew as well as Hazel the shifting boundaries of ownership, how little it mattered in the scheme of things. A wiser woman—a much wiser woman—would have let the bed go, too, and the sweater, and the house, the land. Caroline did.

Hazel picked up the sweater, which was damp, lifeless, and buried her face in it. Nothing. She had so long ago emptied that sweater of every part of Finney, she might as well have eaten it. One day there had been the last trace, elusive and faint, and Hazel had hunted it down and devoured it, not knowing it was the last. But that was okay, she thought, dropping the sweater beside her. If she'd known, she would have done it anyway.

A tap-tap at her bedroom window: Hazel looked up, but it was just a tree branch. She waved her hand at the window, dismissing it. Thirty years. Thirty years since her world had collapsed, and in that time? Nothing. No owls in Jonah. No owls on campus. The windows at her new house? Aluminum, double-paned, diddly for predator birds.

She straightened the coverlet, locked the bedroom door behind her. Two, three, four steps down the hallway, a third key. Hazel unlocked the attic door, turned on the light in the stairwell that was no color, just the remnants of what someone long before her had to spare. She climbed the stairs.

Claudia leaned over the steering wheel, ground her teeth. The radio had bothered her so much she'd slammed her palm against the on/off knob and knocked it to the floor. She needed new windshield wipers and wasn't it always the case that you need new windshield wipers and you don't think of it or notice it until monsoon season? Every mile or so she passed a car off the road, someone who'd tried to drive through standing water and only succeeded in flooding his engine. "Idiots," Claudia muttered, turning the wipers up on high, which streaked the windshield and lowered her visibility. She also turned the defroster on high, in a vain attempt to turn the rain to steam.

The rain was so hard and constant, Claudia could barely see road signs; she missed one turn and had to double back. Her palms were sweating, her fingers icy with fear. She thought of something Amos had said last Sunday morning, about how evil was less a preestablished fact than a failure to respond to God's tug upon our souls toward goodness and harmony. *Imagine the distance collapsed, the one between God and your every decision; it would be like walking down a dirt road in perfectly bright sun, followed by a hawk, or some bees. That is our Messianic dream, no division between God, the light, the road, the Man or Woman.*

Claudia couldn't pray, so she drove.

Rebekah was six years old and had scarlet fever and her mouth was so dry, her skin covered with red bumps. Sometimes she was too tired to cry out for her mother, and at those times Ruth just appeared, it was like magic, and she held a cold washcloth over Rebekah's mouth and let the water drip inside. Her throat hurt too much to swallow, but this was nice, the water on her tongue. A jack-o'-lantern, a pumpkin caving in upon itself late in the season, that's what she had become, although she wasn't allowed to say so because she wasn't allowed to know. She wasn't allowed to know anything about Satan's various holidays, and she wasn't allowed to speak of the way worldly parents allowed him to work through their children. It was as good as inviting him in. Ruth was gone again and Rebekah looked through the haze of fever around her childhood bedroom. She was stunned, even though she was just a child, by Ruth's fastidious care, the straight, tight stitches on the hem of the gingham curtains, the polish of her dresser top. Her mother's love was like a . . . the fever kicked at her, it squeezed her body in a tightening vise, and she felt the water, hot beneath her and flowing from her, and knew then that something was over, and she was at sea.

Claudia didn't recognize the truck following her, and the rain was much too hard for her to see the driver. She tried speeding up and slowing down, thinking she might be in someone's way, but the truck stayed close to her. She turned onto Rebekah's road and crept toward the cabin, knowing the driveway would be difficult to spot. There, finally, was the mailbox.

Peter's car was gone, but Rebekah's was there, covered with fallen leaves and a small branch from the tree it was parked under. Claudia reminded herself to breathe, to stay alert, to take mental note as if at a crime scene. She pulled up the hood of her raincoat and stepped out into the rain just as the truck pulled into the driveway and stopped behind the Jeep.

She stood, letting the rain pound against her, as Vernon Shook stepped out of his truck and walked toward her, his back and shoulders squared in defiance of the elements. He wore a jacket but nothing on his head, and in the strange light of the storm, the green of his eyes reached her first.

"You get on back in your car now," he said to Claudia, almost gently, like a man trying to spare a child something unfortunate.

"I don't think—"

"I said *get on.* You aren't getting near my daughter or the baby."

Even in the rain Claudia could see what she was up against: Vernon was the force that ran everything. She and Rebekah and all women everywhere lived and died according to the whim of men like him. She swallowed against her fear of him and tried to say something, but before she could, he opened the left side of his jacket and showed her the gun he had tucked into the waistband of his work pants. It looked like a .22 to her, the kind of weapon a lot of people kept in a bedside drawer.

"You have till I count to three," he said, lowering his chin and watching her, unblinking.

He just gave me three seconds, Claudia thought, incredulous, as if I were his child or his battered wife. Even though I've got six inches on him and twice the gun. And she pulled the .44 out of the wide pocket of her raincoat. She didn't *show* it to him, she didn't *wave it around,* she extended her right arm and put the barrel against his forehead. A bullet in the first chamber. With her left hand she reached into his jacket and took the .22, dropping it into her pocket.

"You wouldn't," Vernon said, and Claudia wondered if he was right. There was, after all, something so familiar about him, something she felt inclined to hold on to. Then the corner of his mouth rose up in a sneer and twitched, a nervous tic, and Claudia realized, oh, I certainly would.

Vernon seemed to feel it too, that he had given himself away. His shoulders slumped and he let his eyes blink slowly, once, twice. He covered his face with his hands and pushed his hair back, then turned and headed for his truck. Even his walk was defeated. Just before he opened the driver's side door he looked at Claudia and said, "I'd like to have that gun back at some point."

She nodded, said, "You just worry about getting home safely." He started the truck and backed out slowly, and Claudia stood still, waiting until the sound of his truck faded, disappeared.

The screen door was rusted, the mesh pulled away slightly from the frame all around the bottom. She turned the old brass handle and it opened. Now there was the heavy door with a single diamond pane; she raised her hand to knock, let it fall. No one was going to answer. She palmed the doorknob and there was the feeling again, that the weight of an object, or its purpose, offered more resistance than she could overcome. She leaned her head against the door, afraid she would hyperventilate. *Now* she was falling apart. She'd been fine pulling a loaded gun on a man, but now she thought she might faint. A part of her wanted to storm the gate, and another wanted to turn around and go home. What was beyond was not hers, it had nothing to do with her. She saw, again, Hazel's face, her dry lips, the lines around her eyes; saw Rebekah carrying Oliver into the kitchen on a gray morning in December, and Claudia opened the door.

The room was dim, the air was close, and it took a few moments for her eyes to adjust. Here, just as in the kitchen at Cobb Creek, were layers of smells, most of them very bad. There was garbage in the kitchen, dead fish floating in a gray-green aquarium, a smell of sickness, fever, urine.

She took a step into the living room, sweat breaking out on her forehead, her neck. The cabin was so horrible and silent she was afraid to call out. She was about to turn and look for the bedroom when she saw, under an old quilt, Rebekah's hand floating in the air, her skin so white it looked blue.

"No no no no," Claudia whispered, trying to find Rebekah's face in the swirl of hair and quilt. The smell was overwhelming, and when she finally turned Rebekah's face toward her it was swollen, pale. Her bottom lip was cracked and bleeding from what must have been a fever; she was so *hot,* her skin was burning.

Claudia stood up, panting, and began clawing through the debris on the floor for the phone. She traced the wire running around the floorboard and found it on the desk, but when she lifted the receiver, it was dead, of course, it had been disconnected. She kept up a steady stream of verbal panic, beginning with where's the phone where's the phone, and moving on to oh my God oh my God, then Rebekah I'm here I'm here, hold on.

She unwrapped the rest of Rebekah's body and saw that her night-gown was soaked and streaked with pink, as was the futon beneath her. Claudia ran out the door, leapt from the porch to the ground, and opened the passenger door of the Jeep with such force she felt a jolt go through her shoulder. She reclined the seat as far as it would go, then flew—it seemed she was flying—back into the house.

Rebekah was breathing, and her right hand was twitching against her chest, as if she were still running the adding machine at the Used World Emporium. Claudia ran into the bedroom, grabbed a blanket off the bed, and spread it over Rebekah, even her head. Claudia centered her feet just under her shoulders, squatted at the edge of the couch, and slipped her right arm under Rebekah's knees, her left under Rebekah's shoulders, all the while whispering Okay okay bear with me, I'm not very graceful. But when she actually lifted Rebekah up, she felt a hum, deep as electricity, in her thighs. It traveled up her back, through her shoulders, and into her arms, and Rebekah felt like noth-ing, she weighed less than Oliver, less than the groceries Claudia had carried thirty minutes earlier. Fluid ran down Claudia's arm and soaked into her shirt, into the waistband of her pants. She held Rebekah as close to her as she could and took one long step and was over the threshold, another, and was across the porch. Each step brought a moan from Rebekah, a terrifying exhalation, and Claudia spoke constantly, we're almost there, we're almost to the car, I know you can hear me.

Rebekah was telling Claudia that the Mission had been right, the bat-tle was lost and the world was going to end. They'd had this conversation before, and Claudia was impatient. She was impatient but she smiled nonetheless and told Rebekah, as it seemed she had done before, that the world has no end; that it was a trick of Pastor Lowell's, just a shadow flung off his black wing, to suggest that it did. She said Who are you going to believe? And Rebekah sighed and lay back in bed. There were things Claudia might never understand. She had never really known Jesus, after all, she had never slept in a house that was, in essence, His tomb. She thought religion was the honeyed light of Ludie's Christianity, songs about suppertime, jars of bright fruits and vegetables, lined up in a cellar. But that was all fine, Rebekah loved her. You, she said. It's you I believe.

They were still three miles from the hospital when Rebekah began making a strange noise, a concentrated, open-throated hum that was close to a growl. "No no no, Rebekah, wait wait," Claudia said, approaching a low place on the highway where the water was deep. Three cars were already pulled over, either because they'd attempted it and lost, or because they didn't dare. The water rose and rose; she saw now that it was spilling out of an irrigation system in one of Nathan Leander's fields; she was two-thirds of the way through it, almost there. She might make it through the water but she wouldn't make it to the hospital. Three cars at the side of the road: one of them would have a phone.

Claudia coasted to the side of the road, slammed the car into park, left it on with the heater running. She sprinted back to the first car she came to, a green Neon, and knocked, maybe a little too hard. The window came down two inches or so. It was a teenaged girl, dressed in the god-awful fashion of the moment, wherein all of her clothes were made for someone Oliver's size, and they all appeared to have been washed in lye.

"Do you have a cell phone?" Claudia asked, scaring the girl further.

She nodded, and reached into the seat beside her. She wasn't wearing a seat belt, leaving the message on her T-shirt unimpeded: I SUCKED HEAD AT JOE'S CRAWFISH SHACK.

"No, you call. I need an ambulance. Do you know where we are?"

The girl looked around, shook her head.

"We're on Highway 27, eastbound, between exits twelve and thirteen. Can you remember that?" Without waiting for an answer, Claudia ran back to the Jeep and opened the passenger door. Something was definitely happening; Rebekah's body pulled in on itself, and she moaned as if her chest were being crushed. An enormous energy seemed to be gathered just over the baby, and as Claudia began to rub Rebekah's limp hand and say again that everything was fine, she realized Rebekah was pushing. Claudia grabbed the blanket she'd had over Rebekah and threw it over the roof of the Jeep and the open door, making a tent she could stand in without water getting inside.

"Oh no, Rebekah, don't do that, wait wait—" Claudia said, resting her hand against Rebekah's forehead. "Please don't push yet, I have absolutely no idea what to do." She lifted her hand off Rebekah's head and tenderly peeled back the stained nightgown. Her angle was awkward, and she slid the seat back as far as she could, tried to turn Rebekah toward her. She pressed against Rebekah's abdomen, and felt it: a band of muscles tightening, becoming as hard as skin stretched over a stone. The contraction was moving like lightning from the top of Rebekah's stomach to the bottom, and Claudia said, "Push, Rebekah, if you have to, I'm right here." Rebekah pushed, or was pushed, and she cried out again. The contraction eased and Claudia ran back to the girl still sitting in her car. She gave Claudia the thumbs-up, but didn't move.

The next contraction came only a few seconds later, and Claudia inwardly cursed God, cursed Hazel for good measure, and then the third contraction simply didn't stop. Rebekah moaned, turned from side to side, and Claudia saw it: the curve of the baby's head. There wasn't time to think. She slipped her hands, unwashed but soaking wet, in around the head, tearing Rebekah and feeling it as she did so. There was one ear, a second, and she gradually twisted and pulled. The baby's head was almost completely out and he was facedown, so she couldn't tell anything about him, if he was alive or dead. Claudia held on, now reaching for the shoulders. She could hear herself yelling but didn't know what she was saying, and even in the midst of all that, the yelling, trucks driving slowly through the standing water on the highway, Rebekah crying now like a siren, she heard, or felt, the slightest snap between the baby's shoulders, and Claudia pulled him the rest of the way out.

Without warning, there were hands reaching over her, broad-shouldered, well-fed Midwestern boys in the official clothes of EMTs, saying, "Sir, we need to step in here," and then they were under her makeshift tent, clamping the cord, suctioning the baby's face with a handheld pump. Claudia stepped back. She stayed at the edge, watching Rebekah's face through the rear passenger's window. They had placed an oxygen mask over her nose and mouth; the elastic cut into her hair. As soon as the cord was clamped and cut, one boy wrapped the baby in a warm towel as the other pulled up a gurney with a snap that made Claudia jump back a step. She wiped the sweat off her forehead, felt that she'd left a streak of thick, sticky blood. Now the second boy was packing something between Rebekah's legs, and lifting her onto the gurney without half the ease of Claudia. He shouted to the boy with the baby to prepare an IV. Over his shoulder he shouted, "Are you the father?" And Claudia dumbly nodded yes. "You can follow us," he said, slamming the door of the ambulance before she could answer, before she heard anything, anything at all, from the baby.

The attic—what a mess. Hazel had no idea where the trash had come from, or why every time she climbed these stairs she found a new dead bird. It was like an elephant's graveyard, but for pigeons. She stood with her hands on her hips, surveying the damage. Rain was steadily dripping in one pot, but in the larger one, the washtub, it was streaming in. The problem was the slate tiles on the roof—no one would replace them and Hazel couldn't give up and have the roof shingled. When she raised the issue with Caroline, her mother's answer was always the same: let it fall, dear. Let it fall to the ground.

The fans were working—she turned them on and off—and one of the three leaks had stopped, probably because some dead animal was momentarily filling the hole. She walked from one eave to the next, from Edie's Love and Ganga Corner to the bar where her uncle's uniforms had hung. A myth, she thought, running her hand along the boards, that any place is haunted. You walk into an attic, you see a child's wheelchair, a crutch. You think, It's here, the past is here. A few years later you carry the wheelchair and crutch down to a truck, park them in a warehouse, and someone else picks them up—who's haunted now? Where is the past, exactly? Once a week a neophyte, someone from the college, would stand in front of her at the store and say, "My gosh, it's right there, isn't it? I can feel the history of this [eggbeater, bean grinder, tablecloth] in my hands. Isn't that amazing?" And Hazel would nod, try to sound polite as she said, "Oh sure. That'll be twelve-fifty." Maybe she should hang a sign by the cash register, WHATEVER YOU'RE THINKING, KEEP IT TO YOURSELF.

She walked into the eave with the east-facing window. She turned on her flashlight; her mind was blank. If she had been a child and had been asked what she was doing, she'd have said, Nothing. It felt that way. Nothing. I'm just sweeping these flies off the windowsill. I'm just kneeling in front of these boards. She pressed against the seam and pushed, then slid the boards toward her. A bead of sweat slid down the side of her nose, just missing her eye. She stopped. The rain seemed to be slowing, just a bit. Hazel sat down, looked at the opening she'd made. She was a woman who'd tried to figure out what to do with what she'd been given, that was all, and she knew when she was wrong.

She hadn't been wrong to hate Vernon, but she'd been wrong to see him as her rival. What muddied, crazy thinking—true only for her and for no one else. Vernon had said it himself at the entrance to the emergency room, screaming at Hazel and at Albert, who was trying to help the ER nurse get Finney onto a gurney. "*You* killed her," he screamed at Hazel, pointing his finger right in her face. You killed her.

She pulled the boards open another inch, almost enough to slip her flashlight inside. Killed Finney, killed Albert. Caroline had trusted Hazel to know Finney's history—it was *her job,* after all—but Hazel had seen her work as beginning and ending with getting Finney through the door, getting the problem taken care of so they could all start again. A clotting disorder? Who would ask about something like that when Finney had seen the light for just a moment, and Hazel's task was to swoop in and take advantage of it? And how could Hazel not have known about it, anyway?

Her flashlight revealed a crawl space about the size of a closet. In one corner there was . . . it looked like a pile of old newspapers, mostly shredded. There was a cigar box, the lid askew. A pile of old bottles—God, it was the same everywhere—men and their bottles. In the opposite corner she saw half a doll, the other half in shadow. She swung the flashlight across the rear wall . . . nothing else. And then, just to the left of her head, on the opposite side from where she'd begun, an old wooden box.

Vernon had screamed, *You killed her,* and Hazel just stood there, studying the face Finney so adored. She wanted to reach out and lay her hand against his cheek, she'd never seen a more beautiful man in her life. I get it, she whispered, I get it now. It was just a sickness, or no—no—a condition, like color-blindness or a clubfoot. A man so beautiful was necessarily harsh, the Greeks even had a phrase for it. And what was it Finney said? *He can be so tender, you don't know him.* He was a labyrinth, and at the center there was either a trapped hero or a monster. Then he screamed again, "You and your mother killed her and I . . ." and Hazel lost her train of thought about beauty, and kicked him as hard as she could in the groin. He doubled over so fast he looked like a puppet with a broken string. But there was no relief in the gesture, because as soon as she saw his knees hit the ground, she knew Finney was really dead.

She brought the box out of the crawl space and just held it. Hazel was here in Rebekah's name, trying to measure and overcome Rebekah's battle. The little red-haired girl, holiness itself, born less than a year after Finney died. A miracle after all the years they'd waited, Ruth had told her daughter. There was no doubt Rebekah was at risk, and had been since Christmas Day, but this morning when Hazel awoke she felt various strands converging, and she knew she had to act. If there was really a baby in this box, then every step Hazel had taken, every word she'd spoken, had been in good faith. But if there was nothing here . . . then she was a tired old woman with some astrology books and a bunch of cats. Smoke and mirrors. She sighed, slipped her thumbnail under the rusty latch. Her bifocals weren't centered and she couldn't quite see what she was doing. "Ah, dammit," she said, lifting her glasses with one hand while the other fumbled with the latch. Sweat ran into her right eye, then into the left. Why hadn't she just gone out there, to Peter's? Hazel stopped, lowered her glasses. Why was the answer here, in this little casket? She had called Claudia to go because that was a story she was telling called Claudia and Rebekah. And their story didn't start here, in this attic, it didn't start or end with Hazel.

She took a deep breath, lowered her head into her hands, smearing her forehead with rust. She sat that way a long time, listening to the weather. Marguerite Henrietta Post had lived in the house alone until she died at seventy-three. The outline of her story had been easy enough to trace at the county courthouse, but there was no record of a baby, and of course there wouldn't have been. An unmarried woman from old money. You do what you have to do; Caroline had said it herself, it was her mantra in those days. Hazel tried again to lift the latch, halfheartedly. It was no good. A different kind of person would have taken the box with her, might have kept it in her house as a macabre reminder, someone younger or with more nerve. Someone else might have buried it, said some words over the bones. But Hazel just stuck it back in the crawl space, closed the boards.

Outside, she held her hands up to the sky, let the rain wash them. She trudged around to the back of the house, to the clinic entrance. Now *there* was a crime scene: broken windows, ivy crawling through the frame. She walked up the steps, shone the flashlight inside. The plank floor of the waiting room was still stained with blood, Jim Hank's in a wide pool near where the desk once sat, and Finney's over that and all the way to the door. And footprints in the blood—Caroline's, Hazel's, Albert's. Hazel had made one halfhearted attempt to clean it, but barely got as far as the first spot before collapsing, sobbing and sick. She'd been grateful there was no one there to see her. But it hadn't been a crime scene, had it? Albert guaranteed it with his death.

He'd driven home from the hospital raging so furiously, Hazel was more than a little afraid he would harm her. She and her mother had destroyed everything he'd worked for, he yelled, they had robbed him of a lifetime of spotless conduct and honorable accomplishments. The more he screamed at her, the more she told him, not out of fear but because in truth she hated him and she was enjoying watching him change colors and tug at his necktie as if it were choking him, and her life was going to be seriously short of pleasure from that night on, she was certain. At the house they'd found Caroline packing her records into cardboard boxes, and Albert hit Caroline once across the mouth, then strode screaming toward the barn, where he'd grabbed a can of kerosene and used it to start a fire in the fire ring. He intended to burn everything, every trace of evidence. He got the box Caroline was holding by raising his fist a second time, but as soon as he was out the door Caroline said to Hazel, "Tell me what we must do to stop him." Hazel was thinking, thinking, there were guns in this house, there were guns in every house in America, but where? She was thinking but there was a roaring in her ears, too, it wasn't just shock or grief, it was a noise. "Ah, your sister is home," Caroline said coolly, as though she weren't bleeding from the mouth. And just like that, Hazel knew she had an answer.

"Edie!" she'd yelled, running outside. "Charlie! Daddy has hit Mother and he says he's going to kill her! He's gone crazy, look—he's burning medical records."

Edie and Charlie, stoned stoned stoned. They both looked at her a beat too long, as if their electrical devices needed new batteries. Then Charlie said, "What'd you say, man?" just as Albert ran back toward the house, screaming at Edie and Charlie to leave, this was nothing to do with them.

"Oh yeah?" Charlie stepped up into Albert's face.

"You hit Mother?" Edie said from behind Charlie.

"Get out of my way." Albert pushed Charlie away, and for good measure, spit at him.

And then Charlie was backing Albert toward the fire using just his chest, not pushing him, not swinging. Hazel and Edie followed at a safe distance. The men were shouting in each other's faces, and sometimes Albert got the upper hand and Charlie would have to take a step backward, but more often it was Albert backing up. Her father stopped suddenly, just stopped. His face was scarlet, then white. He raised a finger to point at Charlie (or maybe at Hazel) and collapsed to the ground.

Charlie turned back to Edie, rubbed his hands together proudly. "Blew that fucker's gasket," he said.

They loaded Albert in his own car to return to the hospital he'd just left. "Hazel," Caroline said, "stay here. Salvage what you can of that box in the fire ring. Get all my other boxes, put them in my car.

I want you to take them to this address, it's a woman on Washington Street in Jonah. . . ."

"Mom," Hazel said, looking at the scrap of paper in the dome light, "this is on East Washington. That's the projects."

Caroline looked confused. "And?"

"You want me to go there alone?"

"Darling"—Caroline rested her open hand on Hazel's face—"I am so sorry. But you'll survive all of this."

What Caroline had meant, of course—and it had taken Hazel a good long time to figure it out—was that nothing could break *her*. She had married whom she married and stayed with him because she had work to do, and nothing was going to stop her. He was in the back-seat gasping for life and Caroline made sure those boxes were secure.

The rain was slowing down, light returning to the sky. Hazel sat down on the clinic steps, looked out at the barn. Her mother hadn't planned it, but she hadn't even had to lie. Someone broke into the clinic, threatening her and her daughter. No, she'd never seen the man before. Yes, it seemed he'd had Finney, who was suffering a miscarriage, in his truck. No, she didn't know why. The stranger had also assaulted Finney's husband, Jim Hank, with a crowbar; yes, the boy in Critical Care. No, he couldn't speak to the events because he was in a coma. The policeman who'd interviewed Caroline said no one at the hospital had ever seen the man before, the one who'd dropped off the dead girl, he was a complete stranger. Caroline suggested perhaps he was a member of a cult or some such, there were so many of those around these days. And Albert died neatly, his original will intact. The money he'd been saving to donate to the hospital to build a wing in his name was still in their joint savings account. Caroline moved it all, every dime, into an account she shared with Hazel, and off they went, Caroline into a neat, small apartment in town where she began to compile her life's work, and Hazel to the Used World Emporium. Somebody had to do something with all that junk.

Hazel stood, tried to wipe off the back of her coat. The four-story barn was collapsing; the back half was already down, shoulder-hunched against the rain. Hunters had added thousands more holes to the corncrib, and somebody snuck back fairly often and had a fire—there were always fresh ashes in the fire ring. The temple will fall because the temple is always falling, Rebekah had said to her in exasperation, in a conversation about prophecy. Hazel had laughed, said the temple will fall, there will be terrible weather and firstborns will die. A corrupt man will lead the state and there will be blood in the streets. That's the easiest stuff in the world, she'd said to bright-eyed Rebekah. Tell me something harder, like how my next step will set into motion a chain of events I could *never* foresee. Tell me how to live with the outcome.

Hazel opened her car door, paused as she always paused before leaving. She looked at the meadow, the treetops, the old county road, and down the lane toward the mailbox, where she had felt herself filled with spirits in a long-ago month just like this one. As she watched, they streaked past, as they often did, the cemetery dogs, a blur of muscle, fur, and intention. She'd seen them many times before. She remembered asking Edie if she could see them, when Edie was the sort of teenager who had undoubtedly seen stranger things, and her sister had answered, "We live in the damn *country*, Hazel, damn dogs *everywhere*."

Chapter 10

"CAN I COME IN?"

Rebekah pulled back the curtain around her bed to see who it was. Just a puff of orange hair was visible. "Hazel! Come in!"

Hazel fussed around the room a moment looking uncomfortable, as if she wanted to lie down on the bed and cry with relief but instead would just move the breakfast tray over, and then also adjust the chair. "Do you remember seeing me last night?"

Rebekah shook her head. She didn't remember anything. Well, that wasn't entirely true. She had come to consciousness a few times, but there had been tubes in both her arms, she had been catheterized, and a pump beside her released morphine into one of her IV drips. Rebekah opened her eyes every few hours and like a goldfish in a hospital bowl, each time was the first. She would awaken and think, There is Claudia, it worked. How utterly amazing. Then she would sleep, a dark, chemical tumbling from which she brought back nothing. Hours later she would think, There is Claudia, the phone worked. How amazing. Only this morning she had realized the same thing had happened many times.

"Well, it's a good thing you don't remember—I was a fright. You can't imagine what an entire day of torrential rain does to this hair."

"I can well imagine it," Rebekah said.

"Have you seen the baby?"

"He's"—Rebekah lowered her hands to the bed, studied them— "he's still in the NICU." Sometime in the night she had felt a hand on her shoulder—Gil, as it turned out—and she decided to tell him about the fascinating things that had happened to her. But he wanted to do the talking. He said something about toxemia, preeclampsia, an intrauterine infection. All possibilities. He said the baby's clavicle was broken, he was almost four weeks premature, and he was suffering from cephalohematoma. Gil repeated the condition, said it in tongues, *cephalohematoma,* told her there was a blood lake over the infant's skull. Rebekah could see it clearly, the blood lake, and tried to nod. It made perfect sense to her. Unfortunately, she had no idea what baby he was talking about, and believed the clavicle to be a musical instrument. Sad that the baby's was broken. Maybe later his parents could get him a small piano, or a recorder. Claudia was holding Rebekah's feet and it was three in the morning, if not in Indiana, then somewhere. Rebekah turned her head from side to side, tried to open both eyes. She focused on Claudia, opened her mouth and tried to say, *There's been an accident.* She meant . . . she didn't know what she meant—a train wreck, a fallen sky. She couldn't move her legs or feel Claudia's hands on her feet, although she knew them to be there. *Her baby,* that was what she realized with a jolt that cut through the fever; the morphine; her swollen, inert body. Gil had been talking about her baby, the gifted SeaWorld creature who had performed his tricks for months, and then, without warning, had broken through the gates. Rebekah had never stood on a seashore, but thought she was standing there now, watching him swim and swim away.

"Have you seen him?" Rebekah asked.

"I peeked through a window and saw the little cooker he's in, and then I marched to the nurses' station and told them I didn't want him someplace any Tom, Dick, or Harry could just clap an eyeball on him."

"What did the nurse say?"

"She ignored me."

"Hazel," Rebekah asked, "have you ever felt like—has anything ever happened to you and it pushed you so far outside yourself that you almost didn't . . . I mean, have you ever wanted to stop people from going about their daily business, just so you could say to them, I don't know, something like, 'I'm sorry, but I've survived something terrible, and I am not a normal person.' Something like that?"

Hazel waited a moment, said, "Once."

Rebekah sighed, looked back down at the bed.

"You know, don't you, that the baby is going to be fine? He came into the world a little bunged up, it's true, but he's—"

"I know. I know you're right." A tear rolled down Rebekah's face. "He's fine and I'm fine, but barely. If it weren't for Claudia we'd both . . ."

"But you are."

"But almost."

"I see. The Other Universe, right? Right now you are safe and healthy and so's the baby, but in the Other Universe it didn't turn out that way?"

"Yes. Yes! We were so close it might as well have turned out bad as good. And I know you'll say, But it didn't."

"No, I'll just say this: the world is probably divided, like glass-half-full types, between those who, when faced with salvation, revisit the scene and imagine they weren't saved. And the others, who weren't saved, and revisit the scene and make it right."

"So is my glass half full, or half empty?"

"Ha! That's the thing. Your glass is completely full, and you look at it and say, 'What if I'd dropped this just now as I was carrying it from the kitchen? Then it wouldn't just be empty, it would be broken.'"

Rebekah let her head fall back against the bed as she laughed.

"You look good," Hazel told her.

"Thanks, I . . ." Rebekah looked down at the bed self-consciously. "A nurse helped me shower this morning, and Claudia went home last night at some point and brought back this nightgown. She'd been saving it."

"I see."

"And these flowers." Rebekah gestured toward the bouquets on either side of her. "This one is from Claudia and Oliver and Bandit, these are from Millie, who wrote on the card, *Please come home, I like you so much better than Claudia,* and these are from Pete Senior, and Kathy."

Hazel raised an eyebrow.

"Claudia called them last night. I thought she'd done it to be kind—doesn't it sound like something she'd do, be nice like that?"

"It does."

"Well, that wasn't the only reason, I guess." Rebekah lifted her damp hair out from behind her gown. "Kathy was a huge mess when she was here this morning, crying like I've never seen, saying that Peter had left them *a note*—she was desperate for me to understand that. He'd left it on Pete Senior's car the night he left for Florida, but apparently that big windstorm blew it away."

"We've had a lot of wind."

"The note said he was sorry but he had to go, and that one of them should get over to check on me right away, as I wasn't feeling well when he left. She wanted me to know, too, that Peter didn't have the phone disconnected—he just didn't pay the bill."

"Very nice. A good man."

"Yes. I said to Kathy, a note?!? You're asking me to forgive him, and to forgive you, because of a note?"

"Good for you."

"But of course I do."

"Do what?"

"Forgive them. I mean, my goodness, I'm not their responsibility. I wasn't even his, that was all just . . . it was just a mistake, easy to make."

"Are you anybody's responsibility?"

Rebekah studied Hazel's face, thought about it. "It seems Claudia has always thought I was hers."

"But that only works if she is yours, too, I think. Otherwise."

"I know. I know that."

"And what did you decide?"

A nurse bustled in, pulled back Rebekah's curtain with a loud snap. Hazel and Rebekah were silent as blood pressure and temperature were taken. The nurse wrote the numbers in Rebekah's chart, hung it back on its hook. "Grandma, you'll want to be getting this suitcase out of the hallway as soon as you can."

Rebekah covered her mouth, laughed with a sound like a sneeze. "Grandma," she said, pulling her sheet up over her face.

"Don't get started, you." Hazel groaned a little as she stood. She stepped out into the hallway and came back with a trunk on a set of wheels used to pull luggage.

"I've seen that before," Rebekah said, studying the gray trunk with tarnished brass corners. "That's what Claudia and I went downtown to pick up for you, from that—"

"Second Chance. Right. It's yours, actually." Hazel lifted the trunk up and put it on the foot of the bed, released the spring handles. "When Tony and Gretchen, the couple who found this at the dump, went through it, they found letters with my name in them. So they called me, told me I could have it if I'd come get it." She lifted the lid.

Rebekah sat back, took a deep breath.

"Seen a ghost?" Hazel asked.

"Yes." Rebekah reached out, picked up a doll's dress. "I made this. It was the first thing I ever sewed by myself. And this one, too." She turned the tiny hems over, marveled at her small stitches, crooked as they were. "I don't . . ."

"Your mother saved them."

"My mother? This box belonged to my mother?"

Hazel nodded. "It did." She lifted out a battered cookbook.

"I"—Rebekah pressed a hand against her forehead—"never thought I'd see that again. And you say, I'm sorry, you say that your name is in here?"

"I knew your mother." Hazel moved aside a baby's quilt, pulled out a stack of letters bound in a faded yellow ribbon. "We corresponded for a few years, just before you were born and while you were a little girl."

"Hazel?" Rebekah dropped the doll clothes. "Look at me. In five, almost six years you don't tell me this?"

"That's right. It wasn't the right time."

"Not the right time."

"Correct." Hazel lifted her glasses, cheerfully looked for something at the bottom of the box. "Here it is." She pulled out a shoe box.

Rebekah leaned back against the bed, just enough to signal a recoil. She knew it happened all the time in books and movies, that a blood test shows your father couldn't be your father, or the person you thought long dead strolls into a restaurant where you've come by accident, but it didn't need to happen to her. It didn't need to happen today. "I don't want to see this," she said.

"I believe you," Hazel said, lifting the lid of the shoe box. "Now this, this is a story." She took out Rebekah's baby book, the one in which nothing was written. "And it starts," she said, her glasses pushed up on her head as she flipped through the blank pages, "with her." From the very back, farther than Rebekah had been able to go in that long-ago hour, Hazel removed a black-and-white photograph.

It was of a thin, pretty woman standing in front of Sterling's Department Store in what appeared to be a mild season. Her hair was cut in a bob and it curled under her ears. She was wearing a lovely dress with a tuck-waisted white blouse, a full dark skirt, white gloves. In one hand she was holding a small dark clutch purse; with the other she was waving shyly. "Oh," Rebekah said, running a finger over the woman's face. "Sterling's."

"Now this"—Hazel lifted something else out of the shoe box— "is your baby book."

The pink satin cover was faded and stained, the book itself so full of envelopes and letters and cards it was at least three times its original thickness. "This is mine—me? This one is me?"

"Yes."

"Then this"—Rebekah lay her hand on the cover of the empty book—"was my brother's?"

"That's right. Your mother found out she was pregnant with you and she wrote to me, without telling your father, of course, and asked me about her." Hazel pointed to the woman in front of Sterling's. "I wrote her back and that began a correspondence that lasted years. I loved Ruth. She taught me a great deal about humility and kindness, obedience."

Rebekah snorted. "Shame you didn't practice any of it."

Hazel shrugged. "Life is short. These"—she pointed to the letters in the yellow ribbon—"are just mine to her, but I've put hers to me in the box, too, in a blue ribbon. Now"—Hazel stood up—"don't tend to this today. You've got some long nights ahead of you, years and years of long nights."

"Thank you."

"You'll find it all interesting."

"And I can ask you anything?"

"You can ask me anything." Hazel packed the last things in the trunk and closed it. She straightened her lime-green T-shirt, had just settled her voluminous purple skirt in the chair when the door opened and Claudia came in with Amos Townsend. Hazel watched the two of them duck through the doorway, said, "Oh good, two of the Pacers have come to visit."

There was a flurry of activity, a burst of radiance just like the one that follows any disaster averted. Who survived, who chose wisely, who would find a way to live by her own daily lights? Rebekah watched the others talk, Amos describing some mishap at the post office, Claudia laughing that full-throated way that was so rare it felt to Rebekah like the sighting of an endangered bird. Hazel, gathering up her things, getting ready to sneak out of the room. And down the hall, baby David in his special hat, getting baked a little longer in his warm bed. Rebekah knew then that if she taught him only one thing—if there were room for only one—she would tell him to trust her: What feels like the end of the world never is. It *never* is.

Acknowledgments

I'm grateful, as ever, to the fine people at The Free Press and at Simon & Schuster, who demonstrate their support for me in countless ways. I would like to particularly thank Dominick Anfuso, Martha Levin, Carisa Hays, Suzanne Donahue, and Amber Qureshi, for the extraordinary line-edit she did on the third revision of this book.

Fifteen years ago Tom Koontz wrote a poem called "Old Woods," which I told him would make a fascinating novel. He asked me to write it. I tried then and failed. All these years later, two images from that poem have made their way into Hazel's story: Marguerite Post in her rocking chair, and the baby's coral bracelet. I am grateful to him for the depth of that omen, which haunts me still.

This is my fifth and final book with my editor, Amy Scheibe, who has moved on to another publishing house. We have had an enviable professional relationship; Amy gave her heart (not to mention her time) to making each of my books the best it could be. I can never thank her enough for the ways she changed my life.

One image in this book—the dogs running circles into the frozen ground at Cobb Creek—is an homage to Sherwood Anderson's far superior story "A Death in the Wood."

Dear Marcel Proust believed that friendships were a distraction for the real writer, and certainly they can be. That said, I'd rather keep my friends than ever write another book. Thank you: Leslie Staub (who if I never saw you again, you would be the one) and Tim Sommer,

Diane Freund and Joe Galas, Beth and John Dalton, Jody Leonard and Lisa Kelly, Ben Kimmel, Don and Meg Kimmel, Fred Neumann, Suzanne Finnamore, Lawrence Naumoff, Larry Baker, Jay Alevizon, John MacMullen, Tessa Joseph and George Nicholas, my beloved niece, Abby Lindsay.

I owe a much-belated debt to Frank and Barbara Watson. What they gave me and what they taught me is a story in itself. They know.

My eternal love and thanks to my Otters, without whom . . . I can't imagine what. I would be a ruined, leaking basket of crazy and loneliness. Christopher Schelling, Robert Rodi (who was so kind about an early draft of this book, I threatened to have his comments tattooed on my human body), Jeffrey Smith, Dennis Pilsits (Honorary Otter), and Augusten Burroughs, who is my soul's twin, except I have all the hair.

My mother, Delonda Hartmann, reads and reads and reads the drafts of my books and she never tires of them and she never complains and she always makes me feel like a genius, even though she is smarter than I am and a better writer to boot. For that she deserves some huge sparkling award and as soon as I can find one, it's hers.

If I write for one person—if there's one person I really want to please—it's my sister, Melinda Mullens. Anyone who has read my other books knows she often pinches me and calls me names but she loves how I write so it's okay about how mean she is. Thanks to her husband, Wayne, too, who—the first time he saw me after thirty years—said, "My God, I haven't seen you since you were on a bicycle in your slippers and your hair was out to here!"

I've already said everything I can say about my husband, John Svara, but I'll say it again: beautiful, beautiful, you are like Proteus in that old myth. You became exactly the man you wanted to be, and you carried me through that refining fire until what was left was sublime and for the rest of my life.

And finally, I thank my children: the ever-hilarious Obadiah (who never bothers me when I'm writing and makes me laugh like no one else) and my perfect new baby, Augusten James-Anthel, who already shines with some celestial light. But mostly I want to thank my daughter, Kat Romerill, who is the love of my life, the most highly evolved, funny, wicked, brilliant, compassionate woman in the world. How I got to be her mother I can only attribute to my great and rare luck.

About the Author

HAVEN KIMMEL is the author of *She Got Up Off the Couch, Something Rising (Light and Swift), The Solace of Leaving Early,* and *A Girl Named Zippy.* She studied English and creative writing at Ball State University and North Carolina State University and attended seminary at the Earlham School of Religion. She lives in Durham, North Carolina.

The Used World

A NOVEL

HAVEN KIMMEL

Reading Group Guide

A Conversation with Haven Kimmel

ABOUT THIS GUIDE

The following reading group guide and author interview are intended to help you find interesting and rewarding approaches to your reading of *The Used World*. We hope this enhances your enjoyment and appreciation of the book. For a complete listing of reading group guides from Simon & Schuster, visit BookClubReader.com.

READING GROUP GUIDE

Summary

Claudia Modjeski and Rebekah Shook work at Hazel Hunnicutt's Used World Emporium, an antique mall in Jonah, Indiana, that is "the station at the end of the line for objects that sometimes appeared tricked into visiting there." Only Hazel, in her sixties, still has a mother; Claudia, in her forties, is over six feet tall; and Rebekah, nearly thirty, is pregnant, though she doesn't know it as *The Used World* opens. In this heartrending and hilarious novel, these three women are bound together not only by their pasts but also by their futures, finding that long-held truths fall away in the face of newfound realities, secrets never really stop haunting their makers, and that one Christmas and two unexpected babies can turn their formerly used world brand-new again.

Discussion Points

1. The Preface briefly introduces the three main characters and their triangular connection. What do Hazel, Claudia, and Rebekah have in common? In what ways are they different?

2. On page 8, Amos Townsend tells Claudia, "I see people all the time who say they are lonely but it's a code word for something else." Do

you think this is true in Claudia's case? Why or why not? What is loneliness a code word for in the cases of Hazel and Rebekah?

3. Hazel describes vague memories of a world of women, the men all gone off to war. Are the women in this novel different with one another than they are in the presence of men?

4. What is the significance of the flashback to 1950 on page 15, where Hazel has her nighttime encounter with the owl? Where else does this symbol appear in the novel?

5. How do physical descriptions and personality quirks help define the characters in *The Used World*? Identify these descriptions and explain what they reveal about each character.

6. The women in this novel all struggle with motherhood, either through their relationships to their actual mothers or through becoming mothers themselves. Describe the ways in which motherhood poses challenges and otherwise changes these characters.

7. Claudia laments the demise of the Old Mother—exemplified by her mother, Ludie—and the rise of the New Mother, represented by her sister, Millie. What does Claudia mean by these distinctions? How else does this Old/New paradigm work its way into the novel?

8. Because the point of view shifts to let the reader inside the minds of Hazel, Claudia, and Rebekah, we get an opportunity to learn how each woman sees the others. Do you think they have accurate impressions of one another? Why or why not? How does each see herself in comparison to how the others see her?

9. On page 185, Red says, "Children. It don't matter if they're good or bad, they break your heart every time." Compare and contrast the relationships of siblings Hazel and Edie and Claudia and Millie; con-

sider also single children Rebekah and Peter. How have these relationships or lack thereof shaped the adulthoods of these characters? How do you think the presence or absence of siblings changes each character's relationship with his or her parents?

10. The flashback to 1969 on page 210 describes Hazel's attic vision of Marguerite Henrietta Post, the former owner of their house, and her murdered baby. What is the significance of this vision and the information it gives Hazel? How does it influence Hazel's actions as an adult? Why does Hazel return to the attic to uncover the baby's bones near the end of the novel?

11. When did you first guess who Finney's mystery man was? What clues were there leading up to this plot twist? Does this information change your opinion of him? Why or why not?

12. Hazel seems to expect a lot of Claudia. "I thought you were the most courageous person I'd ever known. I trusted you with a baby and a dog and a pregnant woman," she says on page 267. Why do you think she does this? When did you first suspect Claudia was a lesbian? What clued you in to the fact that Hazel was, too? How do you think this commonality influences Hazel's actions with regard to "telling a story called Claudia"?

13. Though *The Used World* is primarily about women, there is much said about the duties of men as fathers, friends, and lovers. Identify the male characters in this novel and describe how they do or do not successfully fulfill their roles. Discuss the consequences their actions have for the women in their care.

14. In two generations, there are two relationships threatened by the presence of a man: Hazel and Finney struggle with the specter of Vernon, while Peter comes between Claudia and Rebekah. Compare and contrast these two triangles of love and despair.

Enhance Your Book Club

1. Rebekah Shook's family is a member of the Prophetic Mission, a small church subset of the Pentecostal movement. Though each local church has its own evangelical perspective, you can find out more about the basic worldview of this Christian tradition by visiting www.religioustolerance.org/chr_pent.htm.

2. Hazel's Used World Emporium is a wonderland of objects that bring the past to life for its employees and visitors, displaying its wares in arrangements that mimic actual rooms. Try visiting a local antique mall with your fellow book club members for a firsthand experience of being enveloped by the past.

3. Most modern towns have spread and evolved as their populations have expanded, but it's still possible to enjoy "Main Street America" disguised as the newly renovated, hipper downtown areas in many cities across the country. Check out your own city's downtown for historic sites and walking tours you can share with your book club members.

4. The author, Haven Kimmel, has written two memoirs and two other novels. To learn more about her and her work, visit her official website, www.havenkimmel.com, and her fan site, www.purityofheart.org.

A CONVERSATION WITH
HAVEN KIMMEL

What made Jonah, Indiana, the perfect setting for this story? Is it a real town? What is your relationship to it?

Jonah isn't a real town (I never base any locations or characters on real places or people), but it shares characteristics with the town where I earned my bachelor's degree, Muncie, Indiana. My relationship to it is mixed, of course. When I'm away from it I think, "Thank God I got away," and then I go back to visit and think, "I love this town."

You are a poet as well as a novelist and memoirist. What prompted the transition from writing poetry to writing book-length narratives?

I moved to the South and lost the ability to write poems. It turned out that my poetic sensibility was entirely connected to the farmland of Indiana. So I turned to prose instead and that worked out okay.

You recently gave a keynote address at your former seminary, the Earlham School of Religion. In it, you said, "I thought a great deal about how, without my seminary education, I could never have written the three novels that compose the Hopwood County Trilogy." Will you expand on that thought?

The three novels are deeply concerned with religion and the religious life of the characters. One of the protagonists is himself a minister. I never could have had the courage (or the authority) to write those novels without those years of education.

During the same speech, you also said, "I thought about how a life spent in the Society of Friends uniquely prepared me to be a writer

altogether." Would you say that your life as a Quaker gave you tools to be a better writer? How did growing up Quaker prepare you to be a writer?

I can sit still for very long periods. I'm used to living in my mind, and to listening to my own heart. I value spiritual truth above all things, and I believe that by practicing discernment, that truth can be heard.

You have written both memoir and fiction. Do you find one medium easier than the other? Do you prefer one over the other? How is your writing process different for each type of book?

Writing nonfiction is much easier for me, because I'm limited by the truth, by what actually happened. I love the frame around which nonfiction is built. Fiction is so much harder because every word, every nuance, has to be invented from nothing, and yet I love writing it so much more.

You are the author of several books, two of which, with *The Used World,* make up a loosely connected trilogy about Hopwood County, Indiana. Did you set out to write a trilogy? How do you see these three different stories working together?

I did set out to write a trilogy and it was a complete act of folly. I had no idea what I was doing, and the books turned out nothing like I expected them to. They're connected in ways I can only allow the reader to discern.

Writing about three women at different life stages seems like a great opportunity to explore various facets of your own personality, or perhaps to imagine the kind of woman you might become (or once were). What elements of *you* appear in the characters of *The Used World*?

There are no elements of myself in *The Used World*. I really try very hard to write fiction; to create out of nothing. If there's one character who periodically reflects my philosophy, it's Amos Townsend, and he's not even a woman. I've said in interviews that if I could choose to be any character in any of my novels, it would be Amos. He's extraordinarily decent and kind; he's a fine minister; and he's overwhelmed with the sort of doubt that marks the true believer.

The relationships between siblings and between children and their parents in this novel are complicated and varied. Were you inspired by your own relationship to your parents or siblings? Has being a mother changed the way you write about family?

In a way, I'm grieving over my own childhood and my grandmother and the mother my own mother used to be. I'm nostalgic for something I perceive as beautiful, which may not have been at all. I miss my grandmother, Mom Mary, who never had an unkind word to say about anyone and she could cook anything and the minute we walked in the door she said, "Let me fix you something to eat; you don't look like you could keep a bird alive." I miss the way we went to church in the winter, and the pleasure of walking in the warm sanctuary. I miss the way my parents gardened, and how we went camping together all summer. By the time my father died he did virtually nothing but sit in front of the television, watching other people live other lives. My mom—who loves working—still teaches full-time at seventy-five. I would love to walk in her house and smell something cooking, and find a bedroom all ready for me and my babies. It's nothing but pure selfishness on my part. And I wish I could walk in a house and see the heirlooms of generations past; antiques and family portraits, and not those plastic-framed Wal-Mart pictures of angels or whatever. It's possible I'm a hopeless snob.

I hate to sound cagey (although I am in fact a cagey person), but I try to keep my children as far from my writing as humanly possible. They deserve their privacy, and I would never reveal them. Once in a while I'll use something priceless my son said, or in one case I dressed baby Oliver in pajamas I love on my own baby. But the bigger question is do I love differently because I have children and the answer is I love more than I thought possible. That shows up in my books, I think.

Religion and spirituality play a major role in these characters' lives. Was it difficult for you to imagine the impact such different reli-

gious paths—such as Rebekah's Prophetic Mission or Hazel's blend of astrology and psychic phenomena—might have on an individual's worldview? What kind of research did you do to bring these elements of the story alive?

I grew up with people who belonged to a sect very like Rebekah's, and my brother is a Pentecostal minister. I was reared a Quaker, but my mother (who is a Quaker minister) is a practicing astrologer and so was her longtime (now deceased) closest friend. So I got it coming and going.

You're from Indiana, but you've lived in North Carolina now for many years. How would you compare your southern home to your former midwestern home? Do you think you will write about small-town North Carolina the way you have about Jonah, Indiana?

It took me a long time to figure out how to answer this question but I finally arrived on it. I was actually raised by southerners, and in a very southern part of Indiana. My father's family was from Kentucky, and I am one of those people who can call myself a hillbilly and not risk being politically incorrect. So when I moved to North Carolina I breathed a sigh of relief and thought, "Ah, *these* are my people."

I don't think I'll ever write about North Carolina because it doesn't belong to me. It belongs to my superiors (and they are my *vast* superiors): Lee Smith, Allen Gurganus, Reynolds Price, Clyde Edgerton, Lawrence Naumoff, Robert Morgan, Michael Malone. More than I could ever name. Oh, and a little someone named Faulkner, for instance, not to mention Flannery O'Connor and Eudora Welty.

You manage to touch on a wide variety of issues in this novel, addressing everything from overindulgent parents to religious cults to homosexuality to the demise of Main Street America. What broader social comment are you hoping readers will take away from *The Used World*?

That what feels like the end of the world never is. It *never* is.

Turn the page to read a chapter from Haven Kimmel's new novel.

The electrifying story of a young woman emerging from layers of
delusion, fantasy, and lies.

Iodine

A NOVEL

HAVEN KIMMEL

Available from Free Press in August 2008

CHAPTER ONE

Two Dogs

Dream Journal

I never

I never had sex with my father but I would have, if he had agreed. Once he realized how I felt he never again let me so much as lean against him while we watched television. I was never allowed to rest my head in his lap, or hold his hand. We gave up our late-night dancing in the kitchen to his favorite records; we stopped camping together. He took away my old hunting rifle, and when I rode behind him on his motorcycle I wasn't allowed to wrap my arms around his waist anymore. I had to let them lie on my own thighs, even when taking sharp corners.

Colt Pennington, Colt a childhood nickname that stuck. He was tall and leggy and too thin. There's just the one photograph of him as a boy, I think—he's standing in a dirt yard in Kentucky with two other boys his age. They are all tanned and barefoot and their hair has been buzzed for the summer, and Colt's head is turned, he's laughing at something one of the other boys has said. Just the *one* picture, and his head is turned. This is a perfect example of, I don't know, I forget, something about . . . Doors that close? Doors that were already closed before anyone knew they were open? The three of them, Colt and his two friends, don't look like boys today, in the same way child soldiers from the Civil War are foreign looking, so long lost. That is another example but I don't know what the word is.

His Gramaw Pennington swept the dirt yard but no one else did. She was the last of her kind in this family, out there swishing a broom around in the fine, dry soil, making patterns. The Last Dirt Yard Sweeper, right up until she killed herself with ant poison. I'm unclear on the details. Colt's mother, Juna? Hold a broom? No. There are a couple of pictures of her around here somewhere; Colt kept them. Juna was a cliché of the worst sort which I know because her type shows up all the time in books and movies, mostly movies, I guess. The too pretty mother who married young and never took to the whole thing, and in the movies there is her rouge and her stockings and the swirl of her skirt as she flies out the door while her little boy begs her to stay—he stands in the door watching as she gets in a stranger's car and drives away. But Juna wouldn't have been cast in that movie; she lacked the necessary . . . refinement. In Colt's photographs she's dressed like a singer at the Grand Ole Opry, the costume party equivalent. All Colt saw going out the door was (I'm guessing) some ratty old shoe and a cloud of cigarette smoke. But he kept those photographs: one where she's holding him, he's about two years old and Juna is so miserable one side of her mouth has collapsed—she has had a stroke of misery. In the other she is modeling her Opry dress (white) (some predecessor to vinyl) and her white boots, along with her big hair which is black like Colt's and does appear to be leading her out of the frame and into whatever her future was, no one knows.

If only he'd been facing the camera you (I) could see his eyes, which were round, irises so black there was no end to his pupil. Hair from Juna, eyes from his father, Clyde Sr., of whom there are a number of photographs but no one is interested in them. Not much to him, as I understand it—he was born to be Juna's victim and live in the same house with his widowed mother and give up on raising his only child after the child's mother left, well what was the man to do but walk slumped over every day to his job at the gas station and . . . am I right— did his teeth eventually melt? I think so, I think his teeth melted. So

Colt let his hair grow long and bought a wrecked 1950 BMW R512, which he worked on night and day in place of a formal education, and was it even running yet when he met L

his hair grew long and he rode that bike all the way from Kentucky, over the Ohio River and through Tell City, up up the middle of Indiana until he landed

a day laborer and then a carpenter but no one ever messed with him or said a word about that ponytail because he was fast as a whip crack, afraid of nothing, he carried a switchblade and walked with a slight left-leaning swagger from a childhood accident, he seemed cool in all ways but he was wound tight. His body rang like a piano string: I could hear him coming from miles away, an A note in an upper register, struck and struck and struck again. His hands were ruined with work and before he stopped touching me he would sometimes run his hand over my back and leave a dozen snags in the material of my shirts, he maybe didn't have fingerprints anymore.

In the winter he drove a '73 Ford truck, an F-100 with a 360, brown—that specific shade of brown of 1973. The muddy dogs jumped in the front seat, barn boots weren't even wiped in the grass before driving. The floor was littered with every imaginable kind of trash and tool and cast-off work glove (they assumed the shape of his hands), and the bed was scarred from loads of firewood and scrap metal. He thought only about what was under the hood, he took care where it mattered.

Cold had

Colt had me, his truck, his bike, his ruined hands, he had his black dog, Weeds. And cigarettes, which maybe Juna left him or taught him, I don't know how it happens. The Marlboro red pack, more of the music of my life: my father's barely in-tune A note jittering down the gravel road and up to the side of the house, and the ritual gestures. Peel away the silver strip that seals the rectangular box; pull off the upper cellophane. Throw it on the ground, in the bed of the truck, whatever. Knock the box against your forearm three, four times to pack the tobacco. Flip the lid with just your thumb, choose the cigarette in the front, in the middle, put it in the corner of your mouth and light it with your hands cupped around the match or the lighter even if no wind is blowing, even if you're standing in your daughter's bedroom and she wakes up because of the sound of the flame, and she doesn't know what you're doing there but she sees you, she would give you anything, she would fillet herself to keep you there, to take you in under the cheap coverlet. She is the dying, the cancerous, the starved or dehydrated, and you, he, Colt: morphine. bread. water. But he turns and walks away, as if he has prevented a disaster, and he takes the smoke with him, but the slight and fading sound of him remains.

✢

Trace Pennington pressed her tingling hands against her forehead, read what she had just written. She was supposed to be starting a dream journal for the class that began on Monday: Special Topics in Archetypal Psychology, an invitation-only course for senior Honors students who had either majored or minored in psychology. She was also enrolled in another senior seminar, Archetypal Analysis of Literature, available only to English or classics majors. Trace was both. At the last meeting with her adviser, a woman in a wig that had seemed deliberately stripped of color (it looked less like hair than fishing line) and styled to flip up at her shoulders, Trace had been told that in addition to her two majors and the psych minor, she had enough credits to declare minors in humanities and philosophy, and was one class away from a fourth in women's studies.

"So," Trace said, nodding.

"So do you want me to add them? You want them listed?"

"How did they happen, those minors?"

The adviser, *Mizzz* Birkle, studied Trace over the top of her half-glasses. "You took the classes."

"Yes," Trace said, trying to remember the past four years. When had she earned minors in four different subjects?

"You declaring them?"

"Wouldn't I?" Wouldn't she? Trace wondered if there was a rule somewhere, a code she had broken.

She tore the pages out of what was supposed to have been her dream journal and stuck them in one of the approximately two hundred unlabeled file folders scattered around the room she slept in. There were three bedrooms upstairs, all oddly shaped and dormered; Trace had chosen the smallest, the one at the back of the house, hoping it would be the easiest to heat. She had found a kind of plastic sheeting that attached to the windows with double-stick tape, and that one then turned into shrink-wrap with a blow-dryer. Having neither a blow-dryer nor electricity, she'd gone to the slick and overpriced store on campus that sold camping supplies (Daredevil Outfitting) and asked a young clerk, who was striving mightily to look gentle and outdoorsy and daring at once, if there was such a thing as a blow-dryer that used batteries.

"Sure," he said, walking toward the back of the store. "We've got curling irons, too, but they use propane inserts."

"Can you weld with them?"

"I'm sorry?"

"Nothing—I'll take the blow-dryer."

It had worked; Trace had turned the dryer up as high and hot as it would go and directed it at the loose plastic, which became tighter at each spot she focused on, until finally the window was completely sealed. There was still the hole in the ceiling, but she'd covered that with cardboard, and in the end she was glad to have the blow-dryer because on the very worst nights she could put it under her blankets and turn it on, warming the sheets just enough that she and the dog didn't shake in the way she hated, the kind of shivering that hurt.

She chose a different notebook to serve as her dream journal. There were stacks available to her, as there were file folders and ink pens and sticky notes and index cards. Working at the campus bookstore for four years had fulfilled her every office supply need. She didn't have to steal a thing: if a box of legal pads came in damaged, she was to take them out to the recycling Dumpster and throw them away, then make a note on the Inventory Loss form, which then went to the higher powers for Trace didn't know what—tax deductions or refunds or perhaps just regret. But in four years at the store (daredevilly named the Campus Book Store) no one had ever watched her recycle anything, nor had they seemed to care. As long as she made the note on the Inventory Loss form, and as long as the CBS superiors were satisfied, everything was fine. Their Loss became her Inventory Gain, just like that.

The scholarship she'd been offered to the University of the Midwest, in Jonah, Indiana, had included room and board, which Trace declined.

The money was refunded to her, and for days on end before her freshman year she drove her father's battered Ford truck up and down country roads so rutted and ruined they might have been Coventry in 1945,
until she found an abandoned farmhouse set back on a quarter-mile
lane she nearly missed. She had been there ever since.

After pulling ivy off the back door (she left the front untouched)
and nearly being killed by a swarm of wasps, she and Weeds had shoul-
dered their way into a domestic disaster. Every room was filled with
trash: broken toys and abandoned cheap clothes and a series of televi-
sions with shattered screens. It appeared that there had been two separate types here before her: whoever initially abandoned the house (that
was the bottom layer—they were fast-food aficionados) and squatters
after them, because there was an old upright piano in the living room
above which someone had spray-painted the words *La Dolce Vita!* with
real feeling, and also she had found a broken-spined and mildewy copy
of Paul Auster's *New York Trilogy* lying on the floor, open in the middle
and on top of a pile of rotting blankets. The first night she was there she
did nothing but read it cover to cover by the light of a hurricane lamp.

There was no heat or electricity, but she had this Inventory Gain:
above the well was a hand pump—not the old kind that required literal
pumping; this one was orange and all Trace had to do for well water was
lift a handle and fill a bucket. That took care of cooking on the Cole-
man stove, washing the dishes, bathing if she had to (she mostly showered at the truck stop out on the highway), and flushing the toilet in the
truly horrifying bathroom just off the kitchen.

Winters in the farmhouse were so cold she often felt as if she were
being lightly stung all over her body by a dentist's drill, even with the
three kerosene heaters she used: a small one in the bedroom, a large one
in the kitchen, where she often worked at the cheap and scarred table
someone had left behind, a small one in the bathroom. She and Weeds
reeked of kerosene, she knew, but there was nothing she could do about
it. At the cheap Laundromat on the south side of town, the one where
no one knew her, she was often afraid to wash her clothes for fear of an
explosion. Kerosene was in her lungs, her bloodstream, but she didn't
have options. Even if the fireplace hadn't been boarded up she wouldn't
have dared use it, in the same way she never used light at the front of
the house.

Using a clean notebook, Trace described the dream: Colt in a billowing white shirt, walking into the kitchen of a house Trace had never seen, juggling oranges. She tried to hold on to the feeling of the dream but it slipped even as she reached for it. Trace closed her eyes, opened and closed her numb hands. It was early afternoon of a bitterly cold January, in the abandoned farmhouse where she was hiding with the black dog, Weeds, who lay against her leg. She would need to leave soon; today was her standing visit with her oldest and only childhood friend, Candy Warner, formerly Candy Buck. The girl and the dog were as close to the heater as they could get, and yet they both shivered and were loath to leave.

✝

It was a long drive to Candy's house outside Mason—sixteen miles— and all of it on rural roads. And Mason was Trace's hometown, it wasn't safe for her to be there, so she ended up taking strange detours and looking for roads that didn't exist, thinking that eventually she was going to find a route she'd missed, a sudden turn, an iron bridge in disrepair.

Candy lived with her husband, Skeet, and their two little boys in a trailer at the back of Skeet's parents' property. Trace drove slowly down the dirt drive, in which there were holes deep enough to break an axle, past the senior Warners', their garage and workshop (which seemed to be missing part of its roof), to the place Skeet's domain began. It wasn't hard to find, marked as it was by dead cars and stripped trucks, lawn mowers that were unrecognizable in any season. There were tires and hubcaps and busted aluminum chairs. There was an old refrigerator and the hulking remains of a coal-burning stove. Trace had long since ceased cataloging or even seeing what was in front of the trailer—Candy's front yard looked like a thousand other front yards in Hopwood County.

Trace parked the truck so it couldn't be seen from the road, and stepped out carefully, Weeds following. Some parts of the ground were snow, some were ice. Everything was muddy, mixed with chunks of salt thrown carelessly, so that most of it was on the vehicle graveyard and not on the path that led to the steps.

From behind the chicken-wire fence attached to the trailer, one of Skeet's hounds, Blue, jumped and bayed and pulled against his chain. He was behind a fence and yet chained to his doghouse. Weeds stopped and looked at Blue. Trace stopped. Skeet had two dogs; where was the other? He called the missing dog Coon but Candy refused and referred to him as Bon Jovi. There was the second doghouse, the second chain, no dog. She took the last few steps and grabbed the handrail of the unsteady metal stairs.

Candy wore her hair in a style known as the Mall: permed on the sides, with bangs curled up into a roll and sprayed with Aqua Net. She had been pretty in high school, cheerful and bright-eyed, but had dated no one but Skeet Warner. From eighth grade on: Skeet's sullenness, his cars, his temper, his boots, the chain he wore connected to a wallet. The Skoal ring in the back pocket of his jeans. The issue of him was not up for discussion, not with Trace or Candy's parents or anyone else; for him she revealed a stubbornness that just grew heavier and more inexplicable as the years passed, and now, seven years later, she certainly had him or he had her but in either case the talking about it was over.

They sat at Candy's Early American kitchen table, which was covered with a plastic tablecloth. Candy smoked one cigarette after another and drank six cups of coffee, three of them so hot she burned her tongue and had to go to the kitchen for ice. The tablecloth was sticky from cereal and baby food and runny eggs and spilled beer and soda, so Trace kept her hands in her lap. As she smoked and drank coffee, Candy also managed to wrangle her eight-month-old son, Duane (named after a dead Allman Brother), who sometimes clung to her and sometimes tried to throw himself off her into the smoky air.

"You know how much weight I gained with this one?" Candy asked, squinting past her cigarette.

"You look fine," Trace said, taking note of the bruises on Candy's forearm, the shadow under her jaw, as if someone had taken sandpaper to her face. There was no denying it—Candy was now officially fat. Her legs were wide, her neck had disappeared. She no longer even had any wrists, just creases where her hands bent.

"*Ninety* pounds. I gained seventy-five with Danny Rae and I thought that was as bad as it could get. And I hadn't lost most of that before I was pregnant with this one."

"That's what happens to pregnant women, right? They gain weight?"

"I'm thinking smoking will help." Candy tucked the baby under her arm and patted the tabletop for the lighter she'd lost. "Dusty's got two girls, she didn't gain weight."

Trace studied her, said nothing on the subject of Dusty, Trace's sister.

"Of course, I don't have what she has to keep me skinny, there's one problem right there." Candy laughed nervously. "Seen her? Or the girls?"

Trace shook her head. "It's been a month or so."

"Them little girls is what makes me sad." Candy joggled Duane fiercely, and he bobbed his head up and down on her fat shoulder and fell asleep.

Them little girls, well yes. Erin and Jessie, five and three. Beautiful surprises, blond like Phil's family. After Erin was born Trace snuck into the hospital in the middle of the night and sat for an hour watching Dusty sleep, the baby tucked up next to her, against hospital policy. The last time Trace saw them Erin was wearing pink fingernail polish she'd put on herself. Half was chipped off but the rest still sparkled, and Jessie had gotten mad at her mother for forgetting to put the chocolate in her milk and cried, in a voice so small Trace couldn't imagine how she was able to imbue it with such misery, *You. Breaked. My. Heart.* Pointing to it, pointing at her chest.

"If it comes to it you'll take them, won't you? You won't let them go to the state?"

"I can't, Candy—I can't even talk—"

"You would."

"You don't know that."

"I've been knowing you since we were six years old and you showed up on Granddad's hilltop outta nowhere."

"You *always* bring that up. You must stop bringing it up."

Candy stood, took the three steps from the table into the narrow kitchen. She came back with a box of doughnuts. Duane snored slightly. The cartoons playing in the living room suddenly got very loud and Candy yelled, "Danny Rae! Turn that TV down or I'll put a hammer through it!" Still the baby slept on, and gradually the television quieted. "Today I'm bringing it up for a reason, not to change the subject, and you're just gonna have to sit your college butt still and listen to me. Now I know you don't hold with almost anything, you think most everything was designed for retards, but I have to tell you about something I heard on the radio last night. Take a doughnut, they're good."

"I don't like doughnuts."

"Take a doughnut."

Trace chose a glazed and ate it. It was good.

"Now you know how there are people who have been abducted by aliens," Candy said, as if she were reminding Trace that there are full moons, or a country called Brazil.

"No, I do not know that."

"Well yes you do and apparently it happens all the time, like *constantly.*" Duane raised his head up and made a sound, a roosterish little squawk, then collapsed back into sleep. Candy pounded on the baby's back as if he were choking, and he just snored harder. "And there was a man on a talk radio show last night, I've forgotten his name already after like five minutes, and it turns out that he spent *years* getting abducted by aliens and he described what it was like, how they could come in through his bedroom window and they're little like dwarves and they dress in blue police uniforms."

"Candy? Were you and Skeeter maybe just the tiniest bit high?"

"We have stopped all of that, Tracey Sue, since Danny Rae was born that funny color." She reached over and took the cup of cold, bitter Folgers Trace hadn't touched and drank the whole thing in three big gulps. A stream spilled down her chin and onto her white T-shirt, which said, in gold letters, SLIPPERY WHEN WET, but the coffee blended with a number of other things that had found their way to Candy's chest over the course of the day. There were stains all over her pants, too, which weren't exactly blue jeans but more like the denim used to cover papasan chairs. "And here's the thing about this guy: he was so sane. He was maybe the sanest person I've ever heard talking on the radio. He was so calm and reasonable and you could tell he was not making up *one word* of what he was saying, he was just telling it like it is: he is a one-hundred-percent victim of alien abduction and they want him for something but he doesn't know what. The poor, poor man. He had the sweetest voice, too. And I kept thinking, If Tracey were here she'd tell me if this person is a bald-faced liar or if he's telling the truth, or if, *even worse,* he believes he is telling the truth but he is lying because he doesn't know the difference, in which case he is not sane in any way."

"A conundrum," Trace agreed, unconsciously resting her elbows on the table. A variety of crumbs ground into her sweater, but she didn't react. "If he truly believes it and he's completely sane, it happened. And if he completely believes it and it didn't happen, he's crazy. And if it happened, we are all in a bind here, where the aliens are concerned."

Candy nodded vigorously. "That is it exactly. I wish you'd been here." She rubbed the rim of her coffee cup with her thumb, a gesture Trace had seen her make a thousand times. "Do you want some coffee?"

"No thanks. But get more for yourself if you want."

"And I've got to tell you something else about that UFO guy." Candy swallowed, lit another cigarette. "One thing he kept talking about was how many people have been abducted and don't know it, because their minds protect them by throwing up a *screen memory*. That's what he called it."

"A screen memory."

"Like this: he has a vivid memory of sitting on his grandmother's front porch and seeing a pack of gorillas come up over the hill in front of the house, coming toward him. He's completely sure that the gorillas are a screen memory for the first time the little midget policemen took him up in the spaceship and stole his sperm."

A high-pitched tone pierced Trace's inner ear and she shook her head as if to dislodge it. The sound stopped. "A pack of gorillas, huh?" Trace asked, smiling. One corner of her mouth twitched and she hoped Candy hadn't noticed. "A spaceship? Just to get some sperm?"

"And that made me think"—Candy spun her Bob Seger Commemorative Concert lighter on the table, spun it around until it was pointing at Trace—"about that time when you were six and you showed up on my granddad's hilltop, and when he asked you where you come from, you said you'd just had a picnic with a coyote, and at the end the coyote had put a little rock in your neck."

Trace's elbows ground against the food on the plastic tablecloth even harder. "Why must we always *talk* about this?"

"Is that rock still in your neck?"

"It isn't"—Trace waved the question away—"it isn't a rock—it's a knot. And anyway it's a calcium deposit or some sort of little, I don't know what. It's a little *knot*."

"Can I feel it?"

"No, you cannot feel it! I should get going. I want to visit your parents today."

"The other thing he saw?" Candy moved the limp, sweaty Duane to her other shoulder. "Tracey? Was a man walking through the train station, he was just a little boy with his dad at the time, and they passed another man walking a wolf on a leash. And eventually"—Candy talked faster, as if to make Trace hear it all, everything that could be said—"he gave up on the screen memories and he began to face what was happening to him, even though he was helpless to stop it. I think that's true. Although I seem to recall a moment at a Halloween party when he thinks he's seeing a child in a costume and it's really one of the dwarves, and that was *really* scary."

Trace reached for her bag, which she'd hung on one of the empty kitchen chairs.

"Doodlebug?" Candy reached over and grabbed Trace's hand, gripped it hard enough that Trace stopped moving. "Sit still a minute."

Trace sat back, let her body go limp.

"Your mother—Loretta, I mean—called." Candy's eyes filled with tears, but even so she seemed that same cheerful girl she'd been at fourteen, fifteen; even under all the weight and the bruises and the terrible color her skin had taken, she was a lovely prize, squandered. "It's not good."

"No." Trace could barely speak. Loretta would have asked, as she had asked Candy (and Candy's elderly parents, and everyone else Trace had ever known) where Trace lived, and Candy would have said she didn't know, because she didn't.

Before he knew the truth about her, Colt used to spin her around in the kitchen, her socks gliding over the slick linoleum floor, and he'd sing, *You with the stars in your eyes*. Sometimes Loretta would be there, sometimes she would hum along. She was the singer, after all—the real thing. If she was there she would slip in between them, between Trace and her daddy, and she would dance with him in a way Trace could only puzzle over. Loretta was so short, her hips were wide, and her breasts were enormous—how could she be graceful at all? How could she move so meltingly, and sing at the same time, and look Colt in the eye and keep him there? What was Trace failing to do, how could she possibly do more than master the finicky old Winchester .22 he'd given her, or catch a bigger fish than that largemouth bass last summer? Out on Lake Chapman she knew not to speak; she cast her line like a pro. She had spent hours working on his motorcycle with him, his truck, handing him tools, rolling cigarettes for him on the arched roller with the rubber grip when his store-bought were gone. Patient hours, patient, silent years she had given him, and all Loretta had to do was slip in and sing a few notes, move her body like a snake with an undigested meal, and his youngest child vanished, the other two already gone.

"They found out where Billy is. But he doesn't know they know."

Trace jumped, hitting her knee on the underside of the table. Billy, gone five years? Her brother? Wild angel boy, now *he* had *loved* Loretta, he charmed her and picked her up off the floor to show her his strength. He had inherited the best of them, of his parents. Funny and tall and a great runner, he would hold open his arms to Trace and she could run and jump and he could catch her as if she weighed nothing; he spun her and read to her, and he was the one who took care of her after—

he got shocked a lot. Was that it, electricity? He took some very bad shocks, once while turning on the basement light, standing in an inch of water, and another time he—there was a guy wire, a storm, a bird, Trace tapped her hand against her ear, there was that sound again, but not as bad. "Where. Where is he?"

Candy shook her head; of course she didn't know.

"Loretta said Marty found him through some buddy. She was crying—"

"This is about Marty." Trace nodded. "Candy? This is about Marty, right?"

Candy swallowed but didn't blink. "Yes."

Trace took a deep breath, rested her hands flat on the sticky table. Weeds, who had been sleeping beside her chair, stood up and slipped under the table, to lie down on her feet. "I was the first to see him," she said, which Candy knew better than anyone as Trace was living with Candy and her parents at the time. It had been a Sunday; Trace had gone home to pick up a few things, hoping her mother would be at church. She had just come through the front door and was about to cross the living room when she saw him walking down the staircase of her father's home, *Colt's* house, Marty Morrison. She already knew who he was—all the girls in Mason knew who he was. He owned an operation that rented out farm equipment; he ran it out of a huge ugly pole barn on 27, the two-lane highway that ran from Mason to Haddington to Jonah. Hell of an idea he'd had, that one, and at just the right time. Because farm equipment did almost nothing *but* break down, and at the worst possible moment, and the time had come when farmers couldn't afford to lose a single minute, and even if everything was perfect—the planting, the rain, the pesticides, the harvest—even then no one could make it anymore. Not one crop turned a profit but everyone was in too deep to sell, and the bank men stopped drinking coffee with the farmers or their hands, and the insurance men stopped coming around at all, and at four in the morning when the combine a man had financed for a staggering six figures threw a belt that had to be ordered, or when a blade broke, and he and his sons and farmhands were bent over in a blinding rainstorm, dropping bolts and wrenches, so afraid of what was right in front of them their chests began to stab, their arms weaken—someone, it didn't matter who, would eventually say, "Call Marty Morrison. Wake him up."

So he wasn't stupid, and he had money—more than anyone else in Mason, which didn't need to be much. He drove a Lincoln Town Car. He was a giant of a man, with a stomach so distended from diner food his back was swayed from supporting it. His hair was always neatly cut; he was clean-shaven and wore white shirts with dark, pressed blue jeans and cowboy boots. He was immaculate, the rarest quality in a man in a farm town, and he smiled and flirted and told jokes that made other men laugh, the men who owed him, and the bankers. At the county fair he always had a big display in the barn, and every time a pretty girl passed he would put his hand over his heart and say, "Come sit on my lap or I'll *die!*" and a few actually did.

Dusty told Trace about him; Dusty, who had never uttered a coarse word in her life. Candy and Trace were walking through the fair barn, and they could hear Marty's loud voice calling out all kinds of things, and then Dusty Ann was beside them. At first all Trace saw was Loretta's red hair, and she froze. But there was her sister's sweet face, and she took Trace by the shoulder and whispered in her ear. She straightened up and glanced in Marty's direction, leaned down, and asked if Trace understood what she'd been told. Trace couldn't answer, and Dusty had to ask again.

I did, Trace thought, her hands trembling on Candy's table. I understood, except I'd never heard of any of it before, what she said. I stood
there like some brain-damaged spy: the message had been delivered to
me and not one word of it made sense and anyway I didn't know what
to do with the information, which government was I working for? Colt
was selling elephant ears in the booth set up by the volunteer fire
department, Loretta was singing at the talent show in the gym. And
where was Billy? If one ride had broken, he was trapped in it. If a single gas line leading to the Italian sausage trailer had snapped, Billy was
standing on it. I forget. I wasn't paying attention. Was it before Dusty's
missing year, or after?

"Loretta was very upset, Tracey, she said that Marty is going to turn
Billy in unless."

She had gone home to pick up a few things and there was Marty
Morrison, walking down the staircase of her parents' home. He was
wearing a white T-shirt and boxer shorts, and because she had come
home at just that moment Trace was the first to learn that Marty carried with him a plastic two-liter Pepsi bottle with the top cut off—carried it up to bed and downstairs in the morning, and sometimes left it
on an end table—into which he urinated, because it was time-saving.
Also it just appealed to him. It was his own bottle of pee, and later she
would learn he defied anyone to say a word about it. However, the
longer nothing was said about it, the more prominently it was displayed.
Perhaps he was conflicted. Someone was discreet about it too long
(Dusty assumed she was the culprit), and the bottle ended up next to
the punch bowl when Marty and Loretta were married in the big hall
at the Armory. (Trace had asked, "How . . . how much was in there?"
Dusty blushed. "A week's worth, maybe? A lot.")

"Why?" Trace asked, leaning toward Candy with a desperate need,
like Duane trying to hurl himself to the floor, where nothing waited for
him but gravity and whatever Skeet had ground into the carpet with
the heel of his boot.

"Why which thing?"

"Why me? I'm not asking in self-pity, I'm not saying, Why me,
Lord? I just honestly don't understand."

Candy stood—her shoulders seemed to be aching—and carried the
baby into the living room, where Danny Rae had fallen asleep in front

of the television. She put Duane in his playpen, stretching her arms and sighing as she walked back to the table. "You"—Candy fell heavily into her chair—"you . . . *denied* him?"

Trace watched Candy carefully, because this woman—a woman who had come to such straits as this—was the sole repository of Tracey Sue Pennington's past. Candy was a Living History project—or, more appropriately, a Civil War reenactor. She lacked verisimilitude and was far too heavy to serve as a soldier, but she knew her lines and every square inch of the battlefield. Trace would soon have a degree, but it was Candy who would say, "This is where you fire your musket, and here is where you fall, and die."

Candy rubbed her eyes and left her hand there, covering half her face. "You were what he wanted all along, Bug, you are the reason he married her. That's a lot, you know, to marry someone and tangle up your money and your business and your . . . everything private to a person. He'll lose half of everything he owns if he leaves her, and you just— you just slipped out of his grasp." She paused, lowered her hand. "You saw him walking down the stairs that day, but he saw *you* long before— years and *years* before. He saw you in early summer, or spring maybe, riding behind Colt on his bike. You weren't wearing helmets—"

"We never wore helmets."

"—and your hair was so long and so black, a black velvet curtain, he said, and you had your arms wrapped around Colt's waist, you were resting your head on his back. You drove past him, past Marty, as he was walking to his car from the bank." Candy had said all of that while looking down into her ashtray, which was overflowing. She looked up.

Trace reached out and took Candy's hand, looping their fingers together. She whispered, "How do you know this?"

Candy whispered back, "Loretta told me."

In the living room the mayhem in cartoon land went on and on and on; mad, hectic music and ceaseless violence. Each moment seemed punctuated with a blow to the head, a shotgun blast, a fall from a heart-ripping height. The babies slept.

"It wouldn't be the worst thing," Candy said, but with hollow spots of hesitation in her voice, "to save Billy. You could close your eyes and pretend you was someplace else—that's what being married is like. And you did it twice before and survived."

Trace clenched her jaw muscles, nodded slightly. True enough. Once for Erin and once for Jessie, and he had kept his word, as far as Trace knew. She stood, nearly knocking her chair over, grabbing her purse at the same time. Weeds was up with her and almost to the door. Hat, scarf. One sweater bigger than the sweater she was wearing, another sweater bigger than that, her long black Australian bush coat, her gloves. "Where's the dog, Candy? Where's the redbone hound?"

Her friend, her only, remained seated, her thumb resting on the rim of her coffee cup but not moving.

"What did your husband do to him? Do you want me to guess?"

Candy shook her head no.

Outside, the air was so cold her lungs ached after a single breath. She walked carefully down the icy steps and onto the path to her truck, Weeds running ahead.

She was nearly there when Candy came flying out the door, jumping down the steps as if she were weightless. She ran to Trace and grabbed the sleeve of her coat, Candy's blue eyes wide and thrilled, as they had been long ago. "That man on the radio?" she asked, gasping in the frigid air. "Tracey? Remember the bobcat? I'm just saying. Do you remember the bobcat you found asleep on your bed?"